A TALE OF TWO PRINCES

A TALE OF TWO PRINCES

ERIC GERON

ISBN-13: 978-1-335-42592-8

A Tale of Two Princes

Copyright © 2023 by Eric Geron

Inkyard Press
22 Adelaide St. West, 41st Floor
Toronto, Ontario M5H 4E3, Canada
www.InkyardPress.com

Printed in U.S.A.

*For anyone pushing an agenda
of equality, inclusion, and acceptance:
keep pushing.*

THE ROYAL HOUSE OF WINDSOR
UNITED KINGDOM

ELIZA II
REIGNING QUEEN OF ENGLAND

(GRANNY)
Prefers my chocolate biscuit cake
recipe to her own.

JAMES
DUKE OF EDINBURGH
· DECEASED ·

♡ GRAMPS

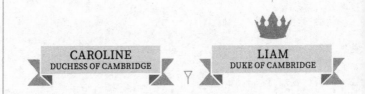

CAROLINE
DUCHESS OF CAMBRIDGE

LIAM
DUKE OF CAMBRIDGE

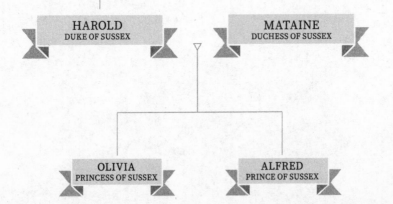

HAROLD
DUKE OF SUSSEX

MATAINE
DUCHESS OF SUSSEX

OLIVIA
PRINCESS OF SUSSEX

ALFRED
PRINCE OF SUSSEX

THE ROYAL HOUSE OF DINNISSEN
CANADA

ÉLÉGANCE ET SIMPLICITÉ

Good ol' Mum and Dad aka "Maple Syrup Sweeties"

FREDERICK
REIGNING KING OF CANADA

DAPHNÉE
QUEEN CONSORT OF CANADA

First comes love,
then comes marriage,
        then comes me
    in the Red Maple Carriage

MOM + DAD
(Connie and Benjamin)

Billy   Mack

EDWARD
~~CROWN PRINCE OF CANADA~~

MOST LIKELY TO SUCCEED
(Get it? Line of succession? Anyway, it's me!)
Out of all the royal Edwards,
I'm undoubtedly the best.

BRITISH ROYAL COMMUNICATIONS

1st March

STATEMENT FROM HER MAJESTY THE QUEEN

We are utterly delighted to announce that my son, Frederick, and his wife, Daphnée, have been appointed to the roles of King and Queen Consort of a new form of monarchy in Canada. The Dominion of Canada has always been a beloved realm of the Commonwealth, and continues to be cherished during this historical shift to member.

As new King and Queen Consort of Canada, Frederick and Daphnée shall maintain their private patronages and associations, uphold Royal duties, and incorporate the codes and conducts of the Commonwealth member of Canada.

We are respectful of their wish to establish a fresh start there as a young family, while very much remaining a valued part of our own.

To that end, we wish them all our very best in the days leading to their foray into parenthood of not only a child, but also of a great nation reborn.

–ELIZA R.

Eighteen Years Later...

Chapter One

EDWARD

"Handsome *and* charming? How is Canada's perfect royal son possibly still single?"

Travis Romano, Dean of Admissions at The Juilliard School here in New York, gives me a meaty handshake. A gigantic grin plasters his face and his green eyes crinkle at the corners. He shifts his stance as if hoping the photographers will be able to capture a few good shots of this moment. It's the same irksome question I've been dodging since the day I went from "Royal Tot" to "Royally Hot."

The clanging of crystal quiets as a hush falls around the dean. A Silicon Valley tech guru sets down her glass of Bordeaux to lovingly place her hand on her husband's arm. The president's son gives me a cheeky grin. Everyone within a three-metre radius is now silent, impatiently waiting to hear how I'll respond.

For a moment, I imagine telling everyone the truth: "Guess what? I'm gay! And I don't *want* to marry a woman and one day have babies to continue the royal bloodline." But I'll never say that. It's too important to my parents—and all of Canada—that I follow in their footsteps.

And as next in line to the Maple Crown, it's too important that I be a good king for my people one day.

So, I'll never find true love. That's the cost of my destiny, and I've accepted it. Besides, I'm already married—to tradition.

MAPLE CROWN RULE 57: Never discuss matters of the heart.

To cover my nervousness, I flash my signature sugar-sweet smile—one befitting the Crown Prince of Canada—at the attentive crowd on the dance floor, letting them drink in the seconds. Over the Juilliard violinists playing softly in the background, I answer the dean's question about how I'm possibly still single with one deadpan word:

"Midterms."

Some people chuckle while others begin a chorus of *aaaaaaw*.

The platinum maple leaf brooch on my jacket lapel sits heavy on top of my heart. It identifies me as the Crown Prince of Canada, but it's also the lock of the box I'm trapped inside. The truth is, I'm single because I'm a closeted gay guy... and I'm a closeted gay guy because I'm the Crown Prince of Canada.

I keep smiling at the crowd, even though the many faces staring back feel overwhelming. I've been gone from the public eye for almost a year, so of *course* everyone is excited to see the "reclusive" Crown Prince return to the limelight. They don't have to know that "reclusive" actually means I've been grounded this whole time, and all because of how poorly I acted at my seventeenth birthday party.

In the fallout, Mum and Dad grounded me for the rest of my junior year, then ordered I be sent away to New York City for my senior year. I've been here for six months, cooped up between my family's private Upper East Side residence and a stuffy private school. Sure, there was public scrutiny over my parents shipping me off to New York, but they passed it off as an opportunity to strengthen their tight bonds with Canada's closest neighbour to the south. No need for anyone to know I had been grounded and sent here as punishment.

Luckily, all my efforts to be a model prisoner have paid off, and my parents have just decided I don't have to be grounded for the rest of my senior year. Tonight they're giving me the chance to prove I really can be a model Crown Prince. And of course, I promised Mum and Dad I would be on my absolute best behaviour. After all, the Investiture Ceremony is in a couple of weeks, which means I have to prove that I'm fully prepared to be heir to the Maple Crown, aka the Canadian Crown. I know I'm ready. I've been training for it since I was a child. But I still need to convince the 38,346,809 people of Canada—and the rest of the world too. No pressure, right?

Dean Romano claps me on the back, wagging his finger at me with a cloying smile. "Well, we look forward to the day you find the perfect girl." The rest of the group applauds politely and clinks their glasses.

I sigh inwardly. Since forever, Mum and Dad have said the same exact thing to me whenever the topic of the future queen has come up. I want to tell my rapt audience that I'm only seventeen years old, and therefore in no rush to marry *anyone*, obviously. But I'm used to near-total strangers interrogating me about my love life, so I wink at the dean and then add, "I promise that you'll be the first to know."

MAPLE CROWN RULE 16: Maintain civility in social settings.

The semicircle of men and women—okay, mostly women—tightens around me, countless sequined arms and shimmering bare shoulders swarming me like voracious sea creatures.

My Adam's apple presses against my stiff collar. "Who

knows?" I add, my sultry smile fighting a twitch as I reach up to loosen my tie. "Maybe I'll meet someone special here tonight."

MAPLE CROWN RULE 46: Make everyone feel heard.

Charity balls are a royal pain in the derrière, but also an unfortunate requirement, along with cutting ribbons and giving speeches. With the Dinnissen monarchy still so new, my parents work tirelessly to endear themselves to the Canadian public, which is still forming opinions on our family as its new fledging figureheads—and as soon as I graduate in June and return home to Canada, the full weight of that responsibility will fall upon my shoulders as well.

Though I suppose I can't be *too* upset with my parents, or as the British press has dubbed them, Canada's "Maple Syrup Sweeties." Tonight, they're off at some admirable conference with our prime minister. Actual important stuff that doesn't involve schmoozing with politicians and celebrities. Well, maybe still *some* schmoozing—Mum always books her reflexologist before traveling with the PM. Then again, I can't complain about standing in for them tonight. I'm still just so glad my time of captivity is finally over.

"To Prince Edward finding true love!" Dean Romano's wife, Rebecca, lifts her crystal champagne flute toward the chandelier, and everyone echoes her words, then drains their glasses.

I manage to keep smiling. Her toast is yet another painful reminder of something I'll never have…true love. But that's the trade-off that comes with getting to be king one day.

It's more exhausting than I remembered to keep pretending I'm something I'm not. I really need to get a breath of fresh air.

Excusing myself, I turn away and scan for the back doors of the Grand Ballroom—combing through a choppy ocean of barons, dignitaries, dukes, and celebrities. All resplendent in sheer gowns and sleek black ties. All elated to speak to me. But I don't care about any of them. I only care about one person. Where the hell *is* Neel, anyway? To think I call him my best friend. And where the hell is the exit?

Gord Lauzon, Canadian secretary to Dad and my personal adviser since I was a child, is laughing up a storm with a group of people against the ballroom's gilded wall. Like always, Gord looks sharp in a luxury suit and tie, his head freshly shaved and gleaming white. He was Granny's ex–private secretary who now controls the press office, acts as the vital channel of communication between my parents and the Canadian government, and manages my day-to-day. Gord also works as liaison to the Institution—or "Firm"—that keeps the Royal Family running like one big business. He was delighted my grounding presented him with a chance to ratchet up his royal lessons. That is, after he got over the sour taste it left in his mouth.

He meets my eyes through his bold-framed glasses. After six months of him being my New York City babysitter, aka my parents' eyes on me, I can tell he's checking in. He subtly extends his arm, pressing fingertip to thumb, our signal for asking if everything is copacetic. I doubt anything foul will happen in this historic hotel's grand old ballroom, other than me breaking a heart or two, so I return the gesture and he nods in understanding. Though, if I'm being honest, I could use his help to point out the exit door.

I check my timepiece and realize I've only been here for an hour. I used to be so good at wowing the crowds at these fundraisers. I've got to get back on top of my game. That is, after I take that much-needed brief break.

"Well, if it isn't Canada's Golden Child," says a sly voice in my ear.

Suddenly, I'm being suffocated by a thick cloud of vanilla perfume as I turn to take in the full lips and chiseled cheekbones of Sephora's latest global ambassador, aka Lady Sofia Marchand, aka Fi, aka my frenemy since childhood. In an exquisite seafoam-blue couture gown with enough tulle to make Cinderella jealous, she looks every bit an ethereal fairy tale goddess.

Click!

The event photographer trips the shutter of his camera before I can even utter a greeting. Seamlessly, Fi throws her head back in laughter as if I've just showed her the most hilarious GIF in the world. Instinctively, I tighten my core, relax my shoulders, and flex my chest.

MAPLE CROWN RULE 13: Have a royal presence.

Gord once told me that the best way to have perfect posture was to pretend someone was pulling a string right up through the top of my head, like a puppet. I was five. That's me, all these years later: Perfect Puppet Prince Eddie, aching mouth unhinged, grin and all.

And Lady Sofia knows just how to pull my strings. With British aristocracy on her mum's side and descending from French nobles on her Canadian dad's side, Fi's been one of my Crown-approved acquaintances since we were kids at Ashwood Elementary in Ottawa. For years, we've attended the same polo and equestrian summer camp, the same celebrity birthday parties, and the same VIP meet-and-greets backstage at sold-out concerts. It's painstakingly evident that our parents are hoping for a romantic spark, but Fi and I are less like maple syrup in milk and more like oil and water. I thought we might be rid of each other when I moved south of the border for my senior year, but no such luck. Her parents put her into St. Aubyn's Prep as soon as they heard I would be attending, which she didn't seem to mind.

Click!

"Well if it isn't New York's hottest crown-chaser," I mutter out the corner of my mouth.

"Given how elusive you are, it's no *wonder* I haven't caught it yet." Fi laughs—cackling this time. "It's only a matter of time." She perches one hand on my shoulder while lightly clasping it with the other, her front leg shifting to elegantly eclipse her back leg. She's all fair skin tinged pink, peachy cheeks, silver-highlighted collarbones, and smoky cat eye.

Click!

Behind the photographer a few yards away, I spy a huddle of girls my age clamouring for my attention, hopping and waving their arms about. I'll have to deal with them soon, I'm sure.

MAPLE CROWN RULE 52: Every person is important.

That includes the fangirls. *Ça va.* Beside me, Fi drops her sculpted arms and shoulders back, puffing out her chest. "What's it been, nearly a year since you've hit the social scene? Glad your 'rents finally let you off the short leash."

I smile very sweetly, keeping my eyes trained ahead. "As am I."

Click!

"I can't wait to get even more photos with you at the gala on Thursday night," Fi continues. "I assume you'll be there."

"Wouldn't miss it."

The photographer lowers his camera and nods, as if to say he's captured enough. *Bien.*

Fi faces me and talks through her smile. "My work here is

done. It's been real, loser. See you in school!" Then she turns to the photographer. "Make sure you tag me—that's *Sofia* with an *f*." She scoffs to herself. "As if he doesn't already know that."

MAPLE CROWN RULE 101: No personal social media accounts.

So, that's a thing, albeit fairly new. My Royal Family has general verified accounts instead, of course. At my last check, the @CanadianRoyals had 20.6 million followers. And photos of me happen to get the most likes.

I look past Fi, lingering despite her goodbyes, and inadvertently lock pupils with one of the girls in the huddle, who takes the fleeting eye contact for an invitation. Gathering her black gown, she rushes forward. Her gaggle of friends follows with hungry expressions, flocking my way in a V-formation.

A crushing weight settles on my chest. Although the pressure of being a royal is ever-present, at least when I was grounded I didn't have to deal with this level of people-pleasing.

Nodding toward the girls, Fi scrunches up her delicate nose. "Good luck with that." She flashes the crowd an enchanting smile, flips her long ombré hair, and strides down a nonexistent red carpet while all heads turn her way and another photographer flails for her attention.

Well. That's Lady Sofia for you, *je ne sais quoi* and all.

"Your Royal Highness!" says the girl in the black gown, who appears to be squatting in what I suppose is her attempt at a perfunctory curtsy. "Sir, may I get a photo with you, too?"

I freeze, trying with all my might not to roll my eyes. Members of the Royal Family must always be gracious. "Of course, *mademoiselle*!" Growing up with a French-speaking nanny clearly rubbed off on me—along with remedial French lessons at school.

"Thank you!" she squeals, then turns to her posse and

mouths, *Mademoiselle!* She angles her phone overhead, and I see my brow wrinkling on-screen.

MAPLE CROWN RULE 102: No selfies.

Another recent rule. My grandmother and the family matriarch, the queen of England, managed to officially deem selfies as unfit for royalty. Too common. Too vain. I agree with *some* of the Maple Crown Rules inspired by Granny's original ones (the Buckingham Crown Rules). But a lot of the traditional values that any Royal Family thrives on are woefully backward.

C'est comme ça.

I gesture at the event photographer still hovering nearby. "Shall we have him take the photo? I trust my friend here will do a fine job capturing your beauty."

"Oh, of course, sir!" The girl titters abashedly and tucks her phone into a sequin clutch. We assume the position while her friends look on, capturing every moment behind their screens. Others move in to watch too, unwittingly revealing the exit behind the photographer. He snaps a few shots and then walks over, showing us the photos.

I smile in approval, then I rely on an old standby and wave to an invisible friend across the packed ballroom. "I'm terribly sorry," I tell the growing cluster of waiting girls. "I must step out for a brief moment. I'll be back very soon! I promise."

MAPLE CROWN RULE 18: Depart at the right moment.

Technically I also broke the rule Royals don't apologize, but I can typically let that one slide. I *am* Canadian, after all.

Flashing one last dashing smile, I make my escape. The good ol' Flash-and-Dash. Works every time. I spin on my heel and bump into a table, sending plates and glasses chattering like teeth (how unlike me!), then course-correct, making my way toward the exit. In my periphery, Gord excuses himself from his coterie of raucous socialites and follows, a long shadow tethered to my every stride, while I search for that pesky invisible friend who conveniently can't seem to stay in one place, weaving in and out and greeting the *crème de la crème* as I go.

"How are you?" I call to a NASA astronaut. I wave at a Scottish minister. *"Hello there! Smart-looking kilt!"*

"Salut! Comment va votre famille?" I ask the French ambassador. I crank my megawatt smile up to an eleven for the prime minister of Japan. *"Sumimasen,"* I say.

MAPLE CROWN RULE 36: Royals should speak multiple languages.

For everyone else, I use my nod/twinkle-in-eye combo that's friendly, but also too intimidating for anyone to do more than reply with a wave, smile, or nod. Otherwise, they'd be on me like flies on maple syrup. I reach the exit, soar through a series of doors, and maneuver past the black-and-white-clad waitstaff wheeling out carts of teacups. Everybody is so busy, they don't even notice me in all the hubbub. I push a swinging aluminum traffic door, stepping past the bustling kitchen, and take a flight of steps down to a door leading to a break room reeking of what I can only assume is the smell of old coffee where I *know* no one will find me.

It's empty, except for a guy my age in a worker's uniform sitting at a rickety little table, gazing at his phone. I drop into a folding chair at a table in front of him, loosen my tie some more, and let out a whoosh of air.

I'm safe. For now.

"Oh!" he says with a start, nervously pushing back his bangs. "Can I help you? Are you lost?"

"I'm fine. It's okay that I'm in here, right?" I ask.

His glimmering eyes dart around. "Umm, normally they'd make me kick guests out for…reasons." He suddenly notices my maple leaf brooch, and blushes. "But it's cool! I won't tell. Your Royal Highness, sir," he adds hastily.

I almost begin to disclose why I'm hiding out in the first place. But then I remember.

MAPLE CROWN RULE 77: Only share what is necessary.

It's technically: *Only share with your subjects what is necessary,* but I've truncated it. I don't have subjects. At least, not yet.

I nod. "Perfect. Thanks."

"D-do you want some privacy?" he stammers. He stands up to leave, and his phone falls from his hand. It skitters across the warped linoleum, coming to a rest at the tip of my shiny black patent leather shoes.

I pick it up and hand it back to him. "No, no, it's fine. Stay. I just needed a tiny break. I'll be out in a jiffy." I give the break room a cursory scan, eyes sweeping cabinets, a sink, a small white fridge. "Do you have any food? I'm famished."

One of his eyebrows quirks in bewilderment. "Oh, you didn't get a chance to eat?"

"At a charity event like this one? Too much schmoozing. Not enough eating. As it goes."

He lets out a little laugh. "Let me see what we have." He vanishes up into the stairwell, then comes trundling back down a minute later with a tray of miniature desserts: everything from frozen mochi and mint sorbet to macarons and bonbons with gold leafing on top.

"Super!" I pinch up a pink mochi and pop it in my mouth. "Have one."

He hesitates, but after darting a glance at the door, he selects a pale green one. "Staff isn't supposed to eat these," he says, but he bites down on it anyway.

"Look at us," I remark. "Me trespassing in employee break rooms and you eating forbidden mochi. We're breaking all the rules." We both laugh. "So, you work here? Aren't you in high school like me?"

"Yeah. But I just work nights. I'm saving up for college. My uncle got me the job. He's a cook here."

I take another mochi. Double chocolate. A favourite. "Do you cook too?"

"I try." He laughs, running his hand through his shiny black hair. "What about you?"

Best not to share how all of my meals are prepared for me at the risk of sounding elitist. Instead, I grin. "Can you keep a secret? I've been working on a chocolate chip cookie recipe that puts Pierre on Park's to shame." I pass it off as a joke, but I actually spent all winter experimenting on just that recipe— along with original recipes for fresh new takes on profiteroles, cream puffs, and croquembouches.

The guy laughs again, briefly covering his mouth. "I bet."

"I'm serious." I select a bonbon from the tray. "It's rather agonizing being a foodie when you're the next leader of a country whose biggest culinary claim to fame is gourmet poutine."

His expression turns contemplative. "Hey, didn't Canada invent the Twinkie?"

"I rest my case."

The guy chuckles and combs his fingers through his hair once more, then locks eyes with me. "I never expected to meet a royal, let alone, well, you. Sorry, you just seem so... *normal*." Reddening, he adds, "Oh. Sorry. I didn't... It's just, you seem so chill. It's like hanging out with...a friend from school." He tucks a strand behind his ear, his eyes downcast, his cheeks practically puce.

"Don't worry about it. I get it." I swallow. I don't know why, but my throat has decided to go bone-dry. "It's easy to talk to you too. Do you get that a lot?"

Silence falls.

My stomach drops as soon as the words escape my lips. Do I sound like I'm coming onto him? What am I babbling about to this stranger?

But much to my relief, a smile washes across his face like sunlight.

I'm wondering what to say next when—

Slam!

The break room door bursts open, and I hear the voice of my best friend. "Edward! There you are!"

The worker and I jump with a start, stepping away from one another as if we were just caught hiding a dead body.

In struts Neel Singh, aforementioned best friend who also happens to be the son of Zubin Singh, Indian ambassador to Canada.

Let me tell you about Neel. People think *I'm* charming, but Neel can get them eating out of the palm of his manicured hand in seconds—including my parents, who bizarrely enough think him being in New York with me is a *good* thing. He grew up all over the world, but stayed in Ottawa long enough for us to become best friends, a relationship which fully crystallized after we built a snowman with a creatively placed carrot. Thank goodness it melted before my parents or Gord saw it. And now, he's in New York for his senior year too. Only *Neel* could convince his parents that he should move to another country for his last year of high school. I guess he griped enough about being separated from his best friend that they eventually caved.

But in this moment, with the worker's eyes still locked on mine, I'm kind of wishing Neel's parents had kept him in Ottawa.

I fold my arms across my chest. "Oh, *now* you decide to show up. Where were you forever ago when I was looking for you, *mon chum?*"

Neel glances at the worker, whose name I wish I knew—*que c'est gênant*—then back at me, grinning. "Oh, you've made a new friend?"

"Shut up," I growl so low that only Neel can hear me. He knows my secret and I trust him to keep it, but sometimes what he says in front of others makes me sweat.

He ignores me and walks across the break room. "Hi. I'm Neel. It's so nice to meet you." He pumps my new friend's hand, lingering for far too long. He has a knack for being overly friendly. And there's no denying Neel looks suave in his tailored black suit, crisp white button-up that contrasts nicely against the warm bronze undertones of his brown skin, and bow tie that perfectly matches his silk pocket square. Probably a look he "borrowed" from the runway he walked in Milan. The perks of being incredibly wealthy *and* good-looking.

"Nice to meet you too." The guy looks from Neel to me, flashes a timid smile, and scurries from the room before I can utter *salut*.

Neel shoots me a knowing smirk then starts washing his hands at the sink. He ditched me all night, only showing up to barge in and scare off my new friend. This is low, even for him.

"Can you believe they had no vegetarian options?" he asks incredulously. "Meat pies for as far as the eye could see."

"Seriously, where have you been? I needed you," I say. "And how did you find me?"

He dries his hands on a dish rag then snatches up a bonbon. "I have my sources," he says through a mouthful.

I glare. I could murder him. Use industrial-strength kitchen cleaner to hide the evidence.

"Fine." Neel sticks his thumb into a vanilla mochi, then jerks it in the direction of the door.

Right on cue, Gord sets foot into the break room, looking less than pleased. "Your Royal Highness."

Rolling my eyes at Neel, I give Gord the signal that all is well.

But as Neel rests a hand on my forearm, I'm no longer sure. He's got that look in his eye. "I'm bored of the ball, so I'm thinking we leave before the raffle and silent auction. Besides—" he beams his radiant smile "—there's a private shindig taking place now at Beauty and Essex—no nonsense this time. Say you'll come? Great! Let's go." Neel hooks his arm in mine and twists in the direction of the door.

He may have made the *Forbes* 30 Under 30 Asia list, but right now, he's number 1 on my naughty list.

I plant my feet. "Sounds sweet, but I'd rather not end up grounded again."

Neel grips my face, pleading. "Please? Pretty please with maple sugar on top?"

I pry his fingers off. "Tempting," I say, "but I'm afraid I'm immune to your charms, my friend."

He grins impishly. "I'll do your AP Chem lab homework," he says in singsong.

He *knows* that's my Achilles' heel. I sigh. "You better not make me regret this."

Gord clears his throat. "Sir." He slowly shakes his head.

Neel knots his fingers together pleadingly. "But I'll have him home by midnight, G!"

I raise an eyebrow. "Who are you, my fairy godmother?" With Neel, "midnight" means 4:30 a.m. Neel's dad still lives in Ottawa, his mum's in India, and he has no chaperone here, so he's pretty much a free agent. The notion of "curfew" is not something he's well acquainted with. While Neel's parents are barely even aware of his zip code, mine like to be in the know, even *with* being busy running and continuing to establish a somewhat new form of monarchy. Hence, Gord, who I'm practically closer with than my own father.

Gord picks a piece of invisible lint off my jacket. "I don't advise it, sir. Your parents gave me direct orders—your name is not ending up in the tabloids." He straightens my brooch. *"Again,"* he adds tartly.

It's true. Dad did say leading up to this event that if I had one more bad run-in with the press, he was going to revoke my going-out privileges for good.

Neel gasps and clutches his chest. "What happened last time was *not* his fault."

Gord turns on Neel. "You mean when His Royal Highness was photographed setting off fireworks for his birthday party on a yacht in the Ottawa River? A little stunt that burned down half the trees on the waterfront? You're both lucky it didn't launch a media blitz."

I feel myself blushing. "I didn't know it was illegal to set off fireworks from a yacht, *pour l'amour du Christ!*"

At this response, Gord clenches his jaw. I know what that means. This conversation is over.

Neel knows it too. He screws up his mouth in defeat, and sighs. "Bye, *bharā.*" His nickname for me, "brother" in Punjabi, never fails to pull at my heartstrings.

I clap a hand on his shoulder. "Have fun for both of us?"

Neel eases back into his radiant smile, eyes playful again. He winks. "Oh, I always do."

"Prince Edward! Prince Edward! Over here!"

Paparazzi surround us, cameras flashing, as we step out into the Manhattan night. A frigid breeze buffets down the avenue, fluttering awnings. My chauffeur holds open the door to my black town car as I duck inside, exchanging the icy air for blissful artificial warmth.

Camera lenses take aim, yards from the tinted windows. Good luck getting a decent shot. The paparazzi here truly are as ubiquitous as rats on subway tracks. Not that I've ever taken the subway.

Gord buckles into the passenger seat, and the chauffeur pulls the car onto 59th while the paparazzi give chase, shouting my name. Before kicking me out of Rideau Hall, Mum and Dad never failed to remind me that the paparazzi in New York would be documenting my every folly, unlike in Canada where the industry isn't quite so rabid and boundaries are better respected (other than the *Daily Maple*, the source for most Royals-related reports and rumours). Going out and about, acting like a delinquent in New York would not only mean my family would find out about it, but the rest of the world as well. Given Mum and Dad's own distaste for paparazzi, they must have felt pretty desperate to have sent me here, but it's been quite effective. That, and being under Gord's constant supervision.

We cross the intersection, leaving Central Park behind us, its naked treetops illuminated by city lights. From the front seat, Gord turns up the radio volume and soft classical music plays. He knows it's one of the few things that relaxes me. I lean back, take a deep breath, and pull out my phone.

A million Google alerts pop up. What? *Of course* I have a

Google alert for my own name. I need to know what people are saying about me after my reentry into the party scene. It's mostly just gossipy tabloid stories, an occasional fashion magazine editorial, and the inevitable message board comments perpetuating age-old rumours and adding to tired conspiracy theories. When it comes to the relatively new Canadian monarchy, people love trying to spill royal Earl Grey tea.

Just before I was born, Mum and Dad fled across the pond to Canada in hopes of escaping the scrutiny of the English press. Waking up to a new disparaging headline every day about Mum being a lowly commoner from Canada was untenable for them—not to mention being baited and badgered by slimy photographers wherever they set foot. My parents had even been prepared to leave the Royal Family and relinquish their official titles—anything to help put an ocean between them and the snaky British tabloids.

A while back, there was a movement to one day replace Granny with a homegrown Canadian Royal Family, but nothing came of it. Our current situation was the result of an agreement with the Canadian prime minister at the time. Apparently, he recognized that Canadian love for the Royal Family was good for business. (Our official merch alone contributes greatly to Canada's bottom line.) The fact Dad was born on Canadian soil before growing up in England made him a natural fit for Canadian king.

On my phone, I'm idly poking around popular royal hashtags and notice that someone has reposted, for the zillionth time, that old and super famous long-range paparazzi photo of my parents arriving home at Rideau Hall with bundled-up newborn me. It was the first time the paparazzi had caught a glimpse of The Canadian Royal Baby. Given my mum's nervousness about paparazzi, my parents had hidden out at the super private Hôpital Royal Jolee in Montreal for the birth, far from where anyone expected them to go.

It's one of the only photos of me as a child to have gotten out. To no one's surprise, it was from a wily and out-of-town photographer who wasn't afraid of being blacklisted. Since that day, my parents have held an iron grip on our private lives, only slightly loosening up the photography ban when I entered high school a little over three years ago. (Hello, *People* magazine cover shoot!)

Despite her secretly difficult pregnancy, Mum appears healthy, rested, and as much a fashion icon as ever in the photo, stepping out of a town car in a formfitting dress with the traditional maple leaf tartan pattern. Dad cradles me in a blanket woven with the same fabric. I've seen this photo so many times that I know it by heart.

I tap back to my notifications. Many of the alerts swirl around the topic of me at tonight's ball, with a few official photos starting to surface, most showing me on the red carpet, hands in pockets. The one of me with Fi is already trending. Just as she'd hoped.

I let out a sigh. It does little to release the familiar feeling of pressure and expectation building in my heart and chest. The whole world is watching, commenting on my every move. I have to uphold the royal Dinnissen glory, or our Canada goose is cooked, because there's a lot to live up to as Crown Prince, aka Prince Royal. Mum and Dad had the perfect modern-day fairy tale love story: prince meets born-and-bred Canadian commoner and falls in love. People have always eaten up and adored their story, even with its darker, nearly-stripped-of-their-titles side to it.

Suddenly, the heat in the car has become stifling. I crack the window for some fresh air.

As much as I love the perks of being Crown Prince, sometimes I want to throw all the rules out the window. But whenever I get that urge, I remember the fiasco that was my seventeenth birthday party. I've learned my lesson. And what choice do I have? I'm trapped.

Gord is always telling me that it's much easier for Canada to get rid of our monarchy than to further change it. I can hear Gord reciting Maple Crown Rule 1, drilling it into my brain like he has my entire life: Duty to the Crown above all else.

I open the faceless alias Instagram account, aka Finsta, that I secretly made for myself—mostly to drool over slow-mo videos of people frosting cakes or pulling gooey, piping-hot cookies apart, and to read baking "top tips" from my favourite *maître pâtissiers*, or master pastry chef—Chef Pierre—who regularly unveils his latest innovative desserts at his culinary school in Paris that end up on the menu of his world-renowned bakery-café here in New York.

Of course, there are also the gay couple accounts I peruse, with varying arrays of cutesy, saccharine selfies. I want what they have.

As I scroll, I can't help daydreaming about going back to the break room, letting the cute guy pull me up onto one of those rickety little tables, his lips parting as we press against each other...

I can never tell a soul, let alone the world, about my *petit secret*.

I am absolutely certain that if I were to come out, the powers that be would find a way to strip me of my title. I can't let that happen. Do I sometimes wish I could have a normal life that allows me to settle down with a nice guy? Yes, I do. But not more than I want that crown. Besides, it would break my parents' hearts if their only son didn't succeed them on the throne.

Sure, my family has had their own fair share of secrets. Hell, there are more secrets than rules (and if you couldn't tell by now, we have a *lot* of rules). My Royal Family tree isn't without its rotten apples—or rotten maple leaves, to keep things on brand. But *I* may just be the worst. A blight, the one to petrify the family tree so that not a single leaf remains clinging to its ancient branches.

It's bad enough that the Firm and current conservative government share a little-known penchant for wanting to streamline the Royal Family, meaning the three of us could be stripped of our titles at any moment.

Selfishly, abdicating the throne would alleviate me of the immense weight to remain in the closet. But I couldn't do that to my parents, even if I *could* find a good way out, and there isn't one—out of the closet *or* out of the monarchy. After the stunt I pulled at my last birthday, Mum and Dad have felt like the three of us are in danger of losing our position in Canada and being sent to live out the rest of our days in a drafty, forgotten castle in Cornwall.

But my parents won't have to worry about the monarchy dissipating to the Chinook winds. I was *raised* to be Crown Prince of Canada, destined to fulfill my royal birthright. Even if it *does* mean no love life.

To bear a crown of power is to be alone, right?

I press my nose to the cold window glass, hearing ambulance sirens blaring in the distance. Normally, traditions imposed on the heir to the throne wouldn't be a huge problem. Except, well...

UNSPOKEN MAPLE CROWN RULE: Don't be gay, eh?

DAILY MAPLE ONLINE

THE ROYAL ROUNDUP
March 2, 06:23 a.m. ET

PRINCE EDWARD SIZZLES BACK INTO THE SPOTLIGHT
by Omar Scooby

Welcome back, Eddie! After ten months of skirting the spotlight following his seventeenth birthday debacle, the Crown Prince of Canada slides back into the social scene with a rare appearance at a star-studded gala.

Entering the ballroom last night at the Plaza Hotel, the Crown Prince of Canada was a sight to behold—wowing in a tailored suit and titillating partygoers with his wit, charm, and majestic magnetism. The world has truly missed seeing that hundred-watt smile. The *Daily Maple* spoke to an insider about what it's like for him, being a teen heartthrob.

When asked about any details surrounding the highly anticipated Investiture Ceremony, our close-to-the-royal-family insider went mum. What has the prince got up his hemmed silken sleeves? We hope to find out and see a whole lot more of him—and his winning smile—in the coming days.

RELATED STORIES
King Frederick Speaks to Prime Minister of Singapore
Queen Daphnée Promises to Lower Housing Costs
Canadian Prime Minister: Hottest Politician Alive?

Chapter Two

BILLY

"Billy!" Pax shouts at me from down the busy hallway of Little Timber High just after the last bell rings.

From my locker, I spy my best friend's DIY acid-washed violet denim jumpsuit standing out against a sea of muted flannels and dark jackets as they push their way toward me. Pax Andrews and I met in Mrs. Smith's first-grade class, where we bonded over a mutual love for Mariah Carey's Christmas album—her *first* Christmas album, that is. We don't speak of the second.

"Hey, Pax." I tip my dad's old mustard-yellow cowboy hat, then use some muscle to yank open my locker. The door gives with a screech, displaying faded rainbow stickers papered up the side, with sayings like **OUT-AND-PROUD COWBOY, LASSO YOUR DREAMS, JOLLY RANCHER**, and **SAVE A HORSE, RIDE A UNICORN**. In the grimy adhesive mirror, I catch my reflection. Patchy scruff. Tired hazel eyes. Strands of brown hair creeping out from under my hat brim. I can shear sheep till the cows come home, but my own hair? Not so much. It's best to keep it tucked under my hat, or tied back with an elastic. Though Pax has been begging to chop my floppy mop for years.

"There he is!" Pax stops in front of me, their face glowing with a sheen of sparkly setting powder. Pax is Black, and one of the few other queer kids in school. And, according to them, probably the only gender-nonconforming, nonbinary teen in all the Plains States. There's not a whole lot of diversity here in Little Timber, Montana. There's not a lot of, well… *much*. It's mostly endless blue skies, wheat fields, and gorgeous mountains dusted with the snow that blows in off the plains this time of year.

Pax thrusts their phone in my face. "Lady Sofia's look at the Gala Apple Big Apple Gala event is giving me *life!*" There's a photo of a girl our age in a ball gown with her hair up. I can almost smell her expensive perfume through the screen.

"Who is she again?" I shrug my old winter coat on over my plaid shirt and fleece sweater.

Pax gasps. "Only *Canadian nobility*."

"My bad," I say. I can never keep track of all the famous people Pax is obsessed with. Celebrities aren't too high on my priority list, not when I've got an after-school job at the general store, livestock to feed at the ranch, and homework stacked to the rafters.

Pax studies the picture again. "The dress is iconic, but it's totally the wrong fabric for the construction. I would've used charmeuse." Pax has been designing and sewing their own clothes practically since birth, using their grandma's scarecrow as their first mannequin.

I root around in my locker for my sheet music. "Literally never heard of charmeuse. Is that a hair product?"

"Oh, honey, that's why *I'm* going to Parsons to study fashion design and you're still trying to make Farmer Chic happen. If you'd just let me play stylist, dress you in anything but flannel…"

See? Relentless.

I laugh. "No way… Flannel is my first and last love."

Truth is, I'm fine just the way I am in Dad's old clothes. I like to think I can still smell him in the fabric. A mix of pine trees and sandalwood aftershave.

For Pax, what they wear *is* their identity. I get that, and I get why it's important to *them*. For me, it's just not as relevant. Call me a sucker, but I just don't see why what we look like on the outside should matter.

Pax simply rolls their eyes at me. "Flannel's your first love, huh? Tell that to Dustin, babe."

We enter the music room and cross to the cubbies, passing battered cellos and an antique upright piano missing a few keys.

"Here she is, honey!" Pax points out my cloth violin case in a cubby, my name hand stitched on the front in fraying white thread. A perk of having a crafty best friend who sews.

I curl my fingers around the handle and lift. From the case's outside pocket, a piece of paper flutters to the floor, and I scramble to grab it. But Pax beats me to it and hands it to me, revealing the Juilliard School of Music letterhead at the top in fancy script.

Dear Billy Boone:

I am pleased to inform you that the faculty has reviewed your prescreening materials and invites you to audition for The Juilliard School. Your **violin** audition has been scheduled for **Tuesday, March 8** at **10:00 a.m.**

"Just one more day and we'll be in New York City!" Pax whoops. "I'm euphoric!"

"Yeah, same." Truth is, I sound anything *but* as I zip the letter back up in my violin case.

Pax tuts. "Relax. The ranch will be *just* fine without you."

"Tell that to my mom." A pang of guilt hits me at the through of being gone for over an entire week. But the fact my audition falls during the same week as spring break was a sign from the universe. It also helps knowing I'll be traveling with my bestie. I'm still reeling that I managed to convince Mom not to come along to chaperone me, after promising her from here to Kalamazoo that we'd follow all her many, *many* safety rules.

"Sweet Mary and Muslin. This is a once in a lifetime experience." Pax points a French horn at me. "Picture it—the two of us taking the Big Apple by storm. *I* check out Parsons. *You* go to your audition. You'll remember it for the rest of your life. I can't wait. I'm *screaming*."

I take a deep breath. "You're probably right."

"Billy…" Pax sets down the horn. "It's not like you're planning on actually *attending* Juilliard."

"I know, I know…"

"Well, I wish you'd follow your dreams. Plus New York is a blossoming fruit. Little Timber is dead on the vine. And I repeat. The ranch will be fine without you for one week."

"One week *and two days*," I correct them, smiling at how hard my best friend is trying. They're usually pretty skilled at mending more than ripped seams, but right now I'm just too overwhelmed for it to work. I'm not going to tell them that, though. "You're right," I say. "Now come on. I told Dustin I'd stop by practice."

Pax glances at the clock. "Uh, don't you have work, like, *now?*"

I sigh. The things I do for Dustin. "Yes. Yes I do. So we *really* need to hurry."

Outside, that cold, dry, 30-degree Montana air hits me, and I shudder, even in my layers, as we head past the painted statue of the marmot, which is basically a mutant squirrel that lives in the ground, and also our school mascot. We step onto crunchy, ice-frosted grass and cross the curving track, dotted with scraggly trees, before entering the heat of the gym.

It echoes with Coach Clark's voice, the thump of basketballs, and the squeak of sneakers on the court.

Even without his gold-and-silver pinnie, I'd be able to recognize Dustin's six-two frame from a mile away. He bursts past a teammate and dribbles the ball to a painted line, then shoots. Pax and I cheer from the sidelines as the ball swishes through the net. Basketball is everything to the Mighty Marmots' forward. Or is it center guard? Power center? Honestly, none of it makes any sense to me. While most people around here aren't into watching college basketball except for maybe the Cats vs. Griz game, Dustin insists we watch the March Madness games every Saturday so he can keep track of his bracket.

Even after what feels like a hundred TV viewings, I still can't wrap my mind around how anyone finds basketball entertaining. But in those moments, it's like the rest of the world is lost to him, and that includes me. It's just Dustin yelling at the screen like he's convinced they can hear him. I don't get sports, and Dustin doesn't get music. But you don't have to get your person's passion to be a good match, right?

All these years, I'd thought that Pax and I were the only queer kids in the county. Turned out, there was at least one more. Dustin had always been friendly, holding doors open for me, picking me for his teams in PE, partnering with me whenever a class assignment called for pairs. I sometimes still can't believe we ended up together. It all started the day he told me he liked the birthmark on my hand, located right at the base of my thumb. I had always thought it looked like a little burn scar, but he helped me see it as a shining heart.

From the outside, it may not look like we have much in common, but like I said, I never put much value into how things look on the outside.

He spins the ball on his finger, then leaps, and dunks. When he lands, he pumps a fist up in triumph, letting out a whoop.

Coach Clark blows the whistle, and the players take a five-minute break, slapping Dustin on the back and showering him in fist bumps.

I call out to him. "Dustin!"

He turns his head in my direction, flashing a perfect white smile, and I grin. Dustin J. Cole. He's like Montana's old state slogan itself: high, wide, and handsome.

Water bottle in one hand, he wipes sweat off his forehead with the other as he runs over, until the big 2 printed on the front of his broad chest is well within my reach. I brace myself. He bear hugs me with his strong arms—and kisses me. My cold nose and lips start to warm after a few seconds, and I pull away, my fingers combing through his slightly sweaty blond hair. He can still make me feel melty, even after dating for over three years, which already seems like an eternity.

"Gaaaay!" yells a teammate.

I've been out since I was ten, so I'm used to it.

"There's always one," I mutter in annoyance.

"Haters gonna hate," Dustin replies with ease.

"Dude, come on! Not in our faces, bro!" another teammate yells, and his friends snicker.

"Okay. More than one," I correct myself.

Truth is, Dustin's teammates don't totally get his being gay, but he's such an incredible athlete that they're not going to mess with a good thing for the team by giving him too hard a time. Though we've been dating for a while now, he's only been out since November. I'm glad we can finally go public. Being a top-secret boyfriend really takes its toll on a person. But getting constantly teased isn't so great either, even if it *is* the lesser of the two evils.

Maybe Dustin's teammates are just grossed out by PDA in

general, or embarrassed about PDA in front of their coach, which I can understand. Either way, it's all small potatoes to me.

I blush, gazing into his bright eyes, so close I can see the unique brown freckle in the green of his left iris. "You're my one and only."

"Yeah, unless Ryder Russell comes to town," Dustin quips, winking. Alright, I admit it. I don't make a habit of crushing on famous people, but I do think that charismatic muscly Canadian action movie star, Ryder Russell, is handsome as all get out.

Pax rests a hand on my shoulder. "As much as I love watching Little Timber's most enraptured couple being all fierce and fab, Billy's going to be late for work, and I'm hoping he could maybe drop me home on the way?" Pax is giving me a sheepish grin. "My grandma's at the eye doctor again, and my dad agreed to pick me up, but he just texted saying he can't now. *The* worst." Pax's parents pretty much disowned them when they first starting designing and wearing dresses.

I'm already cutting it close, but I can't leave Pax stranded. "Yeah. Okay," I offer.

"Thank you! *Look* what he texted me. No explanation. No apology." Pax hands me their phone:

Pax: 4pm pickup! Don't forget!!

Dad: K.

And then, over an hour later:

Dad: Can't pick you up. Find new way home.

"That sucks. I'm sorry." As I'm looking at the screen, an alert notification pops up with the headline, **PRINCE'S ROYAL RENDEZVOUS**. I accidentally tap and it loads a video of a brown-haired boy my age in a suit and tie, climbing out of a limo while bodyguards shove cameras away, the bulbs flashing like a lightning storm in summer. "Oh, hey. Is this that random prince you have a megacrush on?"

"Huh?" Pax flips their phone around and glances at the screen. "Oh! Sorry!" Eyes huge, they hastily try to close the app, but I can still see the guy on the screen.

I squint. "Am I losing it, or does he look a little bit like me?"

Pax's eyes go even wider. "DEFINITELY NOT!"

Dustin elbows me. "Billy, you're more handsome than any old prince."

I grin at Dustin. "But I bet you'd like me better if I *were* a prince."

Pax rolls their eyes and laughs way too hard. "Ha ha, Billy. Very funny. Hey! You've gotta get to work, right? Big last shift before our trip!" They're talking a mile a minute. They must be really embarrassed about crushing on someone who looks like me. I decide to let Pax get away with changing the subject. I'm tired of talking about princes I don't know or care about anyway.

"Yeah," I say. "The store will probably be pretty busy since we're receiving our first shipment of maple butter after countless requests that we stock it."

Dustin's eyes go wide. "No way! This is only the biggest thing to happen to Little Timber since…since Orvin's Vintage opened last summer!" Sadly, it's true. Before that contemporary boutique came to town, all we had was dinky Tumbleweed Thrift Shop, and JCPenney and Dillard's in the next county over. I mean, maple butter is just pure maple sugar—made from maple syrup that's been boiled, cooled, and whipped until it's creamy and spreadable—not really anything to write home about. But one look at Dustin lets me know he'd disagree. He's smiling like he just won a prize pig.

"You maple *butter believe it*!" Pax exclaims.

"I can't wait to get my hands on some!" Dustin exclaims.

"Well, you better come on by the store quick before it sells out!" I say with all the enthusiasm I can muster. "Pax, let's skedaddle."

"Want to hang out when you're off?" Dustin asks me, quirking an eyebrow.

I smile and gently knock my violin case against his thigh. "I have to practice."

"Of course you do. Right." Dustin shakes his head. "I should've realized that." His eyes probe mine. It's like he's asking me to pick between him and violin, or maybe that's the guilt talking. Then again, he's the same guy who'd rather I use my hands to rub his shoulders than to rosin my bow.

My stomach knots up, thinking about my audition. Dustin flipped when I mentioned I'd been thinking of applying. After he eventually picked up one of my frantic calls, I reassured him, like how I'd reassured everyone, that I'm going to my audition just for the experience, and not because I'm seriously considering going to school in New York City.

"I love you," I say, in an effort to smooth things over. It works.

Dustin grins. "I can't wait to graduate," he tells me. "You and I can settle down, maybe eventually start a family right here in Little Timber." He bops my nose, then adds, "And every night, you can play me to sleep on your violin."

Pax pouts, hand on their chest. "My heart," they coo.

I take a gulp of air to help stop the dizziness that comes out of nowhere. Apparently Dustin has our entire future mapped out. I haven't even finished high school yet. Heat prickles in my armpits and creeps up my neck. It's all I can do to give a tight smile and nod.

Coach Clark jogs over. "Hey, quit hogging our MVP!" he only half teases. "Break's over!"

"Sure thing, Coach Clark," I say, almost too readily.

I give Dustin one last squeeze before I go.

After dropping off Pax, I drive Dad's rusty 1988 Dodge Ram through downtown Little Timber, nestled at the foothills of the majestic Rockies. Main Street is picturesque and idyllic, especially with the sun starting to sink into the mountains. It's postcard-perfect. But like a postcard, it never changes.

I roll on past the distressed wood plank held up by rusty poles, with painted block letters that sum up the town:

WELCOME TO LITTLE TIMBER
FOUNDED 1869
POPULATION: 1,149
THE LAST BEST PLACE

In no time at all, I reach the end of my one-road town, which is lined with parked cars tonight, and pull into the tiny but fairly crowded back lot behind Little Timber General situated in an icy clearing of dirt and cottonwood. The old two-story building has peeling white clapboard, pasted with signs advertising things like PAINT & VARNISH, BOOTS & SHOES, DRY GOODS, and ROPE.

The store hosts gear swaps, garage sales, and 4-H meetings year-round, usually led by me, the president of the Little Timber chapter. Over the porch flies an American flag, a Montana state flag, and a tiny rainbow one. An older gay couple, the Howard-Loyolas, own the store. They've been together since they were kids, and they're practically famous around here. But ever since they got married, some locals refuse to refer to them as anything other than best friends, or roommates. Still, nearly everyone in Little Timber loves them, and those who don't pretty much leave them alone. Where else are the locals going to buy their essentials? Especially now that we have maple butter. Practically half the town's here.

Something tells me I'm in for another long, busy shift. But it's worth being able to afford things like violin lessons. Plus I love being around the Howard-Loyolas. It's nice to see how in love they still are after all these long years.

I step inside. It's warm, noisy, and smells like a hot stack of pancakes.

"Billy! Glad you could make it!" shouts Mr. Jackson Howard-Loyola, with his thinning silver hair.

"Sorry I'm late!" I join him and his husband, Isaac, behind the counter, throwing on my apron. On the wall hangs a sepia photo of the general store from when they first built it.

"We're going to miss you next week," Jackson says. The reminder that I'll be visiting New York in a finger snap sends a white-hot spark zinging through my blood—the mix of excitement and nerves stronger than before. "But you are going to love it there—we try to go every year for Pride!" he adds.

"I'll miss you guys too." I get to work, ringing up customers and handing out samples of maple butter on cut-up pieces of toast.

Streamers and balloons hang from the unfinished rafters alongside tools and pots. In the center of the room is a tower of jars, each wrapped in glossy red ribbon. Clearly, maple butter *is* the biggest thing to happen in Little Timber in months, or possibly ever. Plus I think the Howard-Loyolas love any excuse to celebrate.

By the time I close the shop at 9:00 p.m., my feet ache from standing, and I stagger back to my truck, maple butter jar heavy in hand.

Isaac runs up to the window, and I crank it down as he fishes in his coat pocket and hands me a wad of cash. "For your big week in the Big Apple!"

I shake my head. "I...couldn't."

He closes my fingers around the crumpled bills. "Keep it. And make the most of it, okay? Order hotel room service!" He joins Jackson on the stoop, takes his hand, and they both wave.

"Thank you!" I call out, then I roll up the window and peel off.

It's about ten miles to home, down a lonely, wide-open road, with barely another building in sight. Which is just another way of saying "smack in the middle of nowhere."

I slow my truck around a herd of cows, then turn into the long gravel drive. Our horses, cows, and sheep stir beyond the fence in the dark, their barn and pasture around it carpeted with snow. High above me, set against the vast sky of stars, is our rickety wooden sign: OLD BOONE RANCH.

I'm passing the two oaks Mom and Dad planted on the property, then the third oak, then the fourth and final one. Four oaks, one for each Boone. I look forward to when the frost fades and their leaves grow. Mack, my little sister, got her oak planted the same day she was born. Mine was planted a week *after* I was born. That's because Mom insisted she and Dad go to her best friend's wedding in Canada even though I was due the next week. But I decided to show up early.

Shortly after arriving in Canada, Mom and Dad had to rush to a hospital in Montreal, where I was born. I almost died from complications, but emergency surgery saved me. It's why Mom calls me her "Little Miracle." After an extended stay in the NICU, my parents holed up in Montreal before we flew the two thousand miles home. They said I slept the entire time. Healthy, happy, and theirs.

The Boones have always been survivors. At least, until three years ago. I suppose it's too much to ask for more than one little miracle to bless a home. Or to stop cancer in its tracks.

As I rumble on past, I slow to wave at Dad's tree. "Hi, Dad," I say quietly. It's my tradition whenever I come and go. Then

I drive the rest of the way up the path to the house. Mom and Dad built our big ranch house together. Got married here too. We're true country folk.

I park next to Mom's truck and the pile of firewood I chopped yesterday before school. It's silent except for the dripping of icicles on the eaves, and the crunch of my mud-spattered boots over gravel. Then I'm up the two creaky steps and through the screen and front door, unlocked, like always.

Inside, just the foyer light's on, barely illuminating caps and scarves wrapped over hooks. Above them hangs a sign that says **FAITH · FAMILY · FRIENDS**, its letters crafted out of twisted barbed wire and set in wood. With leaving for New York tomorrow, I can't bear to look at the sign. I love this ranch, and part of me has this deep need to carry on Dad's legacy, dedicate my life to it the way he did.

I hang up my keys and pass through the dining room and into the kitchen. From the smell of meatballs in the air, everyone's eaten. Being a rancher means keeping a fridge stocked with beef and trying to think up new ways to prepare it. I place the jar of maple butter on the counter as a nice surprise for Mom, down a cold glass of milk, and step into the den.

It's quiet and dark. Mack is likely in her room, posting life hacks or makeup reviews on her YouTube channel. Since the day she could talk, Mack has said that she wants to be famous, which means she wants out of Montana. She has no interest in running the ranch, and everyone knows it. She's been so jealous that I'm going to New York with Pax for spring break without her. I have faith her day will come.

Mom must be bent over her own computer, wearing her accountant-and-money-manager hat as she reconciles the books or writes emails to vendors. It's a typical Thursday night here at the Boone residence. It's been this way ever since we lost Dad. I don't know how Mom manages to keep the ranch afloat, but she does.

Heaviness weighs on my chest again.

Violin in hand, I stop in front of the mantel and pick up the framed family photo. In it, we're huddled on the back porch, Mom's blond curls swept away from her pale face, Dad's blue eyes squinting against the midday sun, and Mack looking like their spitting image, braided pigtails falling down either shoulder in her faded denim overalls and cowgirl hat.

I study myself in the photo, a hopeful boy with hazel eyes, brown hair, and olive skin, standing next to my fair family with their blue eyes and flaxen-blond hair. I know it's just the result of Grammy Boone's genes skipping a generation, but it didn't stop Mack from teasing the idea that I was adopted back when we were younger. I set the frame back, and trace my fingertip around Dad's smiling face.

"Hi, dear." Mom's voice startles me, and I whip around. She glances at the framed photo, and her warm smile deepens. "I miss him too."

I shake my head. "Yeah. I can't believe it's been almost three years."

Mom walks over and pulls me into a hug. "He was a wonderful man. I know he's still here, watching over us."

I start to say something, but words catch in my throat. I like when my mom talks about him, but it's always just as tough to swallow that he's gone. I like to think he's still here too.

"You gonna practice your violin tonight?" Mom asks in a cheerful way, stepping back.

I nod.

"I still can't believe you're going to New York for an audition at Juilliard." She pauses, and by the look on her face, I know what's coming. The same question that's cropped up every night since she bought my plane ticket. "You're absolutely sure you don't need me to come with you to New York?"

"Mom, I'll be fine. You need to stay here and take care of the place."

"I just keep wondering if I should have asked one of your teachers to go along with you, or Mr. Howard-Loyola—"

"Mom, we've talked about this. I'll call you every night, and I have your typewritten list of what to do and what not to do. All twenty-seven pages of it."

Mom laughs. "You know it's only twenty-two."

I suppress a laugh of my own. "That's right, Mom. Twenty-two pages."

She sighs. "I just worry about you so much when you're not around."

"I know. You've felt this way ever since you almost lost me in that Canadian hospital, but I'm careful, you know that." I give her a big hug.

She hugs me back. "I know. It's just... I could never forgive myself if I lost you too." She smiles fondly. "Well, what are you waiting for, you better go practice. You've got some judges to impress."

I grin. "I'll go now."

"Alright, well, get to it. I'm old. I have to go to bed soon."

My cry comes out as a little laugh, and I wipe my eyes.

"Hey." She pauses in the kitchen doorway, and looks long and hard at me. "Remember you've got a family and a boyfriend here who adore you. Don't fall in love with New York too much."

I laugh. "What do you mean?"

"You know your dad always wanted you to be the one to take care of the ranch."

She's right, which just hurts worse. "I know..." I give a heavy sigh, removing my hat and tossing it on the pullout couch. "You remember I'm not actually trying to get into this school, right? I just want the experience of playing violin for world-class experts in New York City," I say softly.

"I still think it's silly to waste their time and yours on an audition for a school you don't plan to attend, and for a school we definitely could never afford, but if it's that important to you, then go do it. It'll be a memory you'll have for the rest of your life."

I smile. "Thanks for understanding, Mom. You're the best."

She gives a nod of her head. "I'll see you in the morning to take you and Pax to the airport." Then she slips into the kitchen to fix herself her nightly mug of peppermint tea.

In my room, I change into cozy flannel pajamas. I want nothing more than to dive headlong into bed, to cuddle up under my quilt and sleep. But first, I need to practice. If not, I'll end up lying in bed, staring up at the ceiling and going over the notes in my head until dawn. I plan to play better at this audition than I ever have before, or ever will again. It'll be worth the time and the money just for that one epic moment.

I can hear Mack through the wall, recording another vlog. "It's MACK ATTACK! Welcome back to my channel! Today, I'll be ranking the flavor of every glitter Chapstick in this ten-flavor multipack! Let's dig in!" She's super responsible, which is probably why when she asked Mom on her thirteenth birthday earlier this year if she could finally start vlogging, Mom agreed—under three conditions: she has to finish her homework first; she can only vlog about topics Mom approves; and she can't reveal any personal information so that there's no risk of creepy stalkers. I have to say, she's done a really good job of sticking to the rules so far. And as much as she can bug me sometimes, I'm still going to miss her.

I open my case and gaze lovingly at my violin, resting on its velvet lining. For me, playing is a way to relax and escape. To close my eyes and be somewhere else. It's never been a career, or a path forward. I've always known my future is with the ranch. Pax, on the other hand, will crush it as a New York fashion designer, and I'll be rooting them on every step of the way from Little Timber, growing old with Mom, the timeworn house, the land down to its four aging oaks, making the best of things. Maybe even starting that family with Dustin one day.

If I'm being honest with myself, I'm more excited to go to The City That Never Sleeps and play at Juilliard than I am nervous. I'll get to perform in a room where great musicians have played before me, rather than in a high school orchestra room that perpetually smells of bologna and Swiss. To imagine, just once, that I'm living in another life where I can train to become a prestigious musician. I can't deny how much it will mean to me to have this experience, even if it will be bittersweet.

As silly as it sounds, I've always felt like I was destined for something more, and maybe that something more is this audition. Which is why I have to go to New York with Pax. That way, when I'm back in Montana for good, I can at least say I experienced something special. Like Mom said, I'll have the memory of my Juilliard audition for the rest of my life, even if I never leave Montana again. The ranch was my dad's lifework, meaning I'm obligated to keep it going and commit myself to it.

How else can I keep his memory alive?

The audition won't be the start of something new, but it *could* be a beautiful goodbye to the dream.

Closure.

I just hope the memory of New York will be enough.

I resin my bow, lift my old faithful brown solid wood Cremona SV-75 out of its case with great care, tuck into the chinrest, and let my bow glide. My violin emits a note that sounds like the cry of a soaring eagle, and I switch between strings, closing my eyes as the music overtakes me. I feel a smile tug at the corners of my mouth, and I'm no longer alone. I play on, warmed. Alive. With Dad again.

THE ROYAL ROUNDUP

March 4, 07:01 am ET

PRINCE EDWARD AND LADY SOFIA'S
RIVETING ROYAL ROMANCE

by Omar Scooby

Spring winds have arrived to warm the provinces along with our hearts as Prince Edward and Lady Sofia Marchand spark more rumblings about a possible romance. Have these two truly gone from snowbirds to lovebirds?

After a year off the grid, Canada's Crown Prince appeared at Tuesday's star-studded charity ball in New York, as well as at last night's Gala Apple Big Apple Gala, looking better than ever on each occasion. Everyone from Victoria to St. John's wonders if it's due to Prince Edward's growing flirtation with Lady Sofia.

Partygoers got a gander at the two rumoured sweethearts arm in arm, seeming awfully comfortable with one another in a manner that suggests they may be more than friends. One partygoer even claimed she had a picture of him as the wallpaper on her phone.

They both attend St. Aubyn's Prep, also located in New York, but whispers of their budding romance first began long before Prince Edward headed to New York City for his senior year of high school six months ago, when Lady Sofia just so happened to be headed for the very same school then as well… Interesting!

Will we see them together at more future galas and events? Will their rumoured royal romance toboggan toward a swift engagement and royal wedding extravaganza? Order yourself a double-double, and hold on to your toques, folks—you never know when the dry rice will snow down upon their nuptials!

RELATED STORIES

Freddie and Daffy Attend World Bank Soirée
Daphnée Condemns Anti-Asian Hate Crimes
Royal Pooch Evie Gets Pampered
Lady Sofia Revives the Velour Track Suit

Chapter Three

EDWARD

With a slow stretch, I roll over in my high-grade sheets to grab the remote control and turn up the volume of the cheesy romance movie. Propping myself up, I pluck a chocolate tart from my side table with its vase of fresh-cut hydrangeas and old-world-filigree collectables, nibbling as I keep my eyes fixed on the LED TV.

After watching *Canada's Next Great Baker* for hours last night, and eating my fair share of crème fraiche and strawberries, among other sweets, I woke to the TV still on and now running a rom-com movie marathon. This one is about a gay couple falling in love, which is a first for me. I've never seen gay rom-coms on network cable. It's a good thing none of my footmen have come knocking at my door.

The lead actor has burly muscles, an intoxicating smile, and a jawline that could slice diamonds. I daydream about kissing him. I've never kissed anyone before; if I ever did, I'd want it to be special. But the monarchy has never had a gay royal. *Quelle surprise.* It's built on doing things the way they've always been done to maintain their cookie-cutter image, and tamping down any indication of uniqueness in family members. The monarchy is rooted so deep in traditions that it re-

ally should be referred to as the magma core, as opposed to
the upper crust.

So... Duty to the Crown above all else, right?

As I watch the leading man in the movie flirt with the other
leading man at an outdoor candlelit dinner, I realize I need to
hurry and get ready for my day. The life of a Crown Prince
means I've always got things to do and places to go, like school
in T-minus thirty. I swing my legs around the side of the bed
when my phone blares to life with the "O Canada" ringtone.

Crisse. Mum.

Some people have momagers. Me? I am in the unique position of having what I call a "momarch."

I fumble with the remote control to mute the gay couple
now loudly making out on-screen.

"Morning!" I say, while fighting to get the jammed mute
button to work.

"Hello, darling," Mum says. She pauses. "Is everything alright? What's going on over there?"

"Nothing!" The button finally unsticks and mutes the moans.
Fiou! I walk to the latticed bay window, squinting against a
peach-hued sunrise. "Bit early to be calling me, don't you
think?" My voice is light and playful.

"I think it's *lovely* to start off the day with a quick conversation with my darling son," Mum says. I can practically
hear her smiling through the phone. I can picture her seated
at our lavish dining room table in Rideau Hall, our family
motto emblazoned on the crest over the fireplace: *Élegance et
Simplicité.* "Oh, and your father's on the line too," she adds,
along with the clink of her porcelain teacup against its saucer. "Say hello, Frederick!"

"Morning, son," Dad chimes in. "Hope you're well. Gord
tells us you've been a picture of professionalism as of late."

"Huh. I've got both of you on the line," I remark. "And sounding in fine spirits at that. What's wrong?"

"Nothing!" Mum says brightly. How does she always manage to be so chipper first thing in the morning? "We saw the photos. Is it true, darling? Do you have something you want to tell us?"

"About what?" I ask, only half-listening while watching the gay couple silently spooning on-screen.

"You and *Sofia*!" Mum practically chirps.

Hearing her name feels like a splash of cold water. Crashing back to reality, the smile slides off my face. They've got my undivided attention. "Go on…"

"You know, it's so funny. This article says you two may have been dating for a while…" Mum continues. I can tell she's using her famous queenly powers of persuasion, trying to get me to tell her what's going on. "But I wanted to hear it from you. Tell us all about it, won't you?"

"That's right, son," Dad says. "Give it to us straight."

I don't think I can give them anything *straight*.

"Oh! I haven't seen the news. Just a moment." I check the *Daily Maple Online*—the trashiest grocery store tabloid that sprung up in every Loblaws and Sobeys over the years that's now also easily accessible from anyone's phone. Most un-Canadian. I spot a lengthy write-up on me, and decide I prefer the highlights.

So, I open Twitter and there we are: Number 1 trending worldwide. #Edfia. Fi hanging off my arm. Each of us laughing flirtatiously while dressed to the nines. And, do I detect an actual sparkle in her eye? Captions range from **Rumour Patrol: Edward and Sofia Secretly Dating?** to **Canada's Lovebirds Look Stunning at Charity Galas.**

Even *I've* got to admit they're rather convincing photos.

I silently chuckle. While Fi is a clout-chasing schemer, I'm one step ahead. I knew when she came hunting for a photo op both nights that she was hoping to get a bump from being seen acting chummy with the prince. But I've been happy to play her like she's been playing me. And so far, I'd say my maneuvers have been a success—the photos are definitely taking some heat off the old rumour mill about the "Perpetually Single Prince of the Provinces."

I lift the phone back to my ear. "So I see."

"Well?" asks Mum.

Then Dad chimes in. "Is it true, son?" I can picture his cheeky grin, the one the public rarely gets to see.

"Is *what* true?" I ask.

"Darling, are you distracted? I feel like we don't have your full attention," Mum says.

I mash my forehead against the cool windowpane, and shut my eyes. "You know Fi and I have known each other since we were children," I say. "You know that."

"But we didn't know you'd gotten *close*," Mum replies. "When did that happen?"

"Just recently, I suppose." I figure the reply works as both vague and satisfactory. "And since when did you start putting stock into the *Daily Maple*?"

Her voice brightens even more, ignoring my last remark. "Well, what an exciting new chapter!"

"Wonderful! Simply wonderful!" Dad says. "She's got an impeccable pedigree."

"Dad, you can't talk about women like that. She's not a poodle." He should know better. He's married to someone whose antisexism speeches for UN Women made the history books.

"She's a tremendous, ambitious, brilliant young woman," Mum adds. "Oh, you two will be absolutely perfect together!"

I'm fine fooling the world. But a small part of me hates that I'm fooling my parents, aka the real reason I never want to come out.

MAPLE CROWN RULE 15: Follow the plan.

"I'm overjoyed you approve. Now, if that's all, I have school."

"Listen, darling, we'd like to get ahead of this and officially announce it before anything else leaks out," Mum says.

"Sure," I say. Fi is going to love that. And owe me big time.

"Perfection!" Mum says. "We should celebrate. The four of us…a little something at the mansion? Perhaps before your Investiture Ceremony?"

"Wonderful idea, Daphnée," Dad chimes in.

"Great! I'll have Gord send over my schedule. Must dash!"

After hanging up and hurling my phone on the bed, I head for my walk-in closet. In minutes, I'm dressed in my fitted gray slacks, white button-up, and navy blazer with shiny gold buttons and St. Aubyn's opulent crest embroidered on the breast— a red cross with the date 1905 scrawled underneath it. I pin on my maple leaf brooch, lace up my azure-blue luxury sneakers, and then wiggle a bucket hat onto my head. I add giant sunglasses and an oversize black hoodie to complete the look. All to evade any potential paparazzi lurking outside.

MAPLE CROWN RULE 41: Maintain a low profile in daily life.

I flip up the hood, pulling its drawstrings tight, shoulder my knapsack, and stride out of the bedroom, down the labyrinthine corridors of the West Wing (I look forward to moving my stuff into the newly renovated East Wing after the Investiture), and into the marbled lobby. I'm saluting good morning to the doorman when it hits me like a sack of bricks.

I left the gay Hallmark movie on.
Tabarnak!

I rush back upstairs, refusing to let some frivolous Hallmark movie do me in. Gord would blow a gasket if he ever found out my secret. Let's just say the one time Mum proposed part-nering with an LGBTQIA+ organization, he reminded us that it had "potential to become a bit messy in the press." So very *not* Canadian of him, but very on-brand.

I change the channel before switching off the TV. In the darkened screen, I suddenly no longer recognize myself.

St. Aubyn's. The Upper East Side top private school of the elite, typified by its small but powerful student body. It looks inconspicuous enough from the outside. Just another narrow five-story brick building on a quiet tree-lined street within walking distance of my mansion, though of course, my chauf-feur drops me off. And like my place, the sumptuous interiors of St. Aubyn's brim with ornate details, giving it the sophis-tication and elegance of a New England manor, despite the fact that it's a K–12 school with tests, homework, and com-monplace tween and teen gossip.

I duck past the front door and swipe my ID badge. The scent of old books and carpet cleaner fills my nose. In homeroom, I sit through Ms. Dasgupta's ramblings about senior projects before she dismisses us promptly at 8:00 a.m. From the vacant looks on other students' faces, it's clear they've all checked out before spring recess.

Walking to first period, I catch up with Neel in a sconce-lit and carpet-lined corridor. Today he's accessorized his school uniform with a chic silk shirt and velvet loafers, and his dense dark hair's been blow-dried into its gloriously glossy trade-mark pompadour.

"So..." Neel says when he sees me, waggling his microbladed eyebrows. "Don't you want to ask me about the other night, my dear? You know I love telling a sordid story."

We round a corner and pass the giant globe outside our state-of-the-art library. Neel spanks the globe, sending it spinning.

"How was the party?" I ask, indulging him.

"It was fun," he says, hitching up the refined leather satchel holding his tablet. "Very, very fun."

I pull a Neel and clap a hand over my heart. "Is that all I get? *Fun?*"

"Let's just say you missed out on table dancing." Neel shimmies.

"Not *table dancing*," I say with put-on shock.

Neel regards me. "Hey, you doing okay? You seem a bit more down than usual."

"Nothing gets past you," I say, impressed. "My parents called this morning. They saw the photos of Fi and me at the galas and think we're dating. Apparently, everybody does."

Neel guffaws. "That's so perfect. 'Edfia' lives again."

"Actually, though." I laugh. "Speaking of calls, did you ever hear back from that guy about getting a first date on the books? Where did that leave off?" I admire Neel's bravery at being open about his sexuality in ways that I never could. Like how he's on every dating app in existence: private, membership-based ones and otherwise.

"His name's *Leo*, and no, not yet, but we're close to nailing something down. He texted me this morning."

"So, when's the wedding?" I tease.

"You *know* I don't have a romantic bone in my body. Well, maybe one." He chuckles. "Meaning this is just for *fun*."

"Something you seem to have a pretty good grip on," I assert.

We emerge onto the second floor, with its polished medieval suits of armor, antique lamps with green glass shades, and shelves of gilded leatherbound books. Typical St. Aubyn's décor.

"Well, your supposed hetero-hookup is news to me, Edward," Neel jokes. He's clearly peeved I didn't include him in the scheme. "But this is good news, right? I mean, you must be pretty psyched." He knows as well as I do what this publicity stunt does for me.

"It's complicated. I'm glad the news broke. I also despise everything," I say. "Hey, at this rate, maybe we can double date," I joke. I don't bother mentioning how Mum and Dad want a double date of their own.

We start up another staircase, this time joined by some of our chatty and equally well-dressed fellow students, which calls for a topic change. Neel catches on. Another reason we're best friends.

"In more important news!" he exclaims. "Only eight weeks remain before the big day, and for me to find my hot plus-one!"

"Eight weeks? Is that all?" I try to play it off with a smile, although I know *exactly* how many days are left before the Investiture Ceremony that will mark my eighteenth birthday: fifty-seven.

We step onto the third-floor landing and stop outside the St. Aubyn's-crest-adorned school store.

"Well, I hope you have a birthday variety of outfits planned because, naturally, I'm going to kidnap you and take you to Mykonos for a weekend of debauchery to celebrate. I'm telling you now so you can find a way to ditch Gordzilla and make it happen."

"Yeah, wish me luck with that," I shoot back.

"You'll find a way! And if that falls through, we can always slip across the Ottawa River into Quebec and take advantage of the drinking age being only eighteen."

"Of course. You always have a backup plan."

Neel winks, then jerks his thumb over his shoulder. "I'm hitting the café for my morning veggie sausages. Catch you in a few, my love." He saunters off down the corridor.

April 30 is the day of the Investiture Ceremony when I'll be named the official heir to the throne, Prince Royal. I've been in training for it my entire life, intensely so for the past year under the tutelage of Gord.

The very public ceremony will be the culmination of everything I've worked so hard for, just like other Royals before me. During a televised assembly outside Parliament Hill in Ottawa, I'll be reciting the family lineage and promising to help create an even better Canada. Half the speech will be given in French. When I pointed out there are actually seventy First Nations languages spoken across Canada, Gord gave me a withering look and told me not to be "political." After my speech, I'll receive the sword, ring, and scepter, on loan from Granny, along with a newly commissioned gaudy-fabulous Maple Crown and ridiculously garish Maple Mantle to look the part of—what was it Fi called me?

"Canada's Golden Child!"

En parlant du loup.

I whirl around. Fi's standing at the bottom of the stairs. Today, her school blazer is thrown effortlessly on over a magnificent zodiac-printed silk dress, fastened high on the torso with matching belt and buckle.

"Eddie-Bear!" Her voice rings out. "Where'd you run off to last night, cupcake? I had to face the Twittersphere alone this morning when just *think*, we could've been love-scrolling side by side over morning lattes."

"Eddie-Bear?" I smirk. "So, we're on to pet names now, are we? I must have missed the memo, *mon amour.*"

She tucks her embossed hourglass handle bag with a bow-shaped diamante clasp—a one of a kind, I'm sure—under her arm and sashays up the stairs toward me. "In all seriousness, I wanted to say thank you. I'm already fielding calls from Hilfiger and Revlon."

"So glad I could be of service." I move to walk off.

"Eddie, wait!" She lunges at me and pins a finger to my sternum. "What are you doing after school?"

"Hmm, let's see." I pretend to look pensive. "Homework."

She squints at me. "Right. On the Friday before spring recess."

"Then...prince training," I bite back.

"Oh, stop." She laughs and bats the air, as if shooing away a compliment. "Until AP Chem, my dear," she says and then kisses both my cheeks, whispering, "I'm sure it'll be explosive," before sauntering off.

Not even a minute later, I'm halfway down the fourth-floor corridor when my phone dings like all hell. I stop to open my Google alerts and see a bird's-eye view video of Fi and me on the school stairs. As in, from our fleeting tête-à-tête mere seconds ago. If I didn't know any better, I'd say I was watching footage of lovers in a clandestine meeting, exchanging sweet nothings. It's accompanied by the #Edfia hashtag. I join my classmates conspiring outside the door to AP English. They look up over the tops of their phones at me and snicker. Trying not to look visibly ruffled, I smile back, and quickly beeline to Neel who's eating his breakfast across the corridor.

Crashing beside him on the bench, I show him my phone. "It's already trending," I say, watching the view count climb.

Neel scans the video and smiles. "Clever girl."

"What?"

"You can't honestly believe someone randomly caught that moment? Fi clearly orchestrated the whole thing," he whispers. "She knows *exactly* what she's doing."

"Touché. I underestimated her." So, she's capitalizing on

the fake-girlfriend storyline. This means I'm *forced* to play the part of her royal beau to keep up the charade.

Neel's phone dings. "Oh hello, lovely Leo," he says, smiling at his text messages. "Why, yes, I *can* grab coffee Tuesday morning."

I tug the sleeve of his tailored blazer. "You're coming with me to the Lincoln Center Canadian First Nations exhibit on Tuesday morning, remember?"

He closes his eyes and sighs. "Ah yes. How could I possibly forget spending a morning of my spring recess at a museum gallery?" He finishes the last of his veggie sausages, then digs a pot of lip balm out of his satchel and applies it to pursed lips. "Although I'm looking forward to watching this speech you've been stressing about."

On top of preparing for the Investiture Ceremony, I've been putting in overtime training with Gord to give one of the keynote opening speeches at a new museum exhibit that celebrates the 634 different First Nations communities in Canada alongside other representatives of Canadian government and the First Nations. As a dedicated royal representative, I've learned the proper pronunciations for each, from the Tsuut'ina Nation to the Tlingit. Mispronouncing a word during my speech would be far worse than a faux pas—it would be a sign of disrespect. And so, I've spent many nights practicing both with Gord and in front of my bedroom mirror.

MAPLE CROWN RULE 100: The job of a royal is never done.

"Perfect," I say. "So, you'll be there." It's more of a statement than a question.

Neel quirks an eyebrow. "You're my best friend, *bharā*. Do I really have a choice?"

DAILY MAPLE ONLINE

THE ROYAL ROUNDUP
March 7, 04:28 am ET

INVESTITURE CEREMONY:
EVERYTHING WE KNOW SO FAR
by Omar Scooby

The world holds its breath for the Investiture Ceremony of Prince Edward—but what particulars do we know thus far about the biggest royal event of the modern century?

The Investiture Ceremony will mark the day the Crown Prince of Canada officially vows his loyalty and allegiance to Canada. While details of the event have not yet been disclosed to the public, speculation about the theme, décor, location, and guest list has begun to swirl around Prince Edward's most monumental day.

The centuries-old British custom passed down to the Canadian Royals will surely have its own unique flavour and flair. Perhaps The Queen Mother will pass down her own son's investiture coronet? Who will be in attendance? And how is Prince Edward planning on vowing his oath to uphold the values of the Canadian people? The *Daily Maple* will be monitoring the story closely, and posting any and all intel surrounding the mysterious ceremony as it trickles in. More soon, HeirHeads!

RELATED STORIES
Canadian Royals Wax Figures Finally Join British Set at Madame Tussauds
Black Lives Matter Demonstration: Freddie Takes a Knee
Queen Daphnée Announces Indigenous Communities Support Fund
Edward's Birthday Portraits Are Out and About Early!
Duke of Cambridge Feels Unsafe Coming to Canada?

Chapter Four

BILLY

"See, Billy? Isn't New York so cute?" Pax asks from where we sit in the back seat of the yellow taxi on Monday.

All weekend long, they've been pointing out how great New York is, from Saturday's tour of the Empire State Building during which I tried to spot Juilliard from all the way up on the eighty-sixth floor—it was like searching for a needle in a concrete haystack—to yesterday's ferry ride to wave at the Statue of Liberty, to exploring Parsons School of Design. As afraid as I am of what the future may hold, I admit their excitement is finally starting to rub off on me.

"Absolutely," I reply with a grin. I'm all bundled up in my winter coat and thick thermal socks inside my boots, strands of my long brown hair spilling out from my cowboy hat. There's just something about New York City that makes my face ache from smiling so much.

"Oh my God, Times Square is serving *looks*, honey!" Pax jabs a gloved hand toward the window, and we marvel at bright, larger-than-life billboards flashing on the sides of buildings. Crowds of people cross in front of us. A knockoff Hello Kitty and Minnie Mouse beckon to passersby with soggy-looking mitts. Pigeons fight over fallen pretzels. It's beautiful, down to its crumbs.

I lower the window and let the roasted chestnut scent waft in. Although it's cold, it's not Little Timber cold. The muffled sounds from seconds ago are sharper and clearer now. Whistles. Megaphone voices. Clanging bicycle bells. Sirens growing softer as ambulances move away. It's all so different from home, so alive and electric. People walk with purpose, people of all shapes and sizes. I spy a young gay couple holding hands, and can't help imagining living here, being that couple. I already feel at home.

Dad would have hated it, probably. All the noise and chaos. But it still makes me sad that he never got to come here.

My phone trills with a text. I wonder if it's Mom checking in on me again, or Mack asking if I've had any celebrity sightings yet.

Dustin: Miss me yet?

I scrunch up my nose, toying with the idea of replying now or later, and show my phone to Pax.

They flare their nostrils. "Umm, isn't that, like, the fifth time he's texted you that today? He's incessant!"

"Right?" I should reply, but there'll be nothing *but* time for Dustin when I'm back. I close out the text. The taxi passes Madame Tussauds, where a sign features a new epic Royals exhibit.

"Hey, did you want to check out the waxworks of the Canadian Royals?" I ask Pax, reading the sign advertising how they've joined the British collection at long last. Whatever that means.

They shrug. "If we have time! But we also totes don't have to."

"You, not wanting to see something Royals-related?" I joke. "Are you feeling okay?"

Pax swats at me. "What? Of course! I'm feeling a hundred percent times ten! Minus almost stepping on that dead rat."

The taxi dumps us out, leaving us as one with the city. Pax pulls me in for a selfie for this hashtag moment, hand on their hip, hair whipped fiercely back over their shoulder.

It's a short walk to the subway station at Times Square, where a girl on the platform plays "The Lark Ascending" on violin. I'd know those notes anywhere, but I never expected to hear them *here*, of all places. It shatters something inside, but the sharp pain turns into that dull pang that's always there these days, deep down inside me. The song was one of the first I ever learned by heart. It was also the song that Dad loved hearing me practice most, and the song I played at his funeral. He used to say, *The universe works in funny ways.* Guess he was right about that one.

I toss three well-spent dollars into her open case, then swipe my Metro card and breeze through the turnstile like I've been doing it my whole life. I try to tune out Mom's warnings of the dangers of subways, which include a pizza-eating rat. We hop aboard the crowded R train headed to Prince Street. The tourist blog Pax found said there are great cafés there. I'm craving a strong cup of coffee, and Pax wants to check out SoHo for its fancy shops and celebrity hot spots, so we spend the next ten minutes gripping a grimy, germy pole (sorry, Mom!) and trying not to let each grating stop send us sideways.

To pass the time, I listen to my repertoire in my earbuds, starting with Paganini and ending with Bach. The jaunty and plucky nature of the concertos in my ears color the subway car in a calm light, despite its harsh fluorescents. I keep reminding myself, I'm not auditioning to get in. I'm auditioning for the *experience.* For the *adventure.* Tomorrow is purely for fun.

I notice I'm starting to get looks from passengers. It's not just my imagination; one person stares wide-eyed at me, then whispers to their friend, whose eyes sweep sideways till they lock on to mine, then dart away. Another passenger ogles me, but averts their gaze when I turn my head toward them. A kid in a wool cap aims their phone my way…for a secret picture?

Okay, now you're just being paranoid. He's texting.

Still, I shift nervously. "Is it just me, or is everyone staring at me?" I whisper to Pax.

They purse their lips. "Honey, are you honestly surprised with that hat and those boots?" Okay, so they may have a point.

At Prince Street, we head up a flight of steps with the rest of the herd, emerging onto the corner of Broadway and Prince. We wander down Mulberry until a charming brick building with dead ivy clinging to its side catches my eye. I gaze up at an old wooden sign that reads BLUE UNICORN CAFÉ, its logo a unicorn's sparkling horn spearing a croissant.

Pax opens their eyes wide. "Don't you just *love* a fantasy-themed café?" They glow, tilting their head up toward the sign.

Inside, we find ourselves staring at a humongous menu wall that would put the Little Timber Diner to shame.

"So many options…" I muse, reading about a centaur cold brew and then a mermaid mocha.

"Welcome to New York." The barista wipes his tidy apron. He's got square-cut diamonds in his ears, sculpted scruff, tattoos, and the prettiest green eyes I've ever seen.

I laugh, feeling my face growing warm. I wasn't prepared for, well, *this*. And is it really that obvious we're not from around here? Guess so. I unzip my coat.

Pax elbows me and clears their throat. "Tell the nice barista what you want."

Shaking my thoughts, I glance at what a nearby person's got in front of them. A steaming hot mug of coffee with a unicorn's profile pressed in the glittering foam. Without bothering to check the price, I gesture. "That looks good."

Pax glances at the drink, and grimaces. "Coming from the guy who likes maple syrup in his milk," they mutter.

"Hey, I've loved it since I was a kid and it hasn't hurt me yet," I shoot back under my breath. "Coming from someone who'd order an iced coffee in a blizzard." I smile at the patient barista, who's been looking over at the mug. "We'll get two."

The barista nods. "You got it. Staying here?"

Pax glances at me and fights a smile. "Well, isn't *that* the question of the hour?" They're really taking every opportunity to bolster their insistence I'm made to do more than work a ranch for the rest of my life.

"Yeah, for here," I say, glaring at Pax while fiddling with the cuffs of my flannel shirt.

"Coming right up." The barista flashes a contagious smile. He has a sparkly, intense look in his eye as he rings me up, and as he slides the change into my hand, I swear he lingers so that our fingers just barely touch. It sends my heart racing.

We find a dragon table tucked at the back of the café. Pax plunks down and leans toward me. "He was *totally* making eyes at you."

I laugh, brushing it off. "What? No."

"Yaaas!"

The barista appears, setting down our mugs. "Here you go."

I instantly notice two things: one, my latte's foam has been poured to look like a heart. And two, he wrote his number on the napkin. When I look up at him again, he's already back behind the register. Nothing magically unexpected like this *ever* happens back home. It's like what Pax has been telling me the past few days—we were made for New York and its wonders.

Pax grabs my napkin, and their jaw drops. "I *knew* it!" they whisper in excitement.

I grab the napkin back, suppressing a smile. It's nice knowing there's a place in the world where gay people can confidently flirt with one another. I may have a boyfriend, but it's been hard-won. And it occurs to me that I've never had a *stranger* flirt with me in my entire life.

And, dang. It feels good.

Maybe *too* good.

Pax sips their latte and raises one penciled eyebrow suggestively. "You know, for not being iced, this coffee is delicious. Imagine him making you this coffee every morning."

"Oh, shut it," I quip with a chuckle.

"Bet mine doesn't taste as good as yours with that side of phone number, though," Pax teases.

"Hardy har har." I try my delicious latte while peering over at the counter. The barista's serving the next customer. My body's buzzing, like electricity's coursing through my veins. I set my mug down, then check my texts.

Dustin: I miss you. A lot.

Dustin: Hey. You there?

I show Pax, feeling like I've been caught red-handed.

"Did you want to call him and check in?" Pax asks, forehead wrinkled up.

"We can do that later. Come on. Let's finish up here then walk to the West Village." Draining the rest of our lattes, we head toward the door. My heart pounds hard in my chest, and I can't tell if it's the caffeine or the barista. I manage to avoid his gaze as he gives a wave, and I step outside.

"See? I've been telling you that you're profoundly attractive for *how* long?" Pax gushes. "Probably the real reason why everyone's been staring at you."

"Thanks." But when I catch my reflection in the glass of a bookstore next door, I'm not so sure. Between my pilling flannel shirt, faded winter coat, and plain wide-leg jeans, I do seem a bit small-town. I remove my hat. I've always liked my hair on the longer side, but suddenly, I'm seeing myself in a new light. And for the first time maybe ever, I care about how I look. I don't look like someone who would play at Juilliard. I don't look like someone who is even *confident*. As I stare at my reflection, I start to feel this weird, echoey sensation in my gut. I think about how Pax always says what we wear is a form of communication. Studying myself now, I see someone who is lost. Someone who is saying, *I don't know where to go next*.

I turn to Pax. "How about I get a haircut?" I suggest.

Pax gapes.

I shrug, smiling. "New York, new me."

Pax hops in place. "Yaaas! I am *so* here for it!"

"Perfect. I bet we can find a good barbershop nearby."

Pax's eyes gleam with excitement. "Yaaas!"

And so, following a map on my phone, we amble northwest for twenty minutes on the crooked, crisscrossing streets that lead to the West Village. It's as if I'm being pulled by some magnetic force, marveling at the rainbow flags flying in front of every establishment up and down Christopher Street.

Queer people are everywhere, holding hands, linking arms. This'd be a great place to go on a date. A real date too. Not a night of watching Dustin shoot hoops, then grabbing Burger King on the way home. Stomach clenched from the revelation, I bury it down.

The more steps I take, the more I realize I'm walking taller. Strutting, even. I don't hate this feeling. In fact, it's exhilarating. It's clear from the way Pax's lip is quivering and their eyes shimmer they've finally found a place where they can flourish too.

"We're not in Little Timber anymore," Pax breathes.

We get sidetracked and wander into the heavenly scented Magnolia Bakery, where we buy two extremely overpriced cupcakes that we can take back to the hotel and enjoy later. Then we pass the historic Stonewall Inn and end up outside a hole-in-the-wall barbershop, with a rainbow pole out front instead of the common red, white, and blue one.

Pax opens the glass door for me. "After you."

I take a deep breath and stride into the shop. Inside, a tattooed barber with a thick handlebar mustache guides me into a bubblegum-pink chair.

"Right now, he's giving me 'destitute muskrat baby' and we need him to give us 'concert violinist at Carnegie Hall,'" Pax informs the barber. Got to love Pax. The sun slowly sets as the barber gets to work. Pax hovers over him, excitedly pointing out to snip here and buzz there, like they've waited all their life for this moment of transformation…which they have.

The chair spins around to face the mirror, and I find myself looking at a clean-shaven young man, his ponytail lobbed off to reveal tidy, ear-grazing waves. I get all warm inside, not sure if I want to laugh or cry or hug the barber.

"Doesn't that look so much better?" Pax asks, head cocked, hands on hips.

"You look like a prince." The barber clutches the six-inch lock of hair in his fist beside my head.

"Now there's a gorgeous Juilliard-caliber musician," Pax says. "In flannel, but still. It's a start." They squeeze my shoulders. "You look hot! I mean, hello!" Pax gives me their silly over-the-top elevator eyes.

I look up at them and grin. "You told me so. You were right."

After thanking the barber profusely and coughing up thirty bucks for my haircut, Pax and I stumble out into the evening air and take a cab back to the hotel with our pastel-colored cupcakes. When we first arrived at the hotel on Friday, we were shocked by how tiny the room was, but we didn't care. We jumped on the bed, checked out the mini fridge even though we couldn't afford anything inside it, and stayed up late—me practicing violin while Pax watched hours of trashy reality TV, muted with captions, while sketching out garments with their trusty pencil and ruler.

Now, Pax watches TikTok fashion hacks and eats their cupcake on our shared bed in front of the TV while I take my treat to a corner desk. An uneasiness stirs inside me. I need to FaceTime with Dustin. The napkin with the barista's number feels heavy in my pocket, and I toss it into the trash can. I couldn't do that to the same guy who made my name and birthday the password to all his log ins.

Dustin picks up on the third ring, his handsome face filling the screen. I keep the camera focused on the pink-frosted cupcake, suddenly worried how he'll react to my haircut.

"Hey, babe! How's New York so far? Keeping busy, it seems. Is that a cupcake?" He laughs. "You're FaceTiming me a shot of a cupcake?"

"Everything here is fine." I try to downplay just how awesome it's been. "How's Little Timber?" For some reason, I can't get myself to say "home."

He grins wide. "Guess who won against Twin Creeks?"

"No way! Congrats!" I fiddle with the cupcake in front of the camera, unwrapping the paper. "Did you score any goals?"

"You mean *points*?" He laughs. "A few. It was a close game. Hey, seriously, enough with the cupcake. Let me see your handsome face!"

"Uh, sure… But I've got a surprise for you," I say, suddenly nervous. I turn the phone and tilt my head from side to side, showing off my new do.

His eyes bug out for a second. "It's…different." He rubs his jaw. "You know I've always liked your hair long."

"Ouch." I'm starting to regret calling him. "So you don't like it?"

"No. I mean, yes! I think it makes you look… It's just so *different*."

"Yeah, you said that already." A hurt little laugh escapes me. "I'm not allowed to change, is that it?"

"Hey, you know that's not what I mean. You look very handsome."

I let out a breath. I'm never this sensitive. I don't know what's come over me. "Okay." I relent. "Nice save."

"I just miss you," he says with a sigh. "I've waited all day to talk. I didn't want to go there, but…"

"But what?"

"You haven't exactly been that great at texting me."

It's a small comment—and it's the truth. So why does it make me so defensive?

"I'm trying, I just… I wish you could just be happy that I'm getting this chance to live it up a little."

"I *am* happy for you, babe. I'm just jealous is all," Dustin says with that grin that sets me at ease and makes me remember why I love him. Why I'm loyal to him, and to Montana. Why despite what happens in New York City, Little Timber *is* home, and that's reality. There's a safety in the set path ahead there, a familiarity I cling to like a saddle horn on horseback. Dustin's smile is the same one that reassured me in the wake of Dad's death that all was going to be okay, that time heals all wounds.

I rub my forehead. "I'm sorry. I've only been in this city

for a couple of days and already I'm turning into a jaded New York. Look, I miss you too, and I want to talk more, but I have to get ready for tomorrow. Talk soon. Love you."

"Love you." He sounds defeated. I make a mental note to find a great and hopefully affordable souvenir to bring back for him as an apology. Right now, I just can't handle Dustin—and the reminder of everything back home, everything that doesn't and won't *ever* change. Not now that I know just how wonderful it really is out in the big wide world. I hang up, then smash my half-eaten cupcake into a napkin. Too sweet, and too vanilla.

Pax's voice cuts through the quiet. "Umm, that was a five-dollar cupcake."

I'm nestled deep in a dream. Dad is there, and we're laughing like nobody's business. I don't even know what's so funny. Mom and Mack are there too, twirling each other in a circle. It's a beautiful sunny day outside the ranch, the bitterroot flowers in full bloom. Dad's laugh turns into a hacking cough. A cloud covers the sun. Then I remember with a clarity that caves my smile in that he's gone. That I left my family behind.

I'm woken up by Pax bolting up from their own heavy sleep. "Sweet Mary and Muslin!" They shake my shoulder. "Billy, wake up! You're going to be late!"

I drag myself up. The digital clock on the nightstand reads 9:27 a.m. Which means I have exactly thirty-three minutes to get to Juilliard. "Crap. Crap! Oh no. I overslept!" I grab my phone. "Why didn't my alarm go off? I know I set it!"

"It doesn't matter!" Pax yells. "Get up!"

"This is bad. This is so bad!"

Pax rips open the dusty curtains, letting in morning light. "Go! Go! Go!"

I launch out of bed. "I think I'm going to be sick." I wriggle into my white shirt, argyle sweater vest, and navy suit. It's probably the fastest costume change in human history.

Pax brushes my jacket off, and nods. "You look amazing. Now go! Knock 'em dead, honey! I believe in you!"

Violin, cash, and key in hand, I race through the hall, down the stairs, and through the lobby, then burst outside. As if by magic, a taxi pulls right up. I wrench open the door and scoot inside. "Lincoln Center!" I yell. "Please!"

The driver peels off. I've got fifteen minutes on the clock. I run through my repertoire in my head—two contrasting movements, full concerto movement, and a modern piece. But an absurd, hopeful little thought squirms around in my head.

Could attending Juilliard one day be what I was actually *destined for?*

After eight minutes of sitting in bumper-to-bumper traffic, the school's still a good ways away. "Is traffic always this bad here?" I ask the driver.

"Yeah, it is. But today's worse than usual." He swivels around. "Why? You late or something?"

"I'm supposed to be at Juilliard in eight minutes." I check my phone, ignoring an **I love you** text from Dustin. "Seven."

"Buddy, your best option is to get out here and go on foot down West 65th over there." He points out the window. "Can't miss it."

I hand him a twenty. "Thanks! Keep the change!"

Then I hop out and race down the street, the soles of my shoes slapping the pavement, my violin case swinging with each pump of my arms, my lungs aching.

The avenue ahead is blocked off by police cars for some reason. Just my luck! Then to my left I notice a plaza that appears to stretch to the next avenue over. Maybe I can cut through there to get to West 65th. I fly up the steps into the plaza.

Everything has been leading up to this one moment. The beat-up violin Dad gave me for Christmas when I was nine. Learning songs by just listening to them first, and playing them back by ear. Spending hours practicing in my room after I discovered I was gay as a way to pass the time until I grew up and could live a different life. Dad poking his newly bald head in with that soft smile that never changed, even when everything else about him did. His sunken eyes shut, enjoying my song, "The Ascending Lark," and when I finished, he said, "That's the one I want."

I pick up the pace, racing past a big fountain in the center of the plaza that's bursting with water, pigeons taking off at my feet, their wings beating in slow motion. I hope I make it.

It'll be a miracle if I do, though.

Because there's a crowd of screaming people in my path.

CANADIAN ROYAL COMMUNICATIONS

8th March

STATEMENT FROM HIS MAJESTY THE KING

Today, in honour of Commonwealth Day, Daphnée and I provide a special message:

As member of the Commonwealth, which consists of fifty-four countries, we are so very pleased to have such a diverse and wonderful relationship to so many types of peoples.

Over the next week, we celebrate the comradery, spirit of togetherness, and accomplishments of the Commonwealth.

To kick things off, our son is set to give an important speech at an exhibit celebrating the First Nations, Métis, and Inuit peoples, whose cultures and customs are celebrated now and always.

ENDS

Chapter Five

EDWARD

There's nothing worse than spending a morning thumbing through the myriad designer suit jackets hanging in my oversize closet. For most occasions, like for my speech today at the First Nations exhibit, I have help selecting something classic and understated. My royal style adviser was *supposed* to be here at 7:00 a.m. with the outfit she prepared for me, but I've just learned she's at the hospital with stomach cramps and nobody knows where the outfit is, so it's all on me to find the perfect look.

Super. Just what I need. More pressure.

MAPLE CROWN RULE 22: Elegance is effortless.

I keep batting aside sleeves and shoulders, moving down the line of suits organized by colour and shade. "Which one? Which one? Which one?" I pause to yank out two royal blue ones, both with nice, tapered silhouettes. Still, neither feels right, so I shove them back on the rack with a belaboured sigh. I start by the whites again, then sidestep to the reds, fingertips grazing sleeves, until I stop toward the back. Seventy designer suits, and not *one* is right for the event? I know how absurd this sounds, but it's true: I have nothing to wear.

Gord appears in the doorway, looking shipshape in a black turtleneck, grey plaid suit, and bold-framed glasses. His eyes scan the suits. "The green one," he says brusquely. And then he's gone.

I sigh. Thank *God* for Gord. "The green one," I say to myself. *"Classique."*

Then I remember I own *five* green suits, each a different shade of green with a variety of textures and patterns. "Wait. *Which* green one?" I call. "GORD! Which green one?"

"Gold buttons!" he replies from the living room.

"Great." I grab the custom suit, and shrug it on in front of my floor-length, gilded mirror. With the addition of a luxe leather boot, my outfit is complete. Not too shabby.

I practice a genuine-looking smile. Earlier, I diffused my hair and added products aplenty in an attempt to achieve a lustrous, free-flowing, effortlessly tousled mane. Sometimes, my hair looks best if I just do it myself. But today is not one of those days. I tuck a few frizzy strands behind my ears, grateful there will be a hair and makeup team backstage at the event.

Gord beckons. "Time to go, Your Royal Highness!"

Moments later, my town car crawls painfully through atrocious traffic toward Lincoln Center. All the while, I'm mentally running through the lines of my impending speech. *"Welcome to the Canadian First Nations Exhibit..."*

The car slogs through an intersection where a mass of people behind a barrier wave little Canadian flags. A smaller group of protestors holding antimonarchy signs is exactly what the Royals fear. Gord told me at one of our lessons that the Canadian monarchy continues to be in fine standing, despite the many loud voices of dissent. When Mum and Dad first moved to Canada, there was a movement by the francophone population to abolish the monarchy altogether. Other factions hoped the "silly tradition" would phase out. The majority of Canadians saw the establishment of a new monarchy as a *tremendous* step backward for the country. The votes at the time, however, shockingly showed otherwise. Yes, people are still taking bets on when Granny will croak, but even after she does, our new monarchy in Canada will live on.

At least, that's the plan. If all goes accordingly.

The glass facades of Lincoln Center swim into view, along with its gigantic posters showing shirtless male ballet dancers stretching midmoves. What I'd give to meet one of those *danseurs*…but that's playing with fire.

"Just about ready, sir?" Gord asks over his shoulder from the passenger seat.

"Just about," I reply, despite the words drying up in my throat. I slide my index cards out of my jacket to check an Inuktitut pronunciation. When it comes to Gord, I aim to please. Meaning I'd better not mess this up. No member of the Canadian Royal Family has been cancelled yet—granted, it's just me, Mum, and Dad—but I don't want to be the first.

MAPLE CROWN RULE 17: Stick to the script.

My phone dings, and Gord shoots me a look, reminding me to set it to silent. *Oops.*

Neel: Traffic. ☹

Edward: You're on a date, aren't you?

Neel's presence during the ramp-up to my Investiture puts me at ease, because he does ridiculous things like stick his tongue out at me from the audience as I'm giving a speech in an attempt to make me lose composure. He usually doesn't succeed. If traffic truly is keeping him, I'll simply have to make do without his supportive and highly amusing presence.

The car jostles down West 65th Street and stops opposite Lincoln Center. People swarm the car, flashing cameras, whooping and cheering.

"So much for the inconspicuous back entrance," I tell Gord as the screaming intensifies.

The car comes to a full stop and I brace myself. Fans press against the tinted glass, shrieking my name, phones raised, thrashing, standing on tiptoe, as police officers attempt to drive them back.

Hit with the desire to check how my hair's holding up, I stare at my phone screen.

Gord unbuckles his seat belt from up front. "It's go time!"

I bat at a particularly stubborn strand, all while attempting to ignore the frenzied crowd.

A girl bangs on the window. I jump, and my perfect swoop of brown hair falls flat across my forehead. "Excellent. Now I have to redo the whole thing," I mutter darkly, as Maple Crown Rule 23 comes to mind about always appearing neat and tidy.

Gord spins around. "Edward," he says in his calmest tone, "they are going to fix it inside."

"Right, right, right." I give my A–OK signal.

A reassuring smile breaks across Gord's face. "The people love you. You're the reason why the new monarchy's become so popular. You can do no wrong."

If only he knew the truth…

At that, he nods, then slides out of the car in synchronicity with my chauffeur, who then opens my door. I step out, finding myself within the circle of my security detail.

The second my boots connect with the ice-encrusted concrete, the crowd roars. But I can forget clamping my ears in an attempt to drown out the din. Being Crown Prince means not showing any discomfort, physical or mental. In a sick way, I thrive on stressing out by working so hard, but then making it seem totally effortless.

MAPLE CROWN RULE 86: Remain tranquil in times of tension.

I wave. I smile. I button my blazer to block out the chilly air. The crowd goes wild.

Apparently, it doesn't take much.

Reporters thrust microphones at me. Fangirls hold up camera phones, little Maple Leaf flags, and homemade posters.

"Your Royal Highness!"

"Sir! Over here!"

"You look amazing! Can I get a picture with you?"

"Can you please sign this?"

MAPLE CROWN RULE 7: No favouritism.

"Prince Edward! Smile for us! Big smile!"

MAPLE CROWN RULE 32: Smile and wave.

I give a little wave and a coy grin in acknowledgement without breaking my stride.

Gord's hand on my arm steers me like the tiller on a sailboat, guiding me up a set of steps past a tree-lined plaza alongside the concert hall, where more HeirHeads, my self-titled fans, combust with excitement behind the barriers. A fear of mine is that one day the fans will overwhelm the protective measures set, and stampede.

Luckily the doors to the hall aren't far. I strut forward as jets of water erupt from the fountain, making a concerted effort to take everything in stride (Maple Crown Rule 75). Gord leads me through a roped-off path where the crowd shouts my name behind more barriers. Every muscle in my body tenses, and I remember to look completely at ease—a tricky combination. Bending one of the rules, I point and give a thumbs-up at a fan holding a sign that says: I ♥ EDDIE, and laugh good-naturedly. The crowd goes berserk, cheering and screaming, each person vying for me to give them the slightest glance.

"We'll be taking a look at the new exhibit celebrating the First Nations," says a reporter who's speaking into the camera. She sees me passing by and orders the camera to swivel my way. "Your Royal Highness, how does it feel knowing the Canadian monarchy is here to stay thanks to you?"

I smile, gripping the strict directive not to comment, and keep striding toward David Geffen Hall.

"Hair and makeup are in the lobby, waiting to bring you backstage." Gord passes me off to a handler from the exhibit, a man dressed in all-black with a clear plastic coil in his ear.

My handler bows his head. "Very nice to meet you, Your Royal Highness."

"Nice to meet you too." He's cute. I hope he can't tell I'm blushing. If I ever were to have a secret boyfriend, he would most certainly be my type: deep voice, broad muscles, simple attire. I'm wishing Maple Crown Rule 59: No inappropriate displays of affection was struck from the records as I eye his big hands.

Gord stops to give the press their statement while my handsome handler leads me ahead.

The museum guards hold the doors open for me.

"Would you like for me to walk you into the lobby?" asks my handler.

"That's quite alright," I say in an attempt to be polite, as much as I want him to come. "Thank you." He nods and stops short, and I proceed through the glass doors, which close behind me, silencing the energetic crowds.

It's nice and quiet inside, despite the steel-grey lobby packed with guests in informal dresses and suits, milling about or lined up outside the washrooms. There are little covered tables set up, and people eating fruit and drinking coffee, waiting for the theatre to open its doors. Videos on walls preview the gallery art.

But where the hell is hair and makeup...?

I pass through security gates and venture ahead, past velvet ropes, a concession stand, and gaggles of guests wondering if they should chance approaching me, as evidenced by their furtive glances. Before anyone can stroll over, I quickly pull the Flash-and-Dash and find a door marked **BACKSTAGE** that's been left ajar.

The back corridor is long and dark and smells like wet paint. I approach a door marked **DRESSING ROOM 2**. A card insert says **CROWN PRINCE**, aka *moi*. The sanctuary of the dressing room. *Enfin*. Time to spruce up and deliver a speech worthy of everyone's continued support.

After all, our monarchy is always in the balance, as Gord likes to remind me.

I step foot into the dressing room—right before I get the wind knocked out of me.

Chapter Six

BILLY

There's no way in the whole wide world I'm getting through the extreme number of people packed outside Lincoln Center like cattle.

Without missing a beat, I change course and race back down the steps to the street, past enormous banners advertising something called the First Nations exhibit, showing beautiful sculptures, statues, and jewelry. So *that's* what all the hubbub is about.

I hurry past photographers snapping long-range cameras and shouting. There must be a celebrity nearby. Pax and Mack would go hog wild. I glance around on their behalf, but *everyone* on the street looks famous. I can hear Pax now: "You don't know what any celebrities look like, and you don't care to know."

Sprinting along Broadway, I weave and dart through clumps of leisurely, meandering people. Why are they moving so slowly?! *Tourists.* One even stops to take a photo of me. Huh? Weird. I fly around the corner and come to a rest halfway down West 65th Street, panting hard and perspiring in my way-too-hot sweater vest.

Across the street, I spot the entrance to **THE JUILLIARD SCHOOL**, the words in silver letters gleaming on the massive stone building.

I go to cross the street, stepping right in front of a moving taxi. It slams its brakes and honks. And to think I promised Mom that I'd be careful. If New York doesn't kill me, Mom sure will, for breaking more than a few of her safety rules. I luckily make it to the other side in one piece, and stop just outside Juilliard. Through its glass doors, I can see stairs leading up, and people—students?—bustling around.

"I'm cutting it close," I mumble, my hand closing around the door's cold metal handlebar.

"There you are!" shouts a woman in an all-black official-looking suit and dangling earpiece.

I turn to her, frozen. Is she talking to me? I look over my shoulder. There's no one else it could be.

Her eyes sweep the sidewalk. "What are you doing alone?"

Why *wouldn't* I be alone? "Hi! I, uh… I'm—"

"I know who you are!" She winks, then regards my violin. "Violin? Nice." She jabs her thumb toward a gray building across the street. "It's scheduled to be in David Geffen Hall."

I blink, suddenly star-dazzled. "Really?" Visions of Dudamel leading the Philharmonic flash through my head. I'm going to get to play in the same building that *they* do?

The woman is still looking at me. "Of course. Would you please come with me, sir?" She heads onto the crosswalk with purpose. "Right this way. We're lucky the paparazzi aren't all over us here."

I bolt after her, trying my best to keep up, feeling something in my chest swell with excitement. She passes a flight of steps and stops at the corner of a building, where she pulls open a stage door and holds it for me.

Inside, it's dark except for the pale morning light streaming in from the door's tiny rectangular windows.

She bolts the lock. "Follow me, please."

The light is suddenly blocked out by people banging and yelling, though I can't make out a single word.

"I think other people are trying to get in…" I start to say.

"Well, they'll just have to wait," the lady replies without a backward look. "Right this way."

I'm led down a hall and into a dressing room with dandelion-yellow walls. A man in a jean jacket and a woman in a black V-neck and braids scurry toward me, guiding me into a chair facing a mirror and counter covered with makeup and hair products.

I catch my reflection. I look disheveled, with a clammy forehead and rumpled jacket. I'm surprised they provide hair and makeup before auditions, but I'm not going to say no.

The woman in the V-neck begins dabbing products into my hair, while the man in the jean jacket gets to work on my eyebrows. Who knew they needed it?

"We were told to do just a subtle look." He takes the tiniest sponge I've ever seen and pats some light-colored liquid under my eyes, then uses a larger sponge to smear even more of it all over my face, followed by powder the color of a stale chocolate bar. "You've got beautiful skin."

"Thanks." I get sprayed in the face with water that smells like mint. Is this all typical for Juilliard auditions?

"I think we're finished." The man steps back with the lady, and they admire their work.

In the mirror, I'm pleasantly surprised. I look like me, but more refined. Messy, sweaty Billy is gone. My nose is no longer shiny, and my brows look fuller and more even. The tip of my nose and my cheekbones glisten and my lips look fresh as a peach. Pax would approve. They'd also be jealous they didn't get the honor of shining me up themself.

"Do you like it?" the makeup artist asks.

"It looks—" I want to say it looks even *more* like I'm a concert violinist at Carnegie Hall "—great. Thank you." I clear my throat, realizing just how parched I am from running here.

"I'll be right back with some water," the hairstylist says. "Sorry. They usually have water bottles in here." She zips out of the room.

"Alright, just sit tight," says the makeup artist. "I'll go check and see if they're ready for you, Your Royal Highness." *Your Royal Highness?* Before I can ask why he called me that, he's gone too.

I sit staring at my reflection, and wait.

Sure is quiet in here. I study the giant wall clock in the reflection hanging above the couch: 10:08 a.m. Maybe they're running over with other auditions. I strain to hear for the sounds of strings or brass, but it's silent. I rub my finger nervously over my birthmark on my hand. A little voice inside can't help feeling something's off. I should really find someone who can tell me what's going on.

Unsettled, I decide to seize my violin case and barrel out the door when—

Wham! Somebody slams into me. Yelping, we both go down. My violin skitters across the dressing room floor. I pull myself to my feet, turn to face the body-slammer, and freeze.

It's like gazing in a mirror. He has swept-back dark brown hair (just like mine), a heart-shaped face with high cheekbones (just like mine?), and clear hazel eyes (just like mine!).

I'd think this was a ruse if he didn't look just as shocked as I feel.

"We're—" he whispers.

"Identical," I breathe.

"It's *uncanny*," he adds, his expression awestruck. *"Bon dieu."*

"Your Royal Highness, you're on!" a voice says from an intercom in the dressing room.

Your Royal Highness. There's that phrase again.

My look-alike shakes his head, massages his temples, and steps up to the mirror, where he grabs a can of hairspray and spruces up. He eyes me in the reflection. "Listen, if you're some obsessed fan who's trying to turn himself into me, I'm flattered, but no matter how you slice it, it's a little creepy."

Fan? What is he *talking* about?

He smooths down his shirt, then approaches where I'm standing stock-still in the doorway. "Excuse me, I have a speech to give. By the time I come back, it would be in your best interest for you to be gone."

"Wait... *Speech*?" Something felt extremely off before, but now it *screams* off. "This isn't the Juilliard audition, is it?"

Ignoring my question, he skirts around me, shooting another glance my way. I can tell I'm not the only one who thinks this is really, *really* weird.

"Hey," I call after him as he strides away. "Is this... *What* speech?"

But he's already gone.

Suddenly it all falls into place. All this time, people thought I was *this* guy, whoever he is. The glam squad. Being called *sir* and *Your Royal Highness*. What is *wrong* with me?

The wall clock reads 10:11 a.m. I snatch up my violin, race down the corridor, and unbolt the stage door, then burst through it and into the sunlight. The people who were trying to get in are nowhere to be seen. Juilliard is right in front of me. I'm late. I'm so late! I dash across the street and into the building.

A security guard glances up at me and blinks. "ID?"

"I'm here for an audition," I pant, wrestling my driver's license out of my pocket.

"Confirmation of audition appointment?" he asks in a slow, deadpan voice.

I fish out the invitation, which is a crumpled mess by now. The man acknowledges it, chewing slowly on a big wad of gum, then looks at his watch. "You're going to need to reschedule."

"What? But... But..."

He checks a clipboard. "You've been marked as a no-show."

My stomach drops, and I feel like I could both puke and cry. My body shakes. I let out a rattling breath and clench my violin case.

How could I have let this happen?!

"Good thing you have a perfectly logical explanation!" Pax says, trying to cheer me up. We're lying on the hotel bed, watching a Ryder Russell action movie on TV about a heist involving fast cars. Not even Ryder's oiled-up muscles can make me feel better.

"Yeah. Uh-huh." I shove another slice of pizza in my mouth. After taking a taxi straight back to the hotel, I was too bummed to hit the town and explore. Having room service pizza delivered was the right way to go.

"Well, just wait and see if they write back, honey," Pax reassures me, changing the channel. "Oh, *Real Housewives of Ottawa* reruns. Let's see what kinds of salads they'll be discussing."

"You're not even going to ask me about my doppelgänger?" I take another cheesy bite. How could Pax not be more curious about this? "Don't you think this is really, *really* weird?!"

Pax chews their lip and looks at me, their mouth quirking in the corner. "Honestly, I don't think it's that weird. New York is a big city and there are *millions* of people here."

They're right. I must be blowing this out of proportion.

"I don't mean any offense by what I'm going to say, but you've got a common handsome look. Conventionally handsome. That isn't a bad thing! By the way, you seriously look so polished in that makeup," they add. "But you should really take it off before you start to break out." They point at their bottle of makeup remover sitting on the desk. "So when are you going tell your family and Dusty-Boo?"

I reach for my laptop on the bedside table and refresh my email. "That I have a doppelgänger?"

"That you totally missed the audition you came here for in the first place."

"Oh. That." I click refresh again. A new message appears. "Juilliard wrote back!" I gasp and quickly read the reply.

To: BillyBoone@rancher.edu
From: admissions@juilliard.edu
Subject: Re: Makeup Audition?
March 8 at 8:46 PM

Dear Billy Boone:

Thank you for letting us know. We regret to inform you that it is not possible to reschedule.
We hope you consider reapplying in the future.

Sincerely,
Ashley Kosara
Assistant to Dean of Admissions

"What?" I say, crestfallen. "I can't reschedule?!"

Pax narrows their eyes at the screen. "Umm, *that's* not fair!"

"Hence my big meltdown right now!" I slam my laptop and yell into my pillow. I'm livid I missed the chance to perform at Juilliard.

"Calming thoughts. Think of puppies playing in a jungle gym."

I roll my head to the side and shoot daggers at Pax.

"Okay. Sorry. Rage on! Sheesh."

I gaze out the window. "Who knew I'd be this bummed?"

"Hey, you can always visit me at Parsons this fall."

I shake my head, eyes glued to the sparkling, magical skyline. "It's not the same."

"And we have a few more amazing days to explore New York!" Pax adds brightly. "Thursday's the day I have my ticket for the Saint Fang Torsk Pop-Up Fashion Experience. You should come with me. I'm sure we can get you a ticket at the door. Nothing cheers you up like astro-vampire Scandinavian-French fusion couture!"

I laugh. "No, nothing cheers *you* up like astro-vampire Scandinavian-French fusion couture." Then I sigh. "And I love you for suggesting it, but I told you months ago when you were buying your ticket not to get a ticket for me because it's not my thing. Anyway, I don't know what I want to do anymore. I'll probably just wander around the hotel neighborhood." I groan. "What was I thinking coming here, anyway?"

"You were following your heart," Pax says quietly. "It'll be okay."

Maybe it's fate. The universe playing a cruel joke.

Maybe it's Dad, saying: *You don't need anybody else to tell you that you're a great violinist. You knew that already.* He always made me feel better, whether I was venting to him after a hard day at school, or needing him to bandage my scraped knee after slipping on black ice, or calling him after the truck broke down on the side of the road in a blizzard and he came to find me, his flashlight cutting through the thick swirls of snow like a beacon of hope. That was Dad, there to make everything okay again.

I miss him more and more every day.

At least going home will mean returning to him, in a way. Besides, this was always the plan from the start. And I know Mom and Dustin will be ecstatic to have me back for good.

I should find some comfort in that, but oddly enough, I don't.

DAILY MAPLE ONLINE

THE ROYAL ROUNDUP
March 8, 09:34 pm ET

PRINCE DAZZLES AT FIRST NATIONS EXHIBIT
by Omar Scooby

Earlier today, at the opening of the First Nations Exhibit at David Geffen Hall, Prince Edward gave his first speech since reentering the fold—and delivered it to perfection—in an impressive lineup.

"The Indigenous People have faced and do face terrible injustices. So, the question is, where do we go from here?" the first in line to the Canadian throne posed. After touching on the tragedies surrounding Canada's residential schools, the Crown Prince encouraged Canada's First Nations to continue to share their stories.

The new exhibit celebrates the endurance and vitality of Canada's Indigenous People through its one of a kind gallery pieces, created by First Nations artists living in New York, with an emphasis on tradition, diversity, and resilience, as well as cultural contributions and legacy. In two months, the exhibit moves to Canada, where it will find its permanent home.

It's clear that Prince Edward is committed to supporting and fortifying Indigenous languages, arts, and cultures. We've never seen the Crown Prince in finer form.

RELATED STORIES
7 Myths About the Canadian Royal Family
Photos of Queen Daphnée Wearing Jolee's Ruby Ring
Polls Up After Eddie's Surefire Speech
Win for Eddie Spells Longevity for Monarchy

Chapter Seven

EDWARD

The next day, I decide to whip up a batch of flaky sugar-encrusted whale's tail pastries, cracking open my well-worn, annotated cookbook. I'm still relishing in how well my speech went over at the First Nations exhibit, even without Neel there to flare his nostrils at me from the front row. I find myself chuckling about how I ran into my—less attractive—doppelgänger. What had he been hoping for, anyway? While giving the dough time to rise in its lightly greased bowl, an email pops into my inbox from none other than Chef Pierre.

Dear Prince Edward,

I heard you're staying in New York for a time. I'll be in the city for a *Good Morning America* segment on Friday. If you still enjoy baking just as much as you did when we met in my restaurant, I'd be happy to get together with you in the early evening on Friday for that baking tutorial. If you're available, let me know where you'd like to meet. I hope all is well.

My Best,
Chef Pierre

Not only is Chef Pierre one of the finest pastry chefs in the world—he practically put the "profit" in "profiterole"—but he is also *the* chef who piqued my interest in baking to begin with, and the only one who knows about my secret baking bliss. (Well, besides Neel and Gord.) I met Chef Pierre years ago when my parents had a private dining experience at Pierre's on Park, his pâtisserie here in the city, and he promised me one day he'd teach me to bake the way he did. And now...

My thoughts begin racing in excitement. Since Chef Pierre doesn't have his own cookbook, I've been dying to learn his heavily guarded recipes and techniques. Perhaps we'll bake his chocolate-smothered bear claw pastries, or perhaps I can ask him for tips on my own Saskatoon berry pie recipe. We could use the kitchen here at the mansion! I'm sure I can give a heads-up to my senior chef, Jacques.

I draft a response and am just adding my salutations when—

"Can reading up on Canadian history for your upcoming Investiture Ceremony really be bringing you so much joy, Your Royal Highness?" Gord asks from the doorway, gigantic text-book in hand.

"You know it," I quip, minimizing my email on instinct.

God forbid I'm not studying 24-7.

Gord drops the large tome on top of the pile of other books on the kitchen island with a thud. "Why don't you try getting through this one by week's end? A history of Canada's national policy."

I'd much rather be figuring out which dish I want to whip up with Chef Pierre on Friday, but I keep it to myself. "Yippee."

He then drops a newspaper on the table, with the head-line: **PRINCE DAZZLES AT FIRST NATIONS EXHIBIT**. "Nicely done, sir."

I grin. "I have you to thank, as always."

He wrinkles his forehead. "You don't give yourself enough credit, do you?"

My eyes shift back to my laptop. "Hey… Remind me, am I free Friday night?"

Gord shakes his head. "Friday night, your attendance is required at the ribbon-cutting ceremony for Chef Yamamoto's new sustainable sushi restaurant in Brooklyn Heights."

"That's right," I muse, pinching the bridge of my nose as I remember it having been recently slotted into my schedule.

"Something the matter, sir?" Gord asks.

I break into an easy smile. "It's just that Chef Pierre wanted to drop by for a baking session Friday night," I admit. "Can't I skip the ribbon-cutting this time around?" Borrowing a staple move from Neel as a last resort, I clasp my hands together pleadingly.

Gord shakes his head slowly.

MAPLE CROWN RULE 99: Tradition trumps personal preference.

I sigh. "Sometimes I wish I could be in two places at once."

"Not even a prince can be in two places at once," Gord says with a sympathetic smile, his eyes blinking behind his owlish bold-framed glasses. "Oh, and I had your brooch sent to be shined. It was looking a bit tarnished."

"*Merci.*" I close my laptop with a heavy heart.

"You can always visit Chef Pierre in Paris," Gord suggests.

"Yes, once my schedule clears up…which will never happen."

At that, Gord purses his lips. He knows I'm right. It's me, after all—a prince whose funeral was planned since before he was born.

"I'll be meeting with members of the Firm on Friday evening for our monthly check-in," Gord adds. "Good luck Friday evening. You sure you'll manage on your own?"

"Yes, I'll be fine. It's cutting a ribbon, not cutting an artery." Sighing, I slowly pull the thick tome over to me, crack it open to a marked page, and pretend to get lost in it, eyes skimming over how the powers of the governor general were gradually transferred back to Dad. Looks like I have to tell Chef Pierre that I'm too busy snipping silk to be cutting fondant. I was so looking forward to learning more from him.

"Very well, sir. Happy studies." And with that, Gord steps out.

I try to focus. My mind keeps reading the same sentence over and over. What other high schooler is brushing up on national policy during their spring recess? Neel's only still in town to spend time with the new boy he's seeing. Otherwise, he'd be jetting off to Dubai or Bali.

I start reading again from the top.

Anyone who thinks I live a charmed life is sorely mistaken.

"Wait. Start over. He looked just like you?" It's a day later, and Neel is leaning across the armchair in my bedroom, mouth agape.

I'm seated on my fainting sofa, drafting an email back to Chef Pierre and drowning my sorrows over missing his visit in a heaping plate of my freshly made whale's tail pastries.

"Yes. He was the spitting image of me." I take a sugary bite.

Neel holds back a laugh. "Is this like the time you tried to convince me that you and Timothée Chalamet were look-alikes?"

"No, there is someone out there who looks *exactly* like me."

"So, are we thinking he's a stalker who got plastic surgery to look like you, or…?" Neel muses half-teasingly, his teeth sinking into a pastry with a satisfying crunch.

"Actually, that *is* what I was thinking." I study Neel's expression as he chews. "Well? How'd I do?" I gesture to the cinnamon pastry in his hand.

He bobs his head. "They're not bad."

I sigh. "Forget I asked. As you were saying."

"Well, regardless of whether he was a stalker, you running

into someone who looks exactly like you is a bit odd. This is just like in that Lindsay Lohan movie." At that, Gord's words rise unbidden from my memory.

Not even a prince can be in two places at once…

My face lights up. "That's *it*!"

"*What's* it?" Neel implores.

"Why not use this to my advantage?"

"Absolutely," Neel agrees, not listening at all. Then he blinks. "Wait. Slow down. What are you talking about, *bharā*?"

"This is a blessing in disguise! I can swap places with him."

A look of delicious understanding dawns across Neel's face. "He can do all the boring prince things…so you don't have to!"

"Precisely."

"Genius!" Neel claps his hands. "You haven't replied to Chef Pierre's email yet. Let him know he can come by after all! Then this look-alike can go to that tedious-sounding ribbon thing."

I start thinking more about the idea. "No… I could never get away with it. You know that." I gesture to the closed door. Behind it, there's undoubtedly a security guard or two patrolling the corridor, if not Gord himself. "I think all the staff and security would surely notice if a world-renowned chef was coming over to the mansion while I was 'away.' Not to mention they'd see us baking up a storm. Then *poof*! Grounded for all eternity."

"True." Neel grazes the top of his perfectly coiffed thick black hair, then his eyes brighten. "So go to his pâtisserie."

I laugh. "You think me sneaking out of here is going to be easier than hosting him here?" Then I let his suggestion sink in. "You know, maybe you're onto something. If my look-alike and I swap places tomorrow night…then the staff and security will see 'me' leaving for the ribbon-cutting event…and if they don't know I'm still in the mansion, then they won't know to keep an eye out for me, giving me the chance for me to slip away and meet Chef Pierre!"

Neel flashes a self-satisfied smile. "There you have it. You can use my driver. After all, my driver's loyal to *my* parents, not yours."

"There's still the smallest little problem." I groan. "I have no way to get in touch with my look-alike in a city of a million-plus people."

"We better get creative, then," Neel says. "He's your ticket out tomorrow."

I inhale sharply and rub my hands together. "How do I even find him?"

Neel snaps his fingers. "Well, you mentioned he said something about a Juilliard audition."

"That's right! And I know the perfect place to start."

"Really, where?"

"It's perfect. I don't know why I didn't think of it before. My parents have been patrons of The Juilliard School since forever!"

Seizing my phone, I go into my contacts and find the number for a friend in the Firm, or as Neel likes to call it, "the Firm Grip" because of the stranglehold they seem to have over my life. Then I call on speaker and ask for them to connect me to the Dean of Admissions. One of the many perks of royal back channel dealings.

"Hello, The Juilliard School, Dean Romano speaking," a voice says.

"Dean Romano, it's Prince Edward. I do hope all is well."

The Dean of Admissions' tone changes instantly. "Your Royal Highness! It was so nice seeing you at the charity ball the other night. How may I assist you?"

"Do you have a list of the auditions that took place yesterday for violin?"

Neel wiggles his eyebrows at me.

"Well, normally we can't give that information out, but since it's for you... Just a moment, please." I hear the clacking of a keyboard. "We were supposed to have one person yesterday, but he was marked as a no-show."

I sit up straight and Neel grins in delight. "Oh, what's his name? And do you have his contact number?"

"I'm sorry, sir. We can't give that information out."

Time to crank up the charm.

"Of course. I *completely* understand you not being able to provide me with names and numbers. Though it's not as if I would tell anyone that it was *you* who provided it to me," I continue. "But it would be a shame if I told anyone it was you who looked the other way when your nephew played poorly at his audition but you let him in anyway."

Neel gives me an enthusiastic thumbs-up.

It's quiet on the line.

"Well, I don't want to take up any more of your time," I add. I let my words linger.

Then he speaks in a low voice. "His name is Billy Boone." He gives me his number, and Neel jots it down in his notes app.

"Thank you! My lips are sealed! You're the best!" I hop off the phone.

"Well, that was easy enough." Neel eyeballs me. "Was that part true about his nephew?"

I laugh. "Yeah. Rupert in AP Chem? He's the dean's nephew. That's how he got into Juilliard. He told me the entire story."

Neel smiles in approval. "Way to go, Eddie." He grabs my phone. "Call this Billy Boone guy. Right now. Do it!" Sensing my hesitation, he lifts his own phone. "Never mind. *I'll* do it!"

Before I lose my nerve, he dials the number provided and puts his phone on speaker.

My eyes go wide. "Neel, what are we doing?"

It rings once...twice...

"Hello?" says a guy's voice.

Neel gestures for me to talk.

"Hi! Is this Billy Boone?" I deepen my voice. "I'm calling from Juilliard on behalf of the Dean of Admissions to discuss rescheduling your audition." I shoot daggers at Neel.

"Hi! Yes! I got the email. I—I thought I lost out on my chance."

"Oh, no! A mere misunderstanding. We'd like to reschedule."

"Great. Great! Uh…when…were you thinking?"

"Saturday?" I spitball, incredulous that I'm actually participating in this ploy. And, to be honest, that I'm feeling a tad guilty doing so.

"Awesome! Yeah, I'll still be in town! What time?"

"You know, I'll have to check." I catch Neel mouthing conspiratorially: *Ask him to meet you!* "Hey, where are you staying?" I ask. "We'd love to interview you first." I pray that's a thing.

"An interview? I didn't know that was part of the audition process."

Sacrament.

"Oh, well, yes, just an informal one. We do it all the time. Cafés, restaurants, hotels… Shall we meet in, let's say…" I look to Neel, who lifts a finger. "One hour?"

"Yeah… Yeah, okay. Thanks so much!"

"Where are you staying?" I ask evenly.

"The Hilton in Midtown."

"Great. I'll see you in the lobby shortly, Mr. Boone." And with that, I hang up.

Neel rubs his hands together. "Well, this is going to be interesting."

My mind starts playing out all the ways this plan could go south. "Actually… Maybe this is a bad idea after all. Do you know what my parents would—"

"I know, I know. The terrible grounding." Neel flashes his

carefree smile at me. "Do you really want to miss out on finally getting to have your private baking class with Chef Pierre for some trifling ribbon-cutting ceremony tomorrow? This is your chance to get out of it. Live a little. Before things just get busier for you. When else can you do this? I've seen that hairy schedule of yours."

He is good. "I can't believe we're doing this."

"See? Sneaking out with me now—think of it as...a dress rehearsal for tomorrow night."

Before I know it, I'm anxiously shrugging on my bucket hat and sunglasses, aka my disguise.

"I'm glad you're finally loosening up." Neel reaches for the door when—

Knock! Knock!

Gord's signature one-knuckle-double-knock.

I shoo Neel and he crawls under my canopy bed. Then I rip back the covers, flop onto the mattress, and reel them back over me. "Come in," I intone. I quickly remember to snatch off my bucket hat and sunglasses, and stash them under a pillow.

"Your Royal Highness." Gord steps into the room. "Are you...*napping*?"

MAPLE CROWN RULE 8: No rest for the Royals.

"No, no, definitely not." I lift a textbook from my side table as if I've been studying. That's me, working all spring recess long.

He clocks Neel's shoes, which my best friend had removed by the door, and glances around the room with his hawk eye. "Where's Neel?"

"Oh. Left," I lie. "Did you come here to tell me something, Gord?"

"I was just checking up on you." He smiles. "Read up. I'll be quizzing you in two hours on Investiture Ceremony protocols."

"Oh, joy." I manage a smile, casually flipping through the textbook, and then he's gone. I smack the bed frame, and Neel rolls out, stands, and brushes himself off.

Grimacing, he holds up a particularly large dust ball. "And I thought you had a cleaning staff."

"So I guess we can say we tried," I say, ignoring him. "Hungry? Let's go see what the staff's planning on making for dinner later."

Neel shakes his head, then puts on his shoes before carefully opening the door and slipping silently into the corridor. He beckons for me to follow.

"What are you doing?" I whisper truculently. *"You heard Gord. I have reading to do and— Fine, forget it."* I quickly don my disguise again and cram on a pair of loafers.

Against my better judgment, we tiptoe down the corridor and take the servants' entrance to the lobby.

When Neel's driver sees us, he hastily opens the door.

I buckle in. "You are *such* a bad influence," I mutter.

"What's the harm?" Neel cackles. "It'll be quick! Come on, Eddie, other kids our age are doing far worse on their spring recess. You go in, meet 'Edward Lite,' and get out."

"Neel, I'm breaking Maple Crown Rule 94, which *clearly* states that royalty can never just *go* someplace."

"Please. You'll be back before Gord can shave his dome. Besides, what's your mum always telling you about the importance of one's independence?"

The Mum card? *Seriously?* I lean forward. "I'm going to tell your driver to turn around."

"Oh, come on," Neel levels with me. "You have been on your *best* behavior for the past year thanks to the big screwup that got you sent here in the first place. This Billy Boone fellow is your blessing in disguise." He winks. "Besides, think of the chocolate genoise cake you and Chef Pierre will be whipping up tomorrow night."

I allow myself to grin with excitement. "I've been waiting to find out how he makes that cake for years."

This plan is absurd. I'm slouched low in the chair of the lobby lounge of the Hilton Midtown, waiting for Billy Boone. The place is loud and crowded, filled with common tourists, and apparently you have to order something in exchange for a seat. I look up from my untouched clam chowder and glance toward Neel with his beet salad, seated at a little table across the lobby, pretending to be absorbed by something on his phone. Or perhaps he's genuinely scrolling through his dating apps. It's hard to know. I check my timepiece. It's been one full hour since the phone call. Where *is* this guy?

The longer I sit here, the more Gord's concerned voice creeps into my thoughts. *What if you're found out, and a mob of paparazzi descends? Or worse, your safety is threatened?* Not to mention I have less than an hour before my prince pop quiz.

Luckily, people never expect to find a prince out alone among commoners. Especially with my jacket pulled up high and my bucket hat pulled so low over my forehead that all I can see are my hands resting on the wobbly little table. I hope that I don't scare him off when he sees *I'm* the one waiting for him. I feel super creepy. Plus there's the whole bit about our awkward backstage run-in. Suffice to say, I was a bit beside myself.

"Billy, what are you doing down here?" I glance up. Someone my age is standing in front of me with their hands full of shopping bags overflowing with swaths of black velvet and silver feathers, looking at me like we're best friends. They're wearing a fierce lemon yellow ultraslim three-piece suit with a hot pink ruffled shirt and lemon yellow brogues. "OMG, honey, you just got your hair cut and you're hiding it under that…cozy-looking hat? I'll never get the bucket hat trend."

I am highly confused. "Umm…hello. My name isn't Billy."

"Wait—are you…*Prince Edward*? Oh, my gosh! I am *so* sorry!" They bow lower than I've ever seen anybody bow in my life. "Hi, I'm Pax, pronouns they/them! Literally *so* charmed to meet you." They're still bowing. "What are you doing in our random hotel lobby, Your Royal Highness?"

I talk through gritted teeth. *"Trying not to draw a lot of attention in the random hotel lobby."*

Pax comes up from their bow. In the midday light filtering in from the windows, I make out their smooth dark brown complexion, dotted with a constellation of glued-on gems. They're in full glam, with lash extensions, perfectly polished acrylics, and are their earrings shaped like butterflies? From their awestruck expression, I can tell one thing is for certain: they're a total HeirHead.

"Sorry!" Pax hisses, still louder than I'd prefer.

"Do I really strike you as a Billy?" Shaking the offense, I pump up the charm and smile. "Speaking of which, I'm supposed to be meeting a Billy Boone who looks exactly like me."

Pax goes slack-jawed. "Oh, no. Billy wasn't exaggerating."

A stilted laugh leaves my lips. "About what?"

"He did meet someone who looks just like him—" Pax worries the inside of their lip. "You're really… I totally thought…"

I squint harder at them. "So…do you know where he is?"

A sharp gesture from Neel catches my attention, and I realize he's pointing to someone.

There, by the bar, is Billy Boone. Cowboy hat, pale yellow flannel shirt, jeans, and muddy boots. Interesting aesthetic. Not much of a step up from that offensive argyle sweater vest. He's looking this way and that, probably searching for someone who looks like they're from Juilliard. When he sees Pax, he ambles over.

"OMG, Billy!" Pax blurts to him, looking like they've seen a ghost. Then Pax looks from Billy to me then back to Billy, mouth hanging open, confirming our uncanny resemblance. *"Sweet Mary and Muslin."*

I look up the brim of my hat at the young man standing before me. Up close, he's just as I remembered: my (duller) spitting image.

Comprehension dawns on his face at the sight of me. "It's you. You're the guy from the dressing room!"

"Guilty." I survey the details of his face. "We practically look related," I remark, wondering how he's managed to navigate New York without accidentally being mistaken for me. It must be the whole cowboy look. Like with my bucket hat, no one, not even the keenest paparazzi, would think they'd find *my* face under *that* brim.

"Maybe we *are* related," he offers, blinking in rapid succession.

"Doubtful." I smile. "Billy Boone, right? It's so nice to meet you." I gesture to the empty blue chair across from me.

"Yeah?" he says, shoving his hands in his jeans pockets. "Wait, how did you find me? And…and how do you know my—"

"Please sit," I say with a genial smile. "This is no small coincidence. There isn't someone from Juilliard here, I'm afraid."

"So the phone call was…?" Billy eyes me with distrust.

Regardless, Pax urges him, in a rather obvious way, to sit.

"I'm sorry I lied to get you to meet me. I'm not with Juilliard, but I know people at Juilliard. My *parents* know people at Juilliard." I lower my voice. "Pax is right. I'm a prince. Since you don't seem to recognize me, here, let me show you." I pull up the @CanadianRoyals Instagram page on my phone, showing a slew of photos of me with Fi at the latest ball, name in the caption. I point from the image to myself then back to the image. "Get it?"

Billy's hazel eyes widen, and he looks to Pax, who confirms it with a nod.

I catch Neel, who's still playing lookout, pantomiming checking his timepiece, then jabbing a finger toward the exit, which means I don't have long before I've got to wrap this up and return home.

"I can pull some strings at Juilliard and get you an actual makeup audition as soon as Saturday morning. If you agree to take my place at one silly little event tomorrow night."

Comprehension dawns on Billy's face, and he slowly shakes his head. "I'm sorry, I... I don't think..."

"Just *one* event," I repeat, flashing my sweet signature smile.

"He'll do it!" Pax chimes in merrily.

"I... I don't know." Billy tries to take a step backward, but Pax holds him in place.

"Wait," I say. "Please? If it's not the audition you want, just name your price. It's only a ribbon-cutting ceremony. Very easy, trust me."

"I'm sorry. It doesn't seem right to pretend to be someone else," Billy says with a rueful shake of his head.

Ouin, c'est c'que j'attendais.

"Hi there." Neel steps over to us. "I hate to break this up, but Edward, we have to get going." He jerks his head in the direction of the hotel entrance.

"Listen," I appeal to Billy, my composure unraveling. "I have to go to this event to stand in for my parents tomorrow night. I have to uphold the family tradition, or else the Canadian monarchy could someday be revoked. I don't want to let them down, especially not my dad—"

Something in his large hazel eyes lights up, as if he's seeing me for the first time.

I peer at him. "Yes?"

He nods resolutely. "Okay. Just one event. For my Juilliard audition."

"Hooray!" Pax cheers, giving Billy an elated hug.

I sigh, realizing how relieved I am at his answer. "Thank you! You won't regret it."

"Bharā." Neel clears his throat, and taps his timepiece.

"I don't have much time," I tell Billy, "so here's what we'll need to do."

★ ★ ★

Re: Baking Session
To: ChefPierre@macaron.com
From: Edward@CANRoyals.com
March 10 at 4:40 PM

Dear Chef Pierre,

I would be delighted to see you. Let's meet at your pâtisserie. See you tomorrow evening. Say 8PM?

Best,
E

★ ★ ★

To: BillyBoone@rancher.edu
From: admissions@juilliard.edu
Subject: Makeup Audition
March 10 at 6:53 PM

Dear Billy Boone:

Confirming your makeup **violin** audition has been scheduled for **Saturday, March 12** at **9:00 a.m.**
We look forward to seeing you.

Sincerely,
Ashley Kosara
Assistant to the Dean of Admissions

Chapter Eight

BILLY

"There we go." Prince Edward straightens my long silk dress tie and scrutinizes me in his closet mirror. Even the *mirror* is stylish!

It's so surreal standing in a bedroom in the Crown Prince of Canada's mansion. The servants' back entrance that he snuck me through gave no clue as to just how epic this place would be on the inside. As for Prince Edward himself, luckily, Pax was able to fill me in the best they could before we arrived.

My eyes dart from the prince down to the fancy clothes I'm wearing. A red velvet suit with a pale red button-down shirt and clean white sneakers. This whole outfit is probably more expensive than everything I own put together. It's no surprise it all fits me like a glove. The tailor-made look makes me feel ten feet tall, although I'm feeling beside myself…literally.

"Where did you say you'll be while I'm standing in for you?"

"I didn't," he replies, brushing the shoulders of my jacket.

I try to refocus on the task. "I don't need to learn a secret handshake, do I?"

"What?" He scoffs. "All you need to know is that my town car will be here in fifteen, at which point you'll head down-stairs, out of the West Wing, and through the lobby. I'm going to sneak back out the servants' entrance now, so when my chauffeur pulls up, he'll think you're me."

I nod. "Got it."

"Now, once you arrive at the event, you do the wave, you smile the smile, and if anyone asks you *anything*, how do you reply?"

"No comment?" I ask, recalling what Prince Edward had instructed me to say while he was piecing my outfit together.

"Perfect. See? You've got the whole Royal thing down already." He murmurs something quietly to himself in French, then adds, "On second thought, it's best not to say anything. Canadians would notice your accent. Just keep smiling."

I wipe my sweaty hands on my pants, hoping they don't leave a mark. "So I do this 'switch'…and get my makeup audition…" I say, more for the sake of reminding myself.

"Precisely. This ribbon-cutting ceremony will be over before you know it." Prince Edward smooths my shoulders and looks me head to toe again. "Well, if I didn't know any better, I'd say I was looking at myself. Your posture still needs some work, but on the whole I must admit you clean up rather nicely, Billy." His gaze lingers on my left hand. "What's that mark?"

"Oh. This?" I lift it for him to see. "It's a birthmark."

He stares for a moment in silence.

"What?" I ask.

"No. Nothing," he says, then takes in my curious expression. "You're going to need to keep your hand in your pocket."

"Oh. Okay. I… I can do that." I slide it into my pocket.

"Splendid!" He checks the time. "Well, I have to get going. You'll be great." He claps a hand on my arm before gliding elegantly through the door. "See you back here at ten!" he calls quietly over his shoulder. "Remember—just keep smiling! *Salut!*"

He shuts the door behind him, leaving me all alone.

I mosey around the ginormous bedroom that drips with marble and gold, and a laugh escapes my lips. No one is going to believe this, including Dustin, who I still haven't told about my audition *or* this top secret plan. I'm tempted to FaceTime Pax so they can see this place with their own eyes, but who knows if there are hidden security cameras mounted behind paintings? I'll just have to take in every detail, and report back.

Out the wall-to-wall window, New York City twinkles for miles and miles. I'll be venturing out there soon for this ribbon-cutting event. Butterflies fill my stomach. I hope I can pull this off.

Prince Edward already made good on his promise. Juilliard emailed me mere minutes before my taxi pulled up to the mansion—an *official* email saying I can make up my audition tomorrow. I even called from the pristine sidewalk out front to confirm it was real.

I keep perusing the room. There are framed studio photographs all over the walls, of Prince Edward with his parents, the king and queen of Canada. I vaguely know their history now from Pax's rapid-fire overview in our hotel this morning—the Canadian queen, a duchess or something like that at the time, was under harsh scrutiny from the tabloids and was basically run out of England. Her husband went with her, and they built their family right there in Canada as a new king and queen.

I study an enormous grandfather clock. Ten more minutes until I have to head downstairs. I prod an antler of a marble moose statuette sitting on a table. It breaks off. Oh, no. *Crap.*

The sound of approaching footsteps in the hall outside makes me jump, and then there's a faint knock on the door. Did Prince Edward forget something? Or is it his chauffeur, here to get me?

I stick the fragmented antler piece into the marble moose's mouth. I hope no one notices—and that it wasn't a one of a kind gift to him. I quickly straighten up, arms at my sides, heart beating fast.

The door opens to reveal a tall man with a perfectly trimmed brown beard, wearing a designer navy suit with military pins on the lapel. When he sees me, his face breaks into a chipper smile, dark eyes crinkling.

I freeze. Is that…? It is.

The king of Canada.

He strides over to me, throwing his arms out. "Edward!" Before I can actually process what's going on, he wraps me in a hug, smelling of a fresh, leathery fragrance…and money.

I'm being hugged by King Frederick.

This wasn't part of the plan. What ultimately convinced me to agree to Prince Edward's stunt was what he'd said about his dad, about not wanting to let his dad down by missing the event. I never anticipated having to look his dad in the face and…and *pretend*.

"I know this is a surprise, but your mum and I are in town for the ambassador's gala, and I wanted to catch you before you left, to wish you good luck at the event." He beams at me. "I'm so proud of you." Then he roots around in his pocket. "I also wanted to make sure you had *this*. I bumped into one of the staff who shined it up. They were heading here to return it and I said I might as well take it, since I was going to see you anyway." He pulls out a silver maple leaf, which he pins to my jacket. "There it is. Back where it belongs."

This is wrong. I need to tell him I'm not his son. I had a dad. A wonderful, amazing dad. "Uh, thanks," I say, my voice cracking.

His smile wavers, and he folds his arms across his chest. He knows. He has to know. If my awkwardness hasn't given me away, my voice just did.

"Are you feeling okay?" he asks.

"Yeah. Yeah!" I say, trying my hardest to sound like Prince Edward. I clear my throat. "Just…tired." I fight to figure out what to say next, even though I know I shouldn't say another word.

"You don't seem quite like yourself." The king's mouth twists up curiously.

"No!" I fake a yawn and quickly lift my hand to pantomime covering it. "It's nothing. I'm fine. I'm just…a little tired." My voice kind of sounds like the prince's, I think. I hope.

The king's eyes widen, and I realize he's staring at my hand. *Crap.* I jam it back in my pocket, but he's already reaching out.

"Show me your hand," he says softly, and I realize there's no way I can refuse the king of Canada.

I pull my hand back out of my pocket, palm up. I'm trembling. He gently takes it and turns it over, examining my birthmark. His smile vanishes. His brown eyes blink at me. They're swimming with tears. Suddenly, I have the overwhelming urge to comfort him, this complete stranger I've only just met.

"What?" I ask, taking my hand back and pocketing it again.

He straightens up. "It—it can be."

"Can't be…what?"

Footsteps sound, and Prince Edward appears in the doorway. "I forgot my—" When he sees us, he freezes. "Dad! What are you doing here?"

The king looks from me to his son, then back to me, his mouth falling open in a look of shock. He lets out an almost inaudible gasp.

"Dad, I can explain—"

"How did you find him?" the king asks Prince Edward, his voice catching. He turns to me. "Your birthmark." He pauses and floats across the room toward the window. Even with his back turned, I can see him fighting emotion.

The room is silent. I can barely breathe. I glance over at Prince Edward and he's standing perfectly still.

Finally, the king turns back to face us. Shock still fills his eyes, but he's somehow regained his composure.

He slowly exhales. "We had twins. One of them died at birth… Or so they told us." He's staring hard at both of us, his eyes moving back and forth. "Could the hospital staff have lied to us? That birthmark…the other twin lived. It's…you. I know it in my bones. How…could this be?"

Prince Edward stays glued to the spot in the doorway. "Dad, what are you talking about?"

My mind races. Could Prince Edward and I really be related after all? And could this man really be my…biological dad? It's outrageous. But then, so is everything about this. "Wait. Are you saying you're my…?"

"Yes. Yes, I think I am." The man embraces me again. Then he holds me at arm's length, his hands trembling on my shoulders.

I shake my head as a million thoughts and memories reel through my head. Dad teaching me how to ride a bike without training wheels. Dad pointing out bald eagle nests in the tops of trees. Playing catch out in Big Bear Field. Dad helping me with science fair projects, like the time we put an egg in Styrofoam, dropped it from the school roof, and it stayed whole.

Now, my whole world is cracking.

My dad wasn't my biological dad? But we were two peas in a pod. He *had* to have been my dad. This must be some sort of misunderstanding. We shared the same sense of humor, the same quiet thoughtfulness that's easy to mistake for weakness, the same big heart that gives endlessly, even when there's seemingly nothing left to give.

"Do you know what this means?" the king asks me.

I shake my head, eyes sparking with tears.

He regards me solemnly. "You're…the Crown Prince of Canada."

I gawk. "I'm the *what*?!"

"He's the what?!"

Seventeen Years Prior...

CANADIAN ROYAL COMMUNICATIONS

30th April

THE QUEEN CONSORT OF CANADA
HAS BEEN DELIVERED OF A SON

It is with utmost delight that His Royal Majesty King Frederick and Her Royal Majesty Queen Consort Daphnée welcome their son, HRH Prince Edward, Crown Prince of Canada, to the world today. Edward was born on Tuesday, April 30 at 1:14 a.m. in the trusted care of the doctors and staff at the Royal Jolee Hospital in Montreal, Quebec.

He arrived weighing five pounds fourteen ounces. Both mother and child are healthy and well, and settling in at Rideau Hall. The Canadian King and Queen Consort extend their gratitude for all the kind messages of congratulations that have flooded in and ask for privacy as they cherish this sacred time as a family.

The Queen of England, The Duke of Edinburgh, The Duke and Duchess of Cambridge, and The Duke and Duchess of Sussex have been notified and are overjoyed at the news.

ENDS

Present Day…

Aujourd'hui…

re: Baking Session
To: ChefPierre@macaron.com
From: Edward@CANRoyals.com
March 11 at 7:41 PM

Dear Chef Pierre,

I'm terribly sorry, but something's come up.

Best,
E

* * *

To: admissions@juilliard.edu
From: BillyBoone@rancher.edu
Re: Makeup Audition
March 11 at 11:28 PM

Dear Ms. Kosara,

I am so incredibly sorry to inform you that I won't be able to attend my makeup audition tomorrow morning. I really wish I could be there, but something kind of life-changing has come up.

I feel awful about wasting your time and missing out on such a once in a lifetime opportunity. It has been a sincere honor to have been given the chance to audition in the first place (twice!), and I hope and pray that one day I'll be in a position to have the chance again.

Sincerely,
Billy Boone

Chapter Nine

EDWARD

So it turns out Billy Boone is the Crown Prince of Canada.

We know this because the DNA test has confirmed that he's my older twin who didn't actually die in childbirth after all. After a few good talks with Mum and Dad over the past two days about everything that I'm losing as my planned future shifts to Billy, I think I've managed to convince them that I'm perfectly fine, being I'm not one to show a lot of emotion. But the truth is, as I've been sitting here for twenty minutes while Mum and Dad welcome Billy and his family to the mansion, it still hasn't fully sunk in.

I straighten up on the stiff brocade sofa of our formal parlour. Mum and Dad sit on either side of me. Dad is chatting away—and Mum's nodding along as she gently strokes the fur of her Japanese Chin pup, Evie. The dog sits on Mum's lap, staring into space, her big puppy eyes as charmingly vacant as ever.

Across from us, Billy sits on a matching sofa. On one side of him sits his young mother, Connie, who is short and plump, with fair skin and her blond hair pulled up on the top of her head in a classic messy bun. Lounging in the corner of the sofa is his thirteen-year-old sister, Mackenzie (or "Mack"), her blond pigtail braids frizzy with static and flyaway hairs. On the other side of Billy sits Pax, the friend I met in the hotel lobby, whose eyes are outlined in a graphic winged eyeliner.

I size up Billy for the millionth time, taking in his blue denim jeans, faded flannel shirt, sagging sweater, his laugh lines, a permanent crease between his unkempt eyebrows, and his sunburned nose—telltale signs of someone who doesn't know how to temper their emotions…or how to properly apply SPF moisturizer. I still can't believe it. He's not just some random stranger who I bumped into at Lincoln Center. He's my long-lost twin.

I'm a *twin*? Not to mention the *younger* twin.

And to rub salt in the wound, Billy is the straight version of me.

He stares at his rough, blistered hands and knots them together. He's bouncing his knee incessantly, which sets me even more on edge than I already am.

Connie subtly steadies his knee and takes his arm in hers. "We're happy to be here, Your Majesty," Connie tells Dad.

Billy exhales hard. Surely how a straight guy would exhale.

I look away.

MAPLE CROWN RULE 44: Staring bouts are unbecoming.

It's a lot to process…

After forty-eight straight hours of legal debriefings, phone calls, and saliva tests, we've been given the answers. And as much as I hate to admit it, DNA test results simply don't lie.

Gord, standing by the marble fireplace, looks as self-assured as ever, in a sensible cashmere turtleneck. When the DNA results came in, he informed Mum and Dad that it was still early enough that we could keep this under wraps. *Why ruffle feathers? Your Canadian monarchy is still so relatively new. Something like this could really muddy the waters, and I'm sure the rest of the Firm would agree it's best to keep this hush-hush.* But Dad refused.

Dad also didn't bite at my idea to lie about which of us is older so that I could keep my position. Because Gord pointed out, rather begrudgingly, that there is a record of our birth via the hospital, and therefore there's always the chance the information could leak.

Did I mention he's older by a minute?

Mack looks to Gord. "Can I have my phone back, please?" she asks with a lack of deference.

He remains stony, like one of the pedestaled bronze statues throughout the parlour. "Not yet."

Mum sets down Evie, who trots off to the custom Hermès four-poster dog bed. "Well, Edward, I suppose you're wondering why neither you nor the rest of the world ever knew that I had been carrying twins. We have always been private people. We had felt it wasn't anybody's business until the two of you were born. But then the terrible accident happened…"

Mum takes a breath before continuing. "When our first baby was born, he had complications and was rushed to the NICU for emergency surgery. Luckily, our second baby was healthy and perfect. When Connie and I spoke on the phone yesterday, we realized she had given birth at the same hospital at the same time, and her newborn also had complications and was also rushed off to the NICU. But sadly, her baby died. By some terrible mix-up, the nurses told me that *my* baby had died, and Connie was accidentally given *our* baby, who she took back to Montana and raised without ever knowing he wasn't hers."

Connie gives a little sob, and a tear rolls down Mum's cheek, sharing Connie's pain.

Dad takes Mum's hand and squeezes it. "We thought we

had lost one of our babies forever. After that, there was no reason to let anybody know there ever had been twins," he says.

MAPLE CROWN RULE 77: Only share what is necessary.

I know Maple Crown Rule 77 by heart, but this secret
should have at least been shared with me. I'm shocked. Devastated. "And you're certain the DNA test was accurate—" I notice the slight flare in Billy's nostrils. I can tell I've hit a nerve.

Pax places their hand on Billy's arm gently, and I can tell
that Pax has noticed too.

Mum sighs. "Edward, darling, you know the lab worked
overtime. The DNA test results have been checked and double-
checked."

Connie's face crumples, and Gord graciously hands her a
tissue. She pulls Billy in for a hug. "This doesn't change anything," she tells him.

But all I can think about, all I've been *able* to think about,
is how it changes everything.

Being Crown Prince is all I've ever known.

All I've ever worked toward.

And now, it's slipping away before my very eyes.

I hate to think I manifested this fate with all my griping
about preparing for the Investiture Ceremony.

Connie shakes her head, her expression stronger now. She
refuses another tissue from Gord, who's starting to look like
he might need one himself to sop the sweat from his brow.
He's normally unflappable, facing any problem with such calm
equanimity, but now even he is starting to look a bit green
around the gills.

Gord clears his throat. "Please excuse me, Your Royal Majesties, but if I may?" Dad gestures, and Gord goes on. "We
should get started on preparing for this transition right away.

He must begin training for his role and responsibilities immediately."

Billy goes still, his face hard and unreadable.

"Indeed," Dad says. "The boys' eighteenth birthday and the Investiture Ceremony are both right around the corner. Billy will get a crash course in Canadian Prince 101 to get up to speed, and then he'll be ready to be confirmed as Crown Prince." He looks Billy square in the eye. "Don't worry, Billy. With Gord's help, and Edward's, of course, you'll be fully prepared."

I've been training for the ceremony for a year, and even *I* don't feel fully prepared for the big day. Not that it matters anymore… My mind can't seem to wrap around it. The world has slowly had to adapt to the idea of Canadian Royalty in the first place. What—now they have a little over a month to embrace someone new? Someone who's not even Canadian?! We'll see how well that goes over. I bite my tongue.

Billy chews his chapped lip nervously. "Montana is my home. My mom and sister need me. We have a ranch to run. I can't just leave that all behind." Billy looks to Gord. "I can totally head back to Montana. I won't tell anyone about any of this, I promise. We can all…forget this ever happened!"

"What are you talking about?!" Mack whispers to him.

Mum looks like she's been slapped, and I realize Billy's words have truly hurt her.

"We would hope you'd be at least willing to consider your birthright," Dad tells Billy. "Loyalty to responsibility is of highest importance in our family."

Dad's words seem to have struck a chord with Billy. He clenches his jaw. "Then how long do I have to stay in New York City? And what about school?"

"All excellent questions," Mum says. "As your mother and I

have discussed, you'll finish high school here, so that Gord can instruct you and so that you're still close to Edward, and after the Investiture, you'll graduate and live full-time in Canada."

"Of course you'd be able to visit Montana anytime," Dad adds.

"I know this is a lot of information to process," says Mum. "And I fully recognize that emotions are high. But—" her voice softens "—Billy, Canada is your home now. After all, you're our child, and all of this is yours." She gestures around the parlour, with its gilt-wood furnishings and gilded mirrors, its tapestries of moose and elk and coats of arms, its paintings of the Citadelle and Rideau Hall, where Mum and Dad raised me. Dundurn Castle, where we spent our summers. Casa Loma. Craigdarroch. Hatley Park. Everything she and Dad have worked so hard to breathe new life into, all in the name of the Canadian monarchy. Don't they care about its future being left in the callused hands of some...some...*ranch hand*?

Apparently not. My parents are giving him the keys to our kingdom.

Dad smiles. "You three will join Edward at St. Aubyn's Prep starting tomorrow. It's the best private school this city has to offer. You're going to just love it."

Why does the thought of brushing elbows with Billy in class make me want to die?

"I can't wait!" Mack cheers.

Pax grins and nudges Billy with their elbow, but Billy still looks completely overwhelmed.

Billy screws up his mouth. "Then what about our ranch? Who is going to take care of it?"

Connie rubs Billy's arm while he stares at a fixed point on the spotless Aubusson carpet. Does he own my carpet now, too? My mansion? My free-coffee-for-life at Tim Hortons (even if it *is* for commoners)? Will *his* face replace Dad's on the coin and dollar bill one day (no, it's no consolation that we have the same face)? Will *his* Instagram pics rack up more likes than mine?

I've never once considered life without my title. The thought is starting to terrify me.

Dad leans forward. "If you need money to keep the ranch going…"

"I… I have enough to pay our ranch hand, and I can also afford to hire another hand if needed," Connie tells Billy. "At least, for now."

"Then, it sounds like everything's squared away." Dad beams. "Why don't you four enjoy some lunch and then get the grand tour of the place? I've had our senior chef prepare a traditional Canadian dish." He looks at Billy. "How does that sound, son?"

I utter a gasp of surprise. I can't help myself.

Son?

Billy's eyes mist up. His lip quivers. He gulps. Then he gives a subtle nod. "Sounds good."

This can't be happening. Hearing Dad call him "son" nauseates me. I don't know how much more of this I can take.

Mum looks at Dad, that smile of disbelief still on her face. "We have our boy back." It's bizarre hearing them talk about a complete stranger—and a country bumpkin new-kid-on-the-block hoser at that—like he's…like he's me, their son who they raised and taught everything they know about running a monarchy and a country.

"And a reminder," Gord chimes in. "Tonight we will be holding the press conference to introduce Billy to the country."

"Press?!" Mack's eyes positively light up. "Like…on social media?"

Mum claps her hands. "Edward! Darling! Would you please show the Boones to the dining room? Then one of the footmen can give them the tour after. Their bags should already be in their rooms."

Dad nods in agreement. "I'm sure you all will simply adore the East Wing."

My stomach lurches. "But... *I* was going to move into the East Wing after the ceremony."

My words hang in the air.

Mum gives me a small smile. "Billy will be doing the Investiture Ceremony now," she reminds me.

It feels like a knife to the gut.

Mum and Dad rise. "Welcome again to our New York City home away from home." They stride from the parlour with Gord, leaving me alone on the sofa, facing the tight-knit group.

Evie toddles out of her dog bed and barks at me a few times, then jumps on the far sofa, curling up in Billy's lap. She's not the brightest little dog.

I force a smile. "Alright! Marvelous! It's settled then. Welcome to the family."

"Thanks." Billy smiles back, the color returned to his cheeks.

"I think you'll find the mansion here quite comfortable," I add, trying my best to ward off a creeping panic.

He takes a deep breath, looking at Pax, who nods at him reassuringly, then at Connie, who puts her around his shoulder.

Mack pokes Billy, total euphoria washing over her face. "You're the *Crown Prince of Canada*!"

My heart thumps against my rib cage.

It's finally sunk in.

Chapter Ten

BILLY

"Yaaas, queen! I mean, yaaas *prince*! I *love* this for you. Oh, I always *wished* this would happen!" Pax says while digging into the delicious plate of food before them. We're all sitting around a massive dining table, being served by footmen in impeccably pressed outfits. From their fleeting glances at one another, I'm pretty sure they have no clue what's going on—other than the fact they're waiting on someone who looks exactly like Edward in his mansion.

"You always wished I'd find out I was secretly the Crown Prince of Canada?"

Pax pauses—for all of four seconds. "You're so literal. I mean, who wouldn't want the absolute best for their closest-and-gayest friend? From Big Sky Country to Big Apple, am I right?"

Mom doesn't say anything. She just takes a roll from the bread basket and passes it to Mack.

Mack takes two rolls and drops them on her plate. "Anyone else think the Crown Prince of Canada was the same as the prime minister of Canada?"

I chuckle, taking a roll too and some extra butter to boot. I'm not too sure about this whole royalty thing. I actually have no clue what's in store, and about a thousand questions. My guess is a lot of brushing up on Canadian history. At least my family's here with me to figure it all out. And after the ceremony is over, we can all go back to Montana and the ranch whenever we want, which will be *always*, because there's no way they're going to make me live in Canada forever… Right?

Pax chews their lip and shoots Mom a look. "I hope they find the person responsible for the mix-up at that hospital in Montreal."

I take a bite of the special Canadian dish, then another. It's delicious, and a far cry from Mom's homemade meatballs. "You knew the hospital was in Montreal?"

Pax snorts. "Cana-*duh*! Of *course* I did, honey. I'm your bestie. I know everything about you." They lower their voice. "Plus it helps knowing where Edward was born too. Which I shared with you last year, but you probably heard the word royal and tuned me out. Anyway… Ugh! I stan the Royals so hard, I'm sure it's only a matter of time before they come at me with a restraining order."

After making extra sure Edward still isn't anywhere nearby (he ran off to meet up with a friend), I peer at Pax. "If you stan the Royals so hard, how come you never pointed out that I look *exactly* like your royal crush?"

Pax turns away so I can't see their face. "TBH, I always saw the similarity, but that's a super weird thing to say to your bestie." They raise their fingers in air quotes. *"Hey, bestie. The guy I have the hots for looks* exactly *like you."* But I can see from the way Pax laughs awkwardly that they're still not telling me everything.

"Does that mean you think I'm cute?" I ask teasingly.

Pax sets down their fork to stare at me. "Billy! *Gross.*"

We both start laughing.

Pax drains their glass of sparkling mineral water and a footman comes to refill it. "I think *he's* cute. And now we're moving into this killer mansion? And I get to go to private school with him? Somebody pinch me! Oh, thank God my parents are unsupportive and selfish and didn't give two flying *figs* when I told them I was extending my spring break indefinitely."

I think of Dustin, and cringe. He doesn't even know I'm still here. The Royal Family said they wanted the news to be tightly controlled, so yesterday, while being supervised on my own phone, I panicked and told Dustin that I was going camping with my family for the weekend. That is, after I told him I missed my audition. He didn't ask questions, too busy playing some zombie-filled video game. I'm not sure how I'll explain where I am come tomorrow when he doesn't see me walking the dim, noisy halls of Little Timber High.

"I always wanted out of Montana," says Mack. "This is a dream come true!" She shoves another roll in her mouth.

"We'll all be back home soon enough," Mom replies calmly.

"Whatever," Mack mumbles. She catches Mom's warning look. "Sorry."

I sigh. I'm a nervous wreck. It's hard to believe we'll be staying in this mansion. Pax is right. I should be happy. I should be *thrilled*. I'm the Crown Prince of an entire country, and Mom has assured me that the ranch will be taken care of the whole time we're in New York. Mack already fits in here. And hopefully Mom can see it as a vacation—that is, if she can allow herself to relax and just do nothing for once.

But all this is becoming more overwhelming than I imagined. It reminds me of riding a bucking horse that won't let up, my stomach tossing and turning, feeling like I could lose my grip and fall right off at any second.

Sure, I've led 4-H meetings…but an entire *country?*

Suddenly, I'm not so hungry anymore. In fact, I feel like I may be sick.

"Pax," Mom says, cutting through my thoughts, "were you able to figure out who's going to be checking in on your grandma?"

"The Howard-Loyolas offered to help!" Pax says. "I'll miss my grandma, but I was going to leave eventually, with starting Parsons in the fall and all. It's icing on the cake that I get to be here till then! I can't *wait* to start at St. Aubyn's."

"I hope I get to wear a fancy private school wardrobe!" Mack pipes up.

Mom nods. "Oh, you will. Their dress code is very strict."

Pax delicately wipes their mouth and places their napkin beside their empty plate. "Have I mentioned that Prince Edward is very dreamy?"

I shoot them a withering look. "Literally *just* covered it, Pax. He's my identical twin brother!"

They giggle and throw their napkin at me. "Oh, take it as a compliment, honey!"

Giving a good-natured snort, I tuck my own napkin beneath my plate. Despite myself I'm wondering if there's going to be dessert. Maybe once we see the rooms we'll be staying in, things will really start to sink in. Maybe then I'll be able to believe this is *actually* my new reality. Right now? Not so much.

"I'm a *prince*." I have to keep saying it to myself, and even still, it doesn't stick. Me. A prince. If you polled all 1,149 residents of Little Timber and asked which one would be most likely to be secret royalty, I'm pretty sure I'd come in dead last.

Mom sops the last bit of sauce from her plate her with bread crust. She hasn't said a whole lot since finding out. Neither have I. See, I have a lot of thoughts, but the words...they're not coming easy.

Mack, on the other hand, won't quit squawking. "I can't believe we get the *entire* East Wing for ourselves! That was so nice of Prince Edward." *Prince Edward, my identical twin brother...*

I can't blame him for acting rattled. He's obviously just as stunned as I am. But on the whole, he seems to be taking the news fairly well, at least the part about giving up his position in the order of succession.

A footman appears and announces today's dessert will be maple taffy pudding.

"Dessert at lunch!" Mack squeals, arms shooting skyward. "Dad would've loved it here!"

She's right. He had such a sweet tooth. Thinking of him, I recall how he could always put me at ease. Sometimes, I like to imagine what he'd say, the timbre of his voice in my head so clear it's like he's still around. My guardian angel. Right now, I can hear him saying, *Your mom's right, Billy—this changes nothing.*

I look over at Mom and Mack. I keep telling myself it doesn't matter I'm not related to them by blood, but it's still a strange truth to accept. We've been through so much together, from sledding on trash can lids in the winters, to Mack baking me a rainbow cake each June, to slamming doors in all their faces at one time or another but always finding a way to talk it out and come back together. It feels heavy and confusing in a way I can't quite explain. And worse: Dad, who didn't get to live to see this moment, also died without knowing the truth.

Would it have changed anything? Now I'll never know. But I *do* know he'll always be my dad.

Not even a king could fill the space he left behind.

When we first arrived to the mansion this morning, the Royals asked me to call them by their first names—Frederick and Daphnée. But even that felt too familiar. I can't fathom ever thinking of them as my *parents*. It's just too weird.

Even weirder is the fact that I'm also a *twin*. Sitting across from Edward in the parlor felt surreal. The slight look of shock in his big hazel eyes. The quirk of his left eyebrow when something struck him as amusing. It was like the world's most unsettling funhouse mirror—seeing my own microexpressions on someone else's identical face.

I imagine what Dad would say: *Don't look a gift horse in the mouth*. He's right. Isn't more time here a good thing? A once in a lifetime adventure? Maybe even the thing I've been destined to do?

Dessert plates appear in front of us and we all dig in.

"Are you excited for the press conference later?" Pax asks.

"I guess." Honestly, I've been worried about Dustin finding out the big news secondhand after tonight's announcement to the general public. But I still may be able to deliver the news firsthand. He's barely on social media, for one, and nobody in Little Timber cares about what's going on in the big cities of the world. It's actually a point of small-town pride. At least that's what I'm banking on.

One thing at a time, as Dad used to say.

Pushing aside further thoughts of Dustin, I shovel another bite of maple-syrup-soaked sponge cake in my mouth and turn to Mack. "You must both be jazzed that you're finally out of Montana."

"Yep! It's only a matter of time before my channel blows up." Mack picks up her plate to lick it, and Mom gives her a dirty look.

"Mack, you're going to be 'YouTube Famous' in no time!" Pax chimes in.

"Play your cards right, and we can do a collab." Mack drops her plate back on the table with a huff and reaches for my plate. "You gonna finish that?"

"Ooh, a collab about making DIY fascinators for royal weddings!" Pax says. "Or recreations of Queen Daphnée's iconic hats that looked like flying saucers. Loved that era for her."

I glance over at the security detail watching from the door. The Royal Family's having them keep tabs on us, at least until my existence is announced to the world. Or maybe this is just how it's going to be from now on. The Royals are big on privacy.

"Also," I say to Mack, pushing what's left of my maple taffy pudding her way, "you're not allowed to film me, remember?"

She smirks. "Not yet."

After we're done with lunch, a footman appears to escort us into a groaning old-timey elevator, and after it stops on the fourth floor, we enter the East Wing.

It's all twinkling with giant windows, modern, geometric chandeliers, and fresh white walls that seem to reach as high as a concert hall. Glowing sconces bookend an abstract sculpture that is larger than our refrigerator back home. I can only guess it's a multimillion-dollar piece by some artist I've never heard of. Across the hall, I spot gold-framed portraits of pale and pasty people in powdered wigs.

"Wow," Mack says with reverence, pointing at the paintings. "These old farts are your great-aunts and -uncles."

Pax grins. "Talk about some great vintage wardrobe looks!"

"Please don't touch anything." Mom has that edge to her voice. It sharpens when she's out of her element, which she—and *we*—definitely are.

I smile, taking Mom's hand in mine and squeezing, like everything's going to be okay, though I'm not sure which one of us I'm reassuring.

It's mind-boggling how so much space and splendor is

packed inside this brick building. It feels like we're in a sprawling country estate, and not in a mansion smack-dab in the
middle of New York City.

Mack sings some pop song about Royals as she races on
ahead.

I follow the footman, who shows us into Pax's room.

"There's a window in my closet. I'm *deceased*!" Pax yells
from the walk-in. They sink onto the gold-woven canopy
bed. "Okay, seriously, where's the singing furniture? I feel like
I've stepped into a Disney movie. You know, except with a
nonbinary MC."

I chuckle. Pax always has the best one-liners whenever
they're in good spirits, like today. How could anybody *not* be
right now?

By the time we poke our heads into a massive, petal-pink
bedroom with a canopy bed nearly touching the ceiling,
Mack's already flopped onto the comforter. She squeals and
thrashes gleefully around like she's drowning in a creek and
not lying on a deluxe bedspread.

I catch Mom rolling her eyes and cracking a little smile,
and then we head next door to Mom's bedroom. It's cavernous, twice the size of Mack's, and everything's cream with
ocean-blue accents, even the marble bathroom with gleaming gold fixtures. How are these all just *spare rooms*? Back in
Montana, whenever we had guests, it was all about the cheap
pullout couch in the den.

I crane my head back to squint up at the endless ceiling.
"Mom, what do you think?"

"A little small," she says with a laugh, though I can hear how
her voice catches. She's still uneasy about all this, just like me.

There's something comforting about a nearby painting of
galloping horses on a fox hunt. The horses remind me of Lucky

Lady and Junebug. I miss the sight of them trotting toward me when they know I have carrots for them.

Mom sighs. "Maybe this was all fate... How things were always meant to be."

I laugh. "Yeah. Maybe." I find myself kind of nervous at the thought I'm not going back to the ranch after all. How's it going to do without me? Then I let Mom's words truly start to process...

"Shall we go upstairs to your room, Your Royal Highness?" the footman asks, and it takes a second to register that he's talking to *me*.

With Pax joining us, the footman guides us up a set of sparkling, curved glass stairs to the fifth floor. We peek into a private theater, a sitting room and veranda with views all the way up and down Park Avenue, and finally, a huge kitchen with a massive marble bar and island, and more glowing chandeliers. I can only imagine the electricity bill for this place.

We move on to the sixth floor, where there's a beautiful library scattered with worn leather armchairs, a home gym, separate boxing studio, and a portrait gallery featuring a gleaming grand piano, and—why should I be surprised?—an indoor pool. The footman apologizes that the rooftop pool isn't open yet, due to the cold spring temperatures. It hits me as we walk through room after room that though the entrance was modest, the building stretches the entire length of the city block... When I snuck up the servants' entrance to Edward's room that fateful Friday night, I didn't exactly get the grand tour.

I make a mental note to spend my downtime in the portrait gallery with its elegant piano. I taught myself a few simple songs as a kid, plus it would be nice to play my violin in there... Wait, do princes even *have* downtime?

The footman opens another door. "Your Royal Highness, the study."

A person seated at a desk glances over a lofty pile of paperwork at me, one hand clutching a pen, the other adjusting dark bold-framed eyeglasses. Gord, Edward's royal adviser. He stares at me over the tops of his circular glasses, like I'm interrupting him.

"Oh, sorry!" I hasten to close the door.

He knots his hands together and smiles warmly. "It's quite alright, Your Royal Highness. This is where I do most of my work. My central office is actually at the Citadelle."

"Where's that?" I ask.

He's looking at me like I don't know anything, which I don't. "Oh. Right," he says in an understanding way. Then he gestures around the study. "This is also where we'll be regularly meeting for the next several weeks. I look forward to getting you ready for the Investiture Ceremony. The Crown Prince—I'm sorry, I mean *Prince Edward*, will help too. You'll be in very capable hands."

"Cool. Thanks." I nod, then shut the door as quietly as I can.

"Talk about a stiff upper lip," Pax whispers. "Sheesh."

"*There* you are!" Mack bounds over to us. "Did you see your room yet?"

Shaking my head, I think of my cozy little bedroom back home with a view of the beautiful mountains, and can only imagine what lies in store.

The footman leads us to a set of decorative double doors. "Sir."

The bedroom shimmers with ornate crystal chandeliers, gold everything, and could fit an entire basketball court. Blinking, I take in the giant four-poster bed, its gold-painted wood headboard carved to look like a coat of arms topped by a crown with a maple leaf as its centerpiece. The gilded, sky-high vaulted ceiling is portioned into frescoes painted to resemble a pale blue sky with sunlit clouds and frolicking angels. There are tapestries of unicorns and moose wandering through mossy forests, and of orcas splashing in wave-tossed seas, and antlered candelabras as tall as I am. Busts of cupids sit over an extravagant grand marble fireplace.

I feel dizzy. It's all way too much.

"Sweet, sweet fantasy, baby!" Pax croons.

I chuckle to stave off the crescendo of nausea rising up in me. "This is out of control."

"Just wait till the press conference tonight!" Mack says.

"Welcome, everyone," King Frederick—*crap*, I mean just Frederick—says to the swarm of camera crews here inside Carnegie Hall.

My stomach churns with nerves at the thought of walking across that vast stage at any moment. I shift from foot to foot in a suit that probably cost as much as Mom's truck. She, Mack, and Pax congregate behind me, looking on with excitement shining in their eyes.

Gord steps beside me as I watch the Royal Family—*my* family—in the spotlight at a podium with flags hanging at their backs. Frederick stands tall in a somber, steel-gray suit and black tie. Daphnée's hair is up in a braided bun, and she's wearing a sophisticated cinched red dress that shows off her collarbones. Edward wears a suit identical to mine. His style adviser person dressed us in the same ensembles, from our shiny black shoes to our polka-dotted socks, the only difference being the silver maple leaf pinned to my lapel, which is apparently worn as a sign of my status as Crown Prince.

Part of me thinks I'd much rather be about to play my violin onstage at Carnegie Hall, but there's something even more ex-hilarating about announcing to the world that I'm the Crown Prince. That said, bees of anxiety bombard my insides so bad that I can't even appreciate the legendary theater before me. Good thing Dustin won't be seeing this…hopefully. I'll worry about him later.

"Without further ado—" Frederick gestures to me trem-bling in the wings, and my heart races even faster "—we are proud to introduce our firstborn son."

Son. There's that word again. It's unfamiliar on my ear com-ing from Frederick's mouth, and like with the "Royal High-ness" title, it takes a moment for me to register he means me.

Gord gently presses my back just as I hear Frederick speaking my name. Over the sudden roar of reporters shouting ques-tions, I walk out onto the stage and wave awkwardly to the rows of flashing cameras. Frederick and Daphnée part so I can stand between them. I hold on to the podium like it's a buoy keeping me from sinking into an endless void of nerves. I look straight on at the teleprompter, like I was told to, and breathe.

All goes quiet. You could hear a pin drop.

"Bonjour, Canada. Hello, World. I'm Billy. It's very nice to meet you." That's it. Those were my lines. It's a good thing too, because I'm not sure I could've handled much else.

My whole body blushes, down to my toes. If that doesn't give me away as a scaredy-cat, my clenching of the podium sure does. Trying to stay present, I smile along with the oth-ers as more photos are taken.

"Prince Billy! How does it feel to suddenly learn you're royalty?"

"Prince Edward! What's it like finding out you have a long-lost twin?"

"Your Royal Majesty! Can you talk about how the boys came to be separated at birth?"

"Your Royal Majesty! What does this mean for the future of the Canadian monarchy?"

We keep on blinking through our smiles, like we'd discussed. No one answers a single question, but they keep coming.

"Prince Billy! Is there a special young lady in your life?"

A special young *lady*? The question sticks to me like a burr. Why do people always assume straight unless told otherwise? It's heteronormative and ignorant, and something that Pax would tell me to shut down ASAP. But orders were to just stand, silent and smiling and sticking to the script.

"Prince Billy!" the same reporter calls. "Do you have a girlfriend?"

There it is again. Even Edward seems to flinch at the question. My heart is pounding as every fiber of me wants to shut her down. But… I shouldn't. Helplessly, I swivel my head an inch to the left to better see the perpetrator. A pale-faced reporter with a curtain of tawny red locks, cat's-eye glasses, and a frilly purple blouse.

She thrusts a mic toward me. "What's your girlfriend like?"

That's it. I can't take it anymore.

"I'm gay!" I blurt out, feeling my body heat up all over again. *Crap.* So much for sticking to the script.

The reporter's eyes widen behind her lenses, and the crowd goes wild, launching into a series of new questions, all swirling around my sexual orientation. I catch snippets of phrases, about what it's like being the youngest out gay royal, and quite possibly the only.

Who knew it was that big a deal? I face forward again, finding it impossible to slap a smile back on my face. Did I seriously tell the whole world I'm gay? I haven't even had a chance to tell my new family yet. Who knows how they'll react? My body is a furnace.

After what feels like an eternity, but is probably only a second or two, Daphnée steps back up to the mic. "Thank you again for coming. We ask for privacy and space during this emotional time." She and Frederick head offstage, with Edward and I following in the rear. As we round the corner, out of sight from the press, I catch Edward looking shocked. I couldn't stick to simple directions. I hope I didn't mess everything up. But just as quickly as the surprised expression appeared, it's replaced with a serene one as he, Frederick, and Daphnée peel off to talk to a member of their staff. I'm relieved something else has taken their attention.

I can't bear to face them just yet.

Mom embraces me. "You did great," she whispers. I'm glad she's in better spirits. Beforehand, she'd kept asking the security detail how safe it was for me to be standing up there.

"You were amazing!" Pax adds, piling onto the hug.

Mack punches my arm. "Hey! No shout-out?"

I laugh, trying to ignore the pit of doom in my stomach and the fact that I'm shaking all over. "I'm sure you'll get one down the road."

"How was your first taste of the limelight?" Mom asks brightly.

"A little...sour?" I admit. "I'm sure it'll get easier in time."

Even backstage, I can hear the reporters haven't let up calling out questions to a now-empty stage. There's still cheering and hollering and applause.

Maybe I didn't put my foot in my mouth...right?

Maybe coming out is going over just fine.

Maybe I'm worried for nothing.

Edward and our parents rush past us with their security detail.

"Yaaas, Queen! OMG literally. Love your look!" Pax calls out to Daphnée, who smiles at them in kind. Pax wheels on me with the cheesiest doting grin. "Ugh! She's effervescent!" I catch them sneaking a not-so-subtle quick peek at Edward.

On the return ride to the mansion, Mom, Mack, and Pax have fun reading the tabloid headlines that have already started going up, like ones that say: **IT'S A BOY! ROYAL FAMILY OVERJOYED TO ANNOUNCE THE DISCOVERY OF THEIR ELDEST CHILD**, to: **CANADA WELCOMES ITS NEW CROWN PRINCE: SEE THE CELEBRITY REACTIONS**.

The new Canadian Royal Family is basically still just starting out, so I guess it garners a lot of attention these days, maybe even more than the traditional British one. I remember Pax telling me something about that when they sat me down in the hotel room and brought me up to speed on Royalty 101 while we waited for Mom and Mack to touch down in New York. Some of it stuck…maybe?

Pax perches their hand on my shoulder. "So I guess you inevitably have to tell Dustin now."

"Your boyfriend doesn't know he's dating a prince yet?!" Mack squeals at me.

I shake my head. "I wasn't allowed to say anything before the press conference, remember?"

Back at the mansion, everyone's exhausted. We all head off to our separate bedrooms, with Mack's parting words being something about running the world's biggest bubble bath.

I retreat to my airplane hangar of a room, shut the door, and kick off my ridiculously stiff dress shoes. My feet ache. A nice bubble bath of my own actually sounds really nice right about now.

I plug my phone into its charger when I realize I have sixteen missed calls. You'd think it's because he just found out the big news, but I feel like it's just Dustin being Dustin.

Grunting and sinking down onto the bed, I call him back, wondering if there's a security detail listening just outside my door.

"Hey," he says, his voice warm and happy. The sound of it instantly sets me at ease. It also tips me off that he's still in the dark.

"Hey," I say softly. I really have missed him. I take a second to pause. My eyes dart to a portrait of a young Edward in a sweater, cozied up on a marble floor with a young Evie curled in his lap. One more reminder of what my life has become. And Dustin deserves to hear it from me first. "I…need to tell you something."

Before I get cold feet, I share everything, from the accidental mix-up and the surprise run-in with Frederick to the DNA tests and the press conference. "My mom, Mack, and Pax are here too," I finish telling him. "I'm sorry I said I was on a camping trip. I was told to keep it secret, at least until after the press conference."

There's a long silence on the other end of the line.

"Dustin? You still there?"

"Yeah." I can't tell if he's excited or unhappy. "So, what are you going to do?"

"About what?" I ask.

Dustin launches into a whole series of questions. Why had I kept all of this from him over the weekend? What does this mean for our relationship? Am I moving to New York for good? Or to Canada one day? Do royal princes have arranged marriages? Can they even *be* gay? Do I think I'll be back in time for his basketball playoff against Bozeman? Or spring formal? It all seems so unimportant.

I have little to no answers. I mumble something about being certain we can make it work, share a fun fact about Canada I learned about from my quick, basic online research—that Canada invented basketball!—and cut the call short, blaming it on the long day. I honestly do hope everything will be okay. I'm stumped as to why I didn't ask Frederick to relocate Dustin here as part of my conditions, but then I remember that if I had, Dustin would have declined, even for a short time. Not because of playoffs or his fear of flying, but because of his lifelong love for Montana. I'm grateful he doesn't ask me about it, even if he's thinking it.

As I hang up, my phone begins to buzz with notifications from the Google alerts Mack set up for me. I scroll through more headlines like: **BILLY: THE PRINCE OF DAIRIES**; and: **TWINFATUATED WITH BILLY**. There's article after article, each with a long comments section full of people's opinions about me. I can't bear to read any of them, at least not before bed. All this judgment and commentary by people who don't even know who I really am is…a lot.

Releasing a long groan, I put my phone on silent and set it facedown, then burrow under the silky covers.

What have I gotten myself into?

"Billy, we've called you here this fine Monday morning before we jet back to Ottawa to discuss a sensitive matter," Frederick says.

Crap. This can't be good. We're back in the fancy parlor that I'm learning to associate with big news, with the royal trio on their eighteenth-century chairs across from me. Daphnée looks perfect as always, in an expensive-looking pair of pants, high heels, and a cream-colored silk turtleneck, while Edward and Frederick are in slacks and dress shirts. From their blank expressions, it's hard to tell what's going on. It doesn't help that it's so early. Not even this steaming hot cup of Earl Grey is helping. After taking a sip and burning my tongue, a footman (Claude?) refills my cup to the brim.

"Is everything okay?" I gulp, sights landing on Gord.

He slides a tabloid onto the coffee table, and I scooch forward to read it: **NEW CROWN PRINCE COMES OUT IN MORE WAYS THAN ONE**. This confirms it: I *did* put my foot in my mouth. My body tenses like I'm one of the sheep at the ranch right before it's sheared.

Edward stares curiously at me.

Frederick and Daphnée consider me too.

"I—I'm sorry for speaking out of turn," I stammer. "The press conference probably wasn't the best way to share that with you. I wish I had gotten to tell you privately first."

Daphnée sets her teacup down. "It probably wasn't the best way, but we're your parents. We will figure this out together." She tucks a dark tendril of hair behind her ear. "For the time being, you should be aware that this will *unfortunately* ruffle some feathers."

"And lucky for us, that's what Gord is for," Frederick says, gesturing to Gord, who's now standing by the stained-glass windows. "He knows how to navigate any public fracas. We've been through tough times before. Goodness knows when we first left England to come to Canada, it was a media heyday. But Gord smoothed it all out. He has influence."

Edward's eyes dart back and forth between our parents.

I fidget with my fingers in my lap, playing on invisible violin strings. "So it's not as bad as I thought? I didn't make a complete joke of myself?"

"The reality is that we must figure out how to navigate this path," Daphnée says. "Gord will need to address the business side, but of course, we accept who you are personally." She gives me a sincere smile. "And we support you."

"You *do*?" Edward asks with a shocked expression.

"Of course we do," says Frederick, giving me an approving bob of his head.

I let out a big sigh.

Gord takes a step toward us. "As Her Royal Majesty mentioned, this is going to be a problem. It's…" he starts to say, choosing his words carefully "…not a good look for the Firm. His Royal Highness broke protocol, entirely upstaged—in my personal opinion—the more important news of his very existence as rightful Crown Prince, and has stoked the flames of a media firestorm."

I'm so embarrassed I can't even meet his eyes.

"I'm sure we can deal with the PR of it all," Daphnée replies. "And as I said, we have no concern with it personally. But as you know, Gord represents the Firm, which directs many of our decisions as they pertain to public opinion."

"Okay," I say, while not really understanding. I suddenly wish Pax were here to translate all this royal gibberish for me.

"Absolutely," Frederick adds with a chummy smile. "You're our son and we're proud of you being true to who you are." I feel guilty acknowledging it, but this is going over a lot better with him than when I came out to my dad, whose instinct was to storm out. The thought stings. It's still so strange hearing Frederick call me son. Feeling his love and acceptance does something to me, fueling unease at the icy sense of betraying my family by letting him in.

And something worse—my eyes flood with tears as I think about Dad, long gone.

Edward shifts uncomfortably in his seat, his fingers knotting together. "This is okay? How is this okay?" he asks, his voice growing louder. "Isn't the four-hundred-something-year-old Firm going to think it's...? It entirely breaks tradition!"

He doesn't sound very supportive of me being gay.

Gord nods. "Oh, it most certainly does break tradition. That's why we have to do everything in our power to assure the line of succession will continue, to promise that the royal lineage won't be snuffed out after only two generations, and to pledge that Billy isn't going to be pushing a gay agenda."

I blink, taken aback. I can't even process what most of this means right now.

Daphnée bats the air with her hand, shooing off the thought. "Hopefully the public wouldn't be so low as to judge our son like that without getting to know him first."

Our son... Me...

Daphnée shudders. "Then again, we all know the British press tore me apart for being a commoner..." She looks lost in thought.

"Won't the Firm want to cut him off?" Edward asks. "Strip him of his title?"

"It's going to take more than being an out gay prince to strip him of his title," Gord replies. "Depending on how this goes, title-stripping, one way or another, is never out of the question. Never. Not once. As you all know, this applies to each and every one of you. Protocol must be followed to the letter." He looks at me. "Have no fear. We'll work on your professionalism."

Daphnée rests her hand on my knee. "Gord will absolutely figure this out."

"Thank you," Gord says. "On behalf of the Firm, if you're all quite comfortable, I suggest we release a separate statement that addresses Billy's sexual orientation. Something brief. We'll of course emphasize that he's entitled to some personal privacy.

But we need to assure the public that having a gay royal heir next in line to the throne won't pose any threat to the continuation of the Canadian Crown." As a member of the Royal Family, my life is public now. I guess I have to get used to it.

"Which is why it is more vital than ever," Gord continues, "that he begin his training for the Investiture Ceremony at once. We must work overtime to convince the people of Canada that the new monarchy is here to stay."

"I agree completely," I hurry to reassure him.

"Let the adults talk," Gord says under his breath. Despite his put-on cheery tone, I can sense an underlying annoyance. *Ouch.*

"And we'll want to make sure the tabloids don't devour him." Gord takes a deep, even breath. "I apologize for that, Billy. But one more wrong move, and the Canadian monarchy is over."

"I'm sorry again," I say quietly. "I'll follow the rules going forward."

"Splendid! So, that's that then," Frederick says, his voice full of optimism.

"That's all?" My brother sounds incredulous.

"Yes. For now." Daphnée smiles at me, and I look into her clear, kind brown eyes. "Billy, a gay prince is going to inspire so many people in so many ways. Please don't worry about a thing."

Yeah, except for running the risk of single-handedly incinerating the Canadian monarchy.

Not a thing to worry about. Right.

DAILY MAPLE ONLINE

THE ROYAL ROUNDUP
March 14, 07:47 am ET

PRINCE EDDIE'S BAD HEIR DAY
by Omar Scooby

Move aside, Eddie! There's a new Maple Crown in town! The Crown Prince of Canada is forced to make like a maple and *leaf* as his long-lost older twin Prince Billy waltzes in and seizes the crown.

During a surprise announcement last evening at Carnegie Hall, the Canadian monarchs welcomed their firstborn to the world stage—and it wasn't Prince Edward. In a bizarre twist, Their Royal Majesties shared the biggest news ever: the astonishing discovery that they had identical twins who were separated at birth, their eldest being small-town cowboy Prince Billy Boone.

Billy, who comes from humble beginnings in Montana, is gay, unlike his twin—crushing any fangirls' future romantic fantasies.

So what will the newly established Canadian monarchy do about an heir? The answer lies with Edward, the Perpetually Single Prince of the Provinces, who's rumoured to now be dating Canadian nobility and next great fashion icon, Lady Sofia Marchand.

"I can't wait to welcome Prince Billy as my brother-in-law to-be, and future uncle to our kids," said Lady Sofia late last night about rumours that she and Edward may be heading toward marriage and a family one day.

Romantic life aside, it's safe to say things are looking less than Eh-OK for poor Eddie. Word is, he's sweating syrup after being *throne* to the wayside. And Billy, the son of a rancher who seemingly lacks Eddie's natural charisma, may not be up to the challenge of being Crown Prince. We shall find out soon enough, because the Investiture Ceremony will now be in *Billy's* honour.

While the Queen Consort of Canada has asked for "privacy around this deeply personal matter," the public is demanding answers. Had she kept tight-lipped about her pregnancy all those years ago in order to hide the fact she'd been carrying twins? Had she fibbed about how far along she really was? How did the mix-up happen? And what does this "womb bomb" mean for the future of the Canadian monarchy?

Will our "twinces" work out the new arrangement before Billy's Investiture Ceremony in a few weeks' time? Or will the hand that's been dealt result in a royal flush—down the toilet? Stay tuned! The proof is in the poutine.

RELATED STORIES
Eddie Takes a Back Seat as Long-Lost Brother Takes the Wheel
Billy: The Prince of Dairies
Twinfatuated with Billy
All Hail the Homonarch
The Parent Thirst Trap
Eddie: Heir, Apparently Not
Edward: Twinning, But Not Winning

Chapter Eleven

EDWARD

I'm white-knuckling my phone as I scroll through my feed from the passenger seat of my town car on the way to school, trying my best to ignore the dulcet voices of the chatterboxes behind me.

"Hi, fam! It's me, Macky Montana! Welcome back, back, backy to my channel," Mack whispers as Pax holds up a USB microphone. Mack waves and flashes her braces at her phone. *Apparemment*, she's been allowed to vlog under certain conditions after Connie made a special appeal to Mum and Dad. Since she's not an actual member of the Royal Family, they couldn't impose Maple Crown Rule 101 on Mack, though she *is* living within royal walls, which are meant to be our safe haven. After watching several videos of her making slime out of baking soda and glitter glue, however, my parents deemed it harmless enough to let her keep vlogging. Especially with her…*conservative*…number of followers. It has no power to endanger. Only to pester.

"Today, I'm going to do ASMR in an SUV while we're on our way to St. Aubyn's Prep, Prep, Prep…" Mack proceeds to clack her nails painted with tiny red maple leaves across the leather seats, the tinted windows, and the cupholders. Pax and Billy exchange an amused look.

My chauffeur honks and jams the brakes.

"I'll edit that out," Mack says into her phone. "Look! Paparazzi!" She flips her phone to record us maneuvering around a few photographers who've leaped into the street, cameras raised.

Pax presses their face to the glass. "Can they see us?"

"I think the windows are blackout," Billy says. He shrinks down anyway.

"Please check out my newest video in the link below, and I love you guys!" Mack blows a kiss to her screen. Once she's put down her phone, she looks up and announces, "I gained two new subscribers!"

"Congrats!" Billy says. If we didn't look identical enough (I opted not to don my incognito disguise this morning), his school uniform only emphasizes it more. My mirror image smiles at me.

I force myself to smile back. I refuse to let on that I'm livid. Through everything that's transpired, I've tried my best to hide my absolute irritation.

MAPLE CROWN RULE 14: Nation over indignation.

Though I suppose I needn't be so "by the book" anymore…

Who am I kidding? I couldn't convince myself to break the Maple Crown Rules if I tried.

"Oh, honey, just you wait, your subscriber count is going to erupt right out of the tubes!" Pax spins from the window with a jubilant smile. They catch my eye and quickly look away again, turning ashen with mouth pursed and eyes rolling to gaze out the darkened glass. They've somehow found the time to bedazzle their uniform, little gems glued up and down their jacket's lapel. Innovative, I must admit.

"Edward, does going to prep school mean we get to eat lunch at the MET?!" Mack inquires.

"This isn't *Gossip Girl*, I'm afraid," I say tersely, directing my attention back to my phone. I creep onto Mack's Instagram profile and swipe from selfie to selfie, taking in Mack with a slew of barnyard animals. A generic Minnesota sunset. A derelict log cabin. There's only one photo of her and the knockoff version of me. In the photo, they're nuzzling with a sheep in a muddy stall.

Charmant.

It's fair to say the last few days have been a nightmare. What with finding out I had a long-lost twin brother and having my future pried from my hands with not so much as a sorry… To add salt to the wound, my parents tasked me with giving up moving into the East Wing so that Billy's entire posse could inhabit my favourite part of the mansion. The mansion that belongs to me, their biological son.

Oh, right. He's their biological son too.

I hate everything so much.

My vision swims as I keep thumbing the feed on my screen. I need to find something to distract myself. But every Twitter or Instagram post gushes with nothing but support for Billy. Everyone's thanking the gay gods for their Queer of the Realm, with tweets saying: **I Stan My Gay Prince!**; **The Rainbow Crown is Fabulous!**; and **New Gay Prince is Prime-Time Fine**. We're identical, *pour l'amour du Christ*. And yet somehow, the public seems to be fixated entirely on Billy's gayness. Am I chopped liver all of a sudden? There's a graphic of a Canadian Pride flag that everyone is reposting, and even fan art of Billy waltzing with Disney Princes. *Crisse.*

I glance back over at the Gay Crown Prince™. I don't get what's so enchanting about him anyway—even groomed, coiffed, and styled, he still screams grotty barnyard homeboy.

I scroll through his sparse pre-NYC Instagram photos showing him in squalid flannel shirts feeding straw to slobbery cows and carrots to horses on a dirt road. *Flannel shirts*, of all things. And not even designer. I shift back over to Twitter and continue scrolling through far too many ravenous, doting tweets, mostly from Billy impersonation and stan accounts: **I Luv His Royal Gayness; New Crown Prince Being Gay is a Mood!; Billy is the Gay Hero We Need!;** and **He's So Gay, I Love It.** I've got to give it up to the frenzied Twitterverse for its plethora of creativity.

The absolute worst part is knowing I could have been out this *whole* time, and my family, and the country, at least on some level, would have accepted it. If there was ever going to be a revered gay prince, it should have been me. I've trained my whole life, made so many sacrifices growing up in order to do my duty—which included staying closeted—and now, this stranger swoops in and gets all the benefits of being the royal heir without a care? Not to mention that his coming out makes it feel impossible for me to ever come out, like he's stolen my thunder by coming out first. Not that I was planning on ever coming out. I know none of this is technically his fault, or his doing, and I know I shouldn't be mad and resentful at my twin who I just met and barely know, but… I'm horrified to discover I'm somehow on the brink of tears.

MAPLE CROWN RULE 21: Tomorrow is another day.

Like always, I pull myself together, and by the time we're filing out of the SUV in front of St. Aubyn's and security greets us, I'm the quintessence of calm, cool, and collected.

"Welcome to St. Aubyn's," I say over the fracas in the friendliest tone I can muster.

"You're a really good tour guide," Pax blurts at me.

Mack strikes a pose for a paparazzi…by giving the peace sign.

I also smile at the cameras. However, it's fruitless. Their lenses are not aimed at me.

Billy steps forward, oblivious. "This place is so cool."

I'm already dreading having to attend the same classes with the annoyingly perfect Billy. Downsides of a ridiculously small student body.

On se calme le pompon.

After security escorts us safely past a barricade of the overzealous paparazzi, I deposit the motley crew with the secretary, bid them a nice day, then regain my composure as I strut confidently through the halls so no one will notice anything is wrong.

Except for Neel, who can always tell. "Walk with me, *bharā*?" he asks in the corridor.

We link up and climb the stairs. I'm grateful he's back in town after a last-minute jaunt to Miami Beach, which he documented on his socials with gorgeous photos of beaches, pools, and palm fronds.

"Have I mentioned yet how much I've been regretting our little twin swap?" I ask.

Neel bats his eyelashes and grins. "Only every minute *since* then. Tell me again why this change of events is so awful? Other than Gord trying to ban me from ever visiting you at home again? I'm really not *that* bad of an influence!"

"I would never let Gord banish you. You know my home is your home. Or...whoever's home it is now."

"I know, I know." Neel smiles. "You always say that."

"Not only is he moving in on my crown, but he gets my wing of the mansion too?" I fume. "Anyway, the truth is, I miss being Crown Prince. And the worst part is, the people *adore* my interloper."

"You mean your *twinterloper*?"

I sigh.

"Well, I don't have a clue as to why," Neel retorts. "From one look at his Instagram, all he ever wears is flannel, flannel, and—shocker—more flannel. Plus he seems like he's got the personality of a spoon."

I appreciate Neel's interest in opposition research. "Right?! He doesn't exactly put the *fun* in Bay of Fundy."

A group of students made up entirely of the offspring of Oscar winners, presidential candidates, ex-attorney generals, and old-money families harkening back to railroads passes us on the stairs, plodding sleepily as is common the first day back after a week off.

Neel leans in and whispers, "Look on the bright side. If you let him cut the ribbons and speak at the gallery openings, doesn't that offer you freedom? Freedom that you've been wanting since forever? Freedom that *I've* been wanting for you since forever?"

"I'm kind of having a hard time seeing it that way. I've worked too hard for too long to let this tumbleweed roll in and take over," I huff. "He's so ordinary. So…average! Not to mention he doesn't have one regal bone in his body! It's infuriating."

"Twinfuriating?" Neel offers with a cheeky eyebrow wiggle.

I disregard his insertion. "And then there's the whole thing about him being gay and being exalted for it."

"Ah. There it is." Neel simpers. "I knew that'd bug you."

I shoot him a sour look.

"Oh, chin up." He twists up the corner of his mouth. "It'll all be okay, my dear. There's a silver lining, I promise you… somewhere."

"Uh-huh. You're only in such good spirits because you and your boyfriend are now an item." They met up for coffee before Neel left for Miami, and apparently no coffee was consumed, meaning it went well.

We reach the landing. "Yes, but I'm still playing the field. You know I don't like to be tied down. I go wherever the wind blows! Especially since I'm going on my whirlwind world vacation for my gap year, photographing all the beautiful international boys while you're in Canada studying at the boring University of Ottawa."

Neel's love of photography is akin to my love of baking. And like me, he denies he cares about it as anything more than a hobby. A wave of melancholy washes over me as I think about a year without my best friend. Again.

We reach the next floor and split up into our respective classrooms, but I stop short a few feet into mine.

There's Billy, seated at the front of the class…in *my* desk.

Respirer. Le sourire.

"Hey," he says quietly as other students filter in past me and take their seats.

I give a cordial wave and find a desk at the back of the class.

Sloane Fritfeller, granddaughter of an American oil tycoon, leans across the aisle toward him. "Hi," she says. "Sloane. I'm such a fan."

"Really?" he says self-consciously. "Thanks. I'm Billy."

Sloane beams, glancing at our classmates. "We *know* who you are!"

The other students follow suit, introducing themselves with a friendliness that I didn't know existed here. I take out my tablet and stylus, and sit up perfectly straight, waiting for Professor Hildegard to stride in, close the door, and begin lecturing us on our latest read, *Bleak House*. Most found it, well, bleak, but I thought it delightful. After correctly answering a slew of questions, I realize I've practically forgotten my twin seated silently up front. This isn't so bad.

When the bell rings, I snatch up my knapsack and file out into the corridor.

"Edward, wait up!" Billy calls out.

I stop. "Hey. Good class, huh?"

"Yeah," he says. "Though it would probably help if I actually read the book." He takes out a printout of his class schedule, and gazes left and right.

"Looking for your next class? Here. Let me help." I peer at his schedule, and point down the corridor. "The class numbering is *not* intuitive here."

He crumples it back up. "Thanks."

"Billy! There you are!" Pax proclaims, racing up to him. "This place is amazing! And I can't wait for tonight. The event is going to have so many celebs!" They look at me and grow reticent.

"See you both at the gala later," I say with an overly genial wave. Then I turn on my heel and book it.

Neel's by my side within seconds as we descend a flight of carpeted steps toward the student centre, and I fill him in about class. "So, he has no idea you're down about this and hate his guts?"

"None."

He chuckles. "Oh, you are good."

I grin. "I've had over seventeen years of practice."

He pauses outside the student store. "Quick stop? I'm out of pens."

"Sure." We step inside, perusing the aisles of jackets and bags, the school's crest emblazoned across everything.

Neel studies a pack of pens. "Well, what are you going to do?"

"There's nothing *anyone* can do."

"You could come out to your parents..." Neel treads lightly. "Only if you wanted."

"Are you feeling okay?" I run my fingers through my hair and let out a deep breath. "My parents would flip. Sure, they're fine with Billy, but me? The son they've raised since I was in diapers? Come on. Their lifelong wish has been for me to find a wife, remember? Gord would flip too. Ugh. This is horrendous. I need everything to go back to the way it was. I know this is bizarre after all my little rants, but I've never wanted to be Crown Prince *more*."

"Really? I had no idea."

I shoot him a deadpan look.

Neel quirks an eyebrow. "You're seriously telling me you miss having to memorize every Canadian municipality?"

I bare my teeth in a grin. "You know that's not what I mean."

"Sorry," he tells me as the cashier rings him up.

"It's fine." I sigh. "Yes, studying and preparing for being king and for the Investiture was a lot of work, but it would have been all worth it in the end. What else do I have if not the Crown?"

And now, Billy's existence has taken away my destiny.

J'ai mon voyage.

"Your good looks and sunshiney personality?" Neel tries.

I flare my nostrils and half close my eyes.

"Well, what do you propose we do?" Neel asks. "Off him?"

"I draw the line at murder."

Neel finishes paying for his pens. "In all seriousness, is there anything we can do, *bharā*?"

I shake my head. "Not unless the prime minister can get a unanimous vote to alter the Law of Succession for the Crown."

"What are the odds he'll do that?" Neel asks as we head back into the corridor.

"Slim. And even slimmer that all members of Parliament would vote in favour of it. It's not like I can prove to both houses of Parliament *and* the ten provinces and three territories that Billy's not competent enough to wear the crown and that the role of heir should be restored to me." I chuckle. "Though they'd be more likely to strip him of his title if he were to lose public favour."

"Bingo. That's it." Something clicks in Neel's dark eyes.

"What?" Then I see that he's stopped laughing. "Neel, we can't off him."

"No, no, no. We need to bring in the big guns to come up with a dastardly *clever* plan. Something that'll lose him public favour like that." He snaps his fingers.

I narrow my eyes at him. "You don't mean...?"

He smirks. "Oh, I do."

I stun him with a hug, inhaling his woody cologne and fragrant mousse. "You're a genius. A shady genius!"

Neel cackles. "Best compliment you could ever give me."

"A little dose of sabotage from the best of the best?"

Neel nods and flashes a wicked smile. "God save the queer." Off my look, he whispers, "The other queer. Obviously."

Il faut baiser le cul du diable quand il est frette.

"So...does this mean you can come to Leo's rager with me this weekend?" Neel asks.

"Not my priority right now, I'm afraid."

After parting ways, and with several minutes left to spare before the next bell rings, I get to work seeking out the most conniving, devious, morally questionable, *clever* person I know.

"Greetings, Fi." I slide into an empty chair beside her at a library table. "Still glowing from your extended vacation stay in Bora Bora, I see." I glance at her screen and see she has 4,985 new messages in her inbox. "That's a lot of emails to catch up on."

She snickers. "It's my throwaway email."

"Your *what*?"

"The anonymous email I use to sign up for all the promotional deals and gossip mag newsletters. Keeps me informed without giving away my real email to people who want to resell it." She squints at me. "You don't have one? Of all people?"

"I think my Finsta is sufficient."

"Whatever." She closes her laptop. "You ignore my calls for the past week and a half, and now you're interrupting my plan to conquer the four quadrants of fashion, makeup, accessories, and lifestyle. This better be good."

I show her one of Billy's headlines on my phone.

"Yeah. I saw. They *barely* wanted to interview me for that. Your doppelgänger has clearly stolen the spotlight. And just when we were getting some traction with the press. Boo."

"I was hoping you'd see it that way."

"Kind of why I was blowing up your phone, cupcake."

"Sorry. I wasn't ready to talk about it. Listen. I need your help." I glance around at the bookshelves to make sure we're not being overheard, or secretly filmed together—again.

"*You* want help from *me*? Why, Edward, I'm flattered. But make it snappy." She strums her fingernails against the top of her laptop. "Just because I got early acceptance to the University of Ottawa doesn't mean I don't want to end my senior semester with a four-point-oh." Fi has a plan to become the new "youngest self-made" billionaire and knock RiRi off her perch.

I roll my eyes. "Hypothetically, how would one go about eviscerating a new Crown Prince?" I know she's not too thrilled about Billy being on the throne either, for her own reasons. Her becoming queen consort one day won't be feasible with him on the throne. Of course, it won't happen with *me* on the throne either, but if she thinks she and I have a chance of marrying, who am I to crush her dreams? All I know is Billy's standing in the way of the plans she's had with me since forever.

"Walk in the park," she says. "First, what does he like? What does he care about?"

"I don't know," I admit. "Cows. Horses. Ranch…stuff?" I grimace at the thought.

Fi laughs a silent laugh. "Oh, Edward, Edward, Edward." She shakes her head. "What are you, *new* here? You have to keep your friends close and your *twinemies* closer. That's your homework for tonight. I expect an answer when I see you at the gala later. And you're going to need to learn more than just his fave colour. K?"

"Oui, chérie." Lucky for me, I know exactly where to start.

As soon as I get home from school, I enter the darkening East Wing parlour in search of Mack. Strewn pell-mell across the rug and coffee table are her textbooks, loose leaf papers, pens, and pencils, along with my butter tarts. Sugary byproducts of all my recent stress-baking. She's lying on the sofa in a fuzzy housecoat and pig slippers, with a sheet mask on, talking to her phone, a copy of *Anne of Green Gables* open and facedown beside her pink laptop.

Miraculously, the others aren't around.

"And it even has a fro-yo machine!" she says to her phone with a giddy exuberance. Her eyes flicker toward me, then back to her screen. "So, yeah. Someone just got here. So, I have to go. I love you guys! I'll talk to you soon. Macky Montana out!"

"Hello, Mack," I say with as much friendliness as I can scrounge up. "How was school?"

"It was good!" She raises her bushy blond eyebrows.

"I hope you didn't get too much homework." I gesture to her many textbooks. "I remember my first year at St. Aubyn's was a big adjustment. The work load can be intense."

Mack blinks her big blue eyes one too many times. "Mmm-hmm…"

I sit across from her. "Anyway, I'd quite like to get to know you a little better."

She looks taken aback. "Oh. Umm, okay. What do you want to know?"

"What was it like growing up in Missouri?"

"Montana," she corrects me.

"Oh, right, right. Well, I've not been, but I've always wanted to go," I lie, intertwining my fingers together and moulding my expression into one of sincere curiosity.

She snorts. "Oh yeah, after Tokyo and Rome, Montana's right up there on a royal prince's vacation wish list."

This thirteen-year-old is seeing right through me. I'm starting to wonder how I'm going to get her to open up.

"There's just not a whole lot going on in Montana if you don't own a ranch," she adds.

I lean forward. "Tell me about your ranch."

"I mean, it's not *mine*. It's my mom and dad's. *Was.* Now it's my mom's." She folds her legs up and brushes aside a wayward strand of hair that escaped her neon headband.

"It must be an awful lot of work to run a ranch," I say in an effort to keep her talking.

"Yeah, a lot of work. I feed the animals, Mom does the business stuff, and Billy helps our ranch hand with everything else. Even though he'd secretly rather just go play violin after school."

That's right. His violin and obsession with Juilliard. *Of course!*

"Hey, do you want a face mask? I have extra." She holds up a little plastic oval sleeve decorated with a penguin's cartoon face.

A few minutes later, we're side by side on the sofa, fresh sheet masks on our faces. I'm pining for the diamond hydro gel masks I get shipped in from Korea since I can practically feel this cheap thing from a convenience store clogging my pores. Though I have to admit, I'm getting a kick out of Mack. I've never had a little sister, and hearing her gabbing about makeup hacks, cancel culture, TikTok trends, and ridiculous YouTuber drama is surprisingly...*divertissant*.

I lift the flap of my mask at the mouth and sink my teeth into a butter tart. "These are extraordinary, aren't they? At least, until you get one with a soggy bottom."

"Soggy bottom?" She laughs. "They're okay. Best thing I've had here was Shake Shack."

I smooth the mask back over my upper lip. "Only because you haven't tried ketchup chips."

Mack stops striking poses for her Snapchat filters. "Eww! Those sound *narsty*."

"Don't knock it till you try it!" I waggle my eyebrows.

"Seriously, *ketchup chips*? Gross! And that's coming from someone who *loves* ketchup."

"Touché. Well, Canada's got some pretty interesting foods." I stare at the oil painting of Rideau Hall, a large stone building with a fountain bubbling in its roundabout and Dad's royal standard blowing from its roof—aka my family's official residence in Ottawa.

Mack looks from the painting to me. "So when do I get to see a real castle already?"

"We can see one when we're in Canada for the ceremony in a few weeks." I offer her a tart from the tray, and she grabs it between red-and-white fingernails. "I'm glad to see you enjoying my butter tarts. I've finally perfected the recipe."

"You made them?" For a girl who said they were just "okay," she's licking her fingers.

"Don't sound so surprised!" I lower my voice. "I just may have a secret passion for baking. Shh!"

She peels her mask off to reveal a smile. "That's so cool! I didn't know you baked."

I shrug. "As a prince, you don't really get to do much else but prince things."

"Huh. I would think a prince could do whatever he wanted."

I wish, Mack. I wish.

"Besides, who says baking *can't* be a Prince Thing?" she asks. She makes a good point…

I peel my mask off too, gingerly pat my cheeks, and purse my lips. "How do I look?"

Mack scrunches up her face at me then giggles. "Sweaty."

Cringing, I wad up the mask into a damp ball. "How about *I* supply the masks next time?"

"Deal!" she says. "Ooh, there are really cute gel ones you can get at the general store we have back home."

Bless her little heart.

Another night, another gala. On the second floor of the MET, the Hall of Musical Instruments teems with people.

For once, they're not all flooding around me. It's refreshing, I dare say, to hang back in the cramped and dimly lit gallery behind a tanklike case displaying a cello from the year 1824.

"Do you need anything, Your Royal Highness?" Gord asks, startling me.

I turn to reply when it dawns on me. He's talking to Billy, who's passing by with Pax.

"Uh, no thanks!" Billy tells Gord before the pair makes their way to the far end of the room. Pax is a vision, drawing eyes to their maple-leaf-print jumpsuit and maple leaf fascinator. When they turn back to wave at me, I pretend I don't see them.

As if sensing my pang of jealousy about Billy, Gord looks at me, his expression expectant.

I give the A-OK signal, though of course I don't actually mean it.

Still, I'm doing better than expected among the twenty rare and highly valuable stringed instruments from Canada's Musical Instrument Bank. Despite the fact I'm practically invisible. Just another guest. Another body in the sea of bodies here tonight at the star-studded Maple Music Fundraiser Gala—or *Gay*-la, if you will. Instead of focusing on me, or the fifty-million-dollar musical display of violins, cellos, and bows crafted by the legendary Stradivarius, Gagliano, and Pressenda in honor of the *Conseil des arts du Canada*, everyone's been far too busy fawning over Billy, aka tonight's *actual* main exhibit. I admit, it's a strange feeling.

The MET really rolled out the rainbow carpet for him—quite literally—and included the New York City Gay Men's Chorus singing the Canadian national anthem. The amount of love and support for the new Rainbow Crown is palpable.

Hopefully, it can scatter to the winds.

I resent how smooth royal existence seems to be for Billy. He's so easily come out as gay to the world, and here I am, unable to do the same. Which is why I'll be knocking Billy down a peg or two very, very soon...

"You are *such* an inspiration, Your Royal Highness!" Dean Romano exclaims.

I smile when I realize he's looking past me at Billy. I did it again!

I watch giddy gay choral members and Olympic male figure skaters push in front of the dean, approaching Billy to ask for selfies. Which are *not* allowed. Billy agrees happily, flouting yet another Maple Crown Rule. What I'd give to be there when Gord gives him the stern rigmarole about the

Canadian Crown's set rules. Lord knows he's harangued *me* enough times about them.

Admittedly, I've only ever been swarmed by female fans. I always wished I could have guys fawn over me. Though the good thing about being a fly on the wall is that I can revel in watching the masses overwhelm Billy like quicksand. And this doesn't include the people who swarmed the museum steps on our way inside the gala, shouting out his name with neon signs reading **PRINCE BILLY 4EVER**. He looks nervous, hand stuffed in his pocket, lopsided smile paired with furrowed brow. I love it. Surely his rough edges are bound to make headlines. I may not even need to enact my sabotage—he could very well muck it up all on his own.

But I don't want even the slightest margin of error.

A few people interrupt my viewing to ask for a photo, but only because they mistake me for him. *Crisse.* Don't they see *he's* the one with the maple leaf now pinned to his lapel? Or rather, *my* lapel? Did I mention being a twin with a country bumpkin means that *they* can fit into all of *your* nice clothes? For the record, I turn the people away. Call me Bad Cop, or rather, *Evil Twin*.

Yet here I am, pretending to be the admiring and supportive ally. Billy, his face blotchy and sweaty like he just ran the New York City Marathon despite the exquisite suit of mine they've got him in, finishes taking his last selfie when he sees me. I give a nice, welcoming wave, and he excuses himself to walk over to me.

Time to put the *fun* in fundraiser.

My sights sweep the shadow boxes on the clean, smooth white swatches of segmented walls and land on the one instrument *not* in a display case: a 1689 Baumgartner Stradivari violin made of maple with an orange-brown varnish. It's probably valued at over six million Canadian, or five million American dollars. I scan the crowd. Fi's eyes flit toward me, and she gives an imperceptible nod. Across the room, Neel shoots me a saccharine smile.

It's go time.

Soon, everyone will be looking at Billy for all the wrong reasons.

Pax has launched into conversation with a group of regardful people nearby. "The term footman is *so* not working for me! I mean, how about something less gendered…like foot*people*, am I right?" At this, the congregation nods along enthusiastically.

Billy returns to me, his new security detail standing behind him.

I pat his arm. "It seems like you're very popular. People love you!"

"They *do*?" He peers through the glass case and waves at the crowd—a wave that's *far* from regal.

People peep their heads around one another in order to see him, and he bobs his head at them.

He turns back to me, beaming. "Someone just told me that my new official professional Instagram has twenty million followers." He shakes his head in disbelief. "I don't care about all that stuff, but Mack is going to flip." He runs his bony fingers through his hair, and is practically panting, his eyes alight, his smile slightly flagging.

He still has his own Insta profile, albeit a new business one? That's not allowed either. And, last I checked, he had twenty followers on his personal Instagram, not twenty *million*. I bet he's *definitely* getting the most likes on the Canadian Royals account. *Non!* He continues to rain on my parade without even knowing it.

Edward, concentre-toi.

"Did you have a chance to meet Dean Romano? He's here

with Juilliard," I push on. "I'm saddened to hear you weren't able to audition for the school in the end."

"I haven't talked to him yet." Billy sighs even though he's still smiling. "It's okay, though. This is way more fun."

Fun? Being Crown Prince has its perks, but I wouldn't exactly describe it as *fun*. I fight the urge to ask him what part of studying Canadian history is entertaining, but I simply smile and shrug. "Well, just because you didn't get a chance to play for Juilliard doesn't mean you can't still play as Crown Prince." I flick the shadow box in front of us. "Hey, have you managed to check out the exhibit? The instruments are beautiful, right?" I gesture toward the violin lying on a pedestal under a spotlight. No shadow box. Nothing anchoring it. "You see that one?"

He steps toward the pedestal. His hazel eyes widen. "Wow..."

"Go on. Try it out!" I spur from the sidelines.

This *better* work.

He wheels on me, his curious eyes boring into mine. "I can just...*do* that?"

"*Hello*. You're the *Crown Prince* of Canada. Sky's the limit! A *second* of you playing really isn't that big a deal."

He screws up the corner of his mouth. "If you're sure... Okay. Cool." He picks up the three-hundred-year-old violin and nestles it between his shoulder and chin. Then he lifts the bow.

I stand back. My heart starts racing. *Ça y est.*

He peeps at the strings, expression softening, and begins to play the priceless stringed instrument.

MAPLE CROWN RULE 68: Always show respect.

I resist the urge to twirl my imaginary villain mustache. Everyone stops to look on—including a horrorstruck

Gord—and their cacophony of remarks muffles the violin's noise.

"These are just for display!"

"That needs to be handled with care!"

"He's not wearing gloves!"

Qu'il c'est fait avoir!

I cross my arms together, satisfied if not a touch smug. I half consider giving Fi and Neel a subtle thumbs-up...when the crowd's hubbub dies down and a song rises from the ashes.

Billy, who hasn't stopped playing, keeps his eyes shut, his bent arm moving like he's carving a ham, and creates the clearest, most stunning sound—*musique*—I have ever heard. It's rich. Decadent. Absolutely gorgeous. Each note pulls at my heartstrings, making me tremble. Making me...fume.

Because as he plays, there's a look on his face, one of pure happiness, contentment, confidence, and self-acceptance. All things I lack. Not to mention that Billy playing his violin is clearly *just* what he wants to be doing, living for himself. Something I've never gotten to do in my entire life. While Billy already has so much in knowing who he is and living his authentic life, now he's come along and taken the one thing I had: my crown. I hate him for it. I feel the overwhelming urge to fly into a white-hot rage.

Arrêtez.

Billy finishes playing, and the room, which I'd been counting on to deliver the acoustics of Billy's faux pas, resounds with applause and people demanding an encore. Pax whoops and cheers, egging him on. Billy's security detail nods and claps, and...is Gord wiping away a *tear* with the cuff of his suit jacket? Even Fi and Neel are lauding him. I find myself putting my hands together too, not because I don't want to stand out as the only one not clapping, but because it was actually, genuinely beautiful.

So, Billy is the Crown Prince, Out, *and* Talented.

La vie est vraiment pas juste. The only thing I can play is myself for a damn dingbat.

"Thank you!" Billy rests the violin back on the pedestal. "I'm sorry. I promise I meant no disrespect. It's just, instruments as nice as these are meant to be played." He continues over the praise of his raucous onlookers. "It's cool Canada has such a strong commitment to the arts. Anyway, it was really nice meeting so many of you tonight. You're awesome. Uh... yeah. Thank you!"

A little rough around the edges, but spoken like a true prince. Effortless. Graceful, even.

He's a natural.

I grit my teeth and try desperately to bear it.

Pisser dans un violon.

Over the crescendo of applause, he sidles up next to me. "Oh, no. Did I put my foot in my mouth again? Ever since the press conference... I only thought... Was it okay that I did that?"

I manage to smile. "You were absolutely brilliant."

New Crown Prince: 1

Former Crown Prince: 0

DAILY MAPLE ONLINE

THE ROYAL ROUNDUP
March 15, 06:19 am ET

BILLY WOWS WITH BOW
by Omar Scooby

Billy is first chair in more ways than one! The Crown Prince of Canada adds another string to his bow when he demonstrated an impressive skill in violin.

In another string of bad luck for Eddie, HRH Billy amazed audiences last night at the MET through a display of mastery at the violin. In an impromptu performance, he lifted an ancient instrument and began to play a beautiful song—pulling at our heartstrings. From his skills with a bow, the world is ready to bow down while Eddie-Boy bows out. Time to face the music, Edward!

While Billy may not *look* gay, he may just be your typical gay guy after all—which includes being part of a homosexual relationship with another young man back home in Montana. What's next? Will he be put in charge of interior design for Rideau Hall? Will he dump his small hometown cowpoke for more exciting escapades with gay celebrities? Billy is pulling the strings, and royal watchers of the world are here for it!

RELATED STORIES
Prince Billy Pushing Gay Agenda by Flaunting His Homosexuality?
Lil Nas X Asked Billy to Perform with Him at the Grammys
Billy: Unnatural Abomination, or Bomb Dot Com?
Next Oprah Sit-Down Interview with Billy?
Quiz: Who's Your Favourite Canadian Prince?
Which Twin is the "People's Prince"?
Rumours of Prince Billy Signature Investiture Ceremony Doll in the Works?
Commemorative Stamp Planned for Clone Prince
Meet the Boones

Chapter Twelve

BILLY

I'm standing next to Pax at the long, stainless-steel island in the kitchen of a famous New York City cathedral, barely able to keep my eyes open despite how excited I am to be here. It's been a long week, and I stayed up way too late last night.

"Welcome to our fundraiser for the foster care system," announces the host, a woman with red corkscrew curls who stands at the end of the island. "Thank you for choosing to spend your Friday night here. Teen involvement is such a great way to draw attention to this good cause." She clasps her hands together, acknowledging the fifty of us standing around the island, all teenagers from ritzy New York City private schools.

"Sponsors have pledged to donate a certain amount for every brown bag lunch you pack, to go toward a grant for the program, so we'll be staying up all night to pack as many as we can."

All night? I'm already so tired from such a jam-packed week, and everyone knows it—especially Edward, who totally gets it. I feel bad I've been talking his ear off all morning about how sleepy I am. But this charity is worth hanging in there to do the work.

"The lunches themselves will be enjoyed by foster care children who are attending special events all over the region this weekend."

I notice volunteers looking over at me from across the crowded countertop. One waves. Another smiles and nods. I keep finding myself wondering where I know people from before realizing I *don't* know them—they know *me*. So I just wave and smile back.

Pressing my eyes shut a few times, I try my hardest to focus on the host now talking us through the various duties required in order to prepare the food. But with how the week's gone, my brain is mush, worrying about people thinking I'm pushing a "gay agenda," hoping I'm doing right by the monarchy so far, and wanting people to like me—especially after the last *Daily Maple* article that was so rude. Pax just about shrieked when they read it.

"Pssst. Mandy Hathaway is staring at you," they whisper.

I look over at a mousy girl with long dark tresses and expressive doe eyes who's grinning at me over the top of a bin of red apples.

"Is she a celebrity or something?" I ask Pax, waving at her.

Pax buries their head in their hands in response.

"I can't get used to all this attention," I admit. Who would've guessed someone from teeny tiny Little Timber would be the world's next hot topic of conversation?

"Well, get used to it because we're being photographed," Edward chimes in, posing naturally for the event photographer, here to show all the good we're doing to help support this cause.

I stand up a little taller. Gosh, no one warned me this limelight thing was going to be more like a blazing laser. I guess I should have expected it.

The host gestures to the heaps of food piled in front of us. "Alright! Let's get started! We have a *lot* of lunches to pack."

The other volunteers break into conversation.

"Ready to pull an all-nighter?" the person standing to my right says with a sly grin. His cream-colored cashmere sweater contrasts nicely against the warm bronze of his skin. He has perfectly coiffed, thick black hair parted to the side, and mesmerizing dark eyes, the kind where I can't tell if he's wearing eyeliner or if his lashes are just naturally like that.

Before I can reply, he cuts back in. "Pleasure to meet you—" he shakes my hand "—I'm Neel." I notice glittery black nails and twinkling rings on each finger. "Edward's best friend. I've heard great things about you." He smiles a radiant smile, then squints and tilts his head flirtatiously. "Are the rumors true? Are you off the market for the moment?"

"I guess so." I let out a little laugh, taken aback. How does he know? Then I remember how the press found out about Dustin from stalking my personal socials before I had to deactivate them.

"Neel, behave," Edward teasingly tells him.

"Of course." Neel smiles, showing off big white teeth.

A girl in tight, snakeskin-print pants takes a step toward me. "I don't think we've officially met," she says. "Third period AP Calc. Lady Sofia Marchand. Welcome to the squad, cowboy." She smiles sweetly, and I catch a whiff of spicy vanilla perfume.

"Thanks," I say. I know who she is from the headlines boasting about her and Edward's romance. Pax has been obsessed and keeps speculating that the whole thing is a sham.

Wishful thinking, Pax.

Pax acknowledges her with a smile as she cozies up beside Edward. My best friend's smile turns into a glare the second she looks away. Then Pax gives me a look that says they want to send her packing, possibly in one of these brown paper bags.

When Edward catches me glancing over, he breaks into an easy smile and takes her hand in his, which catches the event photographer's eye.

The host gives Neel a box of gloves and asks him to pass them down. I put mine on. After she runs through what should go in each bag once more, the host claps her hands. "Get to it, people!"

"This is going to suck," Lady Sofia mutters, wrestling on a pair of clear plastic gloves over her long nails with difficulty. Then she gives a coy smile as the event photographer takes a close-up.

Neel taps a carrot peeler against a cutting board. "Shall we?"

"Let's do it," I say, hoping my enthusiasm is coming through despite my exhaustion.

Neel starts peeling the carrots, then I start cutting them up into carrot sticks and placing a handful of them in plastic baggies. Pax, who's on sandwich duty, gabs animatedly with Lady Sofia, who absentmindedly slaps mayo on bread. Edward assists with the turkey and cheese while another volunteer bags the finished sandwiches. Others are peeling and slicing apples, or portioning blueberries and assorted nuts. Once bagged in plastic, everything is passed down to the end of the island, where the host packages them in their brown paper bags. It's a pretty solid assembly line.

We keep packing, packing, packing. It takes a long time.

I'm on what feels like my one hundredth carrot and struggling to stay up when I realize Neel is talking to me.

"So, how's being Crown Prince treating you?"

"It's a lot of work, for sure. Just going to a new school is an adjustment. Forget about the whole world knowing my name and forming a zillion opinions about me." I start chopping another carrot. "But it's good. All the love and support is really amazing," I say, the memory of applause at the MET still fresh in my mind from Monday night. "And, you know, being Crown Prince means I get to do stuff I love, like this." I wave my knife. "It's really given me a sense of purpose."

The something *that's been missing all my life…*

I try to remember what Edward had mentioned about Neel. "I hear you're the son of an ambassador. What's that like?"

Neel shrugs, handing me another peeled carrot. "It has its perks. No supervision, which means parties and fun. But it can get a little lonely sometimes." He smiles. "Listen to me, sounding so woe is me. Anyway…" Neel shakes his head. "It's pretty damn neat you're out."

"Thanks. Are you gay too?" I ask, hoping I'm not too bold.

He grins. "I don't care much for labels. Besides, my parents would fly off the handle if they so much as suspected a thing. How'd yours take it?"

"My mom took it well," I say. "My dad…my dad back home…just never really talked about it. He didn't even ask me about my boyfriend, Dustin, when we first started dating."

Why am I sharing so much with someone I just met?

"My dad was a good person," I add, in case I made him sound like he wasn't.

"I believe that." Neel smiles kindly. "I mean, if he was anything like you."

I'm suddenly grateful that he and I are standing side by side.

After two hours more of packing lunches and almost cutting my finger off multiple times as I nearly fall asleep at the island, I realize I have to take a break and sit down. Not take a nap, I remind myself. Just a sit-down. But I'm afraid that I'll look like a slacker if anyone sees me.

"Bathroom?" I ask the host. She points the way. I climb a set of stairs and find myself in the main part of the cathedral, with its softly glowing lights shining up on ornate pillars and stained glass.

Luckily, I'm the only one here. I take the opportunity to collapse on one of the pews, rubbing my eyes. My feet thank me for the brief rest.

I gaze up at the tall ceiling. It feels weird being in a cathedral. I haven't been in one since Christmas—I don't exactly count the Little Timber Chapel as a cathedral. Every year, I light a candle for Dad. I always feel like I can see him in the glow of the warm flame.

Tears prickle my eyes. Sometimes, I feel broken, like why am I still sad? Shouldn't I be healed by now? It feels like I'll never fully heal. I think about him, good memories and bad, just to be with him again. It's like there are two realities: one in which he exists, and one in which he's never existed at all. Sometimes I slip back and find myself wandering the happy halls of that old life with him. It's painful, but at least we're together. I never want to stop remembering.

I can hear his voice: *Everyone heals in their own time.*

My eyes flutter shut. I just need one more minute before heading back down to the kitchen. And besides, it's cold in here, and I convince myself that it will keep me from nodding off.

But I'm wrong, and within seconds I'm fast asleep.

In my dream, there's a whinny from outside, and Lucky Lady comes trotting into the barn. She seems distressed. When I go to pet her, she neighs and bucks, her nostrils wide. I ask her what's wrong. She's covered in a layer of soot. I race out of the barn and spot our house—or what's left of it. It's a charred skeleton, a wisp of smoke rising up from its ruins. Were Mom and Dad inside? Where's Mack? I run toward the house, noticing that the whole yard has been scorched to nothing. The four oaks are ablaze. I see Mom and Dad and Mack standing inside, and when I run toward them, reach out for them, the flames engulf them.

Stomach lurching, I wake with a start in the dim light...to the sound of a *click*? I sit up to find I'm still alone. Phew. How long had I dozed off for? Maybe all of thirty seconds? Definitely not long.

I head back in and start cutting more carrots, apologetic for being out for longer than I anticipated. Luckily, no one asks any questions.

More hours pass in a blur, but I manage to stay awake the whole time. Just after sunrise, the host gets our attention by clapping her hands. She strolls down the length of the island and stops beside the dozens of carts chock-full of bagged brown lunches ready to be shipped off. "The numbers are in of how much you raised," she announces, glancing down at her phone. "Four million three thousand seven hundred ninety-two dollars!"

"Wow," I breathe, my fuzzy brain slowly registering the news.

Edward claps me on the back, jarring me. "Way to go that we stayed awake the whole night!"

Lady Sofia nudges Edward. "Thanks again for inviting me, Eddie-Bear."

If there was ever any doubt, the way my brother looks at her confirms that what they have is real.

Pax must agree because they shoot me a secret eye roll.

I'm just glad I made it through the event without toppling over at the kitchen island, though I sure came close a few times. Now, I only have one thought:

Bed.

Back at the mansion, I spend the rest of the day sleeping. Shortly after I wake up, and after fighting the urge to fall back asleep, I squeeze in a quick dinner with Mom, Mack, and Pax, who's still "rhapsodizing" about Edward, before taking a call from Dustin while rushing to meet Gord. I tell Dustin I miss him, actually meaning it this time, then I enter the study with a notepad and pen.

"Billy." Gord checks his watch. "Welcome to your first royal lesson." He smiles and gestures to a chair across from him at the desk, which is cluttered with textbooks. "I'm glad you're settled in and have taken care of all the basics so that we can finally tackle the truly important things."

I take a seat, barely able to see him over the stacks of books. "Thanks."

He moves a pile aside. "So, here's what you need to know. The Investiture Ceremony. You will be walking when called upon. You will need to know when to pause and bow, when to kneel, when to speak, what to say, when to stand, when to ascend the—"

"Oh, okay," I mumble, flipping open my notepad. "Let me just write that down." He's going so fast, I'll never remember a thing.

Gord takes a deep breath then grins. "Of course." He clasps his fingers together on the desk, and even though he's smiling, part of me wonders if he's frustrated I'm taking so long... and that I was late.

I finish writing what he said. "Okay." I meet his eyes, nodding.

His smile intensifies, and he nods back. "By the by, we appreciate you not bringing your...*friend* to New York at this time. It shows your respect for the delicacy of the situation."

I freeze, not quite sure what he means. Bringing Dustin here was an option, but not one I've considered seriously. The world is my oyster. But I'm still a little lost in terms of what "situation" he's referring to exactly. Maybe this has something to do with the Firm scrubbing through my personal social media—before asking me to deactivate it—and having me take down any photos of me and Dustin, and asking for him to do the same. Who knew that locking lips could shake an institution to its very foundation?

I just nod. "Yeah, of course. I want to be considerate."

Gord pushes a tablet across the desk toward me. "Your uniform design for the ceremony."

I gaze at a fashion sketch of a red cape with furry white trimming with black spots, and a military-like outfit worn underneath it. It looks like something straight out of medieval times.

"Uh, cool," I say, not knowing if Pax would think this outfit was beautiful or plain awful. Either way, they'd jump for joy if they had the chance to see this top secret design.

"It's in line with the traditional British uniforms," Gord adds.

I give a sharp nod. "Right. Got it." I can't let myself think about what lies beyond the ceremony. A forever home in Canada? Leaving Montana behind? And the ranch? Never again visiting our four oaks or Dad's headstone?

Gord grins. "Any questions?"

I keep my eyes trained on the tablet. "That all sounds great," I say quietly.

"Perfect." Gord takes out a bundle of papers. "Now, at the ceremony, the minister of foreign affairs will read the letters patent. After that, you will be reciting your vow to Canada. Half the speech will be in English and the other half will be in French. How's your mastery of the French language?"

I cringe. "I've only ever taken Spanish." I comb through my memory. "*Omelette du fromage?* Cheese omelet?" I let out a little laugh. Gord just blinks at me. I'm not sure he has a sense of humor. He launches into the French alphabet, and verbs, and has me parrot words back.

After that comes an exhaustive history of Canada lesson, at which point I realize I knew next to nothing about Canada, except that certain provinces sell milk in bags. I think I read that somewhere once, and it only stuck because I like milk. I tune back in to hear Gord talking about the history of a place called Hatley Castle. "The king and queen consort almost turned it into a prep school," he says. "This was soon after the governor general's role was dissolved."

He then dives into the king's checks-and-balances role of making sure everything is in the best interest of Canada. His role to provide something called the royal assent, which brings parliamentary bills into law. And his rubber-stamping of… well, everything.

"So, the Law of Succession for the Crown of Canada *can* be changed?" I ask, my pen struggling to form legible words.

"Correct," Gord says flatly. "Through a section 41 amendment."

"Section…41…amendment," I repeat, scribbling it down.

Finally, Gord has me memorize the ten provinces and three territories, and learn the key differences between the country's major lakes. See, the fact I was born in Canada isn't enough to win over the country, so the more I learn, the better. The lesson reaches a point where I'm tipping forward on my chair with exhaustion.

At long last, Gord stands. "We will pick up again tomorrow. Get some rest."

"Thank you," I say groggily, staggering up. I check my notepad. *"Bonsoir."*

At that, Gord gestures to the door with the slightest trace of a smile.

★ ★ ★

I'm back at the diner with Dad, where we always used to go after church. He's looking up at me from his coffee mug, blowing on it; as the steam fogs up his glasses, the warmest smile spreads across his face, and I'm filled with happiness again. And then the steam grows, obscuring him from view.

It clears to show it's not Dad there, but Frederick.

I let out a strangled sob.

I wake up, completely gutted. Those terrible, gnawing thoughts are back—the ones that only appear in the dizzying, disorienting moments after surfacing from a Dad dream: he's dead, and one day it'll be my turn, and we all die. Even Mom and Mack and Pax. *Everyone.*

I take a slow breath, stashing the grim thoughts back into their deep, dark well, and fight the layers of blankets off me, stepping onto the icy hardwood. Then I wrap myself in my silk robe that had been hanging off the bedpost, put on my slippers, and head toward the kitchen for a glass of milk.

My footfalls on the thick, plush rug running the length of the hall are silent, and it's dim except for the glowing sconces on the walls.

There's movement at the end of the hall.

My heart races.

Then I realize it's just my security detail on a routine night stroll. I go to take another step when a flickering light coming from a nearby doorway catches my attention, and I follow it.

I set foot onto the opulent carpet of the library, taking in the crackling fireplace, wood paneling, walls of books, and expansive map of Canada painted across the entire ceiling, adorned with an ornate chandelier.

On the far side of the room, King Frederick is hunched over a tablet and a red-and-white box of paperwork at a lamp-lit

desk, engraved ballpoint pen in hand and cup of tea steaming beside him.

He looks up at me, and smiles. "You're up early." He checks
his designer watch. "About six hours early. Up for a midnight
snack?"

"A glass of milk." I wipe sleep from my eyes. "I guess I'm
having trouble sleeping here. Hey, what are you doing here?" I
ask. "I thought you were supposed to be in Ottawa this week."

"Going to Commonwealth Day service tomorrow here in
town, followed by meetings with some Heads of State." He
removes his glasses and rubs his temples, tapping his finger
on the pile of paperwork. "Right now, I just so happen to be
approving a publicity plan for you. Would you like to attend
the Trevor Project Gala and the GLAAD Media Awards?"

I'm taken aback. My dad never spoke about anything gay-
related. It's so refreshing hearing Frederick talk about these
organizations like they're no big deal…which they're not.

"Definitely."

"Excellent. Let's try that." He red-lines the document.

"Thanks."

He inspects me. "How is life for you as a new Royal going?"

I debate whether I should tell him it's a lot of work, but so
far, so good, like what I told Neel? Or that I've been throwing myself into it all as a way to prove myself to him? And as
a way to fill up the mental space in my head to push away any
sad thoughts about Dad?

"Good," I reply. "Really good."

"Excellent. And Edward is treating you well, I hope? I know
he's adjusting to the shift too."

"Yeah, he's been really welcoming," I say, thinking about
how I'm meeting with him in a few short hours to go over
talking points for an upcoming hockey event. It was at his sug-

gestion, and I'm so grateful. He seems very supportive now. I barely remember the snooty version of him who I met in that backstage dressing room.

"Good. I'm always worried about him."

I laugh. "He's been great."

Frederick squeezes one eye shut in thought. "I hope so. Your mother and I have been treading very carefully with him. His future's no longer what he thought it would be. I'm sure he's hurting, but he'd never admit to it." He shakes the thought. "But nothing you need to take on. You've got enough on your plate."

I consider what it must feel like to have this role taken away. With it, my true sense of purpose has never felt stronger in a way it never could have felt about the ranch...or maybe even violin too.

"Have you decided on your regnal name yet?" he asks.

"My *what*?"

"The name you will be known as from here on out. Edward was almost Duke of Connaught and Strathearn. Granny's full name is Eliza, by the Grace of God, of the United Kingdom of Great Britain and Northern Ireland and of her other realms and territories Queen, Head of the Commonwealth, Defender of the Faith."

"Wow. That's a mouthful." I instantly regret saying it, but Frederick reacts with an agreeable smile.

"You know, your mother and I had settled on a name for you, before you were born. We were planning on going with François."

It's a strange thought. "Edward and *François*?" I chuckle, thinking about how I can't see myself as anyone other than Billy. "Hmm, it's not really me." I give it some more thought. "How about just...HRH Prince Billy?"

"I think that's a fine choice, if that's what you'd like."

"Prince Billy," I muse. "I think that's it. Plain and simple."

"Excellent. Would you like to see something?" Frederick nods toward the tablet on the desk.

"Sure." I close the distance between us, and peer over his shoulder. He smells like new car. On the tablet, there are designs of what look like intricately detailed white plates and bowls. "What's this?"

"I've asked for a design of the new china dishes we're ordering for the ceremony. Look." He points to one of the plates, where there's a moose rearing up on its hind legs. "This plate represents Canada." Then he taps another plate where there's a grizzly bear set against blue sky and mountains. "And this plate represents Montana." He looks up at me. "Do you like it?"

I nod. "Yeah, this is awesome."

"Good." Frederick rests a hand on my shoulder. "It's important to me that you know you're a part of this family."

"Thanks." My mouth twitches as the weight of his words sinks in.

"I take it Gord's told you about the glorious royal regalia you'll be wearing and holding? The scepter and the sword and all that?"

I nod. A strange sensation overtakes me. The more I get to know Frederick and the closer I feel to him, the more *guilty* I feel. All I can think about is Dad. It feels like I'm betraying him, and my bad dream resurfaces. It's not that I want to give the king of Canada the cold shoulder or anything. It's that as much as I like him, I'm also terrified of letting him override that special, sacred place Dad's always held in my heart. "Well, I should get back to bed. I'm meeting Edward for an early prince lesson in the morning."

"You're a great son and a great prince. I just wanted to let you know." He gives my arm a little pat. "Night, son."

"Night…" I can't get myself to say "Dad"—it's not right. "Frederick," I add. Then I quickly turn and head back to bed.

"You know how the Canadians are about their ice hockey," Edward says from across the dining room table over breakfast. "Okay, from your expression, maybe you don't. How much do you know about hockey?"

I take a sip of fresh orange juice. "Umm… Pucks… Sticks… Lots of padded uniform things. And the goal is to get the puck in the net."

Edward quirks an eyebrow, bagel midschmear in his hand.

"Oh, and obviously the skates," I add. Like I've said, I've really never been much of a sports fan. Maybe I should have taken up Dustin on his offer to teach me everything about sports after all…

"I'm really missing my boyfriend right now," I say, sharing. "He knows way more about sports than me."

"Okay. Great." Edward sets down his bagel. "Now that I know your baseline, we can start filling in the gaps so you can trick the world into thinking you're a hockey expert. So, ice hockey is the official national winter sport of Canada. Canada's NHL teams include the Ottawa Senators, the Toronto Maple Leafs, the Montreal Canadiens—fondly known as the Habs. There's also the Vancouver Canucks, Edmonton Oilers, Calgary Flames, and the Winnipeg Jets."

I blink. "Got it. Senators. Maple Leafs. Habs." I give a sheepish wince. "Mind repeating the rest?"

Edward chuckles softly. "Shouldn't you be taking notes?"

"Oh. Right." I dig my notepad and pen out of my pocket, and flip to the last page of notes I took during Gord's lesson.

It's the list of the ten provinces, and the last one on the list catches my eye. "Hey, were you named after Prince Edward Island?"

Edward blinks at me. "Yes, actually. Most think I was named after my great uncle Edward, the Earl of Wessex."

"Nice! Did you know it takes a whole ten minutes to cross the Confederation Bridge into PEI?" I ask, excited to have remembered.

He smiles coolly. "I know everything about the provinces."

"Oh. Right. Sorry."

"Royals don't apologize," Edward corrects me. "The Maple Leafs are going up against the Rangers this week," he says.

"Got it. Why is it Maple Leafs and not Maple *Leaves*?"

Edward spears his fork through a ball of watermelon, then looks up and grins. "No clue."

He launches into all these facts about the various players, and tells me what I need to know and say—and I write it all down. Things about holding the stick. Funny terms like flopper and bender and grinder that I know Pax would find a real hoot.

It's actually going really well until Gord enters the dining room and smacks a newspaper down onto the table. There's a massive, front-page, night-vision photo that shows me snoring on a pew in the cathedral. The headline reads: **ROYAL PRINCE BILLY SLEEPS ON THE JOB**.

"Care to explain?" Gord asks me with venom in his voice.

I gawk. "Uh… Crap." I look at Edward, who calmly dabs his fine linen napkin on his mouth. "I wasn't sleeping *all* through the fundraiser. That's a big lie! I closed my eyes for maybe…two minutes," I say to Gord, not sure I sound very convincing, especially given that it looks like I'm drooling in the photo, with my mouth hanging open like it's trying to catch flies. How was it even taken in the first place?

"I'm sorry," I finally say. "Is this...*really* bad?"

"It's not beyond repair," Gord says, eyes flitting to the unflattering photo, "but you're definitely losing favor in the public eye, and the Canadian Royal Family is going to have to significantly increase their donation in order to make up for it." He takes a seat at the table and knits his fingers together, looking from me to Edward, then back to me.

Edward crumples his napkin on the tabletop. "Well, I'm sure you've got this."

"The Canadian monarchy's existence rests on your shoulders," Gord reminds me.

"I know, I'm sorry!" I say through a mask of horror.

Gord rubs his salt-and-pepper scruff and stands. "I will figure out what's required and commence damage control." Then he leaves.

"Don't fret," Edward tells me. "Out of all the people to trust, Gord is number one most trustworthy. He'll sort this out."

"Okay," I say absently. I realize I am panting and have my knife and fork in an iron grip. I ease up and scan the article, sighing at the photos of the other volunteers peppered throughout, pictures of hard work and determination. "I wish I hadn't taken that rest break. Were there hidden cameras or something?" I let out a contemplative hum.

"The press can spin anything. It's rather bizarre, isn't it? You know... I bet you that event photographer must have been a mole working with the press."

"You *think*?" I peer at Edward, finding myself agreeing with him. I'm pretty sure that drool has been photoshopped. "Hey," I start, "is there anything you can do? *You* know I didn't step out of the kitchen for very long. Maybe a few minutes at the most."

Edward shrugs. "Leave it up to Gord. One philosophy of

his is to never draw more attention to a hot topic, or it only gets hotter."

"What about the other volunteers we were with? They saw me helping cut up carrots all night. Maybe they could chime in—"

"I'm sure the same guidance has been drilled into them: don't get involved." He must see how mortified I look because he smiles kindly at me. "Please don't fret. No one is going to remember this by tomorrow."

"Yeah. Yeah, you're right," I nod emphatically, willing myself to believe him. "I just have to be more careful from now on," I vow.

"This sort of thing happens all the time. From one brother to another, now you see how hard it really is." Edward chuckles. "Being Crown Prince comes with a price. In fact, it puts the 'price' in prince. It requires perfection. *Maple Crown Rule 10.*"

"Maple Crown *what?*"

"Oh, you'll get to those in your lessons with Gord soon, I'm sure." His expression grows serious. Concerned, even. "You sure you still want to take all this on?" he asks softly.

Despite my stomach churning with nerves at my first scandalous headline, it's not even a question.

"Yeah. I'm sure."

I want to be the perfect Royal. I want to make my long-lost father proud. His words replay in my head: *You're a great son and a great prince.*

A part of me feels a pang of guilt when I realize that Dad's voice has been replaced.

DAILY MAPLE ONLINE

THE ROYAL ROUNDUP
March 20, 04:34 pm ET

EDFIA LOVED UP ON NEW YORK STREETS
by Omar Scooby

Edward and Sofia steal the spotlight once again! The former Crown Prince was spotted walking arm in arm with the gorgeous Lady Sofia through the twinkling streets of SoHo. It's clear these two go together like eggs and Canadian bacon.

After keeping a low profile in the wake of Billy sashaying onto the scene, New York City's hottest power couple was captured strolling the streets of Manhattan, looking young and very much in love. The socialite wore a chic skirt, thigh-high boots, and flowy blouse, with her signature silky ombré hair pulled back in a sleek bun. The former Crown Prince donned a lux suit and classic timepiece and appeared to be holding up well considering getting booted off the throne a week prior. The twosome dined after participating in a fundraiser event with proceeds going toward a children's home.

Cause-driven work is vital to the Canadian monarchy and contributes to their good standing in Canada. However, Prince Billy, also in attendance at the star-studded event, was dinged for sleeping through most of it. This less-than-noble act—sneaking off to have a nap while the other volunteers worked tirelessly to bag lunches—has lost him favour with the general public. He simply couldn't resist dozing off in the City That Never Sleeps.

Could Billy be tired of life as Crown Prince so soon? Could he be ready for a royal send-off back to his sleepy little town? Or perhaps he's merely celebrating a belated National Napping Day?

Most are more interested in Edward and Sofia's burgeoning romance than in the soporific tales of a supine snoring snoozer. Stay tuned to keep tabs on everybody's favourite twin flames (Edward and Sofia, that is)!

RELATED STORIES
Royal Prince Billy Sleeps on The Job
Billy: Sleepy Is the Head That Wears the Crown?
Dreamer Not Doer: You Snooze, You Lose!
6 Tricks to Achieving Sofia's Effortless Looks
Prince Billy Flubs on National TV

Chapter Thirteen

EDWARD

I'm starting to appreciate spending study hall without having to make time for an iota of prince work. Especially because, despite it being senior year, the professors are making us work harder than ever with an overabundance of schoolwork. If my senioritis wasn't already dialed up to eleven, my focus is made more scattered by Neel seated across the aisle, jabbing his finger at my tablet, indicating I check my messages.

I open my email and see he's sent me a link to a *Daily Maple* article. I glance over the top of my screen to make sure Professor Hildegard isn't on to me. He's strolling the aisles of students with their noses in books or typing out essays. I click the link to the article.

It's titled: **PRINCE BILLY FLUBS ON NATIONAL TV.**

With the regular hockey season well under way, Prince Billy dropped the puck at last night's Maple Leafs versus Rangers game at Madison Square Garden. But when asked about the matchup between the Maple Leafs and Rangers, the new Crown Prince was on thin ice. He tripped over his words and had his hockey facts so scrambled, it's no small wonder he didn't end up in the penalty box for it.

I snicker to myself. Oh, this is so good. I finish the article, then click on the Canadian Royals' Instagram, where there's nothing about Billy except for Mum and Dad's **Welcome to the family, Billy** post from the day of the press release, and a **Countdown to Investiture Ceremony Weekend** post with a photo of Billy. *Crisse.* I keep scrolling, searching for any indication that the Firm, Parliament, or British Royals are observing Billy's string of mishaps. From the look of things, there's no telling. This just means I have to double down.

I head over to Billy's newly created and verified professional profile. Yesterday afternoon, I raised my inquiry to Gord, asking why Billy has his own account. *Apparemment*, the allowance of the professional account controlled by the Firm is an exception, and only because of Billy's "unprecedented surge in popularity" and what it means for the Canadian Crown. Hearing he's so beloved and gets special treatment because of it is… infuriating, to say the least. Sorry: *twinfuriating*, as Neel put it.

And to think I got grounded for far less. But they need him to show up, attend events, show face, woo the masses. Between Gord taking Billy under his wing and Mum and Dad's blatant adoration for him, I hate to admit that I'm emerald with envy. Somehow, the critique of him in the *Daily Maple* article gives me a shred of hope.

The bell rings, and Neel and I head down the corridor.

Neel keeps his voice low. "Fascinating, isn't it?"

"Looks like people are beginning to question Billy's ability as Crown Prince," I say quietly, a slight joy in my voice.

"'Does he know anything at *all* about Canada?'" Neel says in a mocking tone. "Oh, and did you see the line that said, *'How can he rule a country he knows nothing about?'*"

"What goes up must come down," I say out the side of my mouth as we round the corner. "If the public gives him any more dislikes, the Firm is bound to intervene and strategically strip Billy of his title—and return it to its rightful owner." I mime a crown lowering onto my head. "It's only a matter of time before section 41 is rolled out to alter The Law of Succession for the Crown of Canada."

"English, please?"

"Essentially, Billy's fate will be left up to a vote, and all of Parliament will vote depending on his increasingly rancid reputation," I explain. "That is, if we can pull this off."

"But what will be *the* straw to break the camel's back?" Neel inquires.

Fi joins us on the stairs. "Looks like the tide is turning against Billy. Your plan is working."

"Don't you mean *our* plan?" I quip.

"I'm guessing you liked the photo I took?" Neel asks Fi.

"I shouldn't have underestimated you," Fi tells him.

He grins. "I told you my photography skills work wonders."

"It was perfection," I add.

"Just like you." Fi looks at me a certain way, and reaches for my hand.

Making sure no one else is watching, I swat it gently away. "Wow, you are really good at acting like you like me," I tease.

"Who says I'm acting?" She winks. "Princess Sofia. Has a nice ring to it, don't you think, Neel?"

"Neel, don't you dare answer that." I shudder. "I'd rather marry my cousin."

She scoffs. "So, what's next in store for—"

"Billy!" Neel shouts in greeting.

"Hey, y'all." Billy appears before us. "How's it going?"

"Good!" we all say in unison.

"Good," I say again, firmer, regaining my composure. "How's all with you?"

"Good," he says. "Just heading to lunch in the café."

"Oh, get the chocolate chip cookies. They're baked daily," I offer, flashing a smile. "And don't worry. They're not too sweet."

"Will do," he says. "Thanks. See you after school for that standing meeting thing." He waves and trundles up the stairs.

I look at Neel and Fi, and sigh. "Close call." I grin. "You catch more flies with maple syrup, as they say."

"He seems *way* too happy," Fi mutters.

"We can change that," Neel says with that impish smile I know far too well.

When Mum shared she wanted to spend quality time with me, it took Gord a solid week and a half to find a time when both of us were free—a warm Wednesday afternoon at the end of the month. Luckily, going out in the middle of the week means less crowds.

"Isn't this nice?" Mum asks from a tuffet in the fitting room. She's holding shopping bags and a glass of champagne, with Evie by her side, observing me as I examine the silk ascot on the suit jacket I'm wearing.

"Indeed," I say, turning this way and that in the mirror. "It's lovely to be out on the town without the full entourage for once."

Mum nods. "See? I told you it would get better for you."

"I can't say I miss it." But a big part of me does.

"You're doing a great job," Mum says with gusto, as if reading my mind. "I know it's likely been tough, but your father and I are always here for you." I know penciling this mother-son excursion into her whirlwind schedule was her way of showing that while the press may have left me behind, she hasn't and doesn't plan on it.

I button and unbutton the suit jacket. "How does this look?"

Mum picks up on how I don't want to get into the topic of becoming second string, and she smiles diplomatically. "I think that whole look really suits you, Edward." Her eyebrows rise. "You know, that would be the perfect thing to wear when we finally have Fi over the mansion for dinner." She screws up her mouth. "I just realized Gord never sent us your schedule. We need to get on that."

"Oh, right! Sorry, I must've forgotten to tell him. I'm on it."

We end up purchasing the ascot, the suit, and a few new pairs of shoes in the main room of the department store.

On the way out, I'm able to greet a few fans before Mum and I step into the SUV waiting for us at the curb.

So, *this* is what life will be like from now on. It's…*tranquille*.

Although I froze up at Mum's words of praise back there, I'm thankful she and Dad have really been trying to make sure I'm alright…which is why I think I should finally set up that dinner with Fi. It would make them both so happy—and Fi too. Almost as happy as I was to spend quality time today with Mum, just us two.

But still, not even this pleasant excursion was enough to shake the hell-bent feeling I have about wanting the primo position back.

"I can't believe he keeps making the headline!" I gripe to Neel over FaceTime back on Park Ave. My phone's propped up on the kitchen counter as I slam bowls and measuring cups onto the marble island.

Neel cleans the lens of his mirrorless camera. "Are you referring to the successful bush-planting ceremony he took part in? Or the flag-raising ceremony? Or was it that wreath-laying ceremony?"

"All of the above!" I huff.

"Chill out, it's not that big a deal," he says. "So, for my yearlong vacation, I'm thinking of starting things off in

Madrid, then heading to Ibiza… Or perhaps I should go to Rio de Janeiro first…"

Ignoring him, I look at the paper that arrived earlier, showing Billy shining like a ray of sun. "I worked all of my life for this, only to be pushed aside for the shiny new model." I crack an egg into a bowl. "*I'm* safe. *I* listen. *I* follow the rules!"

"Might I remind you of our little fireworks stunt last year?" Neel asks. "Oh! Maybe I should make China part of my trip…"

"That was an outlier." I sigh. "Fine. I was acting out. But even then, I wasn't a loose cannon!"

"Am I detecting a teeny bit of jealousy, my dear?"

I refuse to admit it, so I deflect. "I wouldn't go *that* far…"

"I get it. You're pissed. I would be too." Neel rubs his cloth against his camera's viewfinder. "Why don't you ply *Pax* for intel?"

"Genius! Why didn't I think of this before? I'll ask them all about Billy. There's got to be a skeleton in that closet of his…" I stare off into space, wondering whether I should also interrogate Mack again.

"Edward," Neel butts in, "you know I love you, but you *have* to relax. Why don't you just take the rest of the night off, kick back, and bake?" He aims his camera lens at me and pretends to snap a photo. "It's only a matter of time before you're back in the saddle."

I cringe. "You're starting to sound like Billy. Maybe you're spending *too* much time around him."

Neel grins and shrugs. "What can I say? I'm taking my assignment seriously! So seriously, in fact, that Leo is starting to wonder if I'm avoiding him."

"I do appreciate it." I pick up my phone and manage a smile. "Alright, talk soon. Dig up some dirt on him already!" I hang up. Maybe I've gone a tad overboard, but it's not like there's anything better to do with my recently freed-up schedule, other than baking, obviously.

Sure, Billy is the shining star that entered the Canadian Royal Family, taking big swings and winning. But the monarchy doesn't like big swings. They like people who are compliant. Consistent. Rule-followers who keep their heads down. That's pretty much me in a nutshell, and it's all going to waste. The thought of him in his prince lesson with Gord right now is aggravating. Who would have ever thought I'd actually miss being the target of Gord's withering stares?

I do what I do when I'm stressed—listen to classical music and bake up a storm. I fling cups of flour into a mixing bowl, letting it puff up like a miniature atomic bomb. With my teeth gritted, I whisk egg whites, combine them with butter and sugar, then fold them in with the dry ingredients, trying to be careful despite the frustration roiling inside me. I pop the cake batter in the oven, and head into the living room, where I throw myself onto the sofa.

I'm about to reach for my AP Calc worksheets when something catches my attention.

Mack's laptop.

It glows on the coffee table, beckoning me. She's probably fast asleep by now, along with Connie and Pax. As for Billy, after his lesson with Gord, he's getting his measurements taken by the Head of Robe before going over steps with the royal dance instructor for the Jolee Jubilee Ball in two weeks… meaning he shouldn't be done for at least another few hours, as has been the case for the past week and half. With all the footage Mack's taken, maybe there's some dirt on him in here…

Non. Neel's right. I need to just relax…or at least start on my homework. I settle into the sofa and get through most of it before my urge to snoop grows too strong.

I look around to make sure the coast is clear, then reach over and pull the laptop close.

Unbelievable. Mack doesn't even have it password-protected.

And she *really* shouldn't leave her laptop unattended like this.

There are a bunch of browsers open. Her surprisingly booming YouTube channel. What looks to be fan fiction sites. TikTok. Email—

I freeze. There are emails from the Firm. These aren't Mack's emails. They're Billy's. He must have signed into his email account on her laptop.

I scroll through his emails, mostly boring correspondence from the Firm about various patronages, events, and ceremonies. He's getting his own royal cypher too. And special commemorative stamps as well as coins saying **CELEBRATING THE INVESTITURE OF HRH PRINCE BILLY**. Of course.

And to think my name on a tea towel set was a big deal.

I open an email documenting all the Investiture Ceremony souvenirs: teacup and saucer. Biscuit tin. Souvenir spoon. Bauble. A collector's edition Ken Doll in my likeness. All things designed for me long ago. Since we have the same face, it was easy enough for the Firm to take my name off and slap his on everything.

Then I spot an email with an interesting subject line: New Canadian Royal China Plates.

Billy,

Here's the latest redesign. I know we looked over the previous iteration in the library together, but it's come along nicely since then. Looking forward to your thoughts.

Best,
HRM

I feel my jealousy flare up again. I'll be *damned* if my desserts are going to be served on plates that I didn't approve!

My thoughts are cut short when I smell something...*burning*.

I throw the laptop back onto the coffee table, and race back into the kitchen. Plumes of smoke are pouring from the oven.

Infuriated at myself, I grab potholders and yank out the scorched cake. Ruined.

Sacrament.

"What's that ominous smell?" Pax wanders into the kitchen, wearing a tank top and yoga pants. When they see me, their eyes widen and they freeze. "Oh! Prince Edward! *Hi!*"

I'm still holding the charred cake in the pan. "Believe it or not, it's a vanilla cake. *Was* a vanilla cake." I open the rubbish bin, about to drop the whole thing in. I don't even want to try to save the pan.

"Wait!" Pax holds up their hands, and I look at them curiously. "If I may?" they say timidly. "You could just cut the flaky burnt part off? I've done that plenty of times before. The rest of it still looks pretty tasty."

"That's blasphemous," I say.

"Oh. It is? I—"

I let myself smile a tiny smile. "I'm kidding." I set it back down on the counter and gently pry it from the pan and onto a serving plate.

Pax takes a knife and begins cutting away the top burnt part. Finally, they stand back with a flourish. "Voilà!"

"It's a little rough," I remark, "but it actually looks edible." I taste a small pinch. It's not terrible. I cut off a chunk and offer it to them. "Try it. Apologies for the lack of frosting. Not my usual."

"Let there be cake!" They knock their cake against mine.

We each take a bite. My tastebuds revel in a burst of vanilla.

"Wow! This is amazing, sans frosting!" Pax says. "You *made* this?"

I nod, surprised by how much the compliment means to me. It sends a warm, fuzzy feeling through my body. "Thank you," I say, blushing for some reason. Somehow, the thought of plying them for information seems wrong. And looking at them, I can't help but wonder if...

Non. Pax is Billy's best friend. And anyone who's a bestie to Billy is an enemy of mine.

But as Pax does a cute little dance after taking another bite of cake, I can't resist smiling.

Pax isn't who I thought would be my type. I'm a gay guy, and Pax is...well, *Pax*. The fact their pronouns aren't *he* and *him* is a bit confusing, because as a gay guy I've only ever thought of *he* and *him* as being crush-worthy. *They/them* is something I've not thought of before. Am I still gay if I'm with someone who doesn't identify as male? Does this make me pansexual? Am I even cis? Now I'm rethinking my sexual orientation *and* my gender identity. Lots to question here.

I shake the sudden surge of thoughts. "You're always in such good spirits," I remark.

"How can I *not* be?!" they say. "I'm here. With you." They stiffen. "Ah. Sorry. You know what I mean. Why do I get so nervous around you? Billy's right, you're human, just like the rest of us, and OMG I need to stop talking now."

I chuckle. "What makes you so sure I'm human?" I give my best vampire-eye smoulder.

Pax giggles.

"What I meant was, you ooze sunshine," I say. "Are you naturally just a happy and ebullient person?"

Pax's smile flags as they go into thought. "I guess so. I mean, not all the time. I wasn't always happy. It took time to heal and figure out how I wanted to live my life. To be honest, I've had my fair share of adversity. Growing up gay and gender-queer in a small and secluded town wasn't the easiest thing. Constantly getting fem-shamed just because I liked eyeliner and floral prints."

"I can imagine," I say, even though I can't, not really.

Pax nods in earnest. "And then there was the whole parents-disowning-me thing."

My eyes widen. "I'm sorry to hear that." Suddenly it puts all my worries about coming out to my parents into perspective. It also hurts my heart to hear it. How can people be so unloving?

"When people used to say invalidating things, I would question why I bothered to fight back," Pax shares. "Then I realized one day that I'm not fighting *against* society's views, I'm fighting *for* myself."

"Good on you," I say, genuinely impressed by their strength and maturity. "But it still must not be a walk in the park," I add.

They grin again. "Hey, I'm still standing, aren't I? So I guess the answer to your question is that yeah, I would say I like to look on the bright side. You kind of have to. Being frustrated really doesn't accomplish anything. Even when my parents didn't allow me to explore my love for fashion, or whenever kids at school heckled me from their cars, I've refused to let other people's negativity weigh me down. Why give the haters the satisfaction? Screw 'em!"

"That's actually really good advice," I muse. "If you let other people's words and actions affect your emotions, then they win." I realize I'm also thinking about myself when I say it.

"Exactly," Pax says. "One's mental health and well-being are so much more important. My grandma always says you can't let anger eat you alive." They eye the remaining cake. "Speaking of eating, could I have another piece?"

"It's either you or that rubbish bin." I slice off a big chunk for them, and they reach for it. "How do you cope with that kind of prejudice?" I press.

Pax finishes their bite. "I design. And I sew. Usually rainbow things. Or sparkly things. Or glittery things. It's the little joys, you know?"

"Certainly," I say, thinking about my stress reliever of baking. It suddenly hits me that despite the fact that they're Billy's BFF, this may be the closest thing to a date I've ever been on—even more so than Break Room Boy at my first gala back.

"I've had a hell of a day," I say, "but you've made me feel better. Thank you."

Pax nearly chokes on another bite of cake. "I... I *have*?" They cough, cake stuck in their throat. "Gah, why can't I function when I'm around you?"

"I think you've been functioning at peak levels," I find myself saying.

Pax looks like a deer in headlights.

What am I doing? I turn and hurry out of the kitchen.

"Night!" I call back to them.

The next day, during lunch in the school café, I lean in toward Neel over my tray of filet mignon and mashed potatoes. "We need to try even harder to find some dirt on Billy," I whisper. "Are you sure you didn't find anything?"

"Nope," Neel says. "Billy really is perfect and adorable and nothing about him is scandalous." He catches himself. "Adorable in the boring sense of the term, of course." He chomps down on his leafy greens, and shrugs. "I don't know. Maybe we should take a break. The tabloids have already been super brutal to the poor guy this week."

"You don't actually feel *bad* for Billy, do you?" I ask, sounding stroppy.

Neel fervently shakes his head. "What? No." But I know him too well. I can see something in his eyes.

"Neel. Do you...do you *like* him?" I feel slightly ill.

J'ai l'impression qu'on me prend pour une valise.

"Ew! No. Never. Trust me, *bharā*."

"Okay." I desperately want to believe Neel. But as I see how he avoids my gaze, I'm not exactly buying it.

Neel prods me. "Besides, I *have* a beau, remember?"

I cut into my filet. "Oh, that's right. How is Lenny?"

Neel recoils. "His name is *Leo*. And he's divine."

"Oh, that's right. Leo. Forgive me, my mind's been a *bit* preoccupied."

Neel raises one perfectly threaded eyebrow. "You don't say?"

Wild laughter cuts through the air, and Billy and Pax enter the café, surrounded by a doting gaggle of giggling classmates. The cowboy boots, albeit chic ones, worn by a few of them don't go unnoticed by me.

"Anyway, what were we talking about?" I turn back to Neel, trying to pretend like I haven't just seen my happy-go-lucky twin waltz in. I can't shake my agitation at his popularity, even here.

Neel sips from his can of seltzer water. "Beaus?"

"Right, right." I glance back at Billy, who's standing in line with his tray, all smiles with his new friends. Then, a thought hits me from out of nowhere like an ice storm in Saskatchewan.

"Neel." I grab his arm, and he nearly spits out his water. I grin, and my grin intensifies. "He's still with his boyfriend, Dustin, right?"

Neel looks blankly at me, and blinks.

"I'll answer. He is. How do I know this? Because I've overheard their inane phone conversations, mostly about basketball." I rub my hands together conspiratorially. "Oh, I am good."

Neel flares his nostrils and looks at me over the tops of his eyes. "What are you nattering on about now?"

"Neel. I have it. The perfect plan to send him back to Missouri."

"Montana," Neel corrects me.

"Sure. Whatever." I lean in. "I'm going to need your help."

Chapter Fourteen

BILLY

"Good morning, Your Royal Highness," says a footman as he wrenches back the curtains.

I groan and yank the covers over my head to block out the blazing sunlight. Is it morning already? It feels like my head just hit my pillow after a packed night of homework, brushing up on the waltz for the ball tonight, and studying with Gord. He's been going over the cue cards with the speech I'll be delivering at the Investiture Ceremony and teaching me about the Maple Crown Rules. Maple Crown Rule 8 rings true: No rest for the Royals. It's intriguing stuff, but it's a lot. Who knew the Royal Family tree was a circle? Interesting how Gord's not going over the British Royals' colonial past, racist present, incest... Pax's Royal Rundown 101 lesson really stuck with me.

As the footman lets in more light, I think about how I'm really starting to miss Little Timber, the ranch, the general store, and even school, down to its silly marmot mascot. Although not having to do dishes, hang up my towels, or muck stalls is still pretty great. Then I remember that *being Crown Prince* is the thing that's been missing my whole life, and suddenly, I feel okay again.

My phone rings, and rings, and rings, and I finally pick up. "Hello?" I grumble.

"I miss you," comes Dustin's earnest voice.

"I—I know." I peek out from the covers, and squint against the glare. "You called to tell me that last night too," I say, rubbing my eyes. "And yesterday afternoon. And yesterday morning."

"I know. I just really miss you," he says tenderly. "What are you up to?"

"Just woke up," I mumble.

"Very nice!" he says, sounding way more upbeat than normal.

"Why do you sound like you're up to something?"

"Who, *me*? I'm not up to anything!" His voice sounds way too playful for me to believe him.

"If you say so." I sit up. "Don't be mad, but is it okay if we talk later? Once I've had a chance to wake up a little more?"

"Yeah. Yeah, of course. I love you."

"Love you too." I hang up and shove my face back into my pillow. I'm so overwhelmed. Dustin's persistence to connect while I've got a million princely duties just feels like one more thing adding to my already full plate. The fact I'm kind of neglecting him, breaking Maple Crown Rule 73: Never neglect family nor friend, is only feeding into my overall sense that I can barely get two minutes to myself before someone is calling for me or telling me what to do. At least being busy is keeping my dad sorrows at bay.

"Breakfast is served, Your Royal Highness," says the footman before slipping back into the hall.

I let out a belabored moan. I just want to go back to sleep. *Oh, it must be so hard being a rich prince*, I can picture Dad saying, and it makes me smile, realizing he's still there living rent-free in my head. *Buck up*, he'd say.

I shuffle through the halls toward the smell of scrambled eggs and coffee, and step out on the veranda, where Mom,

Mack, and Pax are eating breakfast, already dressed for the day. It's the first really warm weather we've had since coming here.

"Morning," I mumble, plopping into a seat at the head of the table and hugging my robe tightly against a breeze.

"Oh, honey, you look worse for wear," Pax remarks.

"You think?" I croak sarcastically, feeling my bad mood lift a little. "I barely slept."

"Again?" Mom frowns, her expression full of concern. "Is Gord being too hard on you? I've told him that you need your rest."

I shrug. "I'm okay."

Mack shoves a syrupy bite of pancake into her mouth. "Well, I'm great, thanks for asking! Gord is actually being super nice to me. He even said I could keep posting on social media… as long as it's not anything 'too sensitive.'" Mack holds up her phone. "Quiet on the set!" she commands all of us. Then she turns to look into the camera. "Hi, fam! It's a beautiful morning here at the mansion." She swipes her phone through the air to get a look at the panoramic view of the treetops of Central Park in the distance. "Did you know the state tree of New York is the sugar maple? I learned that at school." Then she turns it on me. "Hi, Prince Billy! How's it going? Looking forward to the Jolee Jubilee tonight?"

I nod, smile, and give a thumbs-up. What happened to not filming me? I'm pretty sure Gord would consider that "too sensitive."

"Jolee was Canada's OG royal darling," Pax shares. "She preeminently popularized the white wedding dress tradition!"

"Pax Andrews, everybody," Mack says proudly. "They're an amazing clothing designer who designed and made some of the outfits for the event." She turns her phone back on herself. "See you all tonight. It's going to be a blast. Macky Montana out!"

When she puts it down, Pax's fingers alight on my shoulder. "Where's Edward?"

I shoot Pax a bemused glance. "Why do I feel like you're always asking me that?"

"Umm, because I am," they say, pursing their lips. "And because he's elusive."

I shrug. "I don't know. I don't even know what day it is."

"It's Wednesday, April 13." Mom sighs and shuts her paper. "I'm worried about you."

"It's fine." I help myself to a bowl of oatmeal and fresh berries. The balmy spring breeze feels good as it rustles through my hair. It makes me hopeful.

A footman appears to pour me a steaming mug of coffee, along with an extra splash of milk. I desperately drink the hot coffee despite it scalding my tongue. Another footman places a tray of magazines onto the table. The headline on the topmost one makes me do a spit take.

Mack squeals. "Billy! Gross!" She wipes at her face in disgust.

"Sorry." I reach for the magazine. A large photo of Dustin and I is featured on the cover, midkiss outside the ranch at sunset. I recognize the photo instantly—it's an old one from his Instagram. The headline reads: **BILLY AND BOYFRIEND CONDEMNED BY VATICAN**. My stomach lurches. I tear the magazine open, searching for the article. Another bad headline, but this one feels especially invasive. *Oh, no, no, no, no, no.* Edward's words echo in my mind: *Being Crown Prince comes with a price… It requires perfection.*

Pax snatches it out of my hands and shoves it below the table. "Billy, no! Bad Billy! Bad!"

"Wait! What does it say?" I ask, suddenly feeling wide awake, my heart racing.

Pax shakes their head. "Nope. We're adding 'don't read the tabloids' to our list, right after 'don't read the comments.'"

I sigh, recalling the other harsh articles about me, and how I struggled to fall asleep at night after reading them. "I appreciate you," I say, "but I'm also dying inside. Gord is going to see that!"

Pax flings the magazine off the veranda and shrugs. "Oops."

I gawk. "Pax!"

"Yes?" they ask innocently, reaching for another magazine with Ryder Russell flexing his bicep on the cover. Pax flips through it. "This one's in the clear." Something catches their eye. "Sweet Mary and Muslin! I got a mention in the hot topics section!" they exclaim. "'Pax Andrews has been designing and sewing garments for the Jolee Jubilee, which will be shown in their own fashion show early next week...'" Pax squeals, then reads the room. "I can...read the rest later." They tuck the magazine by their side. "Sorry. Where were we?"

I'm proud of Pax's accomplishment, and glad Lady Sofia helped pull a few strings to give them such a great platform to show off their Jolee Jubilee collection at the Museum of Modern Art on Monday. It's a big deal. A *huge* deal.

But I'm too sick to my stomach right now to register that my best friend got their very own shout-out in a magazine when I'm still spiraling over my...shout-out? Callout?

"Why wasn't the press vetted before the staff brought it out to us like they always do?" Mom asks me, clearly annoyed. "I've *explicitly* told them not to send in anything else that paints you in a bad light!"

Mack holds up another magazine that features Edward and

Lady Sofia arm in arm in a box seat. The headline reads: **ROYAL COUPLE WARMS HEARTS AT HOCKEY GAME**.

"How come *they* get the good headline?" she asks.

"This is outrageous." Mom folds her napkin.

"I agree!" Pax says. "I'm as big a Fi fan as anyone, but he's *way* too good for her." They lean in. "That doesn't leave this table."

Mom continues on. "Billy, I thought the king and queen promised to protect you."

"Yeah, I don't know."

"They aren't following through." Mom gives a shake of her head. "Your sister's right. Why does Edward get the good headline, but you don't?"

"Beats me."

"Umm, it sounds like major homophobia to me, peeps!" Mack pipes in.

"Exactly. Why isn't the Firm saying anything?" Mom demands.

"Isn't freedom of the press still a thing?" Pax asks.

"Yeah, I think so. Gord told me that the media is 'capricious,' with the ability of hailing me as the best thing that ever happened to the monarchy one day, and then 'viciously spurning' me the next," I say. "Even the queen of England falls victim. One day, she's a vampire. Another day, she's a lovely lady."

"Well, which one is she?" Mack asks.

"I don't know. I haven't met her yet."

"Not even a phone call?! She's your grandmother!"

"Guess she's being, I don't know, the queen of England?"

"Can't they support you somehow?" Mom looks through the French doors and into the empty parlor. "Where *is* Gord?"

"I don't know," I reply. "Apparently, Fred—er, the king—and queen put in a request with the Firm to help do damage control on stuff like this. But they haven't been returning their calls."

"They're not returning their calls!?" Pax asks. "That fills me with trepidation."

"Maybe they have something out for you, Billy," Mack says.

"I'm sure they're just really busy."

A footman steps onto the veranda. "The car is here to take you to school," he announces.

"Thanks, Claude." I stand, swaying from exhaustion. "I need to get dressed," I tell Mack and Pax. "Meet you in the car in a few."

After trudging back to my room, I get dressed in my school uniform. With an unlimited budget at my disposal, I finally submitted to Pax's pleas to make me over—tossing out nearly all my flannels for dress shirts, my twine bracelets for yellow gold bands, and my cowboy hat for neatly styled hair. My classmates back home wouldn't recognize me. There's something a little thrilling about that. Another perk of my all-over makeover? Fitting in at St. Aubyn's. As I slip on my shoes, I spot my violin on an antique chair in the corner.

I pick it up. It's like a relic from another life, a reminder of who I used to be. I set it back down.

Then I'm on my way, across the hall and into the slow elevator.

It stops on the floor below, and Pax slides the brass accordion door aside and steps in.

"Before you go asking," I say, my voice full of exasperation, "I don't want to talk about any prince stuff please. In fact, how are *you* doing?"

"I appreciate you asking, but as always, you're changing the subject," Pax says softly.

I ignore them. "That's really cool you got a shout-out in the magazine. How's putting all the finishing touches on your

garments going? And when are you finally going to let me
see what you made for me to wear tonight? At the ball itself?"

"How are you *really* doing, honey?" they ask as the elevator
smoothly continues down.

"I'm...struggling," I admit. "There are so many things to do."

"I guess what they say is true." Pax shoulders their tote bag,
blinking. "They say no one really understands what it's like to
be inside the monarchy until they've experienced it firsthand."

"That's a thing people say?" I ask. "Well, it's true. I really
thought I was doing a good job learning to be prince, but
now it seems like I can't do anything right. I fell asleep at the
fundraising event, and made a total clown out of myself at the
hockey game, and they think I'm pushing—"

"What are you talking about?" Pax says. "You're doing
great! The press can turn anything into a juicy story. It's not
your fault. Besides, all that really matters is that you crush it
at the Investiture. And remember, people are going to hate on
you. Let them. Water off your back." Pax always knows just
what to say. They're also speaking from experience.

Still, I can't help sighing. "It's hard enough keeping up with
school, and prince lessons, and getting a full night's rest. Oh,
and I keep putting off calls and texts from Dustin."

"*Who?* I don't know him," Pax jokes.

"Seriously. He's left me eight voice mails. Long-distance is
awful. And we're missing the spring formal. Pax, you *know* that's
all Dustin's talked about for the last two years. He and I making
a splash at the spring formal. Visions of Spring King and King."

"Honey, *honey*! A real prince over a cheesy spring king any
day."

"And now, I'm missing it," I continue. "Maybe Edward was
right. Maybe I'm not cut out for this. I'm constantly breaking
all the Maple Crown Rules, and I can't even—"

"Okay, okay, okay." Pax perches their hand on my shoulder. "Stop. You can do this. You can, you can, you can. Go out there and put the 'can' in 'Canada.'"

I'm only half-listening as I check my phone. "I lost one million Instagram followers!"

Pax covers my screen. "Since when did you start caring about that stuff?"

"Okay." I nod, willing myself to meet their eyes. "You're right. I've got this."

"I know I'm right. Now, just be yourself, and block out the haters. Be like a Shetland pony and prance your way to the top."

I squint at them. "A Shetland pony?"

Pax shakes my shoulders. "Be the queer hero the world needs. Be the queero!"

"Okay, okay." I laugh. "I'll be the queero."

In AP Bio, since Neel asked me to be his lab partner, we've been bent over the counter in our goggles, reading our detailed instructions. Today, we'll be dissecting a frog. I'm still not used to classes with only six students.

But I could get used to partnering up with Neel.

He prods the frog. "You as grossed out as I am?"

"Not really," I say. "I'm used to this kind of stuff. Rancher here, remember?"

"So you dissect frogs on your ranch? Lovely."

I laugh. "Something like that."

Neel squints at me. "Sick." Then he looks back at the frog and grimaces.

"Didn't your parents ever buy you a cow eyeball to dissect or anything?" I ask, turning the page in my science textbook and referencing the diagram showing the frog's various organs.

"My parents weren't exactly involved in my life as a kid…
or at all," he admits.

"Oh." I feel bad for asking him.

"I've never really felt what it's like to have a home. Or at least a
home where I could be myself. Sexuality was never mentioned."

"That stinks. I'm sorry."

I think of Pax, who grew up in a similar situation. I notice
Pax and Lady Sofia paired up, both chatty with each other. It
seems they've fallen into an odd-couple friendship, with Pax
fawning over her outrageous outfits and Lady Sofia twirling
for them to take in all the expensive details. Pax meets my
eye, then waves hello to Neel.

"Did I tell you what I'm doing after graduation?" Neel asks.
"I'm going to spend a year traveling around the world finding
all the best places to party."

"Won't you get tired of being on the road?"

"It's more like *being in the air*. Private jet." He winks. "I'm
used to never being in one place for too long," he adds.

"Well, sounds like fun," I say, trying to be more optimistic.

"I *will* miss Edward," Neel shares.

"Everyone's favorite prince." I sound more downtrodden
than I intend.

Neel laughs. "You two getting along?"

"Yeah. But I feel like he's kind of hard to catch."

"Oh, I'm sure it's nothing personal. Excited for tonight?"

"So, the Jolee Jubilee." I scribble a measurement into my
notebook. "Apparently, after dancing around, there's going to
be a big dinner and I have to give a speech and everything."

"I'll be there, rooting you on," Neel says. "You'll be spec-
tacular. Think of it as practice for your Investiture Speech."

"At least for that one, I'll have cue cards."

Before we know it, we're cleaning up our station when the

bell rings and class is dismissed. Neel ducks out, shooting me a friendly nod, as Pax meets me by my desk. "I was just talking to Fi and she—"

"I'm sorry," I cut in. "*Fi?* Abbreviated-name basis already?"

"Yes."

"What are you, her new gay best friend?"

"Correction," Pax says. "She's my new straight best friend."

"Is that a thing?"

"Is now! She's got undeniably iconic fashion, and by being her friend I'm thinking maybe I can get more of an in with Edward."

Before I can share how that seems a little troubling to me, they press on. "Anyway, she promised to introduce me to *the* Anna Wintour at my fashion show! Billy, I'm on cloud nine!"

"That's amazing! I'm so happy for you!" I cheer, embracing them. "Though I have no clue who Anna Wintour is."

"Of course you don't." Pax smiles at me. "So, ready to see what I'm dressing you in tonight?"

Edward and I walk lockstep into the ballroom and a hush falls over the crowd. The partygoers are all dressed in outfits from the late 1800s, in commemoration of Queen Jolee and her reign, including both of us in breeches, waistcoats, and flat velvet collars, designed and sewn for us by Pax in honor of tonight's festivities. As we continue into the grand ballroom, everyone bows in our honor. Edward and I stop on the dance floor. Photographers appear around the fringe to snap photos of me. I'm used to that by now.

A group of partygoers circling Mack draws my attention, going gaga over her Pax-created gown with lace, ribbons, and bows.

"Mack, you're so darn cute!" a person tells her. "Who are you wearing?"

She grabs Pax and pulls them close. "Pax Andrews!" she replies. People create a space around the two of them, as she holds up her phone and instructs everyone to pose for a group selfie. Celebrities and important people ask her for her social media handle, and add her right then and there on their phones. Another curious crowd flocks to her, and she wins them over too with her sunny personality. Pax is loving it.

Neel steps up beside me. "She's really becoming the darling of the elite New York social scene," he whispers in my ear.

"She's a *total* hit," I agree.

"Not to mention all her socials are booming. TikTok, Instagram, you name it." Neel holds up his phone to show off her YouTube home page. "Her subscriber count is getting up there."

I look at the screen. "Five million? Good for her."

"And climbing," Neel remarks coolly, subscribing.

I turn and bump into a waiter holding a tray of filled champagne flutes. The tray goes flying and champagne sprays everywhere. The flutes smash onto the floor, shattering in an explosion of broken glass. Oh, *no*. This is bad. This is so bad.

All eyes are back on me. Photographers snap their cameras my way. *Crap.*

"Sorry!" I say, turning bright red. I bend to collect shards of glass.

"We do not fetch and step," Gord hisses in my ear, helping me up.

MAPLE CROWN RULE 75: Take everything in stride.

"Sorry!" I say again, blushing even harder. Royals don't apologize. I need to quit it!

Then Fi emerges from the group of onlookers, and I sigh in

relief at the distraction. The crowd turns to ogle at her looking gorgeous in another Pax original: silk gloves, jewel-tone
gown with puffed cap sleeves, the works. According to Pax,
she'd jumped at the chance for them to whip her up one of
their over-the-top, one of a kind creations. It's handy to have
staff who can find whatever fabric you're looking for last minute, and it helped that Pax secretly repurposed outfits they designed from last year's class dance. Apparently, the luxurious
fabrics they have access to now is worlds different from those
from Little Timber General. And it shows.

Edward extends his hand toward Fi, and she takes it. Next
thing I know, they're twirling expertly on the dance floor.

The partner who the Firm assigned me is none other than
Mack, who made lessons with our dance instructor very entertaining. But she's still buried in her admiring crowd, so I
have to wait for her.

I feel totally useless, just standing here in the circle of guests
while my brother and Fi continue to waltz. Waiters are still
scrambling to pick up the broken champagne flutes and wipe up
the wet floor. I try to ignore them and gaze out at the crowd.

Pax is dreamily watching Edward, their crystal flute tipping
so far to the side that cider is practically spilling out. The outfit they'd designed for themself is stunning: a double-breasted
emerald coat that's encrusted with gems.

"Wow. He's so graceful," Pax breathes.

"You can tell he's had years of practice," I whisper.

Pax sighs. "I think I don't like Fi again anymore. She's steal-
ing my man!"

I give Pax side eye.

They rest their hand on my arm. "I can be the one to turn
him gay, Billy!"

I chuckle. "You know that's not how that works, right?"

"I know. But a spirit can dream!"

I'm still stuck trying to move past knocking over the champagne—just another cringy mess-up. Why am I so bad at this prince thing? Edward is graceful. When did I become so clumsy?

Pax keeps reminding me that my MET violin solo went over well, but I know that was a fluke—and I was warned to never attempt something like that again. It was also a fluke that I mixed up my hockey notes, though I could have sworn I jotted down everything Edward said word for word. Given how tired I am, I guess not.

I need to step up my game. I've got a destiny to fulfill.

Gazing back out at the crowd to see if Mack's ready to join me and seeing she's leading a group of people in a TikTok dance, I spot a tall silhouette at the far end of the room, frozen in the doorway.

For some reason, my palms begin to sweat. He takes a step inside, and I see a face that doesn't fit, that can't possibly be…

The bottom of my stomach drops through the floor.

"*Dustin?*" I whisper in total disbelief. Remembering the cameras are still on me, I smile.

There he is, in an old-timey tuxedo with long coattails and a rounded top hat. He strides through the crowd as people move out of the way for him, until he's on the dance floor.

"Surprise," he says, grinning, waiting to see how I'll react, eyes alight. I forgot that his left iris has that brown freckle in the green.

My mouth drops open in shock, and he slides his arm around my waist. Before I know it, we're dancing helter-skelter across the dance floor beside Edward and Fi. Compared to Edward's and Fi's practiced, gliding steps, Dustin and I must look comical.

"What are you *doing* here?" I hiss as he pulls me up from a scarily low dip. I think about how this is going to look to the Firm.

"I came to be your date."

"I can see that." I let out a little laugh. We're spinning now, our feet moving in tighter and tighter circles, and I'm getting dizzier and dizzier.

"I was hoping you'd be a bit more excited to see me," he breathes into my ear.

"How did you even—" But before I can finish my thought, he twirls me, which is met by a smattering of applause.

After what feels like an eternity, the music quiets as the song ends, and Dustin and I, and Edward and Fi, bow. Then I frantically welcome the other guests to join us on the dance floor.

Dustin wraps his arms around my waist from behind, and kisses my neck. I fight the urge to recoil at the touch of his lips. How did he even get into the jubilee? What is he doing?

Gord appears beside me. "Get him out of here!" he whispers in my ear.

MAPLE CROWN RULE 59: No inappropriate displays of affection.

I nod at Gord in agreement.

Then I grab Dustin's hand. "Hey, come with me for a second." I lead him through the crowd and we step out onto a veranda lit up by twinkle lights overlooking a garden. I catch Gord following us, but standing at the door, covering for us. He really is good at his job.

"What are you doing here?" I ask Dustin, no longer feeling the need to smile with photographers no longer in sight.

He snorts. "Spending a romantic night with my boyfriend," he says playfully.

"Sorry. I—I know that. I'm… I just wasn't expecting to see you here," I say, staring at my dress shoes. "Listen, I've been messing up a lot lately, the *prince* stuff, and the *us* stuff, and I was super anxious about this event going well—"

"What are you trying to say?" He laughs. "That I ruined your fancy party?"

I take a deep breath again. "Dustin, I...just didn't expect you to surprise me like this."

"Yeah. We've already established that. But I'm here! I—I flew all the way to see you." He sounds hurt. The last thing I want to do is hurt him.

"How did you even know about this?" I find myself asking.

"Edward."

"Edward?"

Dustin blinks. "Yeah. He said you're always talking about how much you miss me, and he helped arrange this. He thought you'd like it. I did too. But..." He shakes his head and takes half a step back.

"That was nice of him." I study my hands, then look back into Dustin's green eyes. "I want to apologize. I've been so scatterbrained these past few weeks. I don't want to make excuses, but it's been a lot. As you can probably imagine."

"I forgive you," he says.

"You *do*?" I ask, a bit shocked. "Well... Good. I'm glad."

He grins. "Ready to get back to dancing?"

I hum to myself, not sure what to say without hurting his feelings. How do I tell him in a nice way that the whole night's already been carefully laid out for me, and it doesn't include him?

"Great!" He takes my hand and begins to lead me back toward the door. "So, tell me about this mansion I've heard so much about. Can I crash there tonight?"

"What?" I blink at him a bunch of times, trying to register what he's even talking about.

"And who can I talk to about getting myself a new wardrobe?" he asks. "Hey, maybe I can get my own room in the mansion too."

I stop walking. "I'm not sure that's how it works," I say, watching the smile slide off his face.

"Oh. Okay."

"Listen, can we talk more about everything later? I'm really sorry, but I have to get back to the ball, and give this big dinner speech, and I'm not sure hanging out in there with you is something I can do tonight and still enjoy myself."

He looks stung, but then nods in understanding. "Yeah. Of course. Prince things take precedence. But first..." He pulls me in for a kiss.

I gently push him away. "Not now," I say softly, glancing past him to make sure no cameras are taking aim from inside.

He grimaces at me. "Wow. You've really changed."

"I haven't changed," I say defensively, letting out a short laugh.

"You have. Look, I'm trying to be understanding, but you don't seem excited to see me, you couldn't end our dance fast enough, and now you don't want to hang out with me. You're making me feel like a loser. Like you're...embarrassed by me or something." The corner of his mouth twitches. "I don't deserve that. And I don't deserve to be put on the back burner while you...do whatever it is you've been doing."

My mind races with what to say, and I remain frozen.

He shakes his head, taking a step back. "I miss the old Billy."

"I'm still the same person," I say, my face flushing hot. "Maybe...maybe..."

"Maybe *what*?" he asks, his face a look of disgust.

"Maybe we just want different things," I blurt.

My words seem to hang in the silence that follows.

I can't believe I just said it. The thing I've always felt but never could voice. It's true. I've known this deep down all along, but my love for Dustin, and the desire to follow my parents' example, made me push those thoughts aside and hold on to the familiar comfort. My parents met in high school, and had the picture-perfect life. I wanted that with Dustin enough to ignore the feeling deep down that said otherwise. Maybe I *have* changed, but not in the way he thinks. I'm not afraid to speak my truth now. I'm not afraid to choose the unknown, whatever that may bring.

"Wow. Seriously?" His expression becomes unrecognizable.

I maintain eye contact and keep quiet, willing time to pass.

"You go off and become a prince and just leave me behind," Dustin says. "You don't want to move back to Montana. You don't even want to be with me." His eyes swim with hurt.

My heart catches in my chest. It's so much worse hearing him voice the truth than anything I could have ever imagined. It makes what's about to happen feel real, like we're on the edge of a knife.

"Dustin, it's not like that," I start. I've suspected for a while that he and I want different things. It pains me to my core, and suddenly, I'm overcome with the urge to backtrack, to convince him that I'm just having an off night and that we'll be okay again.

But I don't.

My silence doesn't go unnoticed. In fact, it speaks volumes.

Dustin runs his tongue idly over his teeth. "I'm so ashamed of the person you've become," he says softly.

I shudder, taken aback. "*What?* Why would you say that?" My whole body tenses up. "How dare you judge me."

"You're a fancy prince who's too busy to return a peasant's phone calls. A peasant who was only ever good to you." His lip quivers. "If I wasn't enough for you, no one ever will be. You'll never be happy. You did this to us. *You.* And I feel sorry for you."

I fight back a sob, struggling to breathe. "What? Where is this coming from? I didn't— I'm sorry— Listen, maybe we can talk about this—"

"It's over." Dustin bows mockingly. "Your Royal Highness." He turns and goes.

I don't chase after him. And I can't admit I'm heartbroken. Not yet. I still have half a ball to be seen at. I take a steeling breath, trying to compartmentalize what just happened with every fiber of my being. It had to happen. I just hate that it had to be like this.

I pull myself together just as Neel sets foot onto the veranda. "You okay, *bharā*?"

"Who? What? Oh. I'm fine. I just need a minute." I stare at the stars, taking another slow and even breath. Was Dustin right? Will I ever be happy? Will I ever find someone who loves me like he did?

"You don't seem fine." Neel's standing closer to me now.

"The pressure of prince training is getting to me," I say. "I don't know. I'm starting to reconsider accepting my birthright as the Crown Prince of Canada." I sniffle. "But I want it so badly…"

"Anything new is hard," he says. "It'll be fine."

I wheel on him. "How can you be so sure?"

He draws back. "Listen, I was just trying to—"

Tears sting my eyes. "I don't need a pep talk right now," I cut in, my voice hard.

Neel raises his eyebrows. "As you wish." And with that, he turns and stalks away.

I wrap my arms around myself. What is happening to me? Who am I?

Chapter Fifteen

EDWARD

"Hook, line, and sinker," I say, reading the tabloid head-line about last night's delicious debacle: **BILLY'S BOY TOY CRASHES BALL**.

I lean toward Neel, who's seated across the cracked leather sofa from me in the student centre. "Thank you for arranging Dustin's trip here on the back end."

Neel gives a casual shrug, browsing through five-star hotels in Tokyo on his tablet. "It was all your idea," he says smugly.

"That's all you've got to say?" I ask. "How unlike you."

Neel looks up. "We knew Gord and the press would have a field day."

"And did they ever." I smile. "That chump doesn't suspect a thing!" I grit my teeth. "But it still isn't moving the needle. I have to think of what to do that will be just enough to oust him while still keeping the monarchy intact and in good standing…"

Neel grins broadly, setting his tablet on his knee. "What's with you lately? Your obsessive nature is scaring me."

"Hello," I say grumpily, pointing to myself. "Still stripped of his title over here."

Neel rubs his forefinger and thumb together.

"What in the world are you doing?"

"Playing the world's tiniest violin, of course," he quips.

"Oh, shut it," I snap. "Just the thought of the violin makes me want to smash things. That's *his* instrument." I shudder.

Neel cocks his head. "This is starting to go a wee bit overboard, wouldn't you say? Maybe the whole bringing his boyfriend here was crossing the line?"

"What are you talking about?" I flash, overcome with the sudden urge to ruffle and rumple Neel's thick, superbly moussed hair.

"I think we should cool it on the sabotage front, is all," Neel says. "He told me he's really struggling. It was tragic, in the bad sense of the word."

I laugh. "You don't actually feel *sorry* for him, do you?" Then I remember seeing Neel talking to Billy after Dustin stormed out of the ballroom. At the time, I thought he was playing his part, still nothing but a ruse. But now, I'm not so sure.

"Forget I said anything."

"Neel." I scoot to the edge of the sofa and gaze intently at him. "You can't be serious right now. You're supposed to be helping me take him down. He's *this close*—" I move my pointer finger toward my thumb "—to being canceled!"

Neel blinks, his shapely eyebrows arched. "Edward, he's going through a lot."

"Oh. I see." I sink back. "You've changed loyalties."

"Don't be ridiculous." Neel laughs. "What's this 'sides' game you're playing at, anyway?"

I snort. "I *knew* it." My blood begins to boil. "You *like* him."

"I like a lot of people."

"Neel, this is different. He's my *twinemy*." I face-palm. "Wow, Fi is really starting to rub off on me," I mutter. I try to get back on track. "Don't you think it's weird that your crush looks exactly like your best friend? Listen, if you no longer want to help me get my title back, that's fine by me."

I don't mean it, but I refuse to let Neel think abandoning me was *his* choice.

"Excellent." Neel packs up his tablet and textbooks. "Well, I'm off to AP Lit. I'll catch you later, then."

"Great." I pretend to stare at my phone until he's gone, acting like nothing's wrong. Why is everything so awful? What is wrong with me? Did I seriously just get irrationally irate at my best friend because he refused to help me sully Billy's good name? My thoughts are spinning a klick a minute.

I start out for fourth period on autopilot, making my way up the carpeted main staircase, when my phone dings.

It's a text from Pax. A flutter of joy stirs in my stomach. It's as if they *knew* I was in a foul mood and in need of a pick-me-up.

Pax: Thought you would enjoy this pic!

It's a photo showing Pax and Fi making silly faces on the dance floor last night.

So, not Pax checking in on me at all.

The photo is accompanied by a link to an article: **PAX ANDREWS BECOMES THE NEW FACE OF THE FASHION IN-DUSTRY**. I want to be happy for Pax—they're chasing their fashion design dream, and making it happen in no time flat. But I admit that I really wish Pax had texted to ask how I'm doing. I'm feeling so sensitive right now. I know it doesn't make sense, but it upsets me more than I can admit.

I trudge the rest of the way upstairs and slink into my desk for AP Calc. The least I could do is text them back. I pull my phone back out and reply.

Edward: Very cool!

Next, I text Fi.

Edward: Hey, confirming dinner tonight with my parents.

Fi is safe territory. I feel nothing for her, so there's no risk of her making me feel, well, irrationally irate. Tonight, we're finally having the big dinner with my parents. They're *ecstatic* to see us.

Fi: Wouldn't miss it, my love bug.

If I didn't know any better, I'd think she was actually falling for me.

Non. That's ridiculous. Am I really that full of myself?

I'm seated in the formal sitting room with Mum and Dad on either side of our walnut coffee table carved to resemble l'Château Frontenac. They're enjoying a predinner glass of wine, like always, as I nurse my sparkling water, perched nervously on the edge of an overstuffed armchair.

"Oh, Edward, I'm so glad you thought to invite Fi over for dinner while we're in town," Mum says from her chair.

I laugh awkwardly. "It was more Fi's idea than mine."

"I think it's a great idea. What a fun end-of-the-week surprise. We've been hoping to all get together sometime," Dad says. "It's been a while since we've seen her, and it'll be so nice to catch up."

"Wonderful." Tonight's delicious dinner wafts into my nostrils from the kitchen: wild pheasant in mushroom and wine sauce. I check my timepiece. "I'm sure she'll be here any minute now."

"It's fine." Dad holds up his glass of wine. "It's been nice catching up with our son." He takes a sip. "Though I'm still not entirely convinced you're doing as swimmingly as you say you are in light of Billy's arrival."

I brush it aside. "Oh sure I am. I'm better than ever," I lie.

"Edward," Mum says, exchanging an eager look with Dad, "is it alright if we breach the topic of your romantic relationship with her?"

"Uh…"

The doorbell rings. That must be Fi. I jump up.

"A footman will get it, darling!" Mum calls after me.

But I'm already down the corridor. I have to make sure that Fi understands that we're still pretending to be dating in front of my parents tonight. Especially if they're going to be bringing up the whole romantic relationship topic.

Fi arrives, trailed by a footman. She's wearing a polka dot dress with a matching clutch, and bright-red lipstick. "Hello, my love!" She wraps me in a hug, then kisses each cheek.

I smirk. "Don't *you* look radiant…"

"It's dinner with your parents. Did I have a choice to look anything *but*?" She gives me elevator eyes. "You look good yourself." She tugs at the hem of my sleeve and twirls her skirts. "Dare I say, kissable?"

I pull away. "You needn't turn on the charms just yet," I whisper, leading her through the corridor.

She pouts. "But I like flirting with you," she says softly.

Is she falling for me? I narrow my eyes. "This is strictly pretend. Remember?"

"Right," she says, pulling herself together. "Strictly pretend." She winks at me, and it strikes a jolt of unease in my stomach. *Does* she like me for real? Then she strides past me into the dining room. "Your Royal Majesties." She bows, despite Mum and Dad cutting through the formalities with hugs.

As I take my seat at the table, I realize how serious this meal is for everyone else around me. I think about how the original plan was for us to use each other—her using me for power, me using her for cover. But now that we've bonded as "friends" through our pranking of Billy, I've seen another side of her. I'm struggling to find ways to keep her at a platonic distance. Including now, when she sits beside me and interlaces her fingers through mine beneath the table. I resist recoiling. She must really love seeing me squirm.

"Oh, Sofia, you look absolutely stunning," Mum says warmly.

"Thank you." Fi beams. "As do you, ma'am."

"Well, let's eat!" I say.

Dad raises his water goblet. "We're so glad you both could dine with us tonight."

Everyone follows suit.

"I'm so glad you suggested it," I lie through my teeth. Leave it to my parents to be there at every turn, helping this fake romance along. I remind myself how I simply need to make it through this one meal for my parents to get off my case about dining with her.

Fi looks over at me and smiles—it almost looks authentic. She squeezes my hand under the table, and I squeeze back on instinct. *Uh-oh.* Not really helping matters in the realm of making Fi think we're not actually falling for each other. I'm starting to really feel bad for stringing her along, if that *is* indeed what's happening.

"Now, when exactly did you two start dating?" Mum asks, moving her fork around her salad. Ah, here it comes.

We both reply at the same time.

"December—"

"November—"

I laugh. "Sometime between November and December." I shoot Fi a look.

She tucks a strand of her ombré hair behind her ear.

"Wonderful. It's so nice to see young love." Mum smiles

at Dad. "Do you remember when we were their age, honey-bunch?"

"How could I ever forget, my love?" Dad gazes fondly back at her.

"We're the *definition* of young love," Fi chimes in.

"Yes." My eyes dart. "Well, you're hard not to love," I say, swallowing hard.

Dad grins. "You two are already using the L-word, eh?"

"Oh, yes," Fi says, laying it on thick. "We're *deeply* in love." She pecks my cheek.

I turn and kiss her back. This is truly mortifying.

"You two are so adorable." Mum smiles. "The press actually has it right for once."

"You know, when I met your mother—" Dad takes her hand "—I instantly knew she was the one."

"I know just the feeling," Fi says, butting in. "Who better to marry than your best friend?"

I nearly choke on a cherry tomato. This little game has officially gone too far. I feel lousy for faking out both Fi and my parents. People are going to get hurt. It's just a matter of time. But this train has already left the station.

"Sofia, Edward tells us you're *also* gearing up to attend the University of Ottawa in the fall," Mum says.

"Excellent school," Dad says.

"Oh, yes," Fi agrees. "And I hear going to the same university works out terrifically for a lot of couples."

Super.

The rest of the meal goes off without a hitch, meaning we've convinced them we're a couple, even if I don't feel all that happy about the whole charade. Mum and Dad shower Fi in compliments, and dive into a brainstorm of great date ideas for the two of us, including when we're in Ottawa for

Billy's Investiture Ceremony. They ask about her Easter plans this weekend, and the fashion show she's helped arrange for Pax, and Fi answers it all graciously.

After Mum and Dad bid their goodbyes, I walk Fi to the elevator bay, bumping into Pax who exits the elevator.

"Hi." Their eyes flicker from me to Fi then back to me. "Oh! Sorry. I didn't mean to… I'll just be going now. Hi, Fi. Bye, Fi." They reverse back into the elevator, and its doors close.

"They're so sweet and super talented. *Big* fan."

I turn to Fi. "Thanks for tonight," I tell her. "Now my parents will stop breathing down my neck about seeing you."

"No, they won't," she says. "In fact, I'm pretty sure they'll be wanting to see much more of me as you and I continue to date."

I quirk my brow. "You mean continue to *pretend* to date."

"Is this really pretend?" She lightly taps the tip of my nose. "It looks pretty real to me."

"Minus the whole us having chemistry and wanting to make out," I shoot back.

She snorts. "Speak for yourself." As she looks around, I take a deep breath.

"Listen, Fi, this charade has gone on long enough. I think we need to cool—"

"So, I was thinking," Fi interrupts in a whisper. "I have the perfect thing that'll send Billy toppling over like an old colonial statue in a riot. It involves his little speech…"

I sigh. When Neel falls short, leave it to Fi to help me pick up the slack. "Go on."

She shares the delicious details of her plan. "Operation Twinvestiture," that involves taking Billy's precious cue cards moments before his speech in two weeks.

All thoughts of calling it quits with Fi fade away. I grin. "Perfect."

"Hello? It's me." She steps into the elevator. "Talk soon. Nighty night, babe."

I'm too preoccupied thinking of the plan to register my guilt at her use of the pet name and how it felt like she seriously meant it.

I'm soaking in a perfectly sublime lavender-scented bubble bath, scrolling through my Finsta and ogling cake icing videos, hot cookie videos, and cross sections of gooey, loaded brownies, but I can't seem to scrub Fi's plan from my mind. So far, my attempts at sabotage have been child's play compared to the big prank in store for Billy at his Investiture Ceremony...

Que c'est délicieux.

Despite what Neel might have to say about it. Which is why I'm not going to tell him.

I stare into the mound of bubbles before me as classical music floats through the room's surround sound. This stunt is my last chance to prevent Billy from being pronounced heir, and to get back my title—*autrement ça vient de s'éteindre.* I've been so listless and heavy-hearted these past few weeks.

Taking a deep breath, I slide beneath the hot water. I once thrived off the Crown Prince hustle and bustle, being too busy to luxuriate in a fragrant bubble bath. All this downtime breeds too much time getting in my head about literally everything. So, despite feeling hopeful about Operation Twinvestiture, I'm still queasy. No amount of videos of meringues, choux pastries, and financiers can help, and that's saying something.

I dry off and slip into pajamas, then turn off the lights and music and try to sleep. It's useless. My thoughts are reeling in high-definition. Sometimes when this happens, it helps to grab a tall glass of milk from the kitchen. Donning my housecoat and slippers, I travel on over to the East Wing, and am half-way to the kitchen when I overhear something. It's…music.

I strain to listen.

It's a sad, beautiful song being played on a violin.

I follow it up the dark stairwell and to the sixth floor, and come to a halt outside the oak door to the portrait gallery. The classical song is melancholy and heartfelt. I feel like it is exactly what my own heart is feeling.

I knock.

The music stops.

"Come in."

I step into the room and find Billy holding his violin, look-ing disheveled in a crumpled suit with his striped tie loose and askew. "Was that you playing just now?"

"Oh. Sorry! I hope I didn't wake you up. I—I didn't think the sound would carry." He lays his violin in its case.

I find myself sitting on the piano bench across from him along the wall of framed past princes and princesses, kings and queens. "It's quite alright. I rather enjoyed it."

He pauses, hands still on the violin. "Thanks. It's been a while since I've practiced. I tend to play when I'm feeling blue."

I know how that feels, even though I would never admit it to him. And I realize I know why he's doleful. "I'm sorry to hear about your breakup," I say. And I am, even though I was the one who brought Dustin here in the first place. I hadn't meant for them to break up; I just wanted to bring Billy back down to earth.

"Thanks." Billy lets out a beleaguered sigh.

I feel like I have to say something. "I'm guessing you heard I helped arrange his visit. I thought it'd be a nice surprise."

He nods. "I appreciate you thinking of me."

I smile. "I'm sorry it went belly-up." Why am I apologizing so much? How unbecoming. Do I actually feel guilty? Admittedly I can't help imagining how I would feel, if the tables were turned and I had gotten publicly dumped by my first-ever boyfriend. It would suck.

"You know—" he chuckles weakly "—that's not even half the reason I'm feeling down."

"Oh?" I arch my brows, realizing I'm actually interested in hearing what he has to say.

He lets out a sad little laugh. "Being Crown Prince is tough. I don't know how you did it."

"I wouldn't wish the struggles of royal life on anyone," I say without thinking (how uncouth of me!). But it's true.

He slumps over and stares at the wall of portraits.

Neel was right—seeing Billy like this *is* tragic. In the real sense of the word. Against my will, I feel a little pang of pity.

"You've only had a month of this wild life—I've had nearly eighteen years of it. Of the pressure and incessant rule-following…" I wave my hand for effect.

"I'm bad at it," Billy says. "The pressure. The rule-following. But I want to do better. I want this. For my family—my old one *and* my new one."

Spoken like a true Crown Prince. He's not terrible at this, I have to admit. Especially when people like me aren't meddling in an effort to foil his hard work. I push the thought aside.

"If anyone understands you, it's me." I gesture to his violin. "Keep playing. I didn't mean to stop you."

He raises the violin and fits it under his chin, then lifts his bow. He eyes the door I left ajar.

"It's alright," I say. "Go ahead. Please?"

He nods and picks the song back up. I settle back, letting

myself relax. Unlike the station playing during my bath, the live classical music puts me at complete ease. At some point midsong, I notice the look of absolute concentration on Billy's face, the way his mouth is set in a gentle smile, the way his eyes watch the strings, just like when he played at the MET before his fascinated onlookers. When he's done, he rests his violin on his knee.

I clap. "Bravo! Beautiful. You just made my night."

"Thanks. Playing always makes me feel better too." He chuckles. "Usually, I just play for the horses at the ranch."

"I get it," I say. "We all have our passions."

He looks at me. "Yeah? What's yours?"

For a moment, I consider lying, but somehow it feels wrong. What, suddenly I'm Prince Moral Compass? "I love to bake," I confess. "Not a lot of people know that about me. Well, your sister does. And so does Pax, actually. But now you do too."

"Your secret is safe with me," he says with a genuine smile. It nearly makes me feel rotten for all I've put him through and what's still to come.

I jerk my thumb to the door. "Speaking of baked goods, care for a late-night snack?"

Within moments, we're entering the dim, vacant kitchen downstairs. When Billy sees me getting out the milk, he pulls two glasses from the cabinet. I'm impressed he knows his way around—it took me a year to learn where half the things are located in here. I take a tin of freshly baked chocolate-frosted brownies off the counter then pull a glass bottle of maple syrup out of the fridge. I freeze. Billy won't judge me for pouring the maple syrup into my glass of milk, right?

Billy looks at me, open-mouthed. "How did you know I was going to ask you for that?"

I'm confused. "For what?" I slowly pour the syrup into my glass of milk.

He opens his mouth wider. "How did you know I wanted maple syrup in my milk?!"

I laugh. "This isn't for you. It's for me."

"Have you been spying on me?" he demands. "I've been coming in here almost every night for a glass of milk with maple syrup. It's been my comfort drink since before I can remember."

"*What?* I've been doing this since I was a child!" I say, laughing. This is too weird. I've never met *anyone* who puts maple syrup in their milk.

"My dad started putting it in his coffee," Billy says, laughing, but he looks as stunned as I feel. "Then I started putting it in my milk. People always made fun of me for it."

"Same!" I say, shaking my head. "Unbelievable." I want to know more about his dad, but it feels a bit too overreaching. I'm sure he'll share all in good time.

We mix in the syrup with spindly silver spoons, give a toast, clinking our glasses of maple syrup milk together, then chug them.

"That hit the spot," I say, reaching for a brownie.

Billy examines it. "Are those frosted?"

I give a spirited smile. "Brownies should always be frosted. Help yourself." I offer him the tin. "So how are things with Gord?"

"Okay, I guess. He told me to work on my professionalism and that I don't want to become a caricature, whatever that means. He also told me the Firm really wants me to stop pushing my gay agenda. Dustin's visit didn't help things." Billy takes a bite of brownie. "This is amazing!"

"What gay agenda?" I ask, bewildered.

"Exactly. I'm not sure. Apparently they said gay stuff is inappropriate, especially as a role model for little kids. So they want me to ease off on the 'gay stuff.' Oh, and apparently they think people in the Midwest don't accept gay people, which implies there aren't any there." Billy shrugs. "I'm just… being me."

"What?" My blood boils. Am I actually growing defensive on his behalf? "This kind of stuff is exactly why—" I hesitate. Then I realize that I'm about to say something out loud that I've never told anyone before. And I'm about to say it to my archnemesis.

But Billy doesn't seem like my archnemesis anymore, not after the last half hour. I look at him and suddenly it hits me, really hits me: this is my *brother*. And that means I'm not alone. Neel may be my lifelong partner in crime, but if there's anyone who understands about life inside the gilded cage, it's Billy.

I let out a deep breath, check the coast is clear, and look him in the eye. "This is why I've…never come out."

Billy blinks. "You're…?"

I nod. "Indeed."

He keeps blinking. "So, Fi…?"

I grin. "A cover."

"But…" Billy's brow furrows, and then he nods. "Well, I can see why you haven't come out." He gives a sympathetic smile. "I feel bad… Here I am, waving my rainbow flag, while you—"

"Don't worry about it. I'll be okay." I manage to smile back. "Who knows? Maybe the Firm will break their silence and finally speak up in support of you, or allow Mum and Dad to do so in their stead. Now, we've got to be strong. And, well, know that we're here for each other. As brothers."

Billy's still staring hard at me.

Before I realize it, he's embracing me.

I let it happen, stunned, then take a staggering step back.

"I… Thanks for confiding in me," he says. "I'm one hundred percent here for you. I can only imagine how hard it's been, all this time, all the having to pretend." He looks like he could cry.

"Well, when you put it like that!" I break into a sad laugh. I can feel myself truly opening up to him. "Lots of people within the walls of the monarchy are silenced. But me? I'm just silent. I'm not sure which is worse, to be honest. I was afraid what's happening to you is what would have happened to me." I chew my lip. "Truth be told, I think you're braver than I ever could be."

Billy blinks.

Suddenly this is all too overwhelming. I need to be alone with my thoughts. "Now, I'm heading back to bed," I say. "Please, not a word of this to anyone."

My brother nods.

And with that, I retreat to my room.

I lie in bed for hours, unable to sleep.

Have I just made the biggest mistake of my entire life?

THE ROYAL ROUNDUP
April 14, 11:36 pm ET

THE TRUTH BEHIND PRINCE BILLY AND DUSTIN'S BREAKUP
by Omar Scooby

The Jolee Jubilee certainly had its fair share of excitement—as well as its share of heartache. The Crown Prince's BF made a surprise appearance, leading to the couple splitting up!

The ballroom of the Waldorf Astoria glittered with stars, the brightest being Prince Billy. Even Edward and Sofia dancing and twirling on the dance floor wasn't enough to pry partygoers' eyes off the main attraction. And what's a lavish ball without a little drama?

Dustin J. Cole of Little Timber, Montana, stepped onto the dance floor, taking Prince Billy in his arms—and the room by surprise. Despite an ill-fitting suit and well-intentioned appearance, Dustin still managed to turn heads with his whopping height and endearing smile. But that smile quickly slid off his face like a pat of butter off a hot stack of pancakes—by night's end, he was seen fuming and storming from the premises. What happened?

The *Daily Maple* spoke to a party guest who claimed the two were seen fighting out on the terrace in the moments before the fallout. Allegedly, Prince Billy and Dustin had been going through a royally rough patch for some time, but have now officially called it quits.

RELATED STORIES
[Billy and Dustin: Who Was the Man in the Relationship?](#)
[The Inappropriate Gay Kiss That Upset Parents Worldwide](#)
[Billy Proves He's a Hockey Player: Tonsil Hockey](#)
[Edward and Sofia Show Us Their Elegant Dance Moves](#)
[Billy's Little Sister's Social Blade Glows Green After Viral Video](#)
[An Inside Look Into the Colourful Closet of Pax Andrews](#)

Chapter Sixteen

BILLY

"The queen of England is going to be calling you over *Zoom*?" Pax asks in disbelief. "She can *do* that?! I guess she can do anything. She did cut a cake with a superlong sword once. But Zoom? *Zoom?!*"

"According to Edward." I shrug, watching them as they look in their bedroom mirror at my outfit—a perfectly fitted coal-black suit with silk lapels and red stitching. Around us, Pax has swaths of fabric draped everywhere, and a giant, shiny, new sewing machine set up on a wide table. There are also mannequins draped with Pax's designs for their big show.

"Edward," they say dreamily. "My Canadian sweetie… My royal honey!" Pax throws their head back. "Ugh! Why am I so *obsessed* with him?!"

"Pax, I want to know," I sing back. I want to tell Pax about Edward's secret, to see Pax's face break into ecstasy at the fact they were right all along, but I swore to my brother that his secret was safe with me, and it is. Edward's been so helpful to me since day one. Last night felt different, though. We really, truly bonded.

"That would be something…" I muse.

Pax squints at me. "What? You have intel. What do you know?"

"Nothing." I turn to them. "Do I look presentable enough?"

"Why? Do you have an *eerie* feeling about the meeting?" Pax cracks a smile. "Get it? Erie? As in Lake Erie? It's a Canada joke."

I just stare at them, then blink once.

"You look fabulous. And I'm not just saying that because I designed this suit for you." Pax purses their lips. "But seriously, why are you acting ambivalent?"

"I'm not," I say, fidgeting with my maple leaf cuff links. "And if I am, it's because I'm about to meet the queen of England."

They narrow their eyes. "Why, I *Ottawa*..." They grin again and waggle their eyebrows, their silver glitter eyeshadow shimmering with the movement. "Get it? Ottawa?"

I groan. "Pax! Focus!"

"Sorry. I'll stop being a *Mount Royal* pain in the ass. Mount Royal? It's a place in Canada." They laugh, but it's clear I'm not amused. "Okay, okay, officially stopping with the bad jokes. But you have to tell me what she's wearing. My guess is a bubblegum-pink hat with matching suit-dress." Pax smiles then fixes the maple leaf brooch to my jacket. "Go! Good luck." They usher me out of the room.

"What are *you* going to be doing?" I ask, knowing how happy they were to learn we didn't have school today for Good Friday.

"I'll just be here with my girls Organza and Chiffon." They gesture to two of their ballgowns stuck with pins they're working on for their Jolee Jubilee-inspired collection. "Go! Have fun!"

I head down the corridor, full of nerves. This is the first time I'll be talking to the queen of England face-to-face. Will she like me? What will she be like? Sure, I've been learning all about her lately. Her life in Balmoral and Norfolk. How she has someone whose job it is to break in her new shoes (which honestly would have been nice to have had my first week here). How she celebrates two birthdays a year. The fact that she's a living legend and longest reigning monarch ever. But getting to talk to her in real life? I'm terrified.

I step foot into the parlor, where the royal staff bustles all around, dusting furniture, tying back curtains, setting out tiered platters of cookies, finger sandwiches, and scones with clotted cream—as if the queen of England is going to be here in the flesh instead of onscreen.

"Good morning." Edward strolls up to me, looking fresh as a daisy in a perfectly pressed cobalt-blue suit. "It's showtime. You ready?" He sits on the edge of the couch, gazing up at the blank LED TV mounted on the wall, taking up a teacup and sipping with his pinkie out. He shows no signs we ever spoke last night.

I sit beside him. "I'm so nervous," I say. "Being summoned to a Zoom with the queen of England is totally normal, right?"

"Could be totally normal," Edward says, "or could be bad news. We'll find out soon."

I fold my hands in my lap, hoping that it is nothing more than just a friendly call with our grandmother, who simply wants to say hello to her newly discovered grandson.

The screen flickers to life and the queen of England's face appears. She's wearing a giant lavender hat and matching lavender suit-dress, white gloves, pearls, and reading glasses. In front of her, tiny tea sandwiches, scones, and a fruit cake rest on a tiered tray.

My mind races with all the Maple Crown Rules that Gord's been drilling into my head when it comes to Her Royal Majesty the Queen of England, like Maple Crown

Rule 19: Read the room. Not to mention details like how even a second with her requires a ton of careful planning.

Her face breaks into a warm smile when she sees us, which takes me off guard. "Hello, dearies," she says. "Oh, it's so lovely to see you again, Edward. And Billy, it's very nice to meet you."

Edward stands and bows before sitting again, and I quickly follow suit.

MAPLE CROWN RULE 28: When in doubt, bow.

When I take my seat, she's staring at us, a mask of pleasantries. "How are you both doing?"

Before either of us can answer, there's a barking sound coming from behind her.

She twists around in her ornate chair, revealing a bunch of corgis running helter-skelter in the background. "Girls! Hush, now! Bluebell!" She bends away, vanishing, and comes back up with a corgi in her arms, who begins to incessantly lick her cheek. "There, there, Corduroy."

I blink. She's a lot warmer than I'd been led to believe. Comical, even. I find my tense expression softening a little.

"We are doing quite well, Grandmother," Edward replies, his whole demeanor prim and proper. He's so good at that. I try to sit up taller, planting my suede wingtips more firmly on the plush rug, and work on stopping my legs from anxiously jerking up and down.

"Yes, very well," I add, hoping I didn't leave too much of a delay.

"Good, good…" Her smile remains just as taut, as she pets Corduroy in a steady, constant motion, despite the dog squirming in an attempt to break free of her vise grip. Her big brown eyes suddenly move a fraction of an inch to where I sit. "I wanted to chat with you, Billy. We haven't had a chance to talk since your discovery."

I laugh. "Discovery? You make it sound like I'm a dinosaur fossil or something!" I grin, hoping this will break the ice.

Her face is absolutely unreadable. She stares silently at me. I can feel Edward's eyes boring into the side of my head. Oh, no. Is "Dinosaur Fossil" one of her dreaded nicknames?! *Crap!*

I cough. "I'm...uh...glad we're finally getting to chat."

"It's apparent that your start as Canadian Crown Prince has been a bit rocky."

My whole body goes rigid.

"Of course," she goes on, "a learning curve is more than expected." Corduroy yips and she turns the full force of her gaze on the dog. *"Knock it off!"* she growls. Then she smiles pleasantly again. "It has been brought to my attention that the Firm over there is concerned about the mistakes you've made of late."

I catch Edward throwing me side-eye, and he gives a little cough under his breath.

"Oh. I'm...sorry," I say, taking the hint.

My grandmother blinks. "It is amusing how your parents branched off from England with hopes of eliminating scandal, and yet, the Canadian Royals are now creating more scandal than ever. The tabloids are eating up every moment of it."

From my nonstop studying up on the Royal Family history for the ceremony, I am now very well versed in Frederick and Daphnée's move to Canada to avoid the British press, and how it created a strain on the Royal Family, and—to use Gord's phrase—a media firestorm.

"It is what it is," Edward chimes in with a smile. "But Billy has recommitted himself to putting his best foot forward, haven't you, brother?" He grins at me. Wow. He really meant it last night when he said he's here for me as a brother. He doesn't want me to fail. I appreciate him standing up for me, even more than he knows.

I nod. "Yes. Exactly."

"Some friendly advice, not as queen, but as grandmother. Billy can't afford to put another toe out of line. The Firm is going to be watching even more closely." She looks from me to Edward. "You know, you can dig up dirt on anyone. One just has to know where to look." Her expression falls back into the easygoing smile she had at the start of the meeting. Then someone leans in to whisper something in her ear. She grins wider at us. "It was lovely chatting, boys. Please behave yourselves. The world will be watching you."

The screen cuts to black.

I let out a deep breath. "Crap. That wasn't good."

Edward smiles at me. "Pleasant lady, isn't she?"

"She hates me! Why does she hate me?!"

"The queen of England doesn't believe in hate," Edward says, choosing his words with care. "And she doesn't hate you."

"Okay." I spring up off the couch. "You do know her better than I do. Hey, thanks for standing up for me."

"Of course." He takes a cookie from one of the platters. "Those calls are always sufficiently strange."

I stand. "And no more mistakes from me. Hold me to it!"

Edward nods, then dunks his cookie into his tea before biting it.

A footman arrives in the doorway. "Your Royal Highness, your lessons with Gord."

I rub my forehead. "Prince training. See you later, Edward."

"And that concludes your lessons for today." Gord smiles and rests his sleek black fountain pen on top of his neat stack of papers.

I resist the urge to slump over the many textbooks piled around me. Talk about a pathetic Friday night. My brain feels like mush from trying to retain all the information crammed inside it: the names of every Canadian prime minister, the various patronages I've been assigned, facts about the First Nations, speed-learning French pronunciations for when I'll eventually be reading the speech at the Investiture Ceremony... And it's not even 8:00 p.m.

"At this rate, you may just be able to triumph at your Investiture."

"Good!" I reply. "Or should I say...*bien*?" I try with a smile.

Gord blinks. "I take it Her Royal Majesty the Queen of England gave you a little pep talk. She's heard about the stir-up you've caused by being...*out*."

I sit up taller. "Yeah. What's that all about?"

"Billy." Gord steeples his fingers. "As stipulated by the Firm, no one in the family is allowed to discuss the details of your gayness."

"The details of my 'gayness'?" I ask, confused. "What does that even mean?" I don't intend to sound defensive, but I do.

"It is best that we downplay that little aspect of yourself. It's quite divisive."

"My...existence?" I ask, finding it hard to compute what he's saying.

"You know what I mean." Gord stands and gestures to the door. "Good night. Same time tomorrow."

And with that, I head back out into the hallway in a daze.

In her bedroom, Mom is in a bathrobe watching TV, and Mack's on her phone beside her, reading through comments on her videos.

"Someone's living their best vacation life," I say to them, the conversation with Gord still not sitting right with me.

Mom smiles and pats the decorative throw pillow beside her.

I plop down and lean against her, watching one of her favorite game shows. I love how Mom's managed to shed her hard shell and finally start to ease into the glamorous life. I feel like being Crown Prince has brought us all closer together in a lot of ways. It's moments here, like this, that make all the hard work worth it.

"How were prince lessons?" Mom asks.

"Tiring." I sigh, not wanting to think about it.

Mom lowers the volume with the remote control. "Have you heard from Dustin?"

I shake my head. "I can't believe he said I've changed. I haven't changed."

"We just had the yummiest dinner!" Mack cuts in. "Jacques made lobster mac and cheese and ribs and placenta."

"Polenta," Mom asserts.

"Yeah. That. It was so good! This place is the best."

As much as it's nice hearing she's adjusting so well, at the same time, a small part of me wonders if I'm the only one trying to hold on to our old life, to Dad.

I think about him for a split second, and about how I don't want to ever forget about him, to let him fade. But I can't sit in the thought for too long either, so I shake it.

"The staff's been just lovely to us," Mom says. "By the way, you've been so busy, I had to text you about tomorrow."

"Tomorrow?" I ask, trying to jog my memory. "I haven't checked my phone."

"We're dyeing Easter eggs tomorrow," Mom says. "For Easter on Sunday. We're doing it on Saturday because it's…the day we lost Dad."

I sit up straight. Does she actually think I might have forgotten the date of when he died? "I know that. April 16."

"I know," Mom says softly. "You've just been so busy. Remember how much he loved to dye eggs with you two when you were kids?"

A dozen memories surface to mind, of walking into the kitchen the day before Easter every year as kids; Dad would always wait for us with his dish of eggs and cups of colorful dyes. Egg-dyeing was always his thing, from making the little belts that go around each egg to carefully balancing the vivid eggs on their drying rack. He scribbled invisible white crayon on his eggs and after dyeing them, funny sayings would appear that'd make us all laugh. One year, he lined them up so they formed a rainbow.

We didn't talk about it, but I knew it was his way of saying he loved me.

"It's one of the few family traditions we have," Mack chimes in.

"Of course I'll be there." I give Mom a hug, comforted in remembering that we refuse to let him fade, that we'll continue honoring him, blasting his favorite songs while dyeing those eggs. "I wouldn't miss it for the world…" A loud yawn escapes me.

Mom smiles. "Go rest up, dear."

I don't argue with her. "Love you." I head toward my bedroom.

"Love you too," she calls after me. "See you in the morning for egg dyeing! Eleven a.m. sharp! And we'll have lunch together afterward! I'll talk to Jacques about making you some of that delicious placenta!"

Within moments, I'm sprawled across my bed, thinking about how I have less time for all the things I love, like violin. It's a huge difference going from playing every day to playing once a week, if that. I haven't been spending as much time with Mom, Mack, or Pax, or even with my new family. At the same time, I'm missing Montana and simpler times, from the view of the snow-dusted mountains on cold mornings to my own cozy, sunken bed.

Right before I doze off, I check my phone. I look through Mack's latest YouTube videos, with funny titles like **Get Ready for St. Aubyn's with Me**. Her view count on each video is off the charts.

Next, I reread my texts, specifically all my texts to Dustin. It's strange not having any texts, voice mails, or DMs from him, especially since I've reached out a bunch, mostly asking if we can talk.

Over on Instagram, Mack just posted a throwback photo. Even though it's a day early, Mack's post is in honor of the anniversary of Dad's death.

Seeing the photo makes my stomach lurch, wiping all thoughts of Dustin. It's the two of us, ages five and nine, with Dad in the kitchen, a basket of eggs on the table. He's in his soft flannel shirt, an arm around each of us. I can feel the warmth off his smile. Mack and I look so happy, too. I want to tell that little boy and girl in the photo that he won't be there forever, and to treasure the time they have with him. I regret not turning to him then, and a million other times, to freeze the moment by telling him just how much I love him. I should have told him more often.

That was the year we made glitter eggs, and Dad agreed, even though he ended up with glitter in his beard for a week. I laugh and wipe my eyes. I zoom in on his face. That's how I like to remember him. Full head of hair. Full beard. And his smile—that never changed.

I can barely allow myself to read Mack's caption, but I force myself to anyway.

Three years without you, Daddy. I miss you so much it hurts.

I can't wait to see you again someday. Send me a sign in the sky. Send me a rainbow.

I wipe my eyes, power off my phone, and try to go to sleep. But I end up lying here awake, thinking about Dad for a long time. Sometimes, I wonder if he's actually dead, and ask myself if he could still be alive somehow.

But the answer, like the period concluding a sentence, always follows.

The radio blasts. Air rushes into the truck. Dad holds Mom's hand on the center console.

The wind whips our hair. We're singing and laughing, a Sunday drive with my family. Mom's and Dad's wedding bands glint in the sunlight. They turn to each other, belting out the melody. Mack dances in the seat beside me. Everything is perfect, the sky a brilliant blue.

The car slows into town. I wave out the window at the Howard–Loyolas, but they turn away from me, like they can't see me. I holler a hello to Old Man Fletcher the grocer, and to Mr. Gooding my violin teacher, and to Ms. Buyers, the baker, and to Joe, the head cook of the diner, but it's all the same. They keep going about their business, not hearing me.

Something's wrong. The sky darkens and it begins to drizzle.

There's Dustin walking along the sidewalk with his basketball under one arm. He's holding hands with someone. My heart breaks into a thousand pieces, watching as they lock lips. How could he have moved on to someone else so soon? Had he been cheating on me?

I grip Dad's shoulder for help. He turns around in the driver's seat, but it's Frederick's face.

I begin to sob, unable to catch my breath. Where's Dad?

I wake up, surprised to find my eyes are dry.

Thoughts of Dad ebb back into the shadows of my mind, thoughts of the time I assumed we'd always get back, thoughts of how we never did get the chance to experience so much together.

It must be way early, because it's still dark, and no one's ripped back the curtains and informed me that breakfast is ready. I check the clock: 6:13 a.m. A footman with a steaming pot of Earl Grey tea won't come knocking at my door for at least another hour. I'm awake so early. And on a Saturday, of all days. Part of me blames the overall stress and anxiety of wanting to be the perfect prince.

But another part knows it's because today is the anniversary of Dad's death.

I roll out of bed and find my way to the dining room, hoping for coffee. I find Frederick taking a bite of toast spread with orange marmalade as he signs pages from out of his red-and-white despatch box, a cappuccino in front of him. What's he doing back? I thought he was in Ottawa on important kingly business, like usual.

He sets down his paper. "Morning, son."

Son. Typically hearing him use the word grates on my ear, but this morning, it feels even worse. Not on Dad's death-day anniversary. It seems sacrilegious in a way, and makes my chest tight. As much as I'm secretly jealous that Edward has a dad—even though, technically, Frederick is my biological father too—I can't let myself give in, let down my walls for him.

"Good morning," I say politely as a footman pulls out my chair, and I take a seat beside him.

"You must be wondering what I'm doing back," Frederick says.

I nod. "It's nice to see you, but it is a surprise." I dole fresh strawberries and blueberries into my bowl of oatmeal, and the footman pours me a freshly squeezed glass of orange juice.

"Your mother and I are here for Easter brunch tomorrow with you and your brother. We flew in a day early. Daphnée is off meeting with the head of an NGO at their headquarters." He glances at his red-and-white box with paperwork sticking out the top, then at his tablet propped up showing a very full calendar. "I have no morning engagements myself, which is rare. Only a meeting with a British bishop at one." He smiles at me. "You know, we haven't had a chance to do something fun together yet, just the two of us. I feel rotten about not seeing to it. How about a horse-and-buggy ride through the park? I assume you're fond of horses, from your ranch life. What do you say?"

I desperately want to say yes, for a chance to connect with him. But what about dyeing Easter eggs with Mom and Mack at 11:00 a.m.? I do some quick mental math. If Frederick and I left soon, we'd definitely be back by then.

"I'm in," I say through a mouthful of oatmeal, followed by an embarrassed chuckle.

"Excellent." He stands. "You finish your meal. I'll see to it that everything's set for us."

At 8:00 a.m., Frederick and I climb into the SUV taking us to Central Park. When we arrive, I see that the lake area of the park has been roped off in our honor, with security and police patrolling every inch of the perimeter.

Frederick and I step out of his car, where we're met by paparazzi and journalists, along with fans and people protesting a gay Crown Prince—and the monarchy in general. How did they find out we were going to be here on such short notice?

But I have to say, it feels way less scary to face the haters with Frederick by my side.

Still, my skin isn't thick enough for this yet; I feel slightly sick to my stomach.

We climb into the horse-and-buggy waiting for us, and it begins clomping down an incline. The road takes us past bike paths and walkways carved into green grassy hills. Not quite the ranch experience—especially the feather hats on the horses—but it's the thought that counts.

"Lovely spring day for a ride." Frederick closes his eyes in a serene way.

I watch a squirrel run up a tree trunk and a lark sparrow alight on a branch. "It really is," I say.

He blinks his dark brown eyes at me. "So, tell me about Dustin."

"Dustin?" I'm surprised that Frederick cares enough to ask the question. Dad and I definitely didn't talk boys. "Well, we broke up," I admit with a heavy heart.

He nods. "I heard as much. From your brother. How are you doing?"

"I guess I miss him more than I thought I would," I confess.

"And why is that?"

I gaze at my hands. "I guess… Dustin was my lingering connection to Montana. And he played a big role in me learning about myself. Part of me wants to apologize. Or maybe try to win him back."

I hadn't even admitted that to myself until now. But it's true. As flawed as Dustin might be, there's comfort in the familiarity I had with him, and for some reason, I can only seem to remember the good times with him, from the time he showed me a shoebox he kept full of mementos of all of our early dates to the time he surprised me with tickets to my favorite local symphony orchestra.

Then there's the pain of watching him walk away, discarding me so effortlessly, so easily…like trash. Does he see me as a villain now, a monster in his mind? Does he even care about me at all anymore? Did he ever truly?

"If I may," Frederick says, cutting through my thoughts, "I might not have known you in Montana, but you have a good head on your shoulders and an honest heart. That much is abundantly clear to me. I support you in whatever decision you want to make."

"Thanks." I fidget with the seam of my jacket. "My dad was also a connection to home. He died three years ago to the day."

Frederick nods. "I'm sorry, Billy. I understand wanting to feel a connection to home. I'm sure you've read a headline or two about this, but my dear brother and I still aren't on speaking terms, not since Daphnée and I left England. I know how it feels to lose loved ones."

I focus my attention on the clomping sound of the horse hooves on the pavement. "I just miss him." I look away. "I miss him wrangling sheep at the ranch, and shaking mud out of his boots, and making his famous buttered toast in the oven. He was so proud of that toast. It was just toast!" I laugh a little, my eyes misting.

Frederick rests a hand on my knee. "You'll always have a connection to Montana, and to your dad. And you'll always have your mother and Mack."

I'm overcome by his understanding. And talking to him feels surprisingly normal, like I hoped it would, deep down. But the mention of Mom and Mack snaps me back to the present.

"Oh, no! What time is it? I totally lost track!" I yelp. "My mom and sister and I are dyeing Easter eggs this morning."

Frederick's eyebrows rise as he reads his watch. "The morning's just about over," he says, reading my panicked expression. "Let's head back."

Even with the cops on motorcycles flanking the SUV, and despite being escorted up side streets, the way back to the mansion feels like a slog. I'm at least an hour and a half late by the time the car pulls back to the mansion to drop me off.

"I'm off to my meeting with the bishop," Frederick says from his seat. "Thank you for the chance to spend some time together."

"Yeah, thanks." My mind is in an anxious spiral, thinking about Maple Crown Rule 73: Never neglect family nor friend, and how I broke it. *Again.* I race inside the mansion, bypassing the elevators and heading straight up the stairs, taking them two at a time.

Breathlessly, I step into the kitchen, and take in the colorful eggs sitting on a drying rack by a bouquet of fresh flowers. Oh, *no.* I have to find Mom and Mack and apologize.

I spin around and step foot back into the parlor when Daphnée walks in, looking as nice as ever in a beige coat, cream-colored sweater, and black slacks, carrying a simple brown bag with gold clasp.

"Billy!" She grins. "So happy to see you, darling."

I stop short. "You too," I say with a put-on smile. It's not exactly the best time for friendly chitchat.

"Good news." She takes my hands in hers. "Your father and I agreed to let your friend, Pax, redesign your ceremonial outfit for the Investiture," she says. "We think they'll do more than a fine job. Would you like the honor of letting them know?"

I can't believe it. "Oh, thank you! Thank you! This is the best news ever!" My face breaks into a real smile as I squeeze her hand. "Of course! I'd love to tell Pax the good news. They're going to flip!"

Past her, I notice Mom standing in the doorway. We lock eyes. "Mom!"

"Oh. Sorry to interrupt." She turns. I see Mack is with her. They disappear back around the corner.

"We'll talk more about it later." Daphnée grins and releases my hands. "I hate to cut our chat short, but I have to meet the prime minister for an off-the-record chat. Hi to Edward for me." She kisses my cheek before hanging a left into the hall.

I hang a right and chase after Mom and Mack. "Wait up!" I quicken my steps and break into a run, catching up with them.

"You forgot about egg dyeing, doofus," Mack says.

"I know. I feel awful. I'm so sorry."

My mom and sister keep walking.

"It's okay," Mom says. "I understand. You have a lot of new responsibilities."

"Mom." I try to catch my breath. "I feel *terrible*. The king asked me to go to Central Park with him, and there was so much traffic coming back, and then the queen was just telling me—"

"Billy. It's okay." But her voice is cold. She opens the door to Mack's room. "Come on, Mack."

My sister scowls at me. "Dustin was right. You *have* changed." She turns and disappears into her room with Mom.

The bottom falls out of my stomach, and a hot gush of tears runs down my cheeks.

My mom has always been there for me, and now I've let her down completely.

I feel like such a failure. Maybe Dustin *was* right.

Dad would be so ashamed of the person I've become.

Chapter Seventeen

EDWARD

After an agreeable Easter brunch, the clothes fitting at Fi's mansion of our His & Hers garments for the Investiture Ceremony leaves a lump in my throat—a reminder that I'm not the one undergoing the ceremony. A reminder of the life that once was mine.

By the time we're back in our everyday garb and settling down to cram our homework on a sofa in her massive bedroom, we each can't stop staring at the mannequins, one in the start of a maple leaf–printed gold gown, the other in a somewhat complete fitted burgundy tux with a subtle matching pattern. When Pax learned they could design Billy's ceremonial outfit, they volunteered to do an outfit for each of *us* too, even with two weeks on the clock ("Can that even be done?" "Have you *seen* 'Assignment Catwalk'?!"). *Apparrement*, they spent all night stitching up these lovelies, with a little help from the staff.

"You've got to give it up to Pax," Fi says. "Their garments are gorgeous. I'm totally excited for them to debut their Jolee Jubilee–inspired royal collection at the fashion runway show tomorrow." She purses her lips at me. "They're obsessed with you, BTW."

"They are?" I ask, although it doesn't surprise me in the

least. Her comment gives me a funny flutter in my stomach. It's replaced by a kick of guilt as her glance lingers on me. "I get the sense they're Royals obsessed in general," I assert.

"Too bad you're not playing for their team." She moves closer to me on the sofa, and rubs her stockinged foot against mine. "And too bad you're already taken." Her fingers climb up my arm as her lips form a coquettish smile.

I want to tell her that I'm gay, to nip this whole thing in the bud. I'm sick of lying. It felt so good to tell Billy the truth that night, even though a small paranoid voice in my head screams he's going to tell someone, and before I know it, it'll be splashed across the *Daily Maple* with Mum and Dad calling my phone, wanting to chat.

Fi keeps talking. "You know, I *loved* having dinner with your parents, and Easter brunch was fab too." She inches closer to me. She smells like strawberry-scented perfume. It's a nice smell, but not one that makes me want to plant a kiss on her mouth. In fact, I'm inclined to ask her what it is so I can purchase it for myself.

"Fi…" I avert my eyes to my carbon-paper notebook, then look back up at her. "This whole you and me thing…you know it can't *actually* work."

"And why's that?" Her voice has a playful lilt to it, and her eyes smoulder.

I take a sharp breath. "It just…can't." I flash a smile. "Okay?"

"Oh, come on." Her hand lands on my notebook, forcing my eyes back up to hers. "You can't be serious. Is Neel in your ear again?"

"Neel?"

"Please." She glares. "He's had it out for me since day one."

"Truthfully, we haven't really spoken in a while. He's been

flakier than phyllo crust. Probably too busy planning his rip-roaring gap year away and dancing on tabletops with that guy he's been seeing." I sigh. "Plus I think he's decided he'd rather be friends with Billy than with me."

She frowns. "That doesn't sound like Neel. I mean, his party year flying all around the world and taking cool photos, yes. But he's had your back literally since the day you two met. You must have really upset him if he's cozying up with Edward two-point-oh."

Fi might have a point. "I suppose I owe him an apology," I mutter.

She laughs. "I thought you didn't believe in apologies."

I smirk back at her. "I think that's *you*."

"Don't try and change the subject." She attempts lacing her fingers through mine, but I move my hand slowly away. "Ouch, Eddie-Bear. Aren't you having fun fake-dating me? I've been looking forward to you being my real date for the Investiture." She gestures to the impeccably coordinated mannequins. "It's going to be a blast when we pull off our big prank on Billy. But come on, you and I both know we're more than just partners in crime."

More than just partners in crime? Oh, no. Fi *has* fallen.

And I really don't want her to splat.

But I don't have the heart to break hers. "I…should go."

Fi looks stung. "What's wrong with you? We're the perfect match." Her troubled expression gives way to a satisfied smile. "Am I making this all too easy for you, Eddie-Bear? Because I can play hard to get."

I stash my notebook into my knapsack. "I'll see myself out." I give her a prim smile. "Later, Fi."

She smiles. "I see how it is. You're the one playing hard to get. Well, it's working. Later, babe. Happy Easter."

★ ★ ★

"They've just arrived, Your Royal Highness." Gord's matter-of-fact voice carries out into the corridor.

I backtrack and pause in the open doorway to the study. Inside, Billy is seated in an armchair with Pax standing beside him, while Gord wheels over a cart. On top, there's a box covered in a red velvet drape. He moves it aside in a whoosh to reveal a glass box with what is unmistakably the royal scepter, ring, and sword. I realize I'm a little sad as I see what sits in the centre: the gold crown. Happy for Billy, but still a little sad that I won't be the one to wear it.

Billy gives a few short, delighted laughs.

Pax gasps and clamps a hand over their mouth. "O, Canada! They're even more gorge in person!"

Gord gracefully gestures to each object with white-gloved hands. "The sword. The ring. The scepter, otherwise known as the gold rod." At that last one, Pax giggles ("He said 'gold rod.'"). "The Maple Mantle is already with the Head of Robe." Gord unclasps the top of the box. "Let us see how this fits you, sir." He pulls out the crown.

The crown with the metalwork forming maple-leaf peaks.

The crown more sacred than the one used to coronate Dad.

The crown fit for a future king.

The Maple Crown.

"This new crown is just what the world has been waiting for." Gord lifts it over Billy's head, and Billy looks up at it, then gazes over at Pax, breaking into an enormous smile.

As much as I've been dreaming about that crown since I was two, I surprise myself by finding that I'm actually very happy seeing it lowering over Billy's head. He *is* going to make a good king one day. He's a natural.

And in this moment, I realize something that I never would

have expected. But as soon as the thought crosses my mind, I know it's true: Billy deserves that crown. I have to tell Fi that Operation Twinvestiture is off, and convince her to actually listen.

Billy spots me in the doorway. "Edward!" he calls, grinning.

Gord freezes, crown held aloft midair, and looks over at me. "Prince Edward," he says curtly.

I wave. "Just passing through. Lovely crown. Looks great."

"Come in," Billy urges me.

"Yeah! Get in here!" Pax pipes up.

I shake my head. "I don't want to spoil the surprise for the ceremony. You enjoy." And with that, I smile and start off down the corridor before I have the chance to see Gord finish crowning him.

I'm restless for the remainder of the afternoon. I finish my homework, anxiety-pace around my room, and flick through TV shows and movies, changing the channel again and again, not even stopping to settle on a feel-good rom-com or reruns of *Canada's Next Great Baker*. My mind reels with interminable questions that I've been repressing ever since Billy showed up on the scene.

What does my future have in store?

What will my life be like as brother to the Prince Royal?

What will my fate become? I still have no idea.

I find myself padding through the corridor toward the kitchen, knowing nothing makes me feel better than baking something delicious. A part of me wonders if this is what my entire life will be from now on. Aimlessly wandering about. Bathing. Baking. Breathing space.

Maybe that wouldn't be so bad, I realize. It's been nice to have more time to work on my recipes and baking techniques. I'm working on a recipe for the next Canadian classic. I call it the "Queen Daphnée Cake," a twist on the Queen Eliza Cake, but instead of shredded coconut on top (I detest coconut flakes), I use marshmallow, plus a maple syrup base for the icing. In honour of Easter brunch this morning, I made a fig and almond brioche, and I've been itching to try adding more strawberries to my pink champagne cake recipe.

There are so many tasty options, none of which come from dear Britain, in my humble opinion. Every time I see Granny with her jam pennies and Dundee fruitcake, a small part of me dies inside. I definitely didn't inherit my refined palate from her.

As I pass through the parlour, I spot someone standing out on the veranda: Pax.

I open the door and step out into the cool evening, the sun sinking into the city horizon. "Enjoying the sights?"

Pax whips around. "Sweet baby Jesus! Prince Edward! You scared me. Hi!" They're wearing a lime-green housecoat and slippers. The housecoat had slipped open a little when they turned, revealing a sliver of smooth, bare chest.

They're obsessed with you, BTW... Thanks, Fi.

"What are you up to?" they ask.

"I thought maybe I'd whip up some mille-feuille."

Pax blinks hard and fast. "Who's she?"

I chuckle. "It's a puff pastry with cream and chocolate."

"Umm... *Yum!*"

I gaze past them at the orange skyline. "Bit different from Montana, isn't it?"

Pax cocks an eyebrow. "Uhhh, *yeah*!" They smile. "Being here is still surreal, by the way."

"You'll get used to it, I'm sure."

"You know one of the best things about being here?" Pax casts their eyes down, sending their single, geometric hoop earring twirling. "I'm still managing to stand out. I was the

only gay in Little Timber walking around in a muumuu singing Mariah Carey—she's my muse. I absolutely love her music.
Ah, word vomit again!"

"Hey, breathe," I say. "It's cool."

Pax takes a deep breath. My sights flicker to their full lips,
then back up to their intelligent eyes. Is that a knowing look?
Dare I say...*amoureux?*

"All of the garments you've designed are incredible."

They give a silent gasp and grin. "Thank you."

"And I'm not just saying it," I tell them. "They really are."
And it's true. I've had clothes custom designed for me since
before I can remember, but these are some of the most unique
ones I've ever seen.

"Well, good." Pax laughs.

I pause for a moment, then dive ahead. "I have a question,
if I may."

Pax nods enthusiastically. "Oh, go ahead! I'm an open book!
Totally acquiescent. And listen, I just want you to know that
you can totally be your unvarnished self with me." Pax smiles.

Unbidden, I find myself staring again at their lips. This
time, I let my eyes linger. It won't hurt, will it? And they don't
seem to notice. "What was it like growing up in the middle
of cowboy country? I'm genuinely curious."

"Pretty despondent, if I'm being honest. I figured out early
on that people will always judge you for some reason or another. Especially if you're femme. But might as well let 'em
judge your truth, and not give a damn. As for dating, well,
it sucked. But maybe New York will be different. At least, I
hope it will." The vulnerable sadness in their eyes vanishes as
quickly as it came, replaced by a bold smile.

I nod while thrumming my fingers against the balcony banister. "I get that." There's something so appealing about how Pax always seems fully themself.

Before I let myself think about what I'm doing, I step up to stand right next to them.

Their bare arm is so close to mine I can feel the heat radiating off it.

Pax rests a hand on top of mine. "To answer you, I'd say it's probably not so different than being a gay royal prince. Right?"

I pull my hand away, and instantly look around to make sure no one is watching. I can't help it. I've spent my whole life being afraid. "I'm…" I shake my head, slowly, like I'm recalling a good joke. "I'm not…" I smile as broadly as I can. "I'm not gay."

Pax gasps. "Oh, my gosh. No, I was talking about Billy."

"Oh! Right. Of course." I feel my temperature spike.

"There you two are!" Mack exclaims from the door. "Come with me!" She vanishes back into the parlour. I look at Pax, whose mouth is agape, and nod, indicating we should follow her.

Inside, we find that Mack and Connie are seated at the table with steaming porcelain cups of tea. They've pushed aside the vases of Easter lilies to make room for The Settlers of Catan game board.

Connie gives a friendly smile. "How are you, Edward?"

"I'm well, thank you."

Mack jangles an empty chair by its back. "Play with us!"

"Where's Billy?" I ask.

"We're mad at Billy. Apparently, he's too busy for us now."

"He's doing important prince things," Connie interjects, shooting Mack a miffed look.

"Meaning we need *more people, people*!" Mack jabs a finger toward Pax. "Sit!"

"Don't have to tell me twice! I could use a break from sewing!" Pax sidles in between Mack and Connie. "Edward?"

Truth be told, now I'm not in a social mood. "I'm terribly sorry," I say. "I must step out for a brief moment. I'll be back very soon! I promise."

Flashing a smile, I dash from the parlour and take the stairs to the dingy West Wing. Midstep, I hear Pax shouting, "Hey! Wait!"

I spin around. *"Oui?"*

"I'm sorry… I shouldn't have…brought it up," Pax pants.

My heart melts. I already feel bad about ditching them and leaving so abruptly. I shake my head. "There's nothing to be sorry about."

They still look a bit breathless, their eyes wide.

They also look kind of beautiful.

I'm not sure I'm going to regret what I say next, which is why the words flow out easily.

"You weren't wrong."

I'm careful about how I word it. If someone were to record it on their phone, it'd mean nothing at all. But it's still more honest than I thought I could ever be with a person as magnificent as Pax. I gaze into the depths of their clear chestnut-brown eyes. I hope they understand the courage it took.

"Oh, and Billy knows," I add. "Please don't tell anyone."

Pax stares intensely back at me for a split second, understanding swimming in their eyes, locking in that unspoken promise of confidentiality. My stomach is suddenly spinning with butterflies. Are we actually about to…*kiss*?

Then Pax nods. "Your secret's safe with me." They turn away, heading back down the steps.

I watch them go. What was I thinking? Me and *Pax*? Even though I'm no longer Crown Prince, I'm still Edward, closeted and miserable. And then there's the whole labels thing. If I'm gay, doesn't that mean I should be attracted to someone who goes by he/him/his? Maybe "gay," like anything else, is a label, and while labels can oftentimes be helpful, I'm much more than a label, and similarly, can be with someone who uses different labels than my own.

Before I can think about seriously being with someone else, I have to figure out how to be happy with myself, the way Pax is truly happy with themself. I can't hide in the closet any longer.

In the student centre the next day, I find Fi busily studying.

"Listen, Operation Twinvestiture is off," I whisper. "I mean it."

"What?" she asks. "Boo. You're no fun. I was looking forward to seeing Billy's face when he reaches into his pocket and realizes his cue cards are gone."

"No. It's too far. I can't do it."

"Fine," Fi snaps. "What if we swap them out with dud cards so that he ends up reciting all sorts of offensive and silly expressions in French?" She tugs at the hem of my jacket and looks up at me with doe eyes. "Come on. Why the change of heart, Eddie?"

"Believe it or not, I've grown to care about him. I can't stand the thought of seeing him humiliated any further. Especially since the Firm continues to keep quiet when they should be coming to his defense."

"That's rich, being that you're the one who nudged him into the court of unpopular opinion to begin with." For a moment she looks irritated, but then she shrugs and takes my hand. "Fine. As long as we're still the hottest-looking couple there." And there it is, piling onto my mountain of guilt.

I glance at my timepiece. "Class. See you soon." I barge into the corridor and spot Neel walking toward me. When he sees me, he pivots and starts in the other direction. This isn't like any kerfuffle we've had before, like the time we debated if irregardless was a word for a good two weeks. I accelerate my strides until I'm alongside him, overcome with the urge to apologize.

"Hey, are you still coming to the Investiture?" I ask spiritedly.

He doesn't look at me. "I can't *not* go. You know I can't resist an epic party." He quickens his steps.

I figure this isn't the best time to joke about how he's really only going because he's Team Billy and wants to support his new favourite Dinnissen.

"Splendid!" I say, thinking about how he's not making it easy to keep up with him. "Neel, I'm…sorry. I just spoke to Fi and—"

"I can't handle you right now," Neel cuts in, continuing ahead. "Talk soon, okay?"

I stop and watch him fly up the stairs, my mouth slightly ajar.

So, *that* just happened.

After school, I sit in the library at the mansion to start my creative writing assignment but pretty soon am procrastinating by watching one of Mack's YouTube videos where she's ranking all the flavours of Magnolia Cupcakes. It's pretty entertaining, and she's actually doing a great job describing the exact texture of the cake, and the perfect consistency of the buttercream icing. It makes me think about how if I'm ever going to make frosting for any reason, it *must* be buttercream. Whipped frosting is for the grocery store cakes of the world. Special exception shall be made for the cream cheese frosting that tops the red velvet cake at Pierre's on Park. I digress.

The truth is that I haven't been able to stop thinking about Pax.

I wonder if they think differently of me.

If this changes anything, now that they know the truth…

Footsteps fill the library, and I look up.

Pax smiles wanly. "Hey."

My heart thumps in my chest. "Hello there. How's it going?"

Pax beelines to the far windows, a glittery tote bag under their arm. "Good. You?" they say without so much as looking at me.

I sit up tall. "Everything okay?" They seem a bit disinterested.

Pax freezes and turns slowly to me. "Sorry. I… Can we talk?"

I pat the cushion on the cracked leather armchair beside me. "I would like that."

Pax plops down, and I catch a whiff of a wonderful, musky yet flowery perfume that makes me want to move closer to them. "So… I have to tell you something."

I blink at them. I really want to tell them how gorgeous their eyes are, but I resist the urge. "Go on."

"I… I've had you on a pedestal, thinking that you had your entire life together and everything was perfect for you. Learning that you're trying to figure out who you are…it made me realize that we're more similar than I thought. And you know what's wild?" They shake their head. "It makes me feel even *more* gravitated toward you. I haven't told anyone your secret and I *won't* tell anyone! It's yours to tell—if and when you're ready."

"Relax." I smile. "And thank you. I appreciate that."

They give a nervous laugh. "Oh my gosh, of *course*! Well, I'll just be going now—" They begin to stand, and I gently grip their hand.

"I have to tell you something too," I say. "I really admire you." I gulp. Am I going to say more?

But I stop there.

"Oh." They blush. "Thanks." They fumble with their tote bag, obviously trying to change the subject. "Hey, uh, so you said you liked my designs. Do you want to see my design for Billy's new Investiture Ceremony outfit?"

"Sure," I say with a laugh.

Their tablet screen flashes to life, and I'm looking at a smart black suit with epaulets. "Oh, this is just his entrance look. He's borrowing the suit your dad wore at *his* Investiture. You know that already." Pax swipes to the next image. "Here's what *I* designed and what Billy will change into right before the ceremony starts."

I'm looking at a slim, metallic white suit with red epaulets and gold tassels, a red brocade vest, and sash with golden clasps.

"Incredible. I'm sure it will perfectly complement his crown. Not to mention it's sure to capture the public's affection."

"Thanks. I still have a few things to iron out with the pants for the ceremony—literally—and I may have made them a *little* too small, but other than that, I'm really happy with both looks."

"Excellent." Heart pattering, I decide to take the plunge. "Could I...come to your fashion show tonight?"

"Seriously?! Of *course*!" Pax grins. "I just assumed you— Of course! Of course you can!"

"I'm excited," I say. And I mean it.

Pax nods. "Yay! So, uh, I should get to work. See you later!"

After they leave, I sit, thinking about their lips.

And what would have happened if I'd been brave enough to lean in and kiss them.

Chapter Eighteen

BILLY

"You knew and didn't tell me?!" Pax stops combing through my walk-in closet to stare wide-eyed at me. "*This* is why you were acting all cagey whenever I spoke about Edward. How long have you known?!"

"Sorry." I pantomime zipping my lips. "Gay twin brother code of conduct."

Pax huffs and turns back to flipping through my suits, playing the unofficial role of royal style adviser for me for tonight's event at the MoMA. They're already in full hair and makeup, in a short salmon-pink gown with cape that screams famous fashion designer. They take a shirt by the sleeve and draw it under their chin dreamily. "Somebody pinch me! He's gay. Prince Edward! He's gaaaaaay!"

"You don't want him. He's really nice, but I don't think he's good enough for you."

Pax puts their hand to their chest. "What in the disenchanted?! How could you say that about Prince Edward?" They sound as if I've said something criminal.

But I stand by what I said. I've gotten to know Edward, and while I consider him a good friend now, he's so…not out… and Pax is so the opposite… Still, I don't want to say anything more to crush Pax's spirits. "Okay… And once again, I'm going to try really hard to take it as a compliment that you're so at-tracted to someone who's literally identical to me."

Pax looks unbothered. "Yeah, it's not weird at all."

"Yeah, not weird…at all…" My eyes dart as I try hard not to laugh.

"You two are extremely different," says Pax. "It's about his *personality*."

"His shallow, detached, icy-cold, arrogant personality? That personality?" I joke, only half-meaning it.

Pax's dreamy expression shifts, and they glare at me. "You're talking about my crush!"

"Sorry, sorry. I'm just glad you finally took him off his ped-estal," I remark.

"Oh, honey, now that I know he's *gay*, he's intrinsically back *on* the pedestal."

"Of course he is." I can't help laughing at the look on my friend's face. I know them so well. And the truth is, I'm happy for them. Who knows, maybe Pax and Edward will become a thing—even if it's not a public-facing thing.

Pax keeps digging through my expansive closet. They pull aside even more suits, and I see my cowboy boots shoved to the back. I haven't even thought of them since I moved into the mansion. A small part of me suddenly misses the feel of put-ting them on. Which makes me miss the ranch, and the quiet moments spent feeding the horses crunchy carrots in the barn.

"How are you feeling about Dustin?" Pax's voice is muffled by clothes. "Nonchalant?"

"I guess it is what it is." I sigh. "But I do miss him."

"I never liked Dustin," Pax confesses. "He was profusely immature."

"*What?*" I spit. "Why didn't you tell me you felt that way?" I demand, my blood pressure spiking.

Pax pokes their head out of the clothing rack. "Would you have listened?"

"No. Probably not."

"See?" Pax disappears back into the row of hanging garments. "Besides, I don't trust anyone who doesn't pay attention to song lyrics. That told me all I needed to know about him. He wasn't that deep. And if he's over you so soon, clearly his love was conditional."

I wince. "Tell me how you really feel," I say.

Pax reemerges and begins rooting around inside drawers. "So, what about Neel?"

"What about him?" I ask, confused.

Pax unfolds a shimmery shirt and admires it. "It's so obvious he likes you."

I laugh. "What? No! Neel? He's flirty with everyone."

Pax cocks their head. "Here's the part where you listen to your bestie, remember?"

"Maybe. I mean, he's nice and all, but I don't know him that well. Besides, when you asked him to walk the catwalk for you, didn't he tell you he was too busy wining and dining the eligible bachelors in New York or something like that?"

"I think he's actually avoiding Edward, who is coming tonight! At least that's my theory. I haven't seen them hanging out much. Let's say Neel's reason is legit. What says he can't like more than one eligible bachelor in this big old city?" Pax winks.

I find myself blushing. "You're ridiculous. Even if that's true, he's leaving on a world vacation in a few months, so it's moot."

"But he *will* be going to the Investiture Ceremony to cheer *you* on." Pax pulls out a crimson suit. "This is what you're gonna wear to my fashion show tonight."

I nod. "Looks great."

Pax puts a hand on their hip. "Seriously, where is this royal style adviser I've yet to meet? Did she think I was coming for her job and ran?"

"I don't know." I laugh. "I'm so excited for your big premiere."

"And I'm excited you'll actually be able to *be* there," Pax quips. "Mr. Busy Bee." They hand me the suit. "I can't believe Fi is going to be wearing one of *my* gowns on the runway. This is a dream come true! Not to mention I'm so happy Edward is going to be there. *Swoon.*"

There's a knock on the bedroom door, and I go to open it.

Mom's standing there in a purple blouse and black slacks, her hair in a low ponytail with new bangs that the royal hairdresser gave her. They really suit her. "Hi, dear," she says sweetly.

Mack's beside her in a loose paisley dress with her hair on the top of her head pulled up in a blond waterfall. "Hey, Billy." She flashes her braces-filled grin. I've missed that smile.

"Hi! What are you up to?" I ask, smiling. Things have been better with both of them since I apologized this morning.

"We're going to grab a quick snack," Mom says. "Would you like to join us? Or will that fill you up too much for your dinner with the king later?"

My schedule is tight, but I'm determined to make it all work. "Yeah! I'd love that!" I say. "Let's grab a bite. Then it'll be time for me to get ready for my dinner, and I'll see you at Pax's show after."

Mom's face lights up. "Great!"

"And how do you expect to cram all this in again?" Pax asks suspiciously.

"I've gotten pretty good at mastering tight schedules," I say. "Besides, King Frederick says it's important he and I both attend the dinner."

"More important than my show. I get it."

"No! I didn't mean it like that."

"Okay," Pax says, relenting. "You know this means the world to me."

"I've got it all figured out."

"You're biting off more than you can chew, Billy."

"No… I'm not biting any of this off. I didn't choose this. If I had it my way, I'd skip the dinner entirely." My stomach knots with guilt at how excited I am for this dinner. I'd be willing to skip it for Pax's event if it really came down to it…wouldn't I?

A footman appears beside Mom and Mack. "Your Royal Highness, Gord sent me to retrieve you for your lessons now."

"Oh, wait," I say to Mom and Mack, crestfallen. "I have to go. Sorry. I forgot."

Mom's face falls, but she gives a little shake of her head. "We know how busy you are. Don't worry."

"Yeah, it's okay, Billy. We figured you were super busy today," Mack says. "We thought you already had lessons earlier."

"Next time! I promise!" I say. I really hope they can hear the sincerity in my voice.

"No, I know. We understand." Mom smiles. "Love you. Bye, dear. See you at the show."

She and Mack head off down the hall, while the footman remains standing stock-still, waiting.

"Let me just grab my notebook!" I tell him, ducking back into my room. Gord had me replace my notepad for a thick notebook long ago, and after filling up the first two, I'm onto my third one.

Pax hands it to me. "See you tonight! My first ever fashion show! And you *promise me* you won't miss it?"

I give Pax a quick hug, careful not to crush the shape of their sequined gown, and smile. "As Mariah would say, I'll be there."

They let out a jubilant whoop. "If you're not, I will hunt you down," they tease.

★ ★ ★

Dinner at the opulent Crystal Room of the Tavern on the Green goes off without a hitch. It's not every day one gets to eat dinner with *the* Ryder Russell. He tells me what it was like growing up in Canada, and I share what it was like growing up on the ranch, picking horse hooves and raking up their pee spots. I get a lot of laughs. At one point, I'm so in the moment that I almost don't recognize my own voice. I sound…happy. As the remains of the chocolate mousse and cheesecakes are cleared away, I check my phone. Right on time.

I lean toward Frederick and whisper, "I'm going to head out."

He turns to me. "I'll come with you. Nobody will question me for leaving now. Let's go straightaway. You don't want to miss it."

"Cool." See? I *knew* I could handle a tight schedule.

He and I finally begin to say our goodbyes to the celebrities and other high-ranking dinner guests when the president of the United States strolls up and starts talking to us. It's clear a few minutes in that there isn't really a good time to cut her off. What's more important than being in the presence of the president of the USA? And hearing her speak about survivors of a flood in Australia?

But the whole time, I can feel the pressure getting heavier and heavier on my chest, making it hard to breathe. At this point, I'm going to start cutting it close. I appreciate Frederick's efforts, and I feel helpless myself. After what feels like forever, he finally excuses us.

Dodging past a few weaselly paparazzi, we share a town car, and within minutes are pulling up to the steely gray exterior of the Museum of Modern Art. Everyone is pouring out the front door, including photographers and models. There's Fi in a corseted dress with sleeved gloves, a little hat with veil, and silver feathers, soaking up the flash of cameras.

"Oh no! I missed it. I missed Pax's show!" I feel sick to my stomach. First Easter egg dyeing, and now this. I am such a failure. I should have seen this coming. I really need to find a better balance.

There's Pax, stepping out onto the sidewalk as photographers snap their photo. They beam, and answer the questions of eager journalists who wave phones in their radiant face. They turn to another reporter's mic, their gown shining like shimmering rainbow scales.

Frederick looks back at me. "Do you want to get out and congratulate them?"

I shake my head. I'm too heartbroken, but more than that, I'm ashamed.

"Take us back to the mansion, please," Frederick tells our driver.

The whole ride home, I contemplate what to tell Pax, and how to make it up to them. I finally just made amends with Mom and Mack. Now I have to try to do the same with Pax. I can't bear the thought that I hurt them. They must be devastated that I didn't show. I know *I* am.

I lean my head on the cold window. I suddenly miss being back in Montana again, driving Dad's rusty 1988 Dodge Ram home late at night after working at the general store. The night was always full of stars. Here in New York City, they're masked by all the light pollution. And the buildings are closing in around us, making me miss the wide-open roads and skies. How do I keep breaking Maple Crown Rule 73: Never neglect family or friend?

The car pulls up outside the mansion, but I don't move. Neither does Frederick. We just sit in silence, facing forward. Luckily, there aren't paparazzi lying in wait for us beneath the awning.

Finally, he looks over at me. "I remember being your age and struggling to balance my schedule with my friendships."

He reaches out and pats me on the knee. "Your true friends will understand."

I let out a deep breath. "Thanks, Dad."

My smile vanishes as I realize what I just called him.

No. That word is reserved for my real dad, my original dad, the person who raised me.

But then why does it feel right saying it to Frederick too?

He blinks, not missing a beat, and a warm smile washes across his face. I smile back. Maybe it's okay.

Maybe, I think for the first time since Dad died, it's all going to be okay.

I have to do something to take my mind off what a mess I've made of tonight, so I head to the study to practice my French for the ceremony. But I keep getting distracted every time I glance at my phone. Pax still hasn't replied to any of my texts, and I have no idea what time they're planning to get home. I think I remember them telling me they would be going to an afterparty, but I don't even know if that's accurate, which only causes the guilt eating away at me to intensify.

MAPLE CROWN RULE 25: Remain tranquil in times of tension.

Sometime after midnight, when I'm finally surrendering to sleep over the stack of French textbooks, the doors to the study fly open.

There's Pax, covered in glitter and looking exhausted. "You missed my show."

"Hey." Gulping, I straighten up, ready to tell them what happened, the same way that I always tell Pax everything. Then I realize that telling them I missed the most important day of their life because I was having too much fun hanging out with Ryder Russell paints me as an even *worse* best friend.

"You know I had a really important dinner with…" I mumble. I find I can't look Pax in the eye.

Pax crosses their arms. "Celebrities. *Really*, Billy? Last I checked, you don't even care about celebrities!"

I feel my face flame.

"Wow." Pax shakes their head. "That's really uncool."

"Pax, I am so sorry. I *had* to go. I didn't have a choice."

"You're *still* lying! You just wanted to enjoy the perks of being a prince. This isn't about supporting your new Royal Family, this is about you just caring about your fabulous new identity as *Prince* Billy."

I wince. I've never had Pax this upset at me. "That's not true," I say defensively. Although, hearing an echo of what Dustin told me, now from my best friend's mouth, makes my rebuttal sound shaky.

"Is so!" There are tears shining in Pax's eyes. "I feel like I don't even know what's going on with you anymore. You've always been there for me. Now, you're flaking and being super shady about it! I'm sorry, but if you don't hear it from me, then who else around here is going to say something?"

"Oh, I don't know? Maybe… Dustin?" I quip.

"Maybe he was on to something," they shoot back.

"That's not fair."

"Billy, you are so selfish and superficial now!"

My face heats, but this time it's due to a flash of anger. "I couldn't turn down the king of Canada to go to some fashion show. Now *that's* superficial."

Pax looks like they've been slapped.

I instantly want to eat my words.

"Pax, I didn't mean—"

Pax's expression hardens. "You *have* changed. I always knew there was a risk this could happen. That it would all go to your head and…we'd lose the Billy we love."

And with that, they turn on their heel and go.

DAILY MAPLE ONLINE

THE ROYAL ROUNDUP
April 19, 12:18 am ET

PRINCE BILLY ATTENDS STAR-STUDDED DINNER
by Omar Scooby

With just eleven days left until his Investiture Ceremony, Prince Billy was seen rubbing elbows with A-listers at a Tavern on the Green dinner with royal pop at his side.

The Crown Prince of Canada was in fine form—gabbing with the best of them at a private dinner in Central Park. A-listers like Ryder Russell and Blaire Ivy were among those in attendance. On-lookers remarked Billy looked awfully chummy despite his recent split with ex-bf, Dustin, exchanging laughs and easy smiles with his father, the king. "Father's Day has come early!" said a source who spent the night admiring the duo from afar. "It's clear the two have become incredibly close. It's wonderful seeing them bond."

Billy cut a classically handsome figure in custom suit and gold bracelet. As for the king? He wore his signature navy blue suit and black tie, leaving the focus on his son. Royal watchers simply can't wait for the special connection between the King and Prince Royal to continue to flourish as they make up for so much lost time.

RELATED STORIES
Billy and the King's Central Park Carriage Ride
Pax Andrews: Fresh Face of Fashion Industry
Edward and Sofia Engagement Rumours?
BREAKING: Billy Under Royal Surveillance
Crown Prince Orders Seafood and Talks Politics!
Twinces: What Their Handwriting Says About Them
Royal Twinvasion: Are Two Princes Better Than One?
Macky Montana Vows to Free Central Park Horses

Chapter Nineteen

EDWARD

After the thrilling fashion show, I try my best to finish my abysmal AP Calc homework without completely nodding off or letting my thoughts continue to drift. Being demoted from Crown Prince isn't all that different from when I was grounded for almost a year, now that I think about it. There's plenty of time to reflect and ruminate. I learned a lot about myself during that time. Maybe that will happen again?

Suddenly, I hear footsteps passing by my room. Is that the sound of someone…*weeping*? I stop trying to interpret the definite integral and tiptoe through the dim corridor until I find the source of the noise: Pax, crying in a cushioned hallway nook under the portrait of King George VI in his purple cape and white stockings.

I approach slowly, tentatively. "Hello."

Pax starts and promptly wipes their eyes. "Hey."

"Are you okay? What's wrong?" Last I saw them only a few hours ago, they were all smiles on the catwalk, absorbing fervent applause amid their lineup of models and taking a bow.

"Oh, nothing. Never been better! Other than fighting with my best friend and telling him he's become a terrible human being. No big deal!" Pax tries to grin, but it's clear their heart's not in it.

"Okay. Breathe," I instruct them softly.

Pax takes a shuddering breath, tears running down their face. "I'm fine! R-really!"

I fight the urge to crack a joke. "You're clearly not fine," I assure them in a slow, even tone. Without thinking, I take their hand. What am I doing? Somehow, I can't move my hand away. Their perfect buttercup-yellow nail polish is the tiniest bit chipped. "What happened?"

"S-sorry." Tears are clinging to their lashes. "I hate how you're seeing me like this. I'm not usually such a hot mess." Their laugh fades back into the quiet of the corridor. Then their grip in mine tightens just the smallest amount. "How have you been?"

I chuckle. "I've been better."

A slight smile forms on Pax's face.

I smile back, feeling their fingers tense in mine.

"Why is royal life so hard?"

"Isn't that the question of the millennium?" I quip.

"Billy's been so busy doing prince things that he missed my fashion show."

"I thought it odd I didn't see him there. In any case, I'm sorry." I realize that Pax still doesn't truly grasp how much pressure Billy's under to fulfill his royal duties. "It's common for the Crown to take precedence."

"But he was just at some celebrity dinner."

"Sometimes, those happen," I say. "I'm still sorry that he missed your show."

Pax nods. "I should probably try being more understanding." They say it slowly and grudgingly, but I can tell they're really making an effort.

"I wouldn't beat yourself up about it though."

They tug my hand bashfully. "As you say, Your Royal Highness."

We sit quietly. Even with their eyes puffy from crying, they still look handsomely beautiful. I seriously can't stop staring at them.

So much for Maple Crown Rule 44: Staring bouts are unbecoming.

"I'm glad *I* got to see your show," I say quietly. "It was stupendous."

Pax looks my way, and suddenly, I feel like every Maple Crown Rule is out the window—it's just me sitting here, no rules, no inner monologue telling me what I should or should not do.

No voice telling me to check that we're not being watched by any of the mansion's inhabitants, let alone a nosy staff member.

I feel totally out in the open. It's terrifying. I want to look anywhere but their face.

But I can't take my eyes off them.

I gaze at their long lashes and wide, tear-filled eyes. And their lips. There's the slightest trace of clear lip gloss left over from the night. I'm overcome by the overwhelming urge to kiss them.

Pax's eyes flicker to my lips too. A tiny smile lights their face.

"I really like you," I say, finally listening to my pounding, protesting heart.

Pax's eyes go wide, and they clear their throat.

They never take their eyes off mine. And I realize I've always known I liked them, even if there was a small part that didn't know what to think at first.

But now, I'm finally, truly letting myself be who I've been afraid to be for my entire life.

We lean toward each other, closing the infinitesimal gap between us...

Their lips are soft against mine. I close my eyes. I feel my sorrow leech away, feel years of pent-up self-loathing evaporate, like the spell I've placed on myself is finally lifted. My heart is thumping in my chest, and I'm wondering if they can hear it, if they can feel it...and if I'm doing this correctly.

Their hand finds its way to the back of my neck, and their fingers slowly but firmly run through my hair. The way our lips press against each other feels so right. I'm lost in the darkness, walking on air, high in the clouds, my whole body tingling.

Edward, stop. Someone will see.

Oh, *ferme ta gueule.*

After losing track of time, we finally pull apart.

I open my eyes again, dizzy and disoriented.

"That was nice," they say quietly, averting their gaze as a blush creeps across their face.

My lips are practically buzzing. I nod. "It was. Especially for my first kiss."

Pax breaks into an elated smile. "I am so honoured."

I grin. "I couldn't have thought of a better person to share it with."

They squeeze my hands, and I can tell they feel the same way. It wasn't just a kiss for them either. "Does this mean...? Are we a thing?" they ask.

I consider. "I...don't know," I reply. "I've never thought 'a thing' would be possible for me. At least not back when I was Crown Prince. But now..." We intertwine our fingers together. It hits me how right this feels, and how wrong it felt when Fi laced her fingers in mine.

"You don't need to be out, you know," Pax says. "Do whatever's best for you."

"What's best for me is probably not hiding anymore. But it's harder than it sounds. The Firm isn't exactly the warm and fuzzy land of love and acceptance. I do want to do something. I'm just not sure what...or how."

"You do *you*," Pax says.

"It just feels impossible," I say. I can feel the Maple Crown Rules threatening to rise back up inside me like hot, rising bile.

MAPLE CROWN RULE 15: Follow the plan.

"Is that your fear talking?"

I laugh. "Quite possibly." I lightly graze my fingers up and down theirs. "Hey, you're good at this stuff."

They blink. "What stuff?"

"Being authentic. You live and breathe authenticity. You're like this radiant beacon of sunshine. You don't let anything get you down."

Pax points to themself. "Hello? Still upset about the whole Billy thing over here."

"Well, for the most part," I amend. "It's what I like about you."

Pax does a little shoulder dance. "Well, what I like about *you* is who you are when you're being just you. Like right now." They smile, but then look down, unable to meet my eyes, and sigh.

"What's the matter?"

"To be honest, it's not always easy. Sometimes, I have to remind myself that it's okay to not be smiling twenty-four seven. It's just this thing I do, trying to see the world in the best light, because of all the terrible things I've gone through. Most days, I'm truly happy to be alive. There's so much good in the world. But then some days, memories surface, mostly

of home, and I feel like the biggest reject in the world again."
Pax sniffles. "Wow. I've never said that out loud before."

Hearing it breaks my heart. "It's okay to let yourself feel
whatever you need to feel."

Pax takes a deep breath and nods. "This is very true. I promise I'll keep an eye on it."

"Excellent." I can't help smiling. "May I…kiss you again?"

"Do you have to ask? Actually, I always appreciate asking
for consent." Pax leans forward, and our lips connect. This
time, it's short and sweet, but still absolutely perfect.

"And…you don't think I'm too…*extra*?" Pax asks.

I shake my head. "Someone's 'too extra' is someone else's
'just right.'"

"OMG." Pax bites their lip and breaks into a laugh, clearly
smitten. "I like that," they say.

"I'm glad. Well, I should head to bed," I say. I want to stay
here forever with them, sitting side by side in this surprisingly cozy hallway nook that I've only ever brushed past over
all these years, but it's late and I'm starting to realize just how
frightfully exhausted I am.

"Totes," Pax says. "Me too."

I let go of their hand. "Good night."

"Good night."

I head back to my bedroom, feeling light as air. Or as a
fluffy meringue.

Definitely a meringue.

I rise with the sun, and take a few laps in the indoor pool to
help wake myself up after such a late and exhilarating night.
Afterward, I pass the home gym when I hear activity coming from inside.

I hover in the doorway, watching Billy walking to his mark,

two blue pieces of tape crisscrossed on the floor. Then, he pivots, with the exacting movement and perfect posture of a foot guard in the Canadian Armed Forces. He's kneeling on a bench when I step into the room.

"*Très bien fait,*" I say.

Billy starts, nearly falling over. Then he stands up straight and turns to me. "*Merci.* I'm just rehearsing before school."

"I can see that." I smile. "Let me see. Take it from the top."

Billy crosses the room, then begins the long walk toward the bench.

"Try not swinging your arms so much."

Billy adjusts without breaking stride.

"Try holding your head up a smidge higher," I add.

Billy complies.

"Relax your mouth. It's too tense," I instruct.

Billy stops midroom and buries his head in his hands. "Ugh! I can't do this!"

I approach his side. "You can. You've got this."

"How many people will be watching again?" he asks shakily.

"Oh, well, figure that over two billion tuned in for Auntie Caroline's royal wedding…" I try to do the mental math.

He looks at me, face pained and paling. "Am I going to sink the monarchy?"

"No," I assure him. "Go easy on yourself. Being Crown Prince comes with a steep learning curve." A feeling of guilt washes over me as I remember I was responsible for what brought on his recent public blunders. Thank goodness I told Fi that Operation Twinvestiture is canceled.

"I'm just so worried the Firm will want to strip me of my title, and I don't want that to happen."

"If it does, trust me—you'll survive," I say good-naturedly.

"I didn't…" Billy tenses up. "Sorry. I just… Things can't go back to the way they used to be. As stressed out as I am, I'm finally…happy again…for the first time in a long time. Even with the public knocking me every chance they get. This isn't about that." The corners of his mouth pinch down as if he's on the precipice of tears, and his voice quivers. "This is about me, my family, and bringing positive change in the world one day. I won't be able to do that as a rancher in a barn back in Montana. I won't."

"You're worrying far too much," I say in an attempt to calm him. "The only thing you should be worried about is meeting your cousins, aunts, and uncles at the ceremony. They're a dull lot."

Billy's expression goes blank. "I haven't even thought of that. I've honestly been too busy panicking about being closely monitored by the powers that be."

"Why? You don't have any giant secret, do you?"

Billy gives a relieved sigh. "No."

"Good. It would have to be really bad to strip you of your title. Especially if the ceremony goes swimmingly, which it will."

"I think I'm just panicking about *everything*," Billy confesses.

"I think so too."

"Gord says the ceremony has to be perfect." Billy hangs his head. "I don't know if I'll ever feel ready enough."

I rest a hand on his shoulder. "You *will*. You have more than a week to prepare. And what could go wrong in a week?"

DAILY MAPLE ONLINE

THE ROYAL ROUNDUP
April 27, 10:46 pm ET

THE BOONE FAMILY'S GIANT SECRET
by Omar Scooby

Meanwhile, back at the ranch… Juicy details emerge revealing that the Boone family has been hiding dark secrets—namely hiding Prince Billy's true identity for the last three years—and we've got receipts.

Everyone has skeletons in their closet, but Prince Billy's are by far the meatiest. Just over six weeks after entering the world stage, a photo surfaced of Billy posing with his mom, Connie Boone. In the pic, which was confirmed to not have been altered, there's a *People* magazine in the background with Prince Edward on the cover. According to an insider, Connie knew all along that Billy was secretly a prince. "How could she not know? I mean, look at that photo. There's no way she couldn't have noticed her son looked *exactly* like the Canadian prince."

Sources tell us that Connie Boone had been paid off by the Royal Family to keep quiet for the past three years. Which means the Canadian Royals had been trying to keep the truth about Billy being a prince from the public for a while now. Oops.

But why? And why come clean with the dirty little secret now?

"I bet the ranch the Boones knew they'd have the Canadian Royal Family over a barrel and could exact whatever they wanted from them," our royal insider shares. "Those fame-seeking clout-chasers were likely waiting for just the right time—right before the Investiture Ceremony." Things don't bode well for Canada's newest Royal Family member.

Poor Billy can't seem to do anything right these days. Now, after such a negative public reaction toward him and the Boones, can this cowboy ever get back up on the horse?

RELATED STORIES
Connie Looking to Marry into Upper Echelons
Connie the Secret Social Climber
Connie All Along!

Chapter Twenty

BILLY

After debating whether to confront Pax about what they had said, I thought better of it and chose to spend the following week and change going over my lines for the ceremony. Besides, every time I've passed by their room, they've been busy either snipping swaths of fabric or pinning them up. I'd also gotten swept up in royal treatment prep, getting primped and pampered with my first eyebrow waxing and mani-pedi, and a facial using LED light therapy that left me feeling like a fresh-faced baby.

This morning, however, I wake up with a pit in my stomach.

I don't know if it's because the ceremony is in two days or because I had such a bad fight with my best friend in the world and over a week later, we still haven't made up.

And what did they mean by *"We'd lose the Billy we love"*?

Were they really worried that would happen?

Have I really changed that much?

It's been weird not speaking to Pax at school. It's even weirder seeing them in the halls with an obvious spring in their step and not being able to ask why. Maybe there's more good fashion news.

Evenings, I've been attending my training with Gord. I

spent hours rehearsing for Saturday. I even managed to have high tea with Mom and Mack, who pointed out the light from her crystal cup sent a rainbow sparkling on the table-cloth. She's always saying it's Dad sending a rainbow, his way of saying "hi" and "I love you."

Over the past week, there's been no time left for violin, or for me. I feel like a shell, worn thin, and anxious about flying to Canada tomorrow.

But, Duty to the Crown above all else.

At least things with Edward are solid. He just about cheered when I told him that I invited Chef Pierre to the ceremony. I knew how bummed my brother had been after canceling his plan with the chef the night of our failed "twin swap." It was my small way of making sure Edward feels seen. Call it twin-tuition. It's also kind of a birthday present too, since the chef is secretly baking him a cake.

"Can you please pass the orange juice, dear?" Mom smiles at me from across the table on the veranda. Pax is seated next to her, refusing to meet my eyes as they roll berries around in their parfait with their spoon.

"Sure." I hand her the carafe, then continue buttering my toast. I can't look at Pax either. I just need to get through breakfast, and then I'll be off with Gord, rehearsing my steps and lines.

"Somebody's nervous," Mack says in a singsong voice be-side me.

I shrug and start adding orange marmalade to my toast. Pax remains silent.

"How's all your designing and sewing going? Have you con-tinued to receive interest in your clothes?" Mom asks them.

"Tons!" they announce loudly. They finally look at me. They don't smile. Jeez, this freeze out is rough.

A footman glides onto the veranda and sets down the tray of morning papers and tabloids.

I snatch the magazine on top, hoping it'll open wide enough that I can hide behind it. When I see the front cover of the tabloid beneath, my stomach drops. There's Mom and I, posing with arms around one another, cheesing for the camera.

Pax sees it at the same time. We both lunge for it, but I'm faster.

I scrutinize the headline: "'The Boone Family's Giant Secret,'" I read aloud, noticing the burst about exclusive photos being inside.

"Oh, come on, didn't we tell the staff to weed out the drama tabloids about us?" Mack gripes. Then she grins. "So, what's it say?"

Heart racing, I tear the tabloid open to the feature article—an exposé claiming that the entire Boone family is just a bunch of "fame-seeking clout-chasers" who knew all along that I was secretly a prince, and that Mom was simply waiting for just the right time—mere days before the Investiture Ceremony—to come clean with this secret, knowing she'd have the Canadian Royal Family "over a barrel and could exact whatever else she wanted from them."

"This can't be true," I say, gazing up, my hands shaking uncontrollably. I so fiercely want to defend Mom, to tell myself that anything a tabloid publishes isn't real, like what Daphnée's been reassuring me for weeks. Mom could never be that conniving.

Her voice cuts across the table. "Billy, what does it say?" She sounds strangely serene.

"'Sources tell us that Connie Boone has been paid off by the Royal Family to keep quiet for the past three years,'" I read aloud. I look up again. "Is this…*true*?" I ask her.

She looks very pale. She blinks the way she always does when she's trying to figure out what to say.

I can't help reading on. An accompanying article even goes so far as to insinuate that Mom is happy about Dad's death because it frees her up to marry someone in the upper echelons of society. She's painted as a selfish, scheming social climber. A knife twists in my stomach.

"You knew for the past three years that…that…" My vision shimmers.

Mom's eyes mist up, though her expression is still unreadable. Pax begins to chew their lip, looking to her.

I fling the tabloid onto the table. Mom regards it like it might bite her. "This isn't true. Is it, Mom?"

Mom shakes her head, visibly upset. "I don't want to talk about it."

Mack grabs the magazine and studies the full spread article, which is papered with personal family photos of us.

"Then it's true?" I demand. My whole body is shaking. It feels like someone is sitting on my chest. I can barely get a breath in.

"I'm not discussing this right now, dear." Her tone is firm, unwavering. Part of me wonders if she's keeping mum because she doesn't want the footman to overhear us as he clears our plates.

So it *is* true.

Pax peers at the magazine but still says nothing.

"Did *you* know all this time too?" I ask them on instinct.

Pax nods their head, avoiding my gaze.

"Mack? You too?"

"We didn't tell her," Pax whispers.

I gape in disbelief. My mom and my best friend knew I was

a prince and kept it from me for years? Absolutely unbelievable. I can't breathe.

"How did the *Daily Maple* get these old photos anyway?" Mom asks through tears.

Mack cringes and goes beet red. "I've been using old family photos to compile a virtual scrapbook for Billy as a congratulations slash birthday gift for after the ceremony. Someone must have stolen the photos off my laptop!" Mack races inside to investigate.

"Pax? Nothing at all to say?" I glare at them. "That's a first."

Pax looks shocked. They finally speak. "I guess Connie was right not to tell you the truth three years ago."

I fight my own tears, stinging my eyes. "But why didn't *you* tell me?!"

"Billy, I… I always thought you and Edward looked alike, but your styling was so different—and you always kept your hair longer and had so much scruff—I didn't think there was actually anything to your uncanny resemblance."

They give a sheepish smile. "But then one day, I made a joke to your mom and I could tell by her reaction that it wasn't really a joke. I made her tell me. I couldn't believe it. I wanted to tell you, but… I couldn't—"

I cut Pax off. "You've both known my true identity for the past three years? Is that what you're telling me right now?"

Pax slowly nods.

Mom opens her mouth, but just then, the footman reappears holding the teapot. "More tea, ma'am?" he intones.

Mom's eyes dart nervously and her voice drops to a whisper.

"I'll explain everything. Later. When the time is right."

"Explain everything *now*," I say through gritted teeth. "Please."

But Mom's already standing from the table and vanishes

inside, likely not wanting the footman to overhear any more than he already has.

I wheel on Pax. "How on earth did the world get the full scoop before I did?" I'm still trying to catch my breath—my whole body is buzzing. How does any of this make any sense?

Mack returns with her sparkly pink laptop. "I'm going to figure this out..." She flips open the lid and punches at the keys. Then she stops and stares up at us with wide, darting eyes, waiting a beat for the footman to head back inside, giving us privacy once more. "It looks like someone sent the photos from my email," she says in a low voice. "Look at the time stamp! It was sent two weeks ago. Oh, I knew I should have kept this thing password-protected!"

"What email were they sent to?" I ask.

Mack reads the address. "Cupcake28@CAN.mail."

"Edward," I breathe, thinking of his love for baking. "It has to be Edward."

"Yeah! That makes sense!" Mack chimes in. "I'm pretty sure his Finsta handle is 'CupcakeLover4Life'!"

"Edward?" Pax shakes their head. "No, he wouldn't do something so low!"

I shoot Pax a look. "You're one to talk." They flinch. "It *was* Edward. I'd bet anything." My thoughts start racing. "Granny told Edward you can dig up dirt on anyone... That must have been her insinuation that Edward should find dirt on *me.*"

"But why would he do that?" Mack demands.

Why *would* he do that...? I think hard, and suddenly Edward's voice sounds in my thoughts:

You don't have any giant secret, do you?

It would have to be really bad to strip you of your title...

"To justify removing me from the throne," I say, and I can feel it's true, deep in my bones.

"He wouldn't do that, Billy," Pax says softly.

The footman reappears in the doorway and extends a phone to me on a platter. "Your Royal Highness, His Royal Majesty the King."

Ignoring Pax's sudden flip-flop to defending Edward's character, I pick it up. "Hello?" My voice sounds weak and ragged.

"I'm guessing you've seen the *Daily Maple*." His voice is somber.

"Hi." I sigh. "Yeah… It's bad." My eyes lock with Pax's. They look like a deer in the headlights.

Daphnée's voice sounds in my ear. "We don't want to alarm you, but you should know that the story is getting picked up everywhere."

"Is it true?" I ask, sounding suspicious. "Has the Canadian monarchy been paying my mom to keep my true identity a secret?"

"Frederick and I knew nothing about this arrangement," Daphnée says. "That is, if there even was one. We're looking into it to see how valid the claims are, but I'm sure it's just the tabloids doing what they do best."

I sigh, allowing myself to believe her. "So…what are people saying?"

"The tide of public opinion is turning against you," Daphnée says, as gently as she can. "In a very significant way."

My stomach clenches. Here I was worried about single-handedly sinking the monarchy with a slipup during the ceremony. The fact this wasn't my fault feels that much worse. "Will I be okay? Will the Canadian monarchy be okay?!"

"The heat we're taking will cool off," Frederick replies. "We've sent a request to the Firm to see if they can deny these claims, or if the prime minister will be intent on stripping you of your titles and patronages."

My jaw drops.

"This may not come as a surprise," Daphnée adds, "but we have yet to hear back."

What happened? Pax mouths, but I ignore them.

I search for the words. "*Are* they going to take away my titles and patronages?" I think about how they might be gone before I even have the chance to memorize what all of them are.

"There's a chance," Daphnée says. "But it's too soon to know."

"Okay. What can I do?" I ask shakily.

"The show must go on, and the ceremony is still a go. After all, there are always rumors and tabloids. Just focus on the ceremony," Frederick says. "We'll handle the rest."

"That's right. We refuse to let the rumor mill stop us. Even if there's validity to the rumors, we'll find the person or people responsible for it. Keep your spirits up," Daphnée adds. "Please don't worry. Sending so much love your way, Billy."

They hang up, and I stare at Pax.

"You…you all ruined everything," I croak in disbelief.

They stare back, stunned. They've never seen me like this.

"Uh, what about Edward?" Mack pipes in.

"Good question. I'm going to go find out." I stand and stride from the veranda and through the hall, the tabloid crumpled up in my fist.

In the West Wing, I knock on Edward's bedroom door. "Edward?" I knock again. "Edward, it's me. Open up."

When no one answers, I push the door aside and peer into the empty room.

"Hello?" Silence.

I pull my phone from my pocket and call Edward, but no one answers. Surprise, surprise. I decide to FaceTime Neel next.

"Hey," he says, face filling the screen. There's a lot of background noise with bumping music and people passing behind him with trays of food. Who parties at this time of day?

"Where is he?" I demand.

"Well, hello to you too," Neel yells over the noise. "I assume you mean your brother. And how exactly should I know? I'd think he'd be headed to school right about—"

"Have you seen this?" I raise the tabloid in my hand like it's a decapitated head.

He peers into the screen. "Nope! Can't say I have. Does that headline say—"

I cut Neel off. "Seriously, where is he?"

"With his girlfriend, I'd imagine," Neel offers.

"Ha!" I snort. "He does love to lie, doesn't he?"

"Oh. He told you," Neel says. "Why are you looking for him? You think Edward has something to do with that story? No, dearie."

I clench my jaw. "How can you be so sure? All signs point to him."

"No..." he says despite his cheeks flaming.

My words come out fast. "Mack traced the leaked photos back to Edward's email."

"Fine. Maybe it *was* him. It wouldn't surprise me these days."

"Why wouldn't it surprise you?" I demand, narrowing my eyes.

Neel grimaces. "He may have tasked me with spying on you." He pauses, and I stare at the screen, not understanding. "He and Fi may have been sabotaging you this whole time."

"What?" I gawk. "No. That's... He wouldn't..." Then I think about it for a moment. "The Hall of Musical Instruments where he told me to play the violin. He wanted that to go badly, didn't he? The photo taken of me sleeping at the cathedral. He'd planned that too somehow, didn't he? And the false facts for that hockey interview… All those mishaps and near misses w-were Edward's doing."

"I shouldn't have said anything," Neel says hastily. "Listen. I told him to stop—"

"This is unbelievable!" I shake my head. My blood is boiling. I didn't think I could possibly feel this angry. "And you—you spied on me too? I thought we were friends!"

"I'm sorry. It started off as spying, but I genuinely began to care for you as a friend. I was kind of in a tight spot, what with Edward breathing down my neck. But that's why I'm telling you this now."

I scoff. "It's too late for that!"

Neel looks away. "Well, I'll let you go. But Billy, I sincerely hope you can forgive me. See you at the ceremony. Sorry again." And with that, he hangs up.

The silence that follows is overwhelming.

After my last day of school before taking tomorrow and the whole of next week off, I retreat into my room and sink onto the bed, barely registering the staff bustling around, filling my bath, carefully packing outfits for tomorrow's flight in my color-coded monogrammed royal luggage. I can barely look at the tabloid tossed face-up on my bedside table. My friends at school ignored me all day, along with Pax and Neel, and Edward was nowhere to be found. He must have chosen to play hooky after the news broke.

I still can't believe this. I thought I was actually starting to bond with my brother. Even though I've only known him for a couple of weeks, I find that somehow *his* betrayal hurts most of all.

I'm about to slip into the bathroom for my bath when I hear voices in the hall, voices that I recognize. After snatching the tabloid, I fly out the door just in time to see Fi hugging Edward. What are they playing at? Fake-dating…behind the scenes?

I realize I don't care.

She must spot me because she vanishes down the corridor.

He spins around and starts. "Billy! Why do you look so furious?" Is it my imagination, or does he look completely guilty?

I thrust the *Daily Maple* at him.

His face falls. "Oh. That. I heard."

"Fine! You win! Take your shiny crown. I'm done."

Edward shakes his head. "It wasn't me."

"Yeah right," I say, despite some part of me wanting desperately to believe him. The rage building inside me is winning out. "The crown going back to you is a total waste. You're not even worthy."

He scoffs. "What's *that* supposed to mean?"

"You're a total fake person. There's not one *real* thing about you. The Edward that people know…is a lie." I shake my head.

"Well, that's rich coming from you," he retorts, voice dripping venom. "Your family's been lying to you for years about who *you* are. You may want to look at them when you're calling out frauds."

"And thanks to you, everyone found out before I did!"

"I *said* it wasn't me," he snaps.

"How else do you explain the leaked photos and story?"

"No clue."

"You emailed them to yourself from Mack's laptop!"

"What makes you think *she* didn't email them to me?" he asks.

"Oh, please!" I say, exasperated.

"Fine. Believe me or don't. But listen, and I mean this despite how rotten you're being right now, when you say you're done…you know you can't just be a no-show for your big day."

"Watch me," I say snidely, knowing I don't really mean it.

"Me aside," Edward continues firmly, "there *are* other people counting on you. You're still Crown Prince, terrible tabloid article and all. If you won't do it for Mum and Dad, do it for Canada."

As much as it pains me to think it, Edward's right. I don't want to let Frederick and Daphnée down or be responsible for dismantling their newfound monarchy. I couldn't do that to them.

"Fine," I grumble, letting out a heavy breath. "But I'm not talking to you until…until I don't know when!" I turn on my heel and stride back into my room, slamming the door hard behind me.

I wish flying on a private jet was more enjoyable. I know how it may sound—how hard can it be to enjoy a cabin with shiny wood paneling and cushy seats with the Canadian Royal Crest embroidered in gold on the headrests? Full-service kitchen? Wide-screen TVs? But no one's talking, which fills the jet with a palpable cloud of stress. I'm mad at all of them, and with good reason.

Mom pretends to read a romance novel, Mack edits one of her latest videos, and Pax has their eyes shut with their ear buds in, likely listening to a Royals-themed podcast or Mariah. Edward watches what appears to be a Hallmark movie. Is he… *slouching?* I'm able to distract myself by rehearsing my speech.

Weak light from the setting sun slants across my speech cards, which the Firm has been agonizing over for weeks now, to get it just right, tweaking them up to the last minute. With the ceremony taking place tomorrow, there's still so much up in the air, which fills me with dread. Luckily, Gord got to Rideau Hall early this morning to help tie up any loose ends for me.

I feel Edward watching me, so I look away. I just need to focus on my speech and get through tomorrow, like Frederick said.

Just focus on the ceremony...

After an hour and a half, we touch down on an Ottawa runway, beneath a cloudy sky—one I hope will clear up by morning.

"Hello, Canada!" Mack cheers, sunglasses on despite the drizzle starting up and the fact it's basically nighttime.

I nearly slip and fall on the last step of the airplane stairs, but Edward catches me and smiles. Before I know it, photographers swarm us.

Our security entourage of five moves into a protective ring formation as a footman rushes forward and hands me an open umbrella.

Edward and I take it at the same moment. "May I?" he asks politely, his irritating perfect smile forming.

I want to tell him to get lost, but the photographers whistle, vying for our attention. I know by now to smile and wave. Maple Crown Rule 32.

With Edward and I both throttling the umbrella, we turn toward each other and laugh.

"Eat dirt," I say through my teeth.

"You're a pro at this," he retorts through his smile.

I fake another laugh. "Learned from the best."

We duck into the car and slam the rain out.

I stare at the rain-spattered window as the car bumps down one street before careening onto the next. Edward leans over to tell Pax about Ottawa for some unknown reason, and Pax giggles at every little thing he says. *Traitors.* I look out the window and practice breathing—deep, even breaths—unseeing the gray blur of the road.

Mack excitedly connects her phone to the car stereo and plays a jazzy upbeat French song, but it does little to lift my mood.

Eventually, we cross a bridge over a sluggish river, followed by another bridge soon after. A monument of Granny on horseback greets us before we take a narrow drive that winds through wet green lawns dotted with maple trees, and her last message flares to mind.

You know, you can dig up dirt on anyone…

Finally, the road widens, and we pull up beside a fountain in the roundabout outside Rideau Hall. It looms tall above us, glowing softly in the night, its lights illuminating the Canadian Royal Coat of Arms carved below the stone building's gently sloping roof.

House staff bustles to help us from the car and through the grand, arched stone doorway into a dry foyer with a dramatic chandelier. Frederick and Daphnée greet us as the staff whisks our bags off to our rooms.

A footman beckons me and I follow gratefully.

"Night," Mom tries.

I just shake my head and follow the footman. As much as it hurts me to snub her like that, she still hasn't explained anything. She said she'd tell me after the ceremony, that I should only deal with one stress at a time.

Upstairs, I'm relieved to set foot into my own private living quarters, where the house staff is already busying themselves with unpacking my bags and starting a bubble bath. I take in the elegant curtains, fireplace, and delicate crystal chandelier in the enormous room with intricate white crown molding on steel-gray walls.

There, in front of a gated mirror, is a mannequin wearing one of my outfits for tomorrow, steamed and pressed for me. The ceremonial outfit. There's a sparkling ruby red vest and sash, under a shiny white suit with twinkling shoulder tassels. I want to hate it, despite Pax's gorgeous handiwork and how the suit reflects light like fresh snow. I'm impressed they finished it in record time and left it for me to try on yesterday before it was overnighted here.

Tracing my fingers over the sharp crease of the glossy pants, I wonder where the Firm is storing the important items loaned from Granny. I examine the detailing of the vest before me, and the inner pocket of the ceremonial jacket, and think about what I'd give for a special someone to see me in this fancy getup tomorrow, or to be here by my side with gentle warmth and reassurance.

A little crisp white gift bag on the bedside table catches my eye. Inside, through a bunch of cherry-red tissue paper, I find a pair of maple leaf tighty-whities, with a small note in Pax's handwriting:

Happy Early B-Day, Bestie!
Part of the ensemble for your eyes only!
XO,
Pax

If there wasn't house staff flitting around me, I'd fling the tighty-whities onto the floor in anger. I'm too mad at Pax right now to appreciate the gesture.

A double knock breaks my thoughts, and I stash the underwear back down in the bag.

Gord stands in the doorway, wearing a cashmere sweater

and pristine dress slacks. "Welcome to the Hall, Your Royal Highness. How are you feeling?"

I let out a loud exhale, not sure where to start.

"There's no reason to be concerned," he continues. "You'll blink and find yourself at the after-dinner soirée."

I give a solemn nod, watching as the house staff finishes turning down the bed.

Gord smiles. "See you at 6:00 a.m. Get some sleep, and don't worry about a thing. I spent the afternoon personally steaming and pressing your outfit myself. You'll look perfect."

I try to picture Gord holding an iron. Well, that was unexpectedly nice of him. "Thanks." I smile back, despite what I'm feeling. Maple Crown Rule 32.

"Your Royal Highness." He bows then disappears along with the rest of the house staff.

Before long, I'm bathed and in bed, holding my speech cards under the lamp and going over my lines.

The job of a royal is never done.

Finally, I stagger out of bed and tuck the cards safely into the inner breast pocket of the ceremonial jacket, like Gord recommended, so I can easily pluck them out tomorrow, to read from during my speech. Despite having it pretty much memorized, and the fact a teleprompter will likely be there, with the added nerves of the performative aspect, I'm going to need those cards to anchor me in the moment. Maple Crown Rule 17: Stick to the script. I'm not breaking that rule again.

House staff knocks and enters to quietly wheel out my ceremonial outfit to bring it to where the event will be taking place. They replace it with the freshly pressed black suit I'll be wearing for my arrival, the same Frederick wore at his Investiture.

After they leave, I climb into bed and click off the lamp,

plunging the room into a darkness that makes me feel extremely alone.

Even though I know a staff member will be here first thing in the morning, throwing back the curtains to let the light in, I grope for my phone to set a backup alarm. I'm still terrified that by some awful accident I'd oversleep, like I did the morning of my Juilliard audition. I pick up my phone.

The screen blows up with notifications.

Article after article says citizens of the Great White North think I've proven myself to not be Canadian enough to rule the country.

The homophobic bigots who have been lurking on message boards are coming out of the woodwork, even stooping so low as to leave hateful comments on a happy birthday post on the @CanadianRoyals Instagram showing a photo of me at age three.

I shouldn't be reading this. Not now. If Pax were here, they'd smack the phone right out of my hand.

I try to recall what Daphnée told me, that despite the few bigots, I'm a role model for many, and will continue to be. Tomorrow, I'm not only representing Canada, but also the queer community, inspiring young out kids and closeted kids to step forward and shine.

Tempted to check my Instagram comments next, I open the app. The first photo in my feed sends a cold chill through me: Dustin at tonight's spring formal, looking dashing in a peach-colored tuxedo with a daisy in his lapel. He's posing with the whole basketball team. I've never seen him look happier. He's better off with them, and I'm better off with, well...myself.

Still, seeing him so happy while I'm so...*not*? Hurts.

I close the app.

I try again to sleep.

I have to do this. I can't let Canada down.

Tomorrow will be here in a heartbeat.

And I'll be ready.

Dad walks into my bedroom in the Park Avenue mansion, marveling at all the glitz and grandeur.

He sees me, and it's clear I'm the best thing in the room. He breaks into a chipper smile. That dip in his chin. Those bushy eyebrows. That full head of sandy blond hair. He walks toward me, and I run to give him a giant hug. I wish it would never end.

When we part, there are tears in his eyes. "Don't leave me behind."

"I won't," I promise. "I'll take care of the ranch. I won't leave you behind!"

He runs his hands through his hair, and his eyes widen as he lowers a hand to his face. It grips a clump of hair. In seconds, the rest falls out, revealing a sickly bald head. He looks up from his hand and into my eyes, then opens his quivering mouth to speak.

I bolt awake with one thought racing through my head:

What am I doing?

DAILY MAPLE ONLINE

THE ROYAL ROUNDUP
April 29, 10:33 pm ET

STAGE SET FOR CEREMONY: BILLY'S LAST CHANCE?
by Omar Scooby

From the venue to the guest list, here's everything we know about Prince Billy's Investiture Ceremony!

With mere hours to go until the highly anticipated event where Billy will be ceremoniously sworn in as Canada's future leader, the whole world is holding its breath. Earlier this month, Rideau Hall shared the location of the venue—Parliament Hill, a venue symbolic of the heart of the nation, in the nation's capital of Ottawa. It is said the ceremony will be held outdoors, weather permitting, to take full advantage of the Snowbirds' aerial display. Tens of thousands of people are expected to attend in person, while there's a predicted thirty million viewers expected to watch from home. Most of us can't wait to see who shows: the rumour mill expects the queen of England and her family from across the pond will be in attendance, along with the handsome Canadian prime minister. Of course, we'll see King Frederick, Queen Daphnée, and Prince Edward. We're hoping a sidelined Eddie won't be too crestfallen on the big day that was once set to be his.

April 30 not only marks the day of the Investiture Ceremony, but also the twinces' birthday. According to a tweet from Rideau Hall, the Crown Prince asked Chef Pierre, owner of world-renowned Pierre's on Park, to create a celebratory Maple Bacon Cake covered with cream cheese frosting and adorned with sprigs of maple leaves. The sure-to-be-delectable dinner menu remains a mystery, along with details of the private reception following the event. We'll report on everything as we know more!

Above all, most of us are wondering if Billy will be able to pull himself together enough to pull off the ceremony with decorum.

He's lost public favour in light of recent follies, and his defiance of royal protocol, but many have faith he'll put on a good show tomorrow and turn things around.

Regardless, the ceremony of the year starts Saturday at 10:00 a.m. EST—so whip up a fresh batch of Nanaimo bars and maple fudge, and solidify your Investiture Ceremony watch party plans!

RELATED STORIES
What Will Billy Wear for His Investiture?
Red Maple Carriage Set to Carry Canadian Royals
14 Potential Performers at the Ceremony
List of Billy's Charitable Donations
10 Ways to Look Investiture-Ready
Mack's Investiture Ceremony Biscuits for Royal Pup
Easy Recipe for Bombe Glacée Prince Billy

Chapter Twenty-One

EDWARD

Ensuring the coast is clear, I slip into an alcove and wait until the staff wheels Billy's ceremonial outfit into the corridor. They talk about needing to cover it with a sheet for transferring the apparel to Parliament Hill, where Billy will change into it before his speech, and then they're gone, leaving it unattended.

Now's my chance. I can't believe I'm doing this after all, but I bolt out of the shadows and feel for the speech cards in the inner pocket.

Got them!

After slipping blank cards in their place, I slide the originals into my own pocket and dash back into the alcove.

The staff reappears with a garment bag, which they carefully pull over the outfit. And then they're carting it down the corridor and out into the night.

I let out a deep breath. The stage is set.

Ever since calling off the prank, Fi's been pushing for me to reconsider.

"Seize the opportunity," she whispered shortly after arriving at the Hall tonight.

I folded my arms across my chest. "Fi, I can't. It's not right."

"Since when did you become all high and mighty?" she

asked with a mocking laugh. "He thinks *you* leaked that story to the press. He's already villainized you. So, do it. What's the harm?"

A sudden thought came to mind. "Did *you* leak his story to the press?"

"I *wish*."

I've known Fi for long enough to know she was telling the truth.

Fi took the moment to add, "Anyway, strike while the iron is hot. If there was ever a chance to get back your title, this is it."

She was right. As much as I told myself I'd be fine without the title, it's a lie.

Sorry, Billy.

I feel rotten, but this is purely business. Nothing personal.

Besides, I don't exactly feel warm and fuzzy toward him since our last few tense exchanges when his distaste for me has been potent. I haven't forgotten him calling me unworthy of being Crown Prince. I refuse to let his perception of me colour my own any more than it already has.

I'll show him, and the world—and most importantly, myself.

Shifting gears, I dart past rooms where house staff is giving chandeliers a check and polish, heading to the lobby, where Pax is waiting for me. They're wearing a discreet black track suit, but I'm still petrified about 1) people being up at such a late hour to see us, and 2) risking being seen at said hour with said cute human.

I stand beside the sofa they're seated on. "Hey there, hot stuff."

They turn my way, beam, and spring up. "Why hello!"

"Shall we?" I gesture toward the doors.

Within moments, we're skirting past the doorman and out

into the cool night. A security detail discreetly tails us. Lucky for me, all of our guards here can be trusted to keep their mouths shut, and the few out-of-town paparazzi have all gone home for the night.

One of the many wonderful things about Canada is that the pool of paparazzi here is quite small, due to its very strict privacy laws.

Clin d'œil.

We wander lazily through the grounds of Rideau Hall, admiring the neoclassical architecture, and sharing childhood stories, like how my family and I once snuck out of the house in costumes on Halloween, for one anonymous night of trick or treating. Halfway across the bridge over the Rideau River, I stop to lean against the thick stone banister overlooking the dark eddies of water, light from the buildings and lampposts reflecting off its windblown waves.

Pax stands beside me, so close we're practically touching. "Look!" They point skyward.

A shooting star is shimmering across the sky like magic.

"She's beautiful," Pax breathes. Then they bite their lip.

"What's wrong? Is this about that god-awful tabloid? I swear I had *nothing* to do with that."

"No, no, I know that. It's just…me and Billy got into a thing. About me keeping his identity a secret for a while. It'll be okay. I just need to talk to him and explain some things in more detail."

"Believe it or not, I'm not the biggest fan of secrets."

"Me neither!" Pax agrees. They laugh. "But here we are."

"Secret-keeping can also be a good thing," I say. "Why *did* you keep the fact that you knew Billy's real identity a secret from him?"

Pax sighs. "Honestly, it wasn't my secret to share."

I grin. "Fair. Well, I hope you two can salvage what you had."

"I hope so too." Pax turns to me, eyes widening. "Speaking of secret-keeping, can I tell him about…*us?* I'm starting to feel real sketchy keeping it from him! Especially after, you know, keeping his true identity from him."

The thought of us being an *us*, and of someone else knowing about us…unnerves me. "Yes. But can it wait till after tomorrow?" I ask, not sure why the thought of telling him, or anyone for that matter, terrifies me. It hits me: it's because it would make this *real*.

"Sure!" Pax's smile flags. "How are *you* feeling?"

"Happy," I confess, closing the space between us so that our shoulders rest against one another. The air smells wonderful, like sweet honeysuckle, and I'm uncertain whether it's Pax or the river.

Pax blushes. "I meant about tomorrow."

Unease ripples through me at the thought of still planning to move forward with Operation Twinvestiture, and Maple Crown Rule 2 comes to mind. Royal blood is thicker than maple syrup. The ten stolen speech cards weigh heavy in my pants pocket.

"I'll be fine," I reply. "And yourself? Excited to see everyone wearing a Pax original?"

"Yes! EEEEEE!" Pax exclaims. "It's wild to think that just a few months ago, I was sewing silk gowns for baby goats." They laugh.

"You're serious, aren't you?" I ask, deadpan.

Pax nods, stifling another burst of laughter.

"You've come a long way." I nod. "I'm proud of you."

Pax's eyes mist up. "Wow. Thank you. N-no one's ever told me that before."

"First time for everything." I gently take their hand in mine.

Their fingers are ice-cold, but within moments, I can feel them start to thaw.

"So, I know I'm technically a day early," says Pax, reaching into their bag, "but I couldn't give Billy a little gift without giving one to you too. So, this is for you. Happy birthday, honey!"

I take the wad of fabric they hand me and carefully unfold it. It's an apron, one stitched in gold with a cupcake topped by a Maple Crown and the phrase: **KING OF BAKERS**.

"I love it!" I hold it up, admiring it, then look up at them. "Thank you."

"Umm, of course!" Pax giggles. Then they look very serious. "Okay, I'm not good at being all sincere, but here goes: I'm proud of you too."

I try not to snort. "For what?"

"For showing up for Billy. For being such a good brother to him. And…well—" Pax's lower lip trembles "—for opening up to me, and for seeing me—the *real* me—and for being you. The *real* you."

A smile tugs at my lips. "I suppose I have you to thank." My own lip trembles, but it's quickly stilled by Pax's kiss.

I don't know how long we stand here, kissing under the starry sky that flickers with distant red and white fireworks. I allow myself to drift into bliss. We kiss until my lips are raw, and my nose is chilled by the night air.

When we finally start walking back to Rideau Hall, although we're no longer holding hands, I feel closer to Pax than I've felt to anyone.

By the time my head hits my pillow, I'm still grinning ear to ear.

But the smile fades as my guilt around tomorrow bubbles

back up. Even if I can betray my twin brother's trust, can I betray Pax's?

Perhaps I already have.

The next morning, the Investiture Ceremony is in full swing.

Even inside my private town car, I can hear the bagpipes, the drums, the fanfare—not to mention the whistling, roaring crowds packed up and down Wellington Street. Out the window, I see HeirHeads holding up official merch and souvenirs, along with Canadian Pride flags, signs raving about Billy's big day, and posters that say: **GOD SAVE THE QUEENS**. I'm trying to ignore the fact that today has totally eclipsed any and all of my own birthday vibes, but it's still a celebration nevertheless, even without the customary birthday parade to kick things off. I fondly recall my birthday party here last year. Then I recall how it ended. This year, no matter how badly today goes, it can't be worse than last year.

We roll up to the Centre Block on Parliament Hill, which looks every bit the symbolic heart of our nation, with Dad's royal standard atop the Peace Tower blowing proudly against a perfect blue sky, and banners bearing our family crest hanging from the Gothic Revival rooftops on either side. The grassy lawns out front are roped off, with a grand tent erected over chairs for family and friends, and a brimming media tent where camera crews are set up.

There couldn't be a better day for a royal ceremony.

I try not to think about the fact that I am pulling a life-ruining stunt on my innocent twin.

A spray of confetti rains onto the car. I doubt anyone knows who's even in which vehicle, with their tinted windows, but the exuberant fans have that electric energy today that everything is exciting. Neel would say all the hoopla is more over-the-top than a Bollywood dance number. I miss his friendship, *especially* today.

The squeamish feeling intensifies.

Something in the crowd catches my eye: a random stranger waves an antimonarchy sign, but then the HeirHeads swarm over him, pulling him to the ground. He disappears under-neath the crush of bodies. Leave it up to the fervent fans to wipe out any haters from raining on our royal parade.

Now that I'm looking, I notice there's a small smattering of antimonarchists at this end of the street, and a few antigay protestors parading around and waving signs at the opposite end of the street, both groups drowned out by chanting and yelling HeirHeads.

Hopefully, the fans continue their crowd control.

The car turns onto a side street and cruises past buildings until it stops in a petite parking lot roped off by security. I step out, met by a cool breeze blowing in from the Ottawa River, and by the roar of the crowds congregated on the main road, loud even from here. Camera crews gather around me as I'm led by security onto the Red Maple Carpet for a photo op, where I sink into a courtly bow for Granny, and wave hello to Uncle Liam, Auntie Caroline, Uncle Harold, Auntie Mataine, and my snotty younger cousins Alfred and Olivia among the assembly of lofty barons, dukes, duchesses, consulates, vice-roys, and viscounts. I'm astonished Uncle Liam chose to come. He hasn't spoken to Dad since he and Mum exited England, aka "Frexit," as it was so cleverly dubbed. He should make up with Dad, who forfeited his British right as future king and let Uncle Liam jump the line. Perhaps he's here to save face on the world stage. After all, anyone who's anyone is in attendance.

"Who are you wearing?" a videographer asks as I button my jacket.

"Pax Andrews," I reply with my dashing smile. While it's a simple burgundy suit, with a black feather bowtie and white shirt, it fits like a glove, and rivals the likes of my favourite high-end designers.

I join Fi, who looks brilliant in a glossy gown with layers of frothy tulle and inspired by details of famous Canadian landmarks, a diamond necklace on loan from Mum resting on her collarbones, and a maple leaf tiara clipped in her soft waves of ombré hair. "You look gorgeous," I say, striking a pose with her and hoping that if Pax were to look at us, they'd know they'd have nothing to envy when it comes to Fi and me.

"I know," she replies, moving her clutch from one hand to another and taking a few steps down the carpet as a team of people move with her, holding the long train of her dress. "You can thank Pax."

Speaking of my talented crush, I catch Pax's eye. They're standing farther down the carpet, looking amazing in jewel-encrusted loafers and a vibrant red suit with matching butterfly-esque cape. They dramatically flare it open to reveal a pearlescent silk lining, the whole look resembling the Canadian flag...but glam. They're talking to a camera, and the interviewer is loving it. I wish I could hear whatever fabulous thing Pax is saying or, better yet, that I could loop my arm through the crook of theirs. Mariah's "Sweetheart" sounds in my head.

"Earth to Eddie," Fi says, angling me to face a cameraperson.

Fi and I move along the line as news crews snap our photos, screaming out to us to pose this way and that.

The crowd goes wild as Mum, Dad, and Billy arrive, giving regal waves from the gilded Red Maple Carriage drawn by six bay horses with footmen in back and on either side. Ever-adorable Evie is sitting, perfectly posed, on an embroidered cushion between my parents. I realize that Pax has even made a custom outfit for the dog: a frothy tulle princess dress, bedazzled within an inch of its life. She's even wearing a tiny, jeweled crown and a faux-fur cape that drapes onto the carriage floor. Dad looks handsome in his military regalia and sword, hat, and white gloves, and Mum is beautiful in a one of a kind hat and ivory silk sheath dress.

It's apparent Mum and Dad have so much pride for Billy, the way they lovingly look at him seated across from them. My brother wears a smart black suit with epaulets, and medals, all borrowed from none other than Dad, the representation of the future change from old to new. I ignore a hot stab of jealousy. And to think I almost rode along with them, until Gord thought it would steal Billy's thunder. Not even joining the carriage procession in my own coach with Fi was on the table.

As Mum, Dad, and Billy dismount, the crowds reach a raucous cacophony, the voice on loudspeakers continuing to give the play-by-play of the royal cavalcade. Billy steps onto the carpet feet away from me. His smile to the cameras is magnetic, charming, perfect. Which is how I recognize it's put-on. He really is a quick learner.

He approaches me, grinning. "Edward."

"Billy!" I lance my arm around his back, and the two of us smile congenially for the cameras as helicopters loudly circle overhead.

He puts the flat of his hand on my torso and turns out to the news crews. He is *good*. If I didn't know better and were an outsider looking in, I'd think we were thick as thieves. I'd have no idea that Billy thinks I'm a traitorous, untrustworthy... Well, I really can't blame him.

I dial my smile up to an eleven and wave, and for an instant, it feels like old times. But today, the news crews and journalists are only calling out for Billy. A part of me aches at the thought that this event isn't in my honour. "I'm proud you're the one getting sworn in today," I say under my breath.

He ignores me and we begin to walk lockstep to the end of the carpet.

"Are you going to cold-shoulder me forever?" I whisper out the corner of my mouth.

He continues to smile and wave, smile and wave.

My cheeks flame despite my efforts to remain calm. "Regarding the photos, it truly wasn't me."

"I believe you," Billy whispers, and keeps smiling for the cameras. "And as soon as the ceremony's over, I want to hear your side of the story." If there weren't so many cameras trained on me, my jaw would drop.

Billy then leans over and accepts flowers from a little girl who's clutching a Billy doll with its own miniature cape and crown. A little boy hands him a piece of construction paper with a scribble of Billy and the words YOU'RE MY HERO in messy handwriting. I hear the crowds roaring his name, and see all the signs in the distance.

I'm struck with just how beloved and good-hearted he is. He has an admirable way of connecting with people.

Footmen direct Billy to the left, toward a side entrance in the Centre Block, where he will head to the Peace Tower. There, he will change into his ceremonial outfit, then await word to proceed back outside, down the lawn, and to the Maple Thrones lined up on the dais. All things I remember from my accelerated year of training with Gord.

Speaking of which, Gord appears in the doorway, beckoning to Billy. My twin brother.

Billy smiles at the grinning bashful little boy and girl, and stands, then hands the flowers and artwork to a footman for safekeeping. I can tell when Billy glances my way that we're going to be okay after all.

Something snaps inside me. I can't live with what I'm about to do to the brother I'd never even known I had. Blood *is* thicker than maple syrup. I grab his cards from inside my jacket pocket. "Billy!" Taking a shaky breath, I step toward him.

His eyebrow quirks.

I move to hug him. "Good luck out there." At the same time, I angle my body to block the view of the cameras, and drop his cards onto the ground.

We embrace, albeit a bit one-sided, then Billy steps back, staring at the fallen cards. "How did these get here?" He looks at me with distrust.

"You must have dropped them," I suggest with nonchalance.

Billy waits for a footman to rush over, pick them up, and hand them to him. Then he pockets them, glaring at me for a whopping split second. And with that, he disappears into the darkness of the doorway.

Relief washes over me like the sunlight streaming down the long drive as the clock in the tower chimes 10:00 a.m. I've called off Operation Twinvestiture. It's incredible how much better I feel now that the guilt has lifted from my shoulders.

Royal Family members and important persons fill the tent-covered chairs on the sprawling green lawns. The bagpipes drone on; the drums beat. A choir arrayed on the lawn begins singing "O Canada." A flyover from the Snowbirds paints co-lourful streams through the sky.

Flanked by priests, Fi and I begin to walk the solo proces-sion down the path as the drums pound to the rhythm of my own heart, as I think about what Gord once taught me about the importance of being a graceful loser.

"Is this what our royal wedding's going to be like?" Fi whispers.

The earnestness in her voice fills me with shame. At the same time, I realize I'd much rather be walking down an aisle with Pax. The thought makes my cheeks grow warm with surprise.

I spot Chef Pierre in a chair, almost unrecognizable without his white chef coat and black apron. He gestures to a nearby table, where a giant cake stands on a platter. I can't wait to enjoy a slice and catch up with him after the ceremony. I beam, waving. It was exceptionally nice for my brother to have invited him.

I made the right choice to call off the stunt with the cue cards.

On the dais before us, set up in front of the Centennial Flame, Mum and Dad stand at their thrones, a third throne between them ready to welcome Billy.

Fi and I peel off to the right, striding through the fresh-cut grass, and take our seats by the side of the dais alongside Connie and Mack, who are incandescent in their chic rose gold and fuchsia dresses and frothy fascinators, and Neel, and apparently his plus one, whose name is fuzzy to me, looking dapper in matching suits.

"Billy is talking to me again," I whisper to Neel.

"That makes one of us." He glances sidelong at me. I knew today was going to be different for many reasons, but not even being able to enjoy it with my best friend makes it all the worse.

"You know full well I had nothing to do with that story leaking to the press," I retort.

"Mmm-hmm. Sure." Neel keeps on looking ahead, posing smartly for the photographers.

A smile masks my frustration. Why can't I convince Neel, of all people?

But I'm also hit with the realization that maybe I'm a bad friend—I've never even met Neel's beau before today, and I forgot his name. Then it springs to mind. Maybe I'm not such a bad friend after all.

I reach my hand across Neel. "Leo! I've heard so much about you. Edward. A pleasure to finally meet you."

Neel freezes up, eyes downcast, head giving the most infinitesimal shake.

Crisse. What did I do?

Neel's date shakes my hand. "I'm Carlos." His sights flit to Neel, who feigns interest in the pipers ahead. But with his mouth pinched, I know I just totally stepped in it. Who knew Neel's date was an entirely different person? It would've been nice to have gotten a heads-up! Then again, I haven't told him about any of the goings-on in my love life lately… I suppose we're even. I sink back into my seat, loosening my collar.

Carlos softly excuses himself and vanishes back up the aisle. Something tells me he won't be returning. Neel must feel it too.

The music comes to an end. The singing stops. The toll of the clock fades. For a moment, it's silent—even the crowds on the street come to a hush. Fi takes the opportunity to slip her hand into mine. There's no pulling away this time, not with all the eyes on us as the hottest-looking couple here.

I keep facing forward, watching as Dad commands the Earl Marshall to summon Billy from the Parliament building, and the fanfare starts up again. This time around, the brass instruments are joined by the beautiful sound of strings. *Nice touch*.

Now Billy's ceremony can go off without a hitch, like it was always destined to.

☙ DAILY MAPLE ONLINE ☙

THE ROYAL ROUNDUP

April 30, 10:08 am ET

INVESTITURE CEREMONY: LIVE FROM EVENT!

by Omar Scooby

We're mere seconds away from watching Prince Billy get sworn in as official heir to the throne of Canada! Grab a sweet slice of tarte au sucre and your hot chocolate, and settle in, folks!

The Investiture Ceremony held at the nation's capital is well underway! Marching bands with bagpipes and the Canadian Grenadier Guards fill the sunny grounds of Parliament Hill outside the Centre Block, with guests bearing witness to the famous occasion that will symbolically mark Billy as official Crown Prince to the Maple Throne. Crowds of well-wishers line the streets and pack the town, erupting in applause and waving in enthusiasm as they bear witness to a historic occasion. "Long live Prince Billy!" people roared as his carriage trundled into view.

After the pomp and pageantry of getting wheeled onto the grounds in The Red Maple Carriage with his parents, the prince of the blood—or rather prince of the maple syrup—is out of sight, awaiting word to begin the ceremony. Members of the Royal Family continue to walk the Maple Carpet. Outfits are bright and vibrant, fitting for a ceremony full of hope and promise, blending centuries of British customs with a distinguished Canadian sensibility.

We look forward to seeing Prince Billy reemerge from the Peace Tower to proceed to the dais, where the King and Queen Consort of Canada will usher him as their devoted next-in-line. Stay tuned!

RELATED STORIES

How to Watch Prince Billy's Investiture Ceremony
Investiture Live Updates As It Happens
Happy Tidings from the Prime Minister

Wishing HRH the Prince Royal a Happy Birthday!
Royal Arrivals and Celebrity Sightings
How the Investiture Ceremony Will Unfold
Mack Boone's Rise to Stardom
Fab Fascinators for Any Occasion! A Pax & Mack DIY Tutorial
Young Prince Alfred Covers Ears During Loud Flyover
Freddie and Estranged British Brother Patch Things Up

Chapter Twenty-Two

BILLY

My heart feels like it's going to pound right out of my chest.

No amount of training with Gord could have prepared me for the intense panic setting in as I pace around the cavernous rotunda.

I try to focus on what I've learned about which flags are to be flown, which designs of armorial insignia have been approved for souvenirs, which badge of Canadian Herald Extraordinary is decorating the ramparts.

I try not to think of all the ways the ceremony about to take place outside these doors could go wrong, or the multitude of PR nightmare possibilities and what those could lead to.

Around me, the robed officials making up my procession stand in formation, their red-and-white robes bearing my insignia. I catch glimpses of the sword, scepter, ring, and crown resting on velvet pillows in their hands. One of the lords holds a Canadian flag. Another wields my personal flag, granted by Royal Warrant of the king of Canada, featuring grizzlies in blue and yellow squares, and a shield with the Maple Crown and purple bitterroot flowers.

I anxiously rub my thumb over my birthmark, tracing the raised edge. To calm myself, I peer into what must be the Hall of Honour with its Gothic Revival architecture, and notice the

symbols and coats of arms of provinces and territories carved
into the room's high arches. I stop when I start feeling dizzy.
Do I have vertigo?

I steady myself on the column rising from the center of the
room, then smooth the ceremonial outfit the royal style adviser helped me change into immediately after entering the
building: the Pax Andrews elegant snow white suit, plus ruby
loafers with silver maple leaf clasps, maple leaf cuff links, and
silver maple leaf brooch. I think of the custom tighty-whities
I've got on, and find myself smiling.

I put them on last-minute. Even if things with Pax and I
are weird right now, I still love them and know we'll somehow get past this rough patch.

I pull out my speech cards that Edward gave me with trembling hands. *"Votre discours m'a profondément touché. Je promets
de me consacrer entièrement au grand pays du Canada…"* Gord's
voice breaks through my thoughts: *It'll be a media firestorm if
you butcher your French pronunciations.* I can't afford to be so
nervous. And besides, people are on my side—minus a demonstration or two we passed by on the street, holding signs
reading **STOP SINNING** and **GOD HATES YOU**. Why are those
few voices always the loudest?

Truly, I just want the ceremony to be over.

Suddenly, Gord's words comfort me: *You'll blink and find
yourself at the after-dinner soirée.*

A ruddy-faced man wearing a feathered hat and brocaded
jacket with epaulets, with a curved sword in hand, enters the
hall. Everyone straightens up as he approaches.

I recognize him from my lessons as Canada's first Garter
King of Arms. "His Royal Majesty the King has summoned
you."

I nod, fighting the urge to belch. Is that a…*nervousness* thing?

Everything happens in quick succession: the lords and equerry shift into formation behind me, the Canadian Heralds of Arms officers standing at the front of the procession begin to walk down the flight of stairs and pass through the sets of double doors, the minister of foreign affairs for Canada strides ahead next, followed by the Garter King of Arms bearing the letters patent in a long cream-colored scroll of parchment.

And now, it's my turn.

Nothing could have prepared me for the adrenaline coursing through my body.

Out of nowhere, I think of when I was a kid and Dad would take me to breakfast at the Little Timber Diner as a special treat. He always looked over the top of his coffee mug at me as he waited for it to cool.

"I'm so lucky to have a good son like you," he would say, in that no-nonsense way, his big blue eyes boring right into my soul.

Boy, if he could see me now.

Pressing my eyelids shut and quickly wiping away the tears, I lift my chest and chin high, and, with a trembling breath, begin to walk. An unsettling calmness falls over me as my body accepts there's no turning back.

Before I know it, I'm past the flight of steps and through the grand archway of the Peace Tower leading outside. It's a perfect, warm and bright day. The sun hits me straight in the face, and I resist the overwhelming urge to flinch and shield my eyes.

MAPLE CROWN RULE 13: Have a royal presence.

I'm suddenly hyperaware of how my arms swing. How my feet fall on the pavement. I need to keep my strides even, keep up with the rest of the robed figures ahead and behind of me.

I hardly register the blaring fanfare and the shrieks and whistles from fans. This is so much more intense than rehearsals in the home gym.

MAPLE CROWN RULE 25: Remain tranquil in times of tension.

Drawing closer, it's hard to ignore the sea of guests filling the giant green lawns on either side of the path. But I can't let it pull my focus. The Canadian Ceremonial Guards in their red uniforms with fuzzy hats, rifles, and flags salute as we pass. Media crews take aim from under tents. Ahead, past the thrones on the dais and beyond the divide, the street bristles with hundreds of foaming, cheering, poster-wielding fans. But it's nothing compared to the millions—*billions?*—of people watching me worldwide.

Eyes forward. Sights level. Fill your lungs with air.

After descending another flight of steps, I start walking a long drive. I'm in the home stretch. Everyone stands from their chairs as I pass. It sounds silly, but I look for Dad in the audience. I remember how he came to every middle school showing of *The Sound of Music* even though I only played the priest who married Maria and Captain Von Trapp. There he was, front row, a fresh bouquet of flowers ready to hand me after every curtain, night after night after night. I never in a million years would have thought I'd be the one presenting him with a bouquet every April on the anniversary of his death. I know if he were here today, he'd have the biggest bouquet of flowers waiting for me. I let the thought disappear, like I always do, but I know it's never truly gone.

Frederick and Daphnée are tiny at the other end of the drive, where they stand on the dais, joined by the prime minister and people dressed in all black, most likely the members of the Firm. Even from here, I can see the high-backed, walnut-wood thrones with crimson upholstery, the fire of the Centennial Flame rearing up before them. My legs feel like they're going to give out on me.

Mom, Mack, and Pax smile proudly at me from the side of the dais. It's hard not to smile back. I'm glad everyone, including myself, seemed to put aside the drama, at least for today. Next to them, Edward nods with his sly smile, Fi blows a kiss, and Neel looks at me in awe. I can't help the corner of my mouth from upturning.

After what feels like a lifetime, I approach the dais and stop, like I'd rehearsed. My face blushes as I notice a huge camera on a crane homing in on me. *Just keep breathing.*

The Garter King of Arms hands the scroll of parchment off to Frederick, who hands it off to the minister of foreign affairs. Frederick takes a seat on his own high-backed wood throne beside Daphnée. I'm close enough now to make out the little maple leaf pattern of the crimson upholstery of my throne, empty and waiting. I kneel on a cushioned stool facing them, my head bowed low.

So far, so good.

The minister of foreign affairs, in his black suit, with gray hair and glasses, starts to read the letters patent into a microphone at the podium. "His Royal Highness Billy Benjamin Dinnissen, Prince of Canada, by the Glory of God of the Country of Canada, Prince Royal, Member of the Commonwealth..."

I sneak a peek up at Mom and Mack. Despite everything that's happened in the last forty-eight hours, I'm happy to see they're still smiling.

The minister of foreign affairs continues. "By putting a sword on his waist, a coronet on his head, a gold ring on his finger, a scepter in his hand, and also by transferring a mantle onto his shoulders, that he may one day govern there and may conduct and contend those parts. We have produced these our letters to be made patent, observe ourself at Parliament Hill, the thirtieth day of April in the eighteenth year of our reign."

I hear him rolling up the scroll. My flushed face is actually starting to cool, although now I have my aching knees to deal with. Who knew kneeling for so long would be this painful?

Marking the halfway point of the ceremony, the minister of foreign affairs reads the same letters patent, but this time in French. *"Son Altesse Royale Billy, prince du Canada, par la gloire de Dieu du pays du Canada..."*

Although my heartbeat is somewhat back to its normal rate, I desperately need to stand.

I just need to get through the rest of the ceremony.

MAPLE CROWN RULE 37: Patience is gracious.

I tune out the minister of foreign affairs, and study the intricate details of the empty throne before me, from its upholstery's white stitchwork to its pale, polished wood with a decadent royal crown carved onto the high headboard. I go over the rest of the run of the ceremony in my head:

After I'm sworn in, I'll stand, bend into a low bow—the Bow of Reverence—and take my throne beside Frederick. Then I'll step up to the microphone and read the first half of my speech in English, and the rest in French. This will follow with fanfare, and the procession back into the tower with Frederick and Daphnée. The Snowbirds will rip through the sky once more. The town cars will take all of us back to Rideau Hall. And I will be so relieved. Maybe even get my appetite back in time for the reception.

"And now the prince will receive the symbols of the royal office.

First, the sword of the motherland," reads the minister of foreign affairs, followed by the same phrase in French.

Right on cue, Frederick stands from his throne, looming in front of me. A robed person hands him the sword—the symbol of strength. He bends to loop its belt around me, and I help him adjust the sheath over my shoulder. I'm officially an earl now.

His expression remains tranquil, but even from my bowed position, I can see his eyes shimmer with undeniable pride.

At the sight, I'm surprised to fight the urge to cry.

"Then, the Maple Crown signifying sovereignty," continues the minister of foreign affairs.

The pillow bearing the gold crown swims into my periphery, and Frederick takes it—the symbol of sovereignty, its maple leaf peaks glinting in the sun. With the utmost care, he lowers it onto my head. The crown fits easily, then slips. I reach up to adjust it. *Phew.*

Frederick and I exchange a half smile.

"The gold ring signifying unity."

Another robed official brings the gold ring to Frederick, and I hold up my left hand as he fits it onto my finger—the symbol of my "marriage" to Canada.

"The scepter signifying temporal authority."

Next, I'm handed the scepter—the symbol of temporal rule—which I lift shakily in my right hand. I grip the hilt of the sword in my other hand—every miniscule movement rehearsed, practiced, perfect. I can see Gord beside the dais, watching intently, his expression more hawkish than usual, which I didn't think was possible. I know I'm doing him proud. And the rest of the Firm too.

"And finally, the mantle of responsibility."

Robed officials drape the Maple Mantle around me, and

Frederick gently taps each shoulder. Although it's mostly silk, the cape feels heavy, making me sweat. Is it time to stand?

When he's done, the robe is removed. Frederick steps back. Daphnée bows at his side. This all bodes very well.

"...*son Altesse Royale le Prince Billy, Duc Du Canada, est maintenant officiellement prince héritier du Canada*," concludes the minister of foreign affairs. Perfect. Only my oath and speech left to go.

Like clockwork, I hand the scepter to an official, and press my hands together as if in prayer, all the while keeping my head even so my crown doesn't fall off. Frederick closes his big, warm hands around mine. I close my eyes. It's time for my princely oath.

MAPLE CROWN RULE 17: Stick to the script.

"I, Prince Billy Dinnissen..." I say into the tiny mic clipped to my lapel, and stop to hear my voice echoing through the loudspeakers, cutting through the silence over the grounds. "Duke of Canada," I continue, keeping my eyes squeezed shut, "do become your loyal lord, and of temporal devotion, to lead and perish against all nature of hearts."

I open my eyes as Frederick bends and I give him a kiss on his cheek—the Kiss of Fealty.

And now my ceremony as official sovereign prince is almost complete.

All that's left is my speech.

Frederick moves to raise me up, and the celebratory fanfare starts to sound over the eruption of applause. I breathe a long sigh of relief. I can finally stand again. My knees will be so grateful.

I stand, then drop forward into the Bow of Reverence.

As I bend over, I hear a terrible noise.

Riiiiiip!

A gut-wrenching rip of fabric tearing at the seams. *Oh, no.* Did I step on somebody's cloak or dress? But there's no one standing that close to me. Then I feel a gentle breeze on my legs. On my...*naked*...legs... I gaze down at them in horror.

My pants have ripped all along the sides. They're down around my ankles in tatters.

Meaning the thirty zillion people around the world are staring at my tighty-whities too. The ones with the little red maple leaves.

Frederick and Daphnée exclaim something I can't make out. The prime minister and members of the Firm gasp, along with the entire crowd. The tension is so thick, you could cut it with a ceremonial sword.

Silence falls.

I gulp.

Everyone is still staring at me—or rather, at the mini maple leaves on my underwear. This could not get worse. Maybe I can salvage this, laugh it off, turn it into a joke.

"Guess there won't be any more questions about whether I'm loyal to Canada!" I blurt out, trying to smile. Oh, *no*! Did I *really* just put my foot in my mouth at the worst possible moment? I flail, bending to grab my pants in an attempt to scrounge them up.

Instead, I fall over.

My crown tumbles off and lands beside me.

Gord charges over. "Billy! What are you doing? This is wildly inappropriate!"

"I... I..." After I lift my crown from the ground, I leap up and wrap the Maple Mantle around me, my face flaming hot.

All of a sudden, there's shouting. At first, I think it's on my behalf, but then I see that rowdy fans from the main street are hopping the fence and charging toward me, being chased by the armed guards. Cries and yells from the crowd rent the air, mostly words in French I can't make out. The trespassers wave signs saying: **WE ♥ U PRINCE BILLY** and **BILLY PUTS THE CAN IN CANADA**. The HeirHeads stream in like an unstoppable wave.

Mom, Mack, Pax, Neel, and Fi are at my side in seconds, along with Edward, Frederick, Daphnée, the prime minister, and Gord. Who *knows* where the British half of the family's gone?

Armed officials escort us up the drive as guests flee in an ear-splitting frenzy toward the safety of the building.

Mom has one arm around me and the other around Mack, telling us over and over to keep our heads down between the occasional screams as people bump into us, and as we narrowly avoid the outstretched hands of berserk fans.

Pushed and shoved, it's not easy running through the press of bodies with a crown in my hand and a mantle wrapped around my waist. At some point, a fan steps on the hem, and I lose the mantle.

Now, I'm racing beside Mom and Mack in my undies. Hands snatch at my crown. One fan grips it. I yank it free and tuck it under my arm like a football, keeping my head ducked in the tumult of shrieks and shouts.

In front of the Peace Tower, the guards herd us into two SUVs with their engines already running. We roar off the campus, past more rabid fans who hurl themselves at the windows, screaming in excitement like it's a Black Friday sale at Dillard's. Some snatch up lawn chairs and paper programs like they're precious treasures.

In moments, we're heading back up the drive to Rideau Hall. All that matters right now is that we're safe. I look at Mom and Mack, their dresses torn and tattered, barely hearing Mom asking me if I'm okay, barely registering Pax, Neel, and Fi huddled in the back seat behind them.

"I can't believe we almost got trampled by a crowd of fans," I muse aloud, still in a state of shock. "And did I actually just make a joke to the world about my *underwear*?" I try to cover my lap as best I can with my hands, noticing my crown at my feet. "I can only imagine what the people of Canada must think of me now," I groan.

Forget about messing up the French part of my speech; this was unbelievably, horribly worse. The look on everyone's face only confirms it.

"They probably think it's cute and funny?" Pax offers.

I shake my head, wishing I could just dissolve. "I've ruined everything."

"How could this have happened?" Mom asks for the thousandth time.

It's late, but we're all gathered on the coral-colored couches of the Large Drawing Room at Rideau Hall, with its crystal chandeliers, gold mirrors, and portraits featuring the likes of King George VI. Looks like my prince lessons really stuck. Not that any of that matters now. Edward, Frederick, Daphnée, and Gord sit ramrod-straight, facing Mom, Mack, and me. It feels like a terrible recreation of that first meeting back in New York, after they had told me who I really was.

Now, I wish I'd never learned the truth.

"It was Pax's design," Daphnée says delicately. "They must not have sewn it right."

"We should have *never* agreed to that," Gord adds quietly.

Mom shakes her head. "Pax wouldn't have left all those stitches loose."

"No one's blaming Pax." Frederick looks pointedly at me. "What's done is done."

"People think *I* planned it?" I croak. "Wh-what's going to happen?"

Frederick wrings his hands. "Hopefully we'll find out soon."

The door bursts open and men in black uniforms—a mark of the Firm—step into the room. The frontmost man strides up to Frederick and bows then offers him a little scroll of paper tied with a thin red ribbon. "Your Royal Majesty, a decree from the Firm."

Frederick takes it from his gloved hand, unrolls the paper and scans it. "'The Firm, along with the prime minister, has determined that Prince Billy is not fit to rule and will be stripped of his titles, patronages, security, and funds,'" he says, his voice dull. "'Noncompliance will result in the Canadian monarchy as a whole being dissolved.'" Finally, something giant enough to get me the boot.

It's fair to say today is in the running for worst birthday ever.

"'The prime minister has called for a section 41 amendment vote at the House of Commons to push through this change in law so that HRH Prince Edward will be heir to the Crown of Canada.'"

The official salutes, turns on his heel, and vanishes back through the door, his comrades wordlessly following suit. Daphnée bolts up, as if she's about to give chase but thinks better of it, while Mom clamps a hand to her mouth, and looks from the door to me. Frederick slowly turns to us, the letter gripped loosely in his hand, which has fallen by his side. His expression fills me with icy dread.

I've never seen him look so drained, so defeated.

What have I done?

Chapter Twenty-Three

EDWARD

Our Rideau Hall residence is a good place to get lost, with its endless corridors plastered with portraits and art pieces of famous Canadians. It's also great for its sprawling grounds and all they have to offer. Growing up, I roamed the gardens and played cricket with Neel in the summers, and skated on the rink with Fi in the winters. But tonight, I'm not wandering aimlessly.

Tonight, I know *precisely* where I'm headed.

I tread through the central corridor where I cartwheeled as a child, past the door where I added my own crayon embellishments over Queen Jolee's daughter's paintings of tulips, and slink up the stairs to the sleeping quarters until I come to a stop outside Billy's room.

I knock lightly on the door. All evening, I haven't been able to shake the eerie feeling that's settled over my heart. I'm getting back the title of Crown Prince. I should be overjoyed. But the fact the victory was at my brother's expense has made it a hollow one. I need to talk to him.

When no one answers, I try once more, louder this time. It's late, and he perfectly well could already be asleep after such a long and arduous day. I wouldn't blame him. After what the world bore witness to, I also wouldn't blame him if he never wants to show his face again.

After a lengthy stretch of silence, I move back downstairs, striding through the high-ceilinged corridors with their pale yellow walls and ornate, antique rugs over hardwood. I don't know what I planned on saying, but I was certain he could do with more support.

The only other people out and about at such a late hour seem to be the house staff as they pack away food and decor, a dreary reminder that all the festivities have been called off.

There is nothing to celebrate—admittedly, not even for me.

To think I was finally starting to figure out who I was without the high title. A baker living a more relaxed life. Datable. Maybe even lovable.

I pause under an old black-and-white photo of Granny, thinking about what she, the Firm, and the planet must have thought of the whole debacle. I have to admit that it seemed undeniably conspired, from Billy's out-of-pocket comment to his perfectly themed, presumably planned out "ceremonial underwear." Although I still can't believe that he would have done such a thing on purpose.

"Your Royal Highness," says a staff member, slowing to give me a courteous bob.

I nod. "Good evening." The house staff here is always lovely. I watch her continue down the corridor. I'm glad it wasn't Fi, coming to find me to canoodle in the billiard room. A part of me wishes it had been Pax. As for Fi, I know perfectly well why she hasn't gone back to her house yet. She's hoping for a few more chances of being photographed strolling the lawns with me, wherever she is right now.

I keep drifting, no longer sure where I'm headed. I just need to walk. Outside the Long Gallery, there's the portrait of Mum and Dad square dancing, and the painting of me as a toddler, along with one of the former governor general looking a bit miffed, and one of Lord Stanley of Stanley Cup fame. I pause, wondering if Billy's royal portraits have already been canceled, if he's no longer the appointed sponsor of the HMCS *Vancouver*. If not, then it's only a matter of time.

The sound of clattering plates and clinking silverware draws me into the Tent Room, a vast space with pink-and-white-striped walls adorned with gilded portraits. I poke my head in by the entrance sporting Queen Jolee's portrait and see that the room is buzzing with activity: the staff is packing up the new china and wheeling out vases of flowers and a wood-cut beaver statue. It's where tonight's reception would have taken place, followed by an after-dinner soirée in the main ballroom, with tables arranged in formation beneath its dramatic Waterford crystal chandelier. At least the food didn't go to waste. Mum had the good grace to send it to the homeless shelter.

"A real shame. I was so looking forward to the reception."

Neel's voice startles me, and I spin around. I have the urge to hug him, to ask him if he wants to cross the river for a drink.

But he folds his arms across his silk housecoat, and what he said sinks in like chocolate chips falling to the bottom of a too-thin batter. This wasn't how I imagined our time together here going.

"Is *this* what you wanted?" His voice drips with displeasure.

"*Au contraire*. This is far from what I wanted," I reply with a swift shake of my head.

He purses his lips and blinks, unconvinced. "Oh, come on," he protests. "You've wanted this since the day you found out you had an older twin brother." A curious smile tugs at the corner of his mouth. "So, how'd you do it? I can't say I'm not impressed. What. A. Spectacle."

"I didn't have anything to do with Billy's unfortunate wardrobe malfunction. His pants literally came apart at the seams."

"So what, you cozied up to Pax and had *them* do it then?"

"*Sacrament!*" I blurt, and a few staff members momentarily freeze and glance our way before resuming packing.

"In any case, congratulations on getting your crown back."

"What's your deal? You've been so distant and cold to me."

Neel shrugs. "I feel like I lost you to your wicked schemes."

I snort. "Oh, that's *rich* coming from someone who was only too eager to help with most of those wicked schemes."

Neel shakes his head. "You went too far. Even by my standards. Everyone's blaming Billy for what happened. But I think I know the truth." He steps back out into the corridor, then turns around. "I'm leaving first thing in the morning. See you back in New York."

I watch him walk off and grit my teeth. I've regained my crown, but I've lost my best friend—forever, it seems. I don't know how to make him believe me, or how to make things right.

My phone dings.

Pax: Hey. Can you meet?

Edward: Now? Certainly. How's the greenhouse?

Pax: Aren't there, like, ten greenhouses?

Edward: Just meet me in the main hall.

Once I get to the main hall, I take a seat on one of the cool marble steps, and do a quick breath check into a cupped hand. I think it smells mostly fine. One can never be too prepared.

Footsteps sound, and I jump up and peer around the corner.

There's Fi, striding down the corridor in a matching pale-pink pajama set, hair in a French braid. I sprint up the few steps and into the main ballroom, praying she didn't see me. She passes by and keeps going, into the Reception Room. Talk about a close call.

After another minute or so, Pax arrives in glitzy floral pajama pants and a jean jacket on over a lavender tank top.

"Funny running into you here," I say lightly. I'm so happy to see them, especially after my acrimonious run-in with Neel.

Pax smiles. "Hey."

"Hello there." I notice they're holding a polished gold spoon with a maple leaf motif. "What's with the spoon?"

"Oh, it's a souvenir spoon from the ceremony." Pax tucks it into their jean jacket. "My grandma collects spoons."

"That's very thoughtful of you." I gesture down the corridor. "Care for a walk?"

They chew their lip. "Sure."

We head through the front door and pass under the port cochère as I lead us somewhere considerably more private at this late hour, aka the main greenhouse.

"So...how have you been since the blowout?"

Pax sputters their lips dramatically. "Terrible. Woeful. Languishing. Shall I go on?"

My eyebrows rise in a question.

"Even though no one thinks I had anything to do with Billy's wardrobe malfunction, I've been blacklisted. No one wants to touch me with a ten-foot pole. RIP my fashion career."

I turn to them. "Oh, Pax. I am *so* sorry. I hadn't even thought about that."

Pax shrugs. "Who knew nobody would want to work with a fashion designer whose garments fall apart at the slightest movement? Shocker, huh?"

I quirk my mouth, not sure what to say that could lift their spirits.

We keep walking until we enter the greenhouse with its lush green plants and trees, the night sky visible through the glass panels high above, the air smelling of fresh dirt, musk, and mint.

Pax gazes around. "Wow, this is beautiful." They turn to me and look like they're about to say something, but stop.

"What?" I probe.

Pax's eyes mist up.

"I'm sure people will be lining up for your garments again," I insist. "Give it time."

"That's not it." Pax shakes their head. "There's something else. Something...worse."

"What could be worse than that?"

"Billy is convinced *you* masterminded the pants debacle."

"Why does everyone think that?" I ooze exasperation. "Pax, you know—"

"I don't know anything. Maybe I just *thought* I knew."

My head jolts back as I distance myself. "What's that supposed to mean?" I glare. "Why did you even ask to meet? To throw blame on me? Everyone else seems to. Go ahead. Pile it on."

"No, not at all! Besides, you know that everyone thinks *Billy* did this." Pax hangs their head. "It doesn't matter anyway...because we're...we're leaving."

I gape, nearly at a loss for words, and regretful for snapping at them. "What?" My voice comes out hoarse.

Pax gives a little nod. "We're heading back to Montana. For good."

I stare at them in shock. "But you're going to come back, right? To follow your dreams? You're not going to be in Montana *forever*, right?" I start to laugh, then stop. "Right?"

They give a sad sigh. "That's the plan. And you'll be in Canada, so what does it matter to you anyway?" they blurt, their forlorn watery eyes locking on to mine. "Our flight leaves first thing in the morning."

I stare at them. "So, you're just…leaving? Going back home?"

"I have to be there for Billy. He's still upset with me, and I don't blame him, but he needs me." Pax sniffles, wiping their cheek. I can't tell if they're sad about Parsons, or about leaving, or both.

I take a breath. "Well, you're certainly a good friend. I think it's commendable."

They scoff. "Yeah, a good friend who lies to their bestie."

"There's something I have to share with you," I start. "You're not wrong about only *thinking* you knew me. I haven't been completely honest myself, and it bothers me that you don't know."

Pax's eyes widen expectantly.

"When Billy first stepped foot onto the scene, I was a bit jealous, and manufactured his little follies. The catnap fiasco? The hockey game embarrassment?" I raise my hand. "Guilty. I'm not proud of it. But you deserve to know. Now I can say I'm being my real self with you. No more secrets."

Much to my surprise, Pax bobs their head thoughtfully. "I get that. I wouldn't be all that jazzed either if my long-lost twin came to take my crown. Who am I to judge?" They screw up their mouth. "Well, thanks for telling me. So, *did* you do the pants—"

"*That* I did not do," I assert with a smile. But then my smile fades. "Pax, you can't go back home. That place isn't good for you—"

Pax shrugs. "Yeah, going home is kind of terrifying, but I'm an expert at slipping into survival mode. Keeping to myself, facing the hate with a smile and brushing it off. I can't be myself around my family. They don't use my correct name and pronouns, and they're constantly dismissive, but I'm sure I'll figure it out. Maybe I can move in with my grandma. She's actually really accepting of me."

I let out a sigh of relief, but my heart still aches. "That's a good idea. Try not to think about the negativity."

Pax nods. "I get better at it every day."

"Well," I say, fighting to keep my voice from breaking, "keep me posted and please let me know how I can help."

Pax scratches their chin with their shoulder, looking away, like they're done talking.

"What about...us?" I chance to ask, feeling a deepening sense of something I can't place.

Pax bites their lip, and their eyes well up anew. They shake their head. "Anyway, I should head back. If Billy finds out I met with his sworn enemy, he'd...well, he's Billy. He'd probably understand and it would be fine. But I... I should still go. Goodbye, Edward. I'll miss you."

I reach out and place a hand on their biceps, but they shudder. And now, there's clear hurt gleaming in their eyes.

"I just have one ask," they say, their lip trembling.

"Anything," I say, feeling my own eyes stinging with tears.

"Maybe you can...tell your parents that you don't want to be with Fi?"

I freeze. "You know I can't do that."

"Well, then that's that." They sniff. "It makes this that much easier for me."

Before I can say anything, Pax turns and walks straight out of the greenhouse.

They take my heart with them.

I shouldn't be surprised. The realm of the Royals is topsy-turvy. People come and they go. You learn when you're young not to get too attached. (Maple Crown Rule 50).

But this feels different.

"Eddie-Bear!" Fi emerges into the greenhouse, batting aside a row of leafy ferns to reach me.

Super. Just who I didn't want to see right now.

"Hey," I say, trying to hide my foul mood.

"What's wrong?" she asks, coming up short.

"Nothing." I force a smile. "What brings you out here? Come to hurl accusations at me like everybody else?"

"No. Not at all." Fi scoffs. "Housekeeping told me you were out here. They have leftover macarons. Come on, cupcake!" She waves for me to follow her.

Honestly, sweets *would* make me feel better right now. How is it that *Fi* is the one to make me feel a bit lifted tonight? Not Neel. Not Pax. *Fi.* Go figure.

We traipse back inside the building and into the Large Drawing Room, where macarons and tiny cakes glisten on tiered plates beside teacups and a steaming teapot gilded with Dad's royal cypher. There's also Chef Pierre's half-eaten Maple Bacon Cake. It's a shame he left Canada immediately following the mayhem. I'm just glad the cake miraculously survived the siege.

Fi takes a seat beside me and leans forward. *"I can't stop smiling,"* she whispers.

I raise an eyebrow. "Let me guess. Your vision of becoming queen consort is back and stronger than ever?" I cut myself a gooey slice of cake.

"It's within grasp, as long as I've got you." She blushes and sinks her teeth into a strawberry macaron. I'm absolutely convinced she's chosen it to match her pink pajamas on purpose. Then she bursts into a fit of irksome giggles.

"Let's wait and see, shall we?" Pax's words breeze past my

thoughts: *Maybe you can tell your parents that you don't want to be with Fi...* But I shove them down, like I'm so skilled at doing.

A footman fills my cup, and I take a slow sip of cinnamon-citrus tea, furious at myself for not just coming clean and telling Fi she doesn't have me, and never will. It's not fair to her. Every passing moment only accrues more pain for the day all hell breaks loose.

Gord steps into the room. When he sees us, he blinks. "Your Royal Highness. Lady Sofia." He takes a small plate and begins placing pastries onto it.

I take a bite of the Maple Bacon Cake. It's pure bliss. I can actually taste the maple sugar used in the sponge.

Fi wheels back on me with an elated smile. "I heard Billy's going back to Montana first thing tomorrow."

"I know." I squint at her, wondering how *she* knows. "I heard."

She laughs and lightly slaps my knee. "Well, don't sound so excited!"

"This is a good thing," Gord chimes in from behind a tier of treats. "Trust me. The amount of angry letters we've received..."

"Yes. Of course," I reply tartly, surprised Gord's being so candid with us. He's typically more buttoned-up. It's a bit catty, even.

"Heading back to Montana was Billy's decision," Gord continues. "For once, I think it's a good one."

Perhaps Gord's right. Perhaps Billy was never meant to be a member of the Canadian Royal Family, let alone *HRH The Prince Royal.* I simply nod and take another sip of tea. I can tell Fi is eating up Gord's words from the way her lips twist up into a cheeky grin like she's a Grinch GIF.

When I place my teacup back onto its saucer, Fi grips my

hands in hers. "This is everything we've been dreaming of!" she exclaims. "I know he's your brother, but come on, let yourself enjoy the moment. We *won*."

I slide my hands out of hers, reach for my teacup and drain it. "Well, I should head to bed." I stand, bidding Gord and Fi a pleasant night, and head back through the corridor.

As I pass the Small Drawing Room, I glance through the open doorway. I'm stopped short by what I see inside.

Billy's crown. Correction: *my* crown. Resting inside a spotless glass case. The other items of insignia are enclosed in similar boxes around it on little tables. No one else is present. It calls to me like a birthday gift, just waiting to be opened.

I walk over to it, double-checking I'm alone. The top of the box unclasps with ease, and I flip it aside and reach gingerly inside. I've waited my whole life to wear this crown. Why not? What harm would it do? The Maple Crown at long last...

When I place it on my head and catch my reflection in the ornate mirror above the fireplace, a smile spreads across my face.

When everything else fades away, a small sad voice says, *at least you'll still have this. You'll still have your crown. Always and always and always.*

But as my smile melts away, I can't help wondering:

What good is a crown without a heart?

Chapter Twenty-Four

BILLY

I have a throbbing headache that just won't quit.

I can almost hear it drumming against my pillow. Maybe my head hurts because I keep replaying what happened at the ceremony, over and over and over again, like a scab that won't heal because I keep picking at it.

I focus on something new each time. Gord's mortified expression. The minister of foreign affairs blanching. Daphnée taking a sharp breath. A robed official—and every member of the Firm, for that matter—going wide-eyed. A random news anchor rushing toward the dais. Each vivid replay makes me inwardly cringe, and after a while, it feels like I'm a whirlpool, just funneling down further and further. I don't know how long I let myself spiral.

My talk with Frederick and Daphnée only adds to my anguish.

"I want to go back to Montana," I told them. "To my *real* home."

Frederick and Daphnée both froze in surprise.

"You don't have to go. You can stay with us," Daphnée said.

Frederick gestured amicably around the drawing room. "Yes, there's plenty of room here for all of you. We'd hate to see you go, son."

I shook my head and let out a heavy sigh. "I should go back."
Frederick's face fell and he exchanged a crushed look with
Daphnée. "I suppose we can't make you stay if that's not what
you want in your heart."

Daphnée sniffed. "We're still your parents, Billy. No matter where in the world you choose to go, we'll still always be
family. That'll never change."

"Thanks," I said, deflated but unwavering, "but I need to go
back. Besides, I miss the ranch; it's probably where I belong."

"We understand." Daphnée scrunched up her mouth. "The
transfer of your title to Edward will be announced publicly
any day now. Of course, it needs to be put to a vote before
becoming law. We wanted to give you a heads-up in case the
messaging deviates from what actually occurs." She sighed.
"We'll miss you, Billy."

"And we're sorry," Frederick added solemnly.

The dejected look on their faces haunts me.

It's hard to imagine Frederick agreeing to approve the title
transfer. Then again, Duty to the Crown above all else is practically
branded in the mind of every Royal. I can't blame him for
whatever becomes of me. In fact, I probably deserve it.

I flip onto my side, hoping that lying in a new position will
stop the whirring thoughts. Now that my princely duties have
fallen to the wayside, I do that thing I do where I start thinking about Dad. Thinking about how mad I am I didn't spend
more time with him when he was still alive.

I play through scenarios where I wish I had chosen differently, like accompanying him to meet with a vendor in town
instead of hanging out with Pax, or just sitting with him at
the kitchen table and watching as he fixed himself a snack of
chips and hummus, or joining him on the porch in the mornings when he'd spend time alone sipping his coffee in the quiet

while looking out at the cows, instead of breezing past him to watch TV in the den, reruns that would always be there, reruns I had seen a thousand times before and would be fine never seeing again.

As usual, my mind travels back in time, allowing me to join him at the kitchen table as he reads the paper, taking in his messy hair, his every little detail and movement, his hand reaching for his pot of black coffee, the way he'd loudly clear his throat, the furrow of his brows. It's as if, by sitting there, I can soak up the essence of his presence, hold on to it, never let it go. The vision turns into a game of beating myself up. Why didn't I appreciate the little moments more? At least I can appreciate them now, even in the small comfort of a silent, sun-bleached memory. Even though it hurts.

I toggle back to another Dad memory, trying to find comfort in it. One of my favorite things was when he'd sing along to Italian music. His voice would crack on the high notes, and Mack would giggle and join in, and he was happy. We all were. He never stopped singing, until the day he could barely talk from all the chemo, the constant puking making his voice rough and ragged, too weak to utter a single sound. I held his hand. I smiled and told him everything was going to be okay, that he was doing great, that he didn't need to say a single word. Our love was unspoken. The worst part of Dad dying was seeing what it did to us. I grew up real fast, that hopeful innocence gone, marred by worry lines. I realized life is short, and that there wasn't much I found important anymore besides family. And, if I'm being honest, music. I miss playing.

Now I've ruined any chance for a fresh start, for that *something more*. At least I can go back home and forget all this ever happened. But of course it's not that simple. There's my brother, and Frederick and Daphnée. I'm not sure they ever want to see me again, and that's its own kind of heartbreak. If Dustin's still single and is open to making amends, maybe we could finally settle down like he always wanted. At least I'd be closer to Dad, be able to keep the ranch afloat—without any shady back channel deals with the Firm. I haven't forgotten that whole big mess, but it's been eclipsed by all the other troubles.

I've never felt more alone.

You'll always have me. Dad said that to me the day he died. I've survived the worst day. Which means I'm strong enough to survive this too. That's what Dad would have wanted for me.

But, what do *I* want?

I peel back the covers and sit up shakily. The room tips and pitches, reminding me how long it's been since I've eaten.

I'm out of bed and padding down the carpeted steps, trying to remember where the staff said the kitchens were. Believe it or not, this place is bigger and grander than the mansion.

I turn into a long hallway. Light spills from an open doorway. I peer into the room and freeze at what I see. "Edward?" I ask.

He spins around, the Maple Crown on his head, hands up as if showing he's unarmed.

I stare at the crown, how it fits perfectly on his head while it slipped on mine, as if he were born to wear it. *Because he was.*

"What are you doing?"

He hurriedly takes it off but keeps it cradled in his hands, like he can't bear to put it back in its glass box. "I was just walking around and happened upon your crown. Uh, *the* crown." He grimaces, lowering it into the box. I've never seen my brother act so uneasy.

"*'Your crown'* is accurate," I say, but all I can think about is how this is his fault. He's gotten exactly what he wanted. He didn't even have the grace to wait until I'd flown back home to get his hands on the crown. And to think I'd believed he hadn't been the one to leak our story, and was even willing to forgive him for it.

He looks at his loafers, and then glances at me. "Couldn't sleep either?"

I feel my anger subside just a little and shake my head.

He considers me for a long moment, with his too-perfect posture and serene expression, and I'm reminded of the rule: Remain tranquil in times of tension. I have no idea what he's actually thinking right now, but he can't possibly be at peace.

Finally, I can't take it anymore. "Might as well keep the crown on," I say resignedly. "Because I decided I'm going back to Montana."

He looks untroubled. "I heard."

"Pax?"

"And Fi."

"Of course. Word travels fast around here."

Edward lets out a deep breath. "I wish you wouldn't go." He almost sounds sincere.

Almost.

I laugh. "Good one." I start to turn back into the hall.

"I also know what Mum and Dad said to you," he says.

I pause in the doorway, not sure why I'm giving him the chance to keep talking.

"You're still their son," he goes on to say. "This is still your home. Do you even realize how cruel it is for you to leave them? Your decision to go is selfish."

"Whatever," I mumble. He's got real nerve name-calling right now.

"For the thousandth time, I didn't leak your photos and story to the press. I didn't even know about that. And I didn't have anything to do with what happened today."

"Sure." I step back into the hall.

"Connie wouldn't want you to quit. Or your dad."

I stop in my tracks and slowly spin around, feeling my face flush red. "You didn't know him." My voice sounds angry, but the truth is it's fighting back a sob. "Besides, he's not here anymore. And it's not like I have a real choice in the matter. What am I supposed to do? Stick around as Canada's...*screwup*? It's humiliating."

Edward arches a brow. "Fine," he finally says. "You know what? Do what you want. You showed up out of nowhere, took my title, and yes, I didn't like you in the beginning. But I put that aside. I've been there for you, I supported you, and now you're still going to turn around and blame something on me after I stood by you—"

"So all those pranks you pulled on me, what were those? You *'standing by me'*?" I'm so mad that I'm practically shaking. The corner of my mouth twists up in a snarl I don't even recognize. "Good luck with being king one day. With your knack for secret alliances, you're going to be great." My voice is unfamiliar, flat, full of venom.

And with that, I head back to my room to try sleep once more.

But just like earlier, I don't sleep a wink.

"Did they come by and get your luggage yet, dear?" Mom asks.

I slump into a chair in the sunny veranda and take a croissant from a basket. "Yeah," I grumble, thinking how it's far too early, and how the veranda smells far too strongly of fresh-brewed coffee.

"Oh, good." Her cheery demeanor is at odds with the fact she knows I'm still mad at her. We haven't yet talked about her secret dealings with the Firm, or any of the tabloid facts. Maybe it's for the best. At this point, the less I know, the better.

Mack enters the veranda wearing oversize sunglasses, a sparkly top, and jeans. "I don't want to go!" She stomps her sneaker, pouting. "I didn't even get a chance to say goodbye to my new friends at St. Aubyn's." Then she pulls out her phone and a smile washes over her face, her mood flip-flopping. Typical Mack. "At least my channel is doing better than ever. Maybe when we get back to Montana, I can turn it into a fun surviving-out-in-nowhere angle." Her expression shifts to amusement as she flips through her phone. "Billy! You're all over stan Twitter! You're a meme now! And they made a dance out of the whole thing on TikTok and remixed you saying, 'Guess there won't be any more questions about whether I'm loyal to Canada!'"

"Is that good?" Mom looks at me like I've got something to add.

I shove the croissant into my mouth and guzzle orange juice in the grumpiest-looking way possible. Croissant flakes fall onto my shirt but I don't bother flicking them away. I've dug out Dad's old flannel shirt to wear for the trip back home. It seems somehow appropriate.

Mack tilts her head at me. "Oh. He's still sad, isn't he?"

"Wouldn't *you* be?" Mom asks her. "Give him time, dear."

I grunt and rip back into my croissant.

"What about *me*?" Mack cries. "I'm getting sad too! We didn't even get to keep any of the nice clothes, even though no one else here at the Hall can even wear them. And I hate Montana!" She grabs a mini muffin from the basket and looks at it lovingly. "I'm gonna miss you," she whispers to it.

Mom chances a glance at me. "Have you said your goodbyes?" Her sights land on an old portrait of Edward with Frederick and Daphnée, and their little dog.

I shrug and take another bite. "I just want to go."

Pax enters in a lemon yellow shirt and matching capri pants with clean white sneakers. Their eyes bug at the sight of me in Dad's old work shirt. "What the flannel?!"

I look away, studying the ornate metalwork of my fork handle. "I'm not the high-end designer suit kind of person, remember? Never was. Before all this, I didn't even know which high-end designers were which. And I'm definitely no Crown Prince." I sigh loudly. "I should have listened to my gut and turned all this down."

"Well…" Pax tries. "There must be more to this provincial life. Ya know?"

Gord steps onto the veranda and clears his throat. "The car is ready to take you to the airport." He hands our IDs and passports to Mom, who tucks them in the front pocket of her pullover satchel along with our printed-out plane tickets. Mack groans and stamps her foot again.

"Great!" Mom's voice sure has a lot of pep to it. She places her fine linen napkin on the table and stands. "Let's go, dear," she instructs my sister, with that slight warning edge to her voice.

Mack sticks out her bottom lip. "UGH!" she whines, then marches after Mom. I sluggishly rise and head after them. I stop in front of Gord in the doorway, my mind swimming with questions I want to ask. How can I reach Frederick and Daphnée after I'm back in Montana? When will I see them again? *Will* I see them again? I'm still their son, and a Royal by blood, aren't I?

But all that comes out is, "Thank you. For everything."

He blinks his steel-gray eyes and smiles sympathetically. "Of course."

And that's it.

We sit in silence as the car pulls out of the circular drive,

past the Fountain of Hope (how ironic), and down the road
cutting through the sprawling green lawns—a reminder of
all I've just lost.

I look back one last time at the Hall, growing smaller and
smaller. There's nobody there. I feel pathetic for even looking.
Who did I expect to see? Someone running out and calling for
me to come back? Life isn't a movie. Of course there's nobody
there. Just security, following in a car behind us—they'll be with
us at least till we board the private jet. Then it's back to the dol-
drums. Frederick and Daphnee gave me the option of having
security come with us, but I requested they don't. I want zero
reminders of my royal life.

I know it was ultimately my decision to head home, but I
can't stand the thought of staying. I've spent the past several
weeks pouring my heart and soul into what I needed to learn
and become, only to fail. Epically. I went from a no-name
rancher in Montana to the Crown Prince of Canada, thrilled
to inspire the LGBTQIA+ community, a community dealing
with so much hatred every day.

Now I'm headed back to being a no-name again. At least
the ranch is still there, a constant in the chaos. And the whole
Investiture debacle will make one heck of a story one day.

I face forward as we exit through the gates of the property. A
few foreign paparazzi spring out from behind the plaque marking the entrance to the grounds. I wonder how long *that* will last.

I'm starting to see why Mom was afraid of no longer having my security detail around. Hopefully, paparazzi are the
worst of it.

We rumble past them and the big blue signboard that says:
BIENVENUE À RIDEAU HALL.

Au revoir, Canada.

DAILY MAPLE ONLINE

THE ROYAL ROUNDUP
May 1, 9:37 am ET

THE LION, THE WITCH,
AND THE WARDROBE MALFUNCTION!

by Omar Scooby

We see London, we see France, we see *Billy's underpants*? In brief, yesterday afternoon while the Prince Royal held his Investiture, millions worldwide watched Billy drop trow, setting off a full-scale media storm. Most Canadians were amused, but at the end of the day, things aren't boding well on the political stage.

With news of Prince Billy being briefed on how his big day would go down, showing off his Canada-inspired briefs was not what anyone had in mind. The world watched as the now eighteen-year-old made it through most of the ceremony by the seat of his pants.

But after receiving his items of importance and bowing down, his trousers—and our jaws—dropped. The spectacle gave being caught with one's pants down a whole new meaning. The incident hijacked the event, and chaos erupted as HeirHeads bum-rushed the scene. Fortunately, no one was harmed as police moved in.

While some think the brief incident was an accident, most believe it was more than a little slipup. An insider close to the designer alleges intent behind Billy's wardrobe malfunction. "Why else would the briefs have been Canada-themed if they weren't going to be shown? It was clearly premeditated."

Regardless, Billy's botched ceremony coming to a screeching halt can't be good for the Canadian Royal Family, who had looked to the Investiture as a way to secure the future of the Maple Empire. We wouldn't be surprised if Billy's cheeky prank got His Royal Majesty the King's royal knickers in a twist.

In response to furious pleas from parents, officials at the Firm issued a statement: "We are just as shocked, and profoundly apologize to all those offended."

The Undies Stunt begs some questions: What will become of Silly Billy? Will his ceremony be rescheduled? Or were his days as Canadian Clown Prince as fleeting as his peep show?

RELATED STORIES
BREAKING: Outraged Parents Demand Apology
You Too Can Have Ripped Butt Pants: Where to Buy Billy's Briefs
Rideau Hall to Deal with Prince Hill-Billy
Slice of Investiture Cake Sells for $5,000
Fan Arrests at Ceremony: 623 and Counting!
HeirHeads Caught Selling Investiture Souvenirs
British Royals' Harrowing Encounter with Fans

Chapter Twenty-Five

EDWARD

"Get a load of this! The article says, *'An insider close to the designer alleges intent behind Billy's wardrobe malfunction,'*" Fi reads off her phone from the sofa across from my bed at the Hall. "So the world really *does* think Billy was behind it."

Fighting the reflex to shout that Billy would never do something to intentionally humiliate himself, I shake my head and sink back into my pillows. "It wasn't Billy," I say quietly.

"Well, if it wasn't us, and it wasn't him, then…?" Fi narrows her eyes in annoyance.

I'm starting to regret convening in my room to pore over all the controversial headlines. Every media outlet has the same claim: what happened was a planned publicity stunt that Billy set up for scandalous attention, the kerfuffle of his own design.

"Maybe they *were* just really poorly made pants," I offer, not actually believing Pax could ever poorly make *anything*.

Fi shoots me a look. "Oh, please. You're thrilled your brother has finally left so that you can reclaim your precious title."

"You're starting to sound like Neel," I mutter to my coffered ceiling.

"You're avoiding my keen observation. You're thrilled Billy's out of the picture. Admit it!"

I can't make her understand my reality—that I'm truthfully very much torn up about it. Even if Fi *were* to understand, she'd jump to thinking I wasn't on board with her grand plan of becoming queen consort. Not that I *am* on board with that plan. I just don't want to talk about it; I'm missing Pax a lot already.

In fact, I can't stop thinking about them.

"Do remember it was Billy's decision to banish himself back to Montana," I say matter-of-factly. "And quite frankly, I don't blame him. If the entire nation had seen *my* unmentionables on TV..." I don't bother to finish. I can still see the hurt and humiliation in Billy's eyes.

Fi scrutinizes me. "Are you actually going to *miss* him?"

"Perhaps." I idly keep scrolling through my phone.

"Have you seen this one?" Fi lets out a mocking laugh. "This article claims the Investiture Ceremony broke the record for most searched event in a single day. Wow. I'm gagged. How funny!"

"Hilarious," I say flatly, peering over at her. "Honestly, you are cold."

Fi beckons me with a finger, the other hand patting a sofa cushion. "Then come over here, Eddie-Bear."

"*Why* are you still here?" I ask pointedly.

"Your Royal Highness," Gord interrupts from the door. "Your presence is promptly required." I could kiss Gord for saving me.

I slide out of bed and wriggle into my slippers, cinching my cotton housecoat at the waist, and follow him out to the veranda. Dad's reading his daily despatch documents from his red-and-white box, and Mum's sipping her maple ginger tea and perusing the *Ottawa Citizen*. They look up at me, followed by Evie's fluffy head poking up from Mum's lap where she'd been napping, given away by the fur matted on her face.

"Edward." Mum sounds downtrodden.

A footman pulls out my chair and I take a seat.

Dad gives my forearm a little shake. "Morning, son."

"Morning." The footman pours me a cup of piping hot tea as I try to read Dad's expression. "So? What's the latest?"

He rubs a hand back and forth across his forehead. "Isn't that the question of the hour?" He sighs. "As you know, a lot's transpired."

"And more's still transpiring," Mum adds warily, scraping honey onto a scone. "Now, I know you and your brother have grown close, darling, so please don't worry about figuring out how you'll continue to maintain a good relationship with him. We can solve it together, as a family. We want to keep him close in our hearts, but of course we have to respect his decision to return home."

"And we have to do what's best for our monarchy." Dad gives a tired smile. "This is all a complete disaster."

From his spot in the doorway, Gord nods in agreement.

Mum continues. "As much as we'd like to figure out how to keep Billy close at the moment, there are more pressing matters at hand. Yesterday's disaster of a ceremony, and the fact he's returned home, is all anyone can talk about. It has marred our image. Not irreparable, but also not ideal."

Dad groans. "Apparently, it's giving Granny agita. She can't seem to shake the image of him standing there in nothing but his ginches."

I can't help chuckling.

"Edward," Mum says cheerfully, ignoring my bout of laughter. "Your father and I have something to share." They exchange a nervous glance.

I freeze. "If you tell me I'm secretly a triplet, *pour l'amour du Christ*—"

Mum chuckles. "The Firm had a wonderful idea to help

shift the focus back to you." She takes a full breath and holds it, smiling a bit too brightly.

"And…what might that be?" I ask before taking a sip of tea.

"You're in love with Sofia, aren't you?"

I nearly spit out my tea. *"What?"* I check to make sure she's not suddenly standing in the doorway behind Gord.

"Of course he is, aren't you, son?" Dad prompts.

I look from Dad to Mum like they're extraterrestrials. "Where exactly is this going?"

"What do you think of the idea of making things official with Sofia by proposing?"

"Proposing *what*?"

"Well, marriage, of course," Dad says matter-of-factly.

This time, tea sprays from my mouth.

Mum blots her cheek with her napkin, too preoccupied with my reaction to care.

"Think of it as a way to change the media narrative," Dad says. "You're young, but you're in love. What's the harm in speeding up the timeline?"

"The timeline?" I stand. I can't breathe. I need to get out of here. "What timeline?"

"Only if you'd want to go through with it, of course," Mum inserts. "It is just an idea."

"One that the Firm *highly* encourages," Dad adds.

They each look to Gord, who mulls it over. "It's true. It would certainly help matters."

They *can't* all be serious. "What about, oh, I don't know, planning and announcing *my* Investiture Ceremony?"

"We will definitely be having one for you later this year, but there's no way your Investiture Ceremony will be able to supersede Billy's. Not like how a royal wedding can," Dad says.

"We could arrange for Fi's parents to join us for a pre-wedding dinner, encourage well-wishers to send gifts to our charities, give the whole country a day off—" Mum blinks, recognizing my panic. "If you love her, darling, what are your reservations? You know when it comes to true love, we're always for it."

Where to begin? They do recall I'm only eighteen, right? As of yesterday?

I slowly sit back down.

"If I may," Gord interjects with a respectful nod. "A royal engagement would the perfect distraction and would reflect well on the Canadian monarchy. In the wake of Billy-gate, the Firm's decided this is what's best, with a royal wedding to follow."

"*Écœurant*," I say flatly.

"Your father and I are doing our best in light of recent events. So, we'd like to arrange a private dinner for you and Sofia at Casa Loma, but *only* if you're comfortable."

"You're serious?" I say, eyebrows climbing.

"It's what's best for the monarchy," Gord says, and from the affirming looks his words garner on my parents' faces, I know it's the end of the discussion.

"Why are you so opposed?" Mum reaches out and takes my hands. "Let's talk it out."

Every fibre of my being protests. If I'm to be engaged to Fi, what do I do about Pax? I can't think about that now. I'm back in the hot seat, and I don't want to drop the ball—not if my refusal could give the Firm yet another reason to toss the Canadian monarchy as a whole into the old rubbish bin.

"I…suppose I'm not that opposed," I lie, forcing a smile.

Dad leans back, clapping. "Excellent!"

Gord signals to a staffer standing just inside. She enters with a tiny black velvet box that she hands to Mum, who hands it to me. I stare at it, feeling along the scalloped silver edge.

"Well," Dad says, his eyes playful, "open it."

I pop it open and gaze at a gold ring shaped like a serpent with ruby eyes, diamonds, and an emerald. Seeing it suddenly makes this more terrifyingly, gut-wrenchingly real. I think I'm going to be sick. "Mum, this is Queen Jolee's engagement ring," I manage to say.

"Oh, I sent out for it yesterday." Mum beams, looking lovingly at me. "And now it's yours to give to Sofia." She clutches Dad's hand. "So, what do you think, Edward? It would mean our monarchy's reputation would be restored."

"I thought we weren't going to take it out of the royal vault here until I'm ready to get married."

"But honey, aren't you?" Mum asks.

I stare at the ring in disbelief. I want to tell them how I actually feel. It's not too late to back down, to tell them the truth. *Maybe you can tell your parents that you don't want to be with Fi...*

But I can't. I'm not strong enough. Especially seeing Mum's eyes mist up, Dad's toothy grin. They want this so badly. No, they *need* this so badly. *We* need this. I don't have the heart to crush their hopes, not after everything they've gone through these last twenty-four hours. I must keep our monarchy alive and well.

I nod. "Okay," I utter. "I can do that." I suppose I can figure out what to do about Fi later.

"Fantastic!" Dad cheers.

"Terrific!" Mum adds.

"Now, when were you thinking this proposal would happen?" I look to Gord, who shifts from foot to foot.

"Here's the thing..." Mum says slowly, calculatingly. "It should be swift."

"How swift is swift?" I inquire.

"Tomorrow," Dad says. "And we can set up the venue like *that*." He snaps his fingers.

I gulp. *"Tomorrow?"* I grin. "Tomorrow."

Crisse.

CANADIAN ROYAL
COMMUNICATIONS

1st May

STATEMENT FROM HIS MAJESTY THE KING

The monarchy is surprised by the unexpected incident at Prince Billy's Investiture Ceremony.

His actions are being taken very seriously by the Royal Family. We are having private conversations to discover a path forward for Billy and the rest of our family.

ENDS

Chapter Twenty-Six

BILLY

Under the blue Montana skies, the rental car crunches along the dirt path toward our ranch.

It feels so strange to be back. It's greener now, and there's grass as far as the eye can see. The cows look healthy too, with shiny coats and bulging sides, the sheep grazing peacefully, barely stirring as we pass. It was a somber time getting through security and flying for three hours, with the occasional strained question or curt remark. No one's said a word since climbing into the car. Even Mack isn't speaking—unless you count the occasional vlogging of the landscape—and that's saying something.

You really don't know what you have till it's gone. I hate how that message keeps coming around in my life, like a rotating door.

We roll under the sign for the Old Boone Ranch as Pax texts me. After Pax came home with us, we dropped them off, and I had a good talk with them while Mom and Mack hung out in the rental car. Their text says their grandma made welcome-home tuna casserole, which is Pax's favorite, and they ask how I'm doing. I suggest meeting up tomorrow, and that it'd make me happy. Especially since our good talk outside their grandma's house mended our rift.

"Pax, for the last time, why didn't you tell me?" I'd demanded on the sunken stoop.

"For one, I didn't want you to move away and leave us all here in Little Timber."

I huffed and rolled my eyes, thinking of how selfish they sounded.

Pax bristled. "What good would it have done for you to know?"

"It would have meant everything!" My cheeks flushed, and I took off my cowboy hat to wipe my forehead. "You knew I was literal royalty and didn't tell me."

Pax bit their lip. "Billy, I truly never thought of it that way. All I ever thought about was that it meant you weren't blood-related to your dad, and your relationship with your dad was something I always wished I had." Their eyes misted up. "You had the most amazing relationship with him, and I saw how losing him broke you apart. I thought about telling you the truth, but how could I do that to you? You didn't seem like you could handle one more thing. So... I did what I thought was right. And, I'm sorry if I made the wrong call. It wasn't my place to tell you, and I wanted to respect Connie's wishes of keeping it a secret."

I released a shaky breath. "You know," I said softly, "if the tables were turned, I honestly don't know what I would have done. So, I can't be mad at you." At that, I pulled Pax into the biggest hug.

"Oh. And one more thing. I've been dating Edward in secret. Or at least, I was."

"*You what—*"

Mack's voice cuts through my thoughts. "Home sweet home," she says into her video. She's thankful she hasn't lost her millions of followers. I don't bother telling her that it's probably only a matter of time.

Mom stops short at the gate, which the ranch hand opens. It feels strange knowing they've been on the Royals' payroll all this time.

I take the moment to look up at Dad's oak and say my ritualistic greeting to him, this time in my head. I have a hard time being vocal about these things with other people around.

The ranch hand waves at us as we pass by before he closes the creaky gate behind us. A closed gate; a closed chapter.

Is the memory of my whirlwind time going to be enough?

Speaking of closed chapters, I still haven't heard from Dustin, and I don't expect to. The wild thing is, a part of me really does miss him. He was synonymous with home. It's strange being here as a single guy. Not that I'm in a rush to date again. Right now, I just want to hide from the world. To think for a few weeks there I thought my life was going to be different.

"Almost there," Mom says in a playful singsong. "What's the first thing you want to do when we get back?" She likes to use such conversation starters whenever there's awkward tension.

"Nap," I mumble, rubbing my finger along my birthmark.

"Maybe I'll film ASMR in the barn!" Mack muses. "Okay, that sounded way more exciting in my head."

I keep my eyes trained out the car window. There's Junebug and Lucky Lady galloping alongside us. Seeing them brings a smile to my eyes. I've missed them, and it's nice being back around them.

In front of our house, Mom deposits us with our bags, then putters off to park, kicking up a cloud of dust that sends Mack choking and hacking. The temperature is in the high seventies, and I'm wiping sweat off my brow from just standing still.

We stare together at our little ranch home, a far cry from Park Avenue.

"It's weird to be back." Mack turns to me. "Are you sure you don't want to shoot an apology video?"

"I thought you said apology videos are never a good idea and only admit guilt and come off as super insincere?"

"Yeah, but I'm desperate!" Mack whines. "I gained a zillion followers, and I know my surviving-on-a-ranch rebranding isn't going to keep them. Apology videos get a bananas amount of views. Who knows? Maybe people would even... forgive you?"

I snort. "For what?" I shake my head. "It would probably just make things worse. Besides, I don't even have social media any more, remember?" The Firm shut it down, which is all fine and well. It just means I won't be anxiously reading any more vicious comments.

Mom joins us, wrestling the keys out of her bag, and opens the door. We trail her inside, dragging our bags. It smells unfamiliar, musty even. I wonder if it always smelled like this, or if I'd just never noticed before. The foyer is dim, and the hot air feels stale.

"I miss Evie!" Mack moans. "Mom, can we get a dog? Please?"

Mom unshoulders her bag. "We have horses. Why don't you go feed them, dear?"

"Ugh. I hate it here!" She stalks through the den and disappears out back.

I get myself a cup of water at the kitchen sink and see the jar of maple butter sitting on the counter right where I left it, glossy red ribbon and all. A keepsake from another person's life.

I start lugging my suitcases to my room.

Mom catches up to me. "I am so sorry."

I turn around. Her face trembles. With Mack outside, she's finally letting the strain of everything that's happened crack her otherwise solid resolve.

"I think I need to take a nap," I groan, pivoting back around.

"Billy, will you please hear me out? I'd like to explain some things."

"Oh, so *now* you're ready to explain?" I snap. "It's too late. It doesn't matter anymore."

"Billy...may I at least try and explain what happened?"

I stride through the hall and roll my suitcases into my room. Mom appears in the doorway, not giving up.

I kick off my cowboy boots and toss off my hat, then climb under my covers, yanking them over my head.

After a minute, I hear Mom say, "Fine. You don't want to talk." The door quietly clicks shut, and I'm alone.

I wonder how long I can stay under here.

Waiting eventually leads to sleeping.

"Look on the bright side, Billy. You can get back to your music now." Dad slides my violin toward me. His big blue eyes are wide and hopeful as ever behind his wire-frame glasses, and he's got that wide goofy grin on his face that always makes me smile. I nod. He knows just what to say. What I'd give for one shred of advice, or a single word to cling to, to follow like a guiding star.

"Can I take your order?" asks the waiter.

I look up to find it's Frederick. Seeing him in a greasy apron makes me chuckle. What's he doing working at the Little Timber diner? When I look back at Dad, grinning, he has hurt in his eyes.

"Billy, you've replaced me."

My smile goes. "No, I would never! You have to believe me!"

Frederick sits beside me in the booth and puts a possessive arm around my shoulders. "Son," he says, then looks at Dad. "Who's this?"

"Dad, I'd never replace you!"

I wake in the strange gray light of dusk. The sound of Mack's voice filters in from the hall. "So, after I give the horse a glitter mark, who wants to see how to pick dirt out of its hooves? It's gonna be the most satisfying thing you guys have ever watched!" The dream fades back into the muck, in the swamp of memories, losing details with each passing second. Like I know my time as Crown Prince will, little by little.

I stagger out of bed and decide to start unpacking my bags, not quite ready to set foot outside my room. I pull my violin out of its case. I can't believe I've only played violin a few times since we left. I recall the music gala at the MET, and the night Edward came out to me.

I unzip my violin case and begin to fine-tune my strings when my phone lights up.

Dustin: Billy, I wish nothing but the best for you. Take care.

I let out a sigh. *He wasn't a perfect fit, but he was a good first love. And that's okay,* Dad would say.

I heart the text. It's not just his final goodbye making me uneasy. I don't know if it's because I rested and can think more clearly now, but I feel bad about how I treated Mom. I should hear her out.

I pass by Mack in the hall, who's struggling into cowgirl boots, which don't exactly go with the sparkly gown she has on—one she managed to steal from her royal wardrobe, I might add. Typical...

"Want to make a cameo in my vlog?" Mack asks.

"Stop trying to exploit me," I say playfully, rubbing sleep from my eyes. We've already so easily slipped back into our routines.

Like usual, I find Mom seated in the kitchen doing book-keeping—hopefully nothing to do with the Royal Family this time—in her worn lavender bathrobe, her hair in a ponytail, a slice of fresh bread from her bread machine, and a pepper-mint tea steaming in the lumpy old mug I made for her in ceramics class many years ago. I had forgotten how much she loved that mug.

When she sees me, she folds up her reading glasses and blinks.

I sit beside her and sigh. "I'm sorry. If you're ready to talk, I'm ready to listen."

She nods slowly.

"Tell me everything."

"Okay. Where do I begin…?" She methodically brushes invis-ible crumbs off the rough-hewn wooden table. "Starting when you were both in high school, Edward was officially a public fig-ure. The press was hungry to make up for lost time and his pic-ture was everywhere. That's when I realized you and the prince looked identical." She lets out a little laugh and shakes her head.

"Like that *People* magazine cover?"

"Yes. That was the first nonbaby photo of Edward. He was celebrating his fourteenth birthday. I brought that magazine home and couldn't stop staring at it, at the uncanny resemblance."

She takes my hand. "Since you were born in a hospital in Canada too, I started to wonder. I actually became a little ob-sessed with figuring out this mystery. First, I found out you were born on the same day, in the same hospital. Then I called the hospital to track down the nurses and beg them for infor-mation. As you can imagine, I was shocked to discover—" her voice breaks "—my biological son…died. And that you… belonged to someone else." She takes three sharp, shallow in-hales, fighting a cry.

I squeeze her hand. "That must have been awful for you." My own eyes mist up.

Mom laughs. "It was terrible. I felt like I *had* to contact the Firm, which actually worked. I told them all about you—

everything—and well, this part makes me feel just rotten, but the person I was dealing with quickly bribed me with money. He said not to tell anyone about who you really were. He said if I did, there would be a media firestorm. But that's not why I went along with it." This time, tears fall unchecked down her cheeks. I hand her a crumpled paper napkin to blot them up.

"I was so afraid that the second you found out you were a prince, you'd immediately want to leave us. That you'd want to leave *me*. My Little Miracle…" She's trembling, and it hurts my heart to see her cry like this.

"I didn't know what to do," she continues. "I was terrified of losing you, but then your dad got sick and that became my only focus. I wrestled with whether to tell your dad the truth, but I couldn't risk ruining his final days."

In a way, I'm glad he never found out.

I give Mom a weighty nod. Now I understand.

She sniffles. "After your dad died, I was desperate to help keep the ranch going, so I reached back out to the representative and told him that I'd continue to keep the secret if they helped support us. And they did. That tabloid article got it right, for the most part. And I am so sorry. I had planned on telling you. I hope you can forgive me."

I wipe my eyes. "Mom, it's okay. I don't blame you. I forgive you. It's okay."

She takes a steeling breath. "When Pax noticed your similarities, I confided in them. I didn't mean to, but I'd been keeping it a secret for so long, and they kept pressing the issue, and it all just kind of came out." She gives a sad smile along with a sigh of relief. "I'm sorry for keeping the secret from you. It's just that… I love you so much. I was terrified of losing you." She dabs at her eyes. "Especially after losing your dad," she adds softly.

"It's okay. We're back. We still have each other, and that's all that matters. We'll figure out the rest."

"I won't lie. It's nice to be back home with all the memories of you two growing up."

Her mention of childhood fills me with guilt. "I'm sorry again. For missing Easter egg dyeing this year."

Mom shoos the air. "Oh please. I've already forgotten about that." Then she looks me square in the eye. "Remember what I said right after you found out you were the crown prince?"

"Wh-what did you say?" I ask, my mind a foggy, emotional mess.

"I told you that maybe this was all fate. Maybe this is how things were always meant to be." She smiles. "Watching you in New York, I saw what an amazing prince you would have made."

I avert my eyes. "Well, thanks. But it's moot now. I pretty much ruined any chance of being Crown Prince. All signs point to the title officially going back to Edward. They should be announcing it any day now."

Mom shakes her head. "You'll always be a prince in my eyes. No matter what happens." She grips my other hand.

"I love you, Mom." I take in the details of her, bookmarking this memory, from her happy smile to the steam rising like a ghost from the chunky mug I made for her so long ago. "I can tell you're glad to be back."

She fights a sob. "I really am. I'm sorry."

"There's nothing to be sorry for." I hug her. "I know how much you love this place."

She kisses my cheek. "Thank you for understanding. You've become a wonderful young man. Your dad would be proud."

CANADIAN ROYAL COMMUNICATIONS

2nd May

STATEMENT FROM HIS MAJESTY THE KING

Today my family had very productive conversations on the future of my sons and our family.

We honour and accept Billy's wish to step down as a full-time working member of the Royal Family. He has made it apparent that he does not want to be dependent on public funds. It has been agreed that he will move back to his home in Montana.

Edward is being counseled regarding the possibility of reinstating his royal title as Crown Prince.

These are complicated circumstances for my family to settle, and there is much work to be fulfilled, but I have requested for a final resolution to be decided upon in the coming days.

A vote will take place in the House of Commons, where a unanimous result will confirm the right for the title of Crown Prince to return to Edward.

ENDS

Chapter Twenty-Seven

EDWARD

"Are you going to tell me what this is all about?" Fi rests her head in her hands, a bemused expression creeping across her face. "I'm not getting any younger."

The queasy feeling that's settled over me has ruined my appreciation for the beautiful night here at Casa Loma. The place is one of my absolute favourites. It used to be a tourist attraction until Mum and Dad made it a home away from home after the city of Toronto practically gave it to them as a gift for the new monarchy. Typically, I'd be curled up inside reading a book, or taking a nighttime stroll through the gardens, admiring the trimmed hedges.

But tonight is certainly no typical night. Far from it.

The staff has set up a table for two outside in the main garden, with radiating heat lamps that are a bit too turned up. The fountain spurts anxiously in view. Beyond it, spotlights throw a sickly glow up onto the stones and turrets of the medieval castle estate. The night would be so much more romantic were I with Pax instead, but I shove the thought away.

"Will you please relax?" I reply in a low voice.

Across the table, Fi looks like a vision in a black velvet dress with a plunging neckline and a set of pearls resting on her collarbones. She wears matching drop pearl earrings, and her sleek hair is up in an elegant bun, two loose tendrils framing her face. She looks the part of a prince's fiancée. I'm wracked with guilt. But what else is new?

I just want to pop the question and be done with it already. She quirks an eyebrow at me. "Well, fine then." All during our flight, she ruthlessly needled me for details. She guessed correctly at one point, but I didn't let on a thing. She forces a giggle. "At least try to look a little less constipated. We have an audience," she says through her blindingly white veneers.

Lo and behold, the paparazzi invited here tonight have been strategically planted around the premises. "I'm pretty sure I saw a drone hovering overhead when the staff brought out the hors d'oeuvres," I say with a syrupy sweet smile.

Fi nods. "The more drones, the better." Under the table, her foot finds mine.

I resist the urge to move it. "You look dashing, Fi. Truly." She scoffs. "Ditto, cupcake." Her smile lessens a smidge. "Well, we don't have all night. Get on with it. Whatever it is you want to say…or *ask*… You're seriously killing me."

Ditto, cupcake.

Thankfully, we lean away from each other like a parting bascule bridge as the staff clears away our dishes and refills our goblets with ice water from a sparkling crystal carafe, and then it's just the two of us again.

I grope the little box in my inner jacket pocket. "I have—"

"I always forget what a charming place it is here," she cuts in, not paying attention to me anymore. She takes in the hedges, the rows of tulips, the fountain. "We haven't been back since we were kids." She shoots me a simmering look. "Remember? We'd play tag? And one time, I pushed you into the fountain and you ran off crying?" She snorts. "Dork."

I narrow my eyes at her. "How is it every story ends with me crying? In fact, I don't know if *you're* even *capable* of crying."

The photographers continue to snap away, the shutters like clicking insects in the fringes of the night.

Fi gives them a cursory wave. I take the moment to slip the box onto my lap. I realize that my throat's gone cotton dry.

"It's wonderful how they're shifting the focus back onto you," she says in a low voice. "Or should I say *us*." She licks her lips at me.

"Quite," I say, mustering my strength. I take a few quick sips of ice water, which isn't nearly enough. "Now—"

"I couldn't have planned it better, even if I *hadn't* tried," she continues softly.

I fidget with the box on my lap, my expression inquisitive. "Right. Anyway. I have to ask you something—"

"Oh, me first!" She grips the edge of the table and tips toward me, eyes smouldering.

"Alright then," I submit, my racing heart thankful for the momentary reprieve.

"Well, I wasn't going to say anything," Fi confides, "but since you're making this dinner way more cryptic than it needs to be, I may as well spill some tea." She brightens. "Okay… Guess what?"

I tilt my head down and twirl a hand for her to get on with it.

"I was the one who leaked the Boones' embarrassing family photos." She beams as if expecting me to compliment her.

But my whole body stiffens and my face falls. "Fi, that was a rotten, terrible thing to do."

"Edward." She taps the skin between her eyebrows. "Frown

lines." She looks over her lustrous shoulder and blows a kiss to a paparazzi, her French manicure twinkling.

I don't care that I'm less than camera-ready. I keep glaring at her, clenching my jaw.

"I want to make sure they have some candids and some posed photos. Give them options." She laughs when her sights land back on me. "Oh, please. You know you secretly love what I did. He's out of the picture, isn't he? I couldn't trust you to take care of matters, so I took them into my own hands."

"Why would you do that? And how did you learn about the payoff?"

"I only sent the photos." She giggles devilishly. "Mack really should have that laptop of hers password-protected. It was just sitting there on the coffee table. The *gardener* could have gotten into it. Anyway, when I saw the photos she had open, I sent them to my dud email, hoping to find something useful. They turned out to be *uber* bland, and not the most flattering, so I sent them to the press hoping they'd use them somehow." She shrugs. "I have no clue who leaked the story part of it, but if that isn't serendipity, I don't know what is."

I snort. "You really expect me to believe all that?"

She smirks. "It's pretty unbelievable, isn't it?"

"You don't get it," I say flatly. "I'm actually really upset."

And that's when it clicks. This is how Neel must have felt when he said I took things too far. I can't even believe it. She unwittingly made Billy and everyone else think *I* was to blame.

Not to mention doing something arguably so much worse.

I let out a deep, measured breath. "You *ruined* Billy's life."

And others' too, I think. *Like Pax's life.*

Fi titters. "Edward, who *cares*?" She shakes her head and laughs. "Honestly."

"*I* care!"

Fi stares wide-eyed at me, delicate hand to her chest. "Edward, your reaction is surprising, to say the least. I was just trying to help. Besides, like I said, I didn't cause the scandal—I just shined a light on it."

I pocket the ring box under the table. "It's over," I say.

"Edward." Fi angles her head and gives a put-on pout. "You can't be serious."

"Whatever we have, I'm sorry." My voice trembles. "But I'm done." Not *quite* what I had in mind for this evening. I can't say a small part of me doesn't feel some relief in the rift.

Fi's hand goes to her pearls. "I thought this was what you wanted! I...love you. I'm *in* love with you."

Now, it's my turn to laugh. "You *love* me? You're—*what*?"

"Yes." She looks genuinely wounded. "Aren't you?" I've never seen her look genuine *anything*. She isn't joking. She loves me in a romantic way. Guilt gnaws at me, unnerving me. Unfortunately, I don't have feelings for her, try as I might (blech!). I hope Fi can forgive me for what I'm about to say.

I lean across the table. *"I'm gay!"* I whisper.

The words feel foreign on my lips, but also right at the same time.

Fi falls back. "I thought we... Wow." Tears spring to her eyes.

"I'm sorry I didn't tell you sooner," I say, deflated but still trying to be truthful.

She uses her ring finger to blot the inner corner of her eye. "You dragged me into this mess. You led me on. You...you *liar*."

She looks repulsed. Pretty rich coming from her. Regardless, I owe her decency now.

"You know it's not like that," I try. "Think of my environment. Not exactly lenient."

She shakes her head. "I'm so clueless," she mumbles, sniffling.

"You know if this got out, it would ruin me," I add in a low voice, eyes darting to the hedges.

"Save it!" Fi snaps, her sorrow replaced by ferocity.

"I was aiming on telling you sooner. I—I never meant for you to get hurt—"

"It's too late for that."

"Fi, I'm so—"

She lifts her water goblet and chucks its icy contents at me.

I stand, gasping, before registering that my face and chest are dripping wet, my shirt clinging icily to my skin.

She stands too, throwing her napkin onto the table, before turning on her heel and clomping toward the rose garden. "Hey, you can say you've seen me cry now!" she calls back.

"Where are you *going*?" I hiss, flicking water from my chin. How do I explain to my parents why they ended up with distressing water-in-the-face photos versus romantic proposal photos?

"I'm sure one of these shutterbugs can give me a ride to the airport!"

The paparazzi chases after her, asking for a statement. I *pray* she doesn't give them one about my *petit secret*. Not when I'm looking for smooth sailing as reinstated Crown Prince…

Even *she* wouldn't be so low as to out someone. Right? I'm pretty sure she knows that's a cancelable offense in the public sector.

But the more I think about it, the more I begin to kick up a worry wind into a worry *vortex*. My heart is racing.

Did I seriously just come out to her?

And is she going to tell everyone?

Tabarnak.

Inside the castle, changing out of my soaked suit and into dry cotton pajamas never felt so good.

I climb into my dark-wood canopy bed, warming my shivering body, and stare at my phone, considering what to do. My incessant fretting hasn't lessened. Although I know things aren't entirely back to normal with Neel, I still hope my best friend will support me when I tell him about what happened.

Edward: Hey, I came out to Fi. It didn't go well. Call me back?

I'm surprised at how quickly my phone rings. Maybe Neel isn't so mad at me after all?

But then I see his face. He's obviously still not feeling particularly understanding right now—still upset at me for roping him into my schemes with Fi and likely ruining any sort of friendship he had with Billy—and quite possibly his romantic relationship with Carlos now that I think about it. I comfort myself with the thought that he obviously still cares about me too or he wouldn't have called.

"What happened?" His voice is flat.

I tell him about the whole fiasco.

He sniffs. "Sorry to hear it."

"Thanks…" A thought comes to mind. "Well, at least I have some good news. I kissed somebody."

His eyebrows rise as high as a perfect soufflé. "What! Who?"

"Pax," I say, feeling myself blush.

"Wow. Well, good for you." He doesn't look particularly surprised. It stings.

There's a long silence. It's clear he feels he's fulfilled his friend duties by checking in on me. I can't blame him for still being upset.

"Text me if you need anything else." He hangs up.

"I miss you," I say to the darkened screen.

I contemplate texting Billy next, but after some pondering, I think about how ridiculous that would be.

I haven't said a word to him since he basically told me to drop dead.

Maybe Pax would be open to hearing about my predicament, and be impressed with me for finally choosing to come out to Fi. Oh, *God*. Am I really that self-absorbed? Do I seriously need a pat on the back to validate what I did? Regardless, and despite how much I've wanted to reach out, I've been giving Pax space. Sending a text out of the blue sounds like a flimsy idea.

I place my phone on my nightstand beside the ring box, and space out, gazing at the hardwood floor. I've burned my bridge with Fi, pushed Neel away, and Pax and Billy are back in Montana.

I have no friends left, fake or otherwise.

Edward, you're doing great. Nice start to your new chapter.

I'm also still ruminating on how I explain to my parents why they got photos of waterworks instead of a monarchy-saving engagement. I'm relieved that I was able to be honest with Fi, but how it went down was less than ideal. I hope nothing more comes of it. And I hope Fi can forgive me. I don't know what this means for our fake-dating—but that's

the least of my concerns. She'll bounce back. It's who she is.
But I'm strangely still riddled with a biting remorse.

I decide to send a text to her.

Edward: I know I'm likely blocked, but I hope you're OK.

Edward: I'm sorry.

The next morning, I sip a bitter cup of hot coffee in Casa
Loma's Edwardian dining room, ignoring calls from Mum,
Dad, and Gord.

The staff hands me the tray of tabloids and papers. Taking a deep breath, I lift the topmost one. To my shock and
relief, the tabloid in my hand shows Fi and I looking cutesy
at dinner, with a favourable headline: **LOVEBIRDS SHARE
ROMANTIC NIGHT AT FAIRY-TALE CASTLE**, while another
tabloid features an old photo of Billy smooching his ex-boy-
friend Dustin with a jagged line drawn between them and a
less-than-favourable headline: **ARE GAY BREAKUPS EVEN
MESSIER THAN STRAIGHT ONES?** I honestly don't have the
stomach to read it. Not to mention the question is ignorant.

My phone lights up. It's Gord. I let it keep ringing.

So, they're calling me to simply inquire about last night.
No coverage on the disaster.

What do I tell them? That I chickened out? They're just
going to insist Fi and I do it all over again. But next time, I'll
need to follow through. Who knows, maybe Fi would even
be amenable. Keep the secret. Marry me despite our romance
being a complete and utter falsehood.

All of which would be contingent upon whether she chooses
to forgive me.

Maybe I need to rethink my priorities. Sure, she could end
up being queen consort, but her entire life would be a sham.

I know a thing or two about that and wouldn't wish it upon anyone.

Deep down, I already know Fi is too hurt to play pretend anymore, regardless of the lofty title it could afford her one day—at least for now. It started as an innocent game, but I'm through playing it, and through with my life being a sham.

I sincerely regret stringing her along. Who ever thought I'd live to see the day when Fi had my sympathy?

Hiding my true identity isn't just hurting me anymore. It's hurting those I care about.

I'm done hiding.

After the swift ride back to New York on the private jet, I'm reclined on a sofa on Park Ave, doom-scrolling on my phone while gnawing on an éclair.

It's not easy taking my mind off my last phone call with Mum, even as I tap away from the slew of defamatory posts about Billy and browse my trove of baked-good posts. Not even gorgeous photos of Opera cakes, pearl-sugar-sprinkled chouquettes, or powdered beignets can put my mind at ease.

"What do you mean, things with Fi are as sticky as buns?" Mum had inquired.

"I accidentally upset her before I could propose. A mere hiccup."

"Oh, Edward, what did you say to her?"

"Something about her necklace," I lied. "It was nothing. Truly." *I suppose old habits are harder to break than I'd imagined.*

"I hope you haven't scared her off. We'll look into rescheduling with her."

"Sounds good." And with that, I hung up.

Why can't I just be honest with them? Fi was right—I *am* a liar. More than figuring out what do about Fi, I wish there was something I could do to help salvage what little is left of Billy's reputation, and talk with Pax. But it's like I'm on a train, chugging along on the tracks, with no way out and no way to stop it from barreling full-steam ahead. On top of all that, I'm still longing for Fi to text me back to assure me that she's okay.

My phone dings, but it's an email.

Dear Prince Edward,

Sincerest apologies for the delay. No hard feelings about missing each other a few weeks ago. It was nice to see you at the ceremony, which reminded me to reply to your last email.

I hope we can bake together soon. You see, I am working on my very first cookbook featuring recipes both old and new, and I would like if you could contribute something like a foreword, or at the least taste-test my latest innovations. In fact, I wanted to ask if you would like to collaborate with me on an idea I have for a dessert beverage that I concocted in your honor: the Mapleccino.

My Best,
Chef Pierre

This certainly lifts my spirits. Mapleccino sure sounds like it involves milk and maple syrup. Did *Billy* tell him about our shared love for the unique drink? Possibilities race through my head. Maybe Chef Pierre and I could finally collaborate on my Queen Daphnée Cake recipe. Before sending my resounding yes, I take a moment to consider putting my name in the public eye as a baker.

The thought horrifies me, but also thrills me. It makes sense when not much else does. Taking back my title of Crown Prince is great and all, but none of the fallout with Billy has felt right. He never deserved the way I treated him, or what happened to him in Ottawa. The Undies Stunt? Those anti-monarchist protestors and anti-LGBTQIA+ protestors? The fans who stormed the grounds? Not to mention the grace with which he's faced the world after losing his dad… He's not just a good prince. He's a good person.

A good brother.

It hits me, the thought I'd had seconds before his ceremony: Billy deserves to be Crown Prince. Again.

I don't always respect tradition, but I respect this one: he's the older twin (even if it *is* only by a minute). It's his birthright. And it's not fair that was pried away from him through no fault of his own.

Allowing Billy to step back into the picture would be the right thing. I wish there was a way I could help make it happen instead of continuing to dig myself deeper into the royal role.

Chewing it over, and thinking about what Pax would say to do, I respond to Chef Pierre with an enthusiastic yes.

Then I'm back to thinking about Billy and Pax. I miss them. I shift over to my Finsta, where I've been stalking them. No new posts or stories. In fact, the Firm shut down Billy's official Instagram with its 30+ million followers.

In my grid, a post of Mack catches my eye, taken preceremony, hours before things went AWOL. She looks fresh-faced and full of aplomb, seated in a pile of synthetic maple leaves, her fuchsia dress ballooning up around her, her lacy fascinator glittering.

I tap it and am stunned to discover her Instagram account has 21.4 million followers. Her numbers on TikTok aren't far off from that either. She truly *has* become New York's newest social darling. With this kind of influence, she could do anything…

Ça y est!

I scramble into a seated position, pressing my back against the mound of silken pillows, and FaceTime Mack, who should be available since we were all told not to go out and about until further notice. *"Please pick up… Please pick up…"*

The screen fills with Mack's face. She's got her hair in pigtails, and she's standing in a barn.

I ease into a casual smile. "Hello there! How…rustic!"

"Uh… Hi." She wipes a frizzy flyaway from her forehead. "Why are you calling?"

"Can anyone else hear me?"

She looks around, then says, "Nope. Well, unless you count our horses. Billy's working, and Mom's meeting with the butcher in town. We're not raising the cows as pets here. So, what's up?"

"Terrific. Listen. I have a plan, and I need your help."

"My help?" She juts her head back. "This better not be about Billy making an apology video. Those are never a good idea. Besides, I already tried convincing him to make one. It's a no-go."

"Hear me out. I need your help to execute a media blitz."

"A media *what*?"

"It's when TV, tabloids, and social media all pick up the same story."

"Why can't you do that yourself, Mr. Crown Prince? Why do you need *my* help?"

"Because one, I don't have the right social media reach, and two, you're Billy's sister with a huge following. Believe it or not, the goal of my plan is to turn favour back to Billy."

She narrows her eyes at me. "And…move it off *you*?"

"Yes. I'm of the mind that Billy deserves to be Crown Prince. This might be how to help."

"Why should I trust you? Billy told me that you're to blame for what happened."

"Well, once I tell you about my plan, you can use your judgment to decide if you think I'm still being dishonest."

"What makes you think he even *wants* to be Crown Prince again?"

"Come on, Mack," I implore. "You saw how happy he was."

"True...he's never been happier. Before he got cancelled, obviously. And he does keep sighing and saying he didn't know what he had till it was gone..." Mack makes a contemplative humming sound. "I'm in!" She scrunches up her mouth. "But what exactly do I have to do?"

I look to my door, talking low. "Could you post a photo of Billy? Any photo, totally up to you. But flattering. Preferably not one of him picking his nose. And then simply use the hashtag #CrownBillyBoone."

She stares, and the silence stretches on. "Done."

"Perfect!" I cross my fingers onscreen. "Here's hoping it goes viral. Public opinion always sways the votes, especially if we can get people writing to their members of parliament before the vote. Take it from me. And the fact that negative public opinion is mostly to blame for his excommunication from the Royal Family. The Firm receives a few angry letters and calls demanding my dad strip Billy of his title, and suddenly he's being kicked to the curb. If the public can affect big decisions, then so can we. We can flip the script!" For someone who never goes off-script, this feels good.

"And you're sure *you* want to do this? Let Billy take back the crown?"

I nod. "It's what he deserves. Wouldn't you agree?"

"Yup! Plus, if he's Crown Prince again, I can ditch this place again for the high life!" Her screen goes blurry as she minimizes it. "Gimme a sec. Looking for a good photo..."

I get off the sofa and stand at the window overlooking Central Park.

"Got it. I'll post the photos I was planning to use for Billy's gift. The photos that *weren't* leaked. Creating a photo dump now... Okay, now adding the caption and hashtag...and, posted!"

My stomach flutters with excitement. "Thank you kindly, Mack. Let's take a look." With my heart racing, I gaze at my phone. A Google alert lets me know that the extremely expedited House of Commons session in two days will determine the fate of the Crown. Apparently, Mum and Dad will be in attendance, presiding over the room. There isn't much time to right the wrongs. I hurriedly close it out and reopen my Finsta.

The first photo in her carousel shows Billy with his arm around Mack at the ranch, maybe taken a year or two ago, back when he had much longer hair. The second photo shows him playing the violin, his passion for music evident in his expression. The third photo shows him with Mack and their parents in a grassy field, the wind whipping their hair, their smiles effervescent. The fourth photo is a selfie of Billy and Pax in Times Square. And the fifth and final photo shows the two of us posing together on the Red Maple Carpet. If I didn't know any better, I'd say we look like the best of friends.

"The likes are coming in!" Mack cheers.

"Excellent."

"The people are loving it!" she squeals.

"Great work, Mack! I owe you one. Keep me in the loop. And not a word of this to Billy or your mum. I'm sure they'll see the post eventually. Hopefully it brightens their spirits." I hang up, bursting with hope, and wander into the kitchen.

I refresh the post, again and again, watching the number of comments slowly climb before I set my phone down. *Give it a little time, Edward.*

To keep busy, I pull my cookbook from its hutch and flip

through its flour-spattered, stuck-together pages. What shall I bake to pass the time? I land on my chocolate biscuit cake recipe, the one that gives Granny's senior chef's recipe a run for his money. It's her all-time favourite, easy to make, and nonbake. I usually make it for her on her official birthday.

After clearing my workspace and turning on some classical music, I get to work, feeling any tension start to slough away as I break up tea biscuits into a bowl, then go on to whisk the eggs, and add in softened butter and sugar. I have the recipe practically committed to memory. I dump the mixture into a separate bowl of dark chocolate I've melted, stirring it together till it's nice and glossy, all the while resisting the urge to obsessively check my phone. In go more crumbles of tea biscuits. Last but not least, I add my Edward signature ingredient that makes my recipe way better than Granny's old tired one: two tablespoons of maple syrup. It makes all the difference. I lick the batter. *Délicieux!*

I pour everything into a stainless steel cake pan and pop it in the fridge to chill, then wipe my hands off. Shall I begin on the chocolate frosting just yet? *Non.* I snatch up my phone greedily.

There's Mack's post—this time with 31,767 comments.

Just what I was hoping for.

My phone rings, and I nearly drop it in the sink in surprise. There's Mack over FaceTime again. "Lil Nas X just reposted to his story! And Ariana Grande! It's catching on!"

I glance at the comments. Everyone is recounting all the great things Billy did over the past several weeks, with even more comments pouring in about what a fine Crown Prince he'd make once more. #CrownBillyBoone and #JusticeFor-Billy are spreading like wildfire. My heart is pounding, and a warm sensation traces a ticklish trail in my stomach.

"Talk about a media blitz! Let's see if our little groundswell reaches the Firm."

"I sure hope so!" Mack says wistfully. "I can't stand seeing Billy so sad." She gazes around at the horse stalls where I'm pretty sure I saw a mouse scamper by. "And I can't stand sweeping up one more cow poop or horse pee."

"You sweep up horse pee?"

"Actually, you shovel it." She looks at me, and the corner of her mouth twists into a smile. "Edward, this was a great idea. Glad I could help. I'm starting to think you're not an evil twin after all."

I laugh. "Thank you again. *Au revoir* for now." I hang up. I'm realizing that I will be perfectly okay if it turns out I'm no longer heir apparent to the throne. In a strange way, this step was my first move toward trying to truly love and accept myself. It may be a long road, but I'm finally ready. And if my future involves more of what I love to do—baking, and possibly dating Pax?—even better.

Now, as far as Billy goes, what more can I do?

I've tried everything.

Well…not *everything*.

The next day, the royal private jet lands on a small strip of runway in a flat green field. It's a good thing Mum and Dad didn't bat an eye when they assumed I wanted to borrow it for the afternoon to set up a lovey-dovey surprise for Fi, to apologize for our "argument." (I know—more dishonesty. I'm working on it.)

Not to mention Gord is flying up to Canada early, too preoccupied with preparing for tomorrow's debate to give me much thought.

Security guides me into a car waiting on the runway with

the lack of usual urgency required in places more…populated. There's no paparazzi lying in wait to snap my picture. In fact, there's barely anyone. I only see one person in the distance.

No, wait. That would be a scarecrow.

Regardless, I'm in an inconspicuous baby blue velour zip-up hoodie, designer jeans, pristine azure-blue sneakers, oversize sunglasses, and a simple one-tone baseball cap.

Okay, so maybe not all that inconspicuous.

We start down a main road with more endless blue sky and a mountain ridge in the distance. There is something charming about it all, along with the smell of fresh grass wafting in from the open window. On second thought, perhaps that's what's making me sneeze. I roll up the window.

We pass a one-road town with shops and restaurants festooned with festive flags in honour of Billy I'm sure. A man steps out of a shop and sits on a stool in front of vegetable carts. I sigh in relief. I was starting to think this eerie small town was haunted by flag-hanging ghouls.

Pax wasn't kidding about this place being secluded.

The thought of them being in the same state as me again makes my heart pitter-patter.

As we start on another seemingly endless, curving path, I can't help but wonder which part of town Pax lives in—the town part with the shops, or somewhere out here in the wilds among the livestock. There doesn't seem to be an in-between, at least none that I've laid witness to so far.

I'm tempted to text, letting them know I'm in town, but I remind myself there may still be time for that later. It will all depend upon how my surprise visit goes over with Billy.

The car slows beneath a decrepit wood sign: OLD BOONE RANCH. There's a bit of shuffling as the driver hops out to open the entrance gate, and then we're driving through a fenced-in pasture of sorts, before he hops out again to open a second gate. This time, he fends off a curious brown cow who takes ahold of his sleeve in the process while more cows push past him. By the time we park outside the log-cabin-looking home, there are cows all around it, grazing in the window boxes and chewing the grass by a screen door.

I search the peeling wood for a bell, but there isn't one, so I open the screen and knock. And I wait.

There's a pile of logs to my left, into which I'm pretty sure something furry just scuttled. An insect lands on my neck, and I slap it, hitting myself a bit too hard in the process. Thinking about tiny flying bugs makes my whole body itch.

Let me in *already...*

Mack opens the door. "Edward!" She gives me a big hug, then pulls back, her expression soured. "PU. You stink."

"I do?" I sniff my armpit. All I can smell is the woodsy outdoors.

She looks past me. "Aww, hogs! You let the cows in!" Mack takes a step onto the drive with her bare feet, shouting at the cows crowded around the house. "Shoo! Shoo!"

"Apologies." I let out a laugh, inhaling a mouthful of gnats in the process. "Blech!"

"It's fine. I'll take care of it. Good thing Mom still isn't home." Mack jerks her hand. "Billy's out back. He's going to be so confused you're here."

"I'm hoping that works to my advantage."

"Come on in. Follow me." Mack retreats back into the relative coolness of the home.

I follow her past knickknacks and a mantel prominently showcasing a framed photo of Billy's family, the same one Mack posted in her Instagram carousel, and another framed photo on a table of her dad alone. It sends an unexpected pang through my heart. He has bright blue eyes, and a smile that looks like it's never met pain.

He was Billy's dad too. Suddenly, I no longer feel the wave of envy that came with contemplating his budding relationship with our dad. He could still use a father, and ours is pretty great too.

Mack opens a back screen door for me. "Head on out. You'll find him. He's finishing herding the sheep. I'll go take care of the cows." She wags her finger markedly at me. "Good luck. This better work." Then she's gone.

I step off the porch and into an endless grassy field, and then I see him.

There, across the pasture, in the distance, just beyond a little copse of oak trees, Billy is riding toward me on the back of a glossy, muscular chestnut horse. In his jeans, pale yellow flannel, and cowboy boots and hat, he looks at one with the horse, and I envy how connected he seems with the steed, something no official riding lesson can teach.

As he gallops closer, I see a glimmer of why Billy might have wanted to come back, and realize he's always been the prince of his own domain, even if he never knew it.

My face breaks into a gentle smile.

He pulls the reins to stop short in front of me, looking less enthused. I don't know what kind of welcome I expected. A tip of his tattered cowboy hat? "Edward? What are you doing here?"

I shield my eyes from the sun. "Hey, brother. I've never met anyone who was more in tune with their horse than Granny, yet here you are!"

He looks past me at the house, as if expecting to find an entourage and security detail.

"It's just me." As long and hard as I've thought about what

to say, I decide it's best to just wing it. "I'm here to apologize for pulling all those pranks on you, and to convince you to come back to New York and fight for the throne."

His horse whinnies, as if objecting on his behalf.

"There, there, girl." Billy pats her neck, then shakes his head at me. "You flew all the way here just to ask me that?" He taps the horse's muscular flanks with his heels, yanking the reins, and she starts to trot away.

"Hey! I didn't come all the way to Podunk, Nowhere, to be turned down, at least not so swiftly. Let me just—" I make to move after him, and step into a giant, steaming pile of cow poop. "Not my custom-made Giuseppe Zanotti!" I try wiping it off on the grass.

Crisse.

Billy has returned, trying not to laugh. "Watch your step."

"Little late, don't you think?" I mutter.

He reaches his hand down. "You did come all the way here. I can't send you packing just yet. Even if you are morally shaky."

Fair. Though from his tone, I can tell that he's forgiven me. I begrudgingly take his hand, and he hoists me up onto the horse.

I look for something to hold. "Well, this is certainly—"

"Giddy up, Junebug!"

The horse breaks into a trot.

I grip Billy's sides, holding on for dear life. "Where are we going?" I call out.

"Thought maybe you'd want to see the place." Billy effortlessly gestures. "This is our ranch." We gallop through the field and eventually pass two oak trees on our left. "Mom and Dad planted four oaks, one for each of us." He points to the two oaks full of leaves. "That oak was planted for me and that oak was planted for Mack." The trees bend and rustle in a balmy spring breeze.

"Beautiful," I say. "They remind me of the ceremonial trees planted at Rideau Hall."

Billy turns Junebug around and sets us on course back for the house. He pulls on the reins in front of the gate, and the horse halts. Then he gestures to two oaks on either side of us. "Mom and Dad planted these when they first built the place." He dismounts and runs his hand over the peeling bark. "This one was Dad's." He looks at me, and I can see sorrow return to his familiar features.

I reach over from where I still sit atop the horse and gently touch the trunk as if feeling for a pulse. "I would have liked to meet him."

Billy stoically unlatches the gate and guides Junebug through without a word. Moments later, the horse slows beside a water trough outside a barn, and Billy helps me dismount. He takes the reins and looks on as the horse drinks, stroking her silky brown mane.

"It's a nice home you have here," I say in an attempt to connect.

He keeps his gaze fixed on the trough. "Home is where the heart is."

"Speaking of which…" I say, trying to choose my words carefully. "Please come back to New York with me. Get back on the horse, or the saddle, or whatever that expression is." I reach into my pocket and unfold the piece of construction paper with the crayon drawing of Billy and the scribbled words YOU'RE MY HERO.

Billy regards it for a long moment, looking pensive before locking eyes with me. "I *want* to go back."

"I *knew* it!" I cheer. "Yes! Of course you do! Great. So, what's stopping you?"

He looks at the house, the green pasture. "All this. The ranch. It's the last thing keeping my dad's memory alive. If I don't work to take it over, it'll get sold off to someone else—especially if we're not getting secret money wired to us to keep it going."

"Still not over that, I see."

He drops the reins to wring his hands. "Mack sure as heck isn't going to step in. And Mom can't keep going at the rate she is. It's all on me." He sighs. "Maybe I'm destined to stay here forever. Besides, the world clearly isn't ready for a gay prince." He stops, flushing. "Sorry, I didn't mean—"

"No one is ever ready for change." I hand him the construction paper, and he carefully tucks it into his shirt pocket. "But it's needed. That's why you've got to come back and keep going."

"*Me?* Why not you?"

"Billy, you were made for it." I take the maple leaf brooch out of my pocket and offer it to him.

"I appreciate what you're doing," he says, eyeing it, "but even if I were to come back, the Firm—and Parliament—still doesn't want me. I mean, how were you expecting to get around that?" Billy gives me a knowing look. "Mack's hashtag?"

"Oh. You saw that."

"You're not the only one who can make a Finsta," he says. I give a sheepish chuckle. "Clever, right?" I smile, but he still looks stoic despite my attempt to lighten the mood, and I instinctively slide the brooch back in my pocket. "Listen. I don't exactly know. But that hashtag is catching fire. Public opinion matters—you know that. That's why I flew here. So we can figure it out together. For starters, how did the great pantsing stunt occur if it wasn't you?"

"And if it wasn't you?" Billy shoots back.

"Touché." I stare off into the blue sky, thinking about how if I had the chance to snag the speech cards from the ceremonial outfit in the corridor, then perhaps someone else could have tampered with the pants while the outfit was being moved... "I'm determined to know," I say. "Let's retrace what happened leading up to the ceremony as it pertained to your ceremonial garb."

"Fine. I'll humour you." Billy screws up his mouth. "Pax designed and finished the outfit, and a footman brought it in on the mannequin the day before the ceremony. I tried it on, and the Head of Robe made some minor adjustments. And then it was bagged and overnighted to Rideau Hall."

"And then?" I urge.

"The day before the ceremony, Gord came to steam and press it, and then the staff transported it to Parliament Hill that night."

I suppress the memory of my interfering with its nightly transfer. Not that it ultimately mattered. "Gord's pressing suits now? For all the years I spent trying to impress him, he never did that for me." I try not to feel hurt. "Wow. He must have really taken a liking to you."

"Doubtful. Besides, it was only the one time," Billy admits.

"Still, the Gord I knew would never act that way." My envious tone betrays me, despite working on trying to quell it.

Billy shrugs. "I mean, he was adamant about going to the Hall before me to help get everything in order. When I got to my room, he told me he took care of it. But that doesn't mean anything, right?"

"Hmm. That doesn't sit right with me." I try to picture it, Gord pressing a suit. It feels all wrong.

"But hasn't Gord been your family's most loyal adviser since forever? I remember you telling me that out of all the people to trust, Gord was number one most trustworthy."

I shake my head. I can't put my finger on it, but there's something very amiss. And the more I think about it, the deeper my suspicion grows.

I fix Billy with a stare. "I have a bad feeling about this."

Chapter Twenty-Eight

BILLY

"Something definitely doesn't smell right," I tell Edward.

We both look down at his fancy blue sneakers, then he looks up at me, his eyebrows raised.

"I meant about Gord. But, that too." I lead Junebug to her stall. "Do you think *Gord* leaked those photos of me?"

Edward flushes. "That part...wasn't him."

I step back out of the barn. "How do you know?"

Edward swats at a gnat. "Honestly, how *did* you survive so long living here?"

I'm not amused at his obvious attempt to change the subject. "Edward," I say flatly.

"Sorry. Sorry. So about the photos for the Billy-gate article. Those...would have been Fi."

"Fi?" I guess I shouldn't sound so surprised. "Why would she have done that?"

He hangs his head. "You seriously have to ask?"

I kick a clump of grass. "Oh. Right. Maybe it has something to do with her undying love for you and the future you two might've had were it not for me?"

"Well, that charade's all over now. She and I. Don't go telling anyone though—it's not exactly reached the public sphere yet."

I look at him. "Which scheme of hers finally did it in for you? Was it Billy-gate?"

"Actually—" Edward rubs his neck "—she broke up with *me*."

"Oh." I can't tell if he's happy about that.

Edward grinds his shoe into the dirt then examines the underside. "I might have let slip…about me…to her."

It dawns on me what he's referring to. "Oh. Wow. Are you nervous she's going to tell people?"

"She wouldn't." Edward laughs. "But only to protect her own reputation. How would it look that she's been 'dating' a gay prince all this time? At least, I hope she wouldn't. Then again, her motto is all publicity is good publicity. Regardless, we still don't know who leaked your story, with absolute certainty."

I chew over what he says, but something still isn't adding up. "Let's say Fi leaked the story too. How could she possibly have known about my mom's backhanded deal? She's Canadian nobility, but…she doesn't have access to royal records or anything like that, right?"

"She doesn't," Edward muses. "I suppose I could ask her, but I don't think she'd be very receptive to a call from me right now, considering the circumstances. She's a bit torn up. Rightfully so. I feel rotten about leading her on." He strokes his chin. "Tell me anything peculiar you know about the hospital mix-up."

I try my hardest to recall. "My mom said when she figured it out three years ago, she immediately reached out to the Firm and told someone all about me. The man she spoke to said he would pay her off for her keeping quiet about the mix-up because he didn't want a—"

"Media firestorm?" Edward cuts in.

We look at each other, our eyes going wide.

"Gord!" we say in unison.

My heart races. "So…what? He wanted to keep my existence under wraps?"

"Sounds like him, wouldn't you say?"

"And obviously that didn't work," I continue. "So then he did orchestrate my wardrobe malfunction. But why?"

"You said your mum told him all about you?" Edward asks. "Three years ago?"

I nod. "She said she told him everything."

"Everything?"

"Yes." Something clicks, and I wonder if he's thinking the same. "You don't think—"

"Gord kept out a gay prince for a 'straight' one?" Edward uses air quotes for the word *straight.*

"Well, joke's on Gord, isn't it?" I say. "I mean, that totally checks out. He was always going on about the newly formed Canadian monarchy having the best chance at taking root and upholding the traditions of the British Royal Family. I'm pretty sure that doesn't include a history of gay Royals, out or otherwise. On top of that, he's molded you from a child. He's been rooting for you since day one. And from everything you've told me, Gord has no idea you're gay."

Edward takes a breath. "Precisely. Fi sent the tabloid the photos, and Gord likely got wind of it and contributed what he knew about the payoff." His face lights up. "Do you know what this means?"

I take a breath, my thoughts reeling. "What?"

"Now that we know Gord has been trying to kick you off the throne, and succeeded, we stand a fighting chance of re-instating you as the rightful heir!"

I fight the hopeful flitter in my stomach. "Don't we need evidence?"

Edward's smile wavers.

"What about Fi?" I suggest.

"What about her?"

"I'm not certain, but I do know she's good at digging up

dirt on people." I recall Granny's words. *"One just has to know where to look…"*

"You're brilliant! If we can get our hands on some hard, cold evidence, it'll be the final nail in the coffin. And hopefully, we can get it in front of Mum and Dad before their session tomorrow at the House of Commons."

"What are you talking about?" I ask.

"Tomorrow, Mum and Dad will be presiding over the House of Commons at Parliament Hill to decide the official transfer of the title from you to me. If we can get them to see the light ahead of then, hopefully you can get the crown back."

I take a deep breath and nod.

Edward smiles. "So, shall I tell them to fire up the jet for two?"

I try to slow my heartbeat, and gaze out over the field. "Under one condition."

Edward folds his arms coolly. "And what might that be?"

"From here on out, you have to promise to be honest. No more sabotage—"

"Done."

"Or *self*-sabotage."

Edward squirms. "I'm pretty sure you just said one condition. Technically that would be two."

I tilt my head at him and stick him with a hard glare.

He lets out a quick breath. "Fine. No more sabotage or self-sabotage. Now, is that all?"

"Oh. No. Sorry. I buried the lede," I say. "Pax really likes you. Don't be a jerk."

I think back to Pax explaining everything to me, and how Edward and Pax gave "a whole new meaning to the 'royal we,' honey!" I felt sorry to hear it had to break off, and was warmed to hear that Pax chose our friendship over their relationship in the end. Now, I want Pax to be happy, especially knowing my twin isn't a total jerk.

"So, they told you about us." Edward blushes. "Luckily, *I* really like *them*." He runs his hands through his hair. "I've...seriously messed up, haven't I?" He jams his hands in the pockets of his designer jeans. "I have to make things right with them. And I need to start by finally being honest with my parents about not wanting to marry Fi."

"I'll have your back when you tell them, and the country, if and when you decide you're ready. After all," I say, smiling, "what are brothers for?"

"But what about all the vitriol that's bound to follow? And the haters?"

"There's always one," I say with another smile. "The cruelest voice is always the loudest. As Pax would say, 'Don't cater to the hater.' It'll be okay."

"Thank you. You're right. And for all those commentators saying you're too gay," Edward says. "Well, one can never be too gay. So, in time, I'd like to squash that rhetoric."

"One thing at a time." I grin. So he *does* care about more than just surface things.

"Hopefully, we can save Pax's reputation in the fashion world too," he adds softly.

We gaze out over the beautiful Montana hills and mountains, the gorgeous robin's-egg-blue spring sky, the four oaks rustling in a perfect breeze. I feel as if they're letting me know, for the first time, that I'm free to set off and do whatever I want—with my brother by my side.

I turn to him, something igniting within me. "Fire up the jet."

"Excellent." Edward's eyes sparkle.

"But before we go, there's someone I still need to see," I tell him, thinking about how ever since I've been back, I've been wanting to visit Dad's gravestone. Now, I'm compelled to let him know how I'm doing, to let him know it's not goodbye, but I'll see you soon. "I'll need a few hours," I add.

Edward flares his nostrils. "Under one condition," he says smugly.

"Yes?"

"Actually, two," he says. "One, do you have a change in shoe?" He turns up his nose in disgust at his dirty sneaker.

"Yes." I don't mention they're not much of a step-up.

"Great. Now two, where can I find a certain special somebody?"

Little Timber Cemetery is green and smells unsurprisingly of soil.

I stand in front of Dad's grave—a stone block carved with his name. I run my fingertips along the edges of the roughly etched letters, the right angles of the simple carved cross.

✝

BENJAMIN BOONE
LOVING HUSBAND AND FATHER

I open my mouth to speak. The words don't come. I want to tell him everything that's happened, everything that could happen. But most of all, the very real possibility that this *is* goodbye. I swallow the lump forming at the back of my throat.

I stand for a very long time, grappling with what to say, how to say it.

Eventually, the sound of a nearby bird stirs me. I rest a hand on the headstone, and the words come out. "You'll always have me by your side too. No matter what." I stay rooted to the spot until a weight lifts, until I feel Dad gently squeeze my shoulder. Then a breeze stirs through the trees. Would you look at that? Oak trees.

And just like that, all is well.

Chapter Twenty-Nine

EDWARD

I stand in Billy's spare pair of cowboy boots on the porch of the quaint grey house at 17 Bitterroot Road.

I knock, then take in the property as I wait. It has a little green lawn with a flower bed hugging the front of the house, scraggly trees, and an American flag blowing over the front door.

Charmant.

There's movement through the warped oval of glass set into the door, which then opens to reveal a heavyset older woman in a vibrant floral muumuu with a cloud of white hair piled atop her head. Her orange, bold-framed glasses hang from a string of beads around her neck.

She peers at me. "Hello. Can I help you, sweetheart? You Pax's friend from the 4-H? Billy, isn't it? I think we've met before."

I smile, my eyes flitting past her into the cluttered interior of the house. "Hello there. I'm another friend of Pax's. Are they home?"

"Oh, so you *are* here to see my Paxy Flaxy! Well, they didn't say they were expecting any guests. Come on in, doll." She calls over her shoulder. "Pax! Pax, sweetie! You got a visitor!"

Their voice comes from somewhere upstairs. "What, Grandma?"

"You got a visitor!" She turns back to me. "What's your name, sweetheart?"

"Edward," I reply.

"Edwin!" she yells up the stairs. Close enough. Bless her.

I step through a mothball-smelling foyer with a huge collection of decorative spoons hanging on the wall, all carefully dusted, and into a cramped yellow kitchen. Pax's grandma points out a chair for me and then ambles into the next room as I take a seat.

I hear the sound of Pax trundling down the creaky steps. They appear in the kitchen doorway in a loose pink blouse and overalls with one of the straps undone.

"What in the beef Wellington— What are you doing here?" They are completely shocked, and I can't blame them. After all, their grandmother did say "Edwin." Their mouth opens and shuts like a goldfish.

I stand. "I've come to kidnap you!"

Pax grimaces. "Huh? What now?"

"You heard me. Come on, let's go." I stride past them and toward the front door, then turn back around. Pax is still rooted to the exact same spot in the cramped hall.

"Well, are you coming or aren't you?" I sigh. "Billy knows I'm here. We've mended fences. I've cleared my name with him. In fact, he's the one who gave me your address."

"And those boots, clearly!" I see a smile creeping over their face. "Okay, fine. But…where are we going? And what should I wear?"

"What you've got on is perfect. But you may need a jacket."

"Okay. Give me two seconds!" Pax jets back upstairs.

I realize their grandmother has reappeared and put on her bold-framed glasses. She looks shocked as well. I guess she finally figured out who I am, because she drops into a deep bow.

I grimace and wave a hand. "Oh, that's really not necess—"

"Your Royal Highness! My goodness, pardon the mess. I knew you looked like Billy, but I can't see that well without my glasses on. Oh, I should have put two and two together. Of course! Of *course*! Can I get you a, uh, spot of coffee?"

I stifle a laugh, watching as she moves backward into a cabinet, sending its plates chattering.

"I've got Oreos. You want an Oreo with some peanut butter? Or how about a vanilla wafer?" She straightens up and begins prying open cabinet drawers. "Oh, my gosh. The prince. Here! Here! Where did I put those doilies?"

"Let's not advertise my visit to the whole town, shall we?"

"Oh, I'm not gonna say nothing! My lips are sealed." She runs her thumb and pointer finger across her mouth and flings away the invisible key.

I smile. "Excellent."

Pax thunders back downstairs in a bedazzled jean jacket and high tops. "Ready!"

"Excellent." I turn to their grandmother, who's bowing again. "A pleasure."

"Oh, the pleasure was all mine, ya Majesty," she says, her nose to the floor.

"Grandma," Pax remarks. "Get ahold of yourself!" They kiss her cheek. "I'll be back!" Their eyebrows rise as they look at me. "I *will* be back, won't I?"

Their grandmother shakes her head. "Oh, take your time! Take all the time you need!"

"Thank you. Pax will be in good hands." In a flash, we're out the door and seated in the back seat of my car. The driver clocks us in the rearview mirror then pulls out of the gravel driveway.

Pax squeals. "This is out of control! Where are we going?"

"It's a surprise," I say. "Are you opposed to me blindfold-ing you?"

"Do it, honey!"

I fish into my jeans pocket and bring out a red kerchief that Billy lent me. Wrapping it over Pax's eyes, I make sure it's not too tight. Then I sit back.

Our hands meet on the middle seat, and our fingers inter-twine.

It feels right.

We drive out of the quiet suburbia, along a dirt road, and come to a stop in a meadow of purple and yellow wildflow-ers, with the mountains ringing us in the distance.

"Stay put," I tell Pax as the driver opens the door for me. I step out into the hot, fragrant field, pop the trunk, and lay out a horse blanket with a picnic basket. It was the best I could scrounge up on the fly given what Billy had lying around the ranch. I hope Pax likes it.

I open the door for them. "Come on out."

Pax unbuckles, and I steer them out of the car and onto the edge of the blanket. Then I untie the makeshift blindfold.

Pax takes in the meadow, and the picnic. "Edward!"

I signal the driver, then all the car windows open as Mariah Carey's voice reverberates out into the meadow.

"OMG! This is one of my all-time favourite songs." Pax starts singing along in delight.

"A little birdie told me you quite like this particular meadow."

"I do! I used to come here all the time as a kid and chase bumblebees. Well, until I finally caught one and it stung me." Pax giggles and sits on the blanket. I follow suit. They brush their hand over the tops of flowers.

"I'm glad it brings you such fond memories." I pause. Am I actually going to say it? Yes, yes, I am. I take their hands in

mine. "I want to tell you something. Being apart from you…
it's been driving me out of my mind."

Pax turns to me with a trembling lip. "Me too."

I pull them into a hug. When we finally part, I gesture at
the basket. "Shall we?" Pax nods. I pull it open, and hand Pax
a frosted brownie.

"Sweet Mary and Muslin!" Pax takes a bite and smiles.
There is chocolate frosting all over their lips. Perhaps this
wasn't the best treat to eat on a date.

"You've got a bit of chocolate. Just there."

Pax blushes and runs their tongue over their lips, then
smiles. "Better?"

"Perfect."

"They're delicious. Did you make these?! They have Edward written all over them."

I nod. "I was pleasantly surprised with Billy's kitchen supplies. Luckily, brownies are just sugar, eggs—"

Pax cuts me off with a kiss. A wonderfully sweet kiss.

"That was nice," I say when they pull back.

"It was simply perfect," they say breathlessly. They pause.
"Does this mean that we're…?" Pax's words trail off into the
warm spring air.

Being gay, I thought I'd always wanted a boyfriend. But
Pax is not a boyfriend.

They're even better.

I jump in. "Would you like to be?" My heart is thumping
a million miles an hour.

Pax explodes into the biggest grin I've ever seen on their
face. And that's saying a lot. "Oui. Oui! And this means we're
officially the Royal We!"

"Indeed. Speaking of which, what term would you like to
use to describe our relationship? Are we…partners? Significant others?"

"How about Maple Hearts?" Pax laughs. "Too sappy?"

"I actually really like that." My smile flags. "You should know… I haven't exactly told my parents about Fi yet. But I'm working toward it. I told her the truth about me being gay. Or, actually, I think queer is a better word to describe me."

"You told Fi?!" Pax blurts.

"It went terribly. But I felt awful for lying to her for so long."

Pax takes my hand. "I am so proud of you, Edward."

"Thanks. I couldn't bear to keep stringing her along." I keep holding on to their hand. "Or you. I've had feelings for you since the start, but I was scared to dive into a relationship for fear of people finding out. Plus, up until now, I've felt like I had to stay in the closet for the good of the monarchy, and I didn't want to subject you to that. I admire your ability to love yourself and be yourself, and I know that you deserve the same in someone special. I want to be that person for you. I can do it. I'm finally ready to be who I am, with or without a title."

I pause and take a deep breath. "In fact, I'm also ready to tell my parents the truth." I find myself grinning. That was easier to say than I had expected.

"Wow. Well, thank you for saying all that. I don't know what my future holds either, but I know I'd like for you to be a part of it," Pax says.

"I'd like that."

Pax's light dims. "But Crown Prince is the most important thing in the world to you."

"There are more important things, like being able to be myself."

"I love that for you."

We kiss. And kiss again. This time, there isn't any more fear. I allow Pax in, allow my feelings to flow through me, unhindered and without internal monologuing. We just…are.

Pax laughs. "Did you really come all the way here for one sweet picnic with me?"

"I convinced Billy to help me reinstate him as Crown Prince. And if we can do that, hopefully it'll also clear your name as the wardrobe malfunctioning fashionista."

Pax's face lights up. "And hopefully Parsons will reconsider my admission!" They grin. "I belong in New York... with you."

"Billy and I are heading back to Ottawa tonight. There's a debate happening tomorrow in the House of Commons that we'd like to influence, if possible. Coming with?"

"Umm, let me think..." Pax pauses. "Of course! I can't wait to tell my grandma."

"That's probably a wise idea."

Pax shudders. "I love her, but she can be a little intense."

"Oh, I know all about intense grandmothers," I quip.

Pax laughs.

I lock eyes with them. There's a terrifying sensation bubbling up, making me want to roll into a ball. But I push through it, and let the words rise.

"I'm in like with you, Pax."

Pax gasps.

My cheeks flame but I try to act cool. "Well...it's true."

"I'm in like with you, too."

We kiss, and kiss, and suddenly, I'm thinking Montana isn't so bad after all.

"If there's time, I'd love to show you around town," Pax says. "You can meet the Howard-Loyolas, and we can get maple butter! That is, if there's any left. Hot commodity here."

"If that's what you'd like, then that's what we'll do." I kiss them through my smile. "As long as we hurry," I add with a little laugh.

The picnic is all packed up, and we are climbing back into the car when my phone rings.

I hold it out at arm's length, shocked at the caller ID. "It's…Fi."

Pax ushers me out of the car. "Take it! Take it! I'll wait in here."

"Alright. If you don't mind." I gently close the door and take a few steps into the grass.

"Hello there," I say as Fi's poker face fills my screen. My hand is shaking.

"Nice background. Where are you, Switzerland?"

"Montana." I laugh, letting loose a bit. "It's good to see your face."

Her lips pinch and she nods. "That's not something I thought I'd ever hear. Hey, listen, I'm sorry I've been ignoring your texts. And I'm sorry I 'Real Housewives of Ottawa'd' on you at Casa Loma. You know. With the dramatic water-throwing. Not my finest moment."

"I have an apology of my own." I let out a deep breath. Royals don't apologize if it can be helped, but I've been starting to realize lately how much I strongly dislike that particular custom. "I'm sorry for leading you on."

She laughs and fiddles with her chunky gold necklace. "It's not your fault. Don't worry—we'll always be friends."

I bristle. "Um, Fi, were we *ever* friends?"

"Shut up. And yes." She examines her French manicure. "Besides, I'll just find another hot prince to social climb with. Unless you want to keep up the charade. I'm not against it."

"Something tells me that's not the best idea." I blink at her. "So, you forgive me?"

"Obvi." She rolls her eyes. "Listen, in all seriousness, you're the truest friend I've ever had. I value our friendship. Not to get all mushy on you, but you're the only one who hasn't left me. I've pretty much burnt bridges with everyone else I've ever known. I don't know how you tolerate me." She laughs, but there's a sadness.

"I've been asking myself the same." I chuckle. "Also, if my parents ask, I told them I'm with you. Not *with* you. With you *geographically*. They...don't know I'm here in Montana."

She shrugs. "What are friends for if not for corroborating false narratives?"

"Well, thanks, friend. And the feeling's mutual. I'm serious this time."

She smiles. "I mean, the fact I didn't rat you out to the press that night just proves our friendship is real. I told them what they wanted to hear. It was so tempting to say otherwise."

"Much appreciated."

"Good, because believe it or not, there's a nice person in here somewhere. One who knows just how important being Crown Prince is to you. Uh, and why *are* you in Mon—"

"About that... Me wanting to be Crown Prince has taken a permanent back seat."

"What?!" Fi's eyes go wide and her jaw drops. *"Spill. Now."*

After filling her in, I hang up and duck back into the car.

"How'd it go?" Pax asks.

"Surprisingly well." I buckle my seat belt as the car rolls forward.

Pax takes my hand. "I think you have one more call to make."

I give them a quizzical look. "I do?"

"Come on. It's so obvious you and Neel had a fallout! Call him. Clear the air. Besides, we're going to need his help too."

I smile. "I've been trying, but he's not picking up."

Pax hands me their phone. "So call him from mine!"

I take the phone, laughing. "Genius!"

DAILY MAPLE ONLINE

THE ROYAL ROUNDUP
May 4, 08:14 pm ET

EDDIE TO STEAL BACK TITLE OF CROWN PRINCE?
by Omar Scooby

Way to go, Eddie! After reallocating his coveted title of Crown Prince to Billy weeks ago when his older twin first appeared, Eddie is about to be confirmed as Crown Prince—once more!

A tweet from Rideau Hall confirms what everyone's been thinking: the Crown Prince of Canada may be switching back from Prince Billy to Prince Edward. It's still a mystery as to when Billy's title will be returned to his brother, and when Eddie's Investiture Ceremony will be scheduled, but the *Daily Maple* is eating it up! Rumour has it that Frederick and Daphnée will be present during the official debate at the House of Commons that will determine if the title will indeed go back to Eddie, requiring a unanimous vote. The very nature of the Maple Empire teeters on the precipice.

When asked about how Edward is doing in light of this recent news, our source said he seems overjoyed at the prospect of getting back in the game—and we'll be here to root him on.

As for Billy? A source said that in the meantime, the dark horse has headed back to the stables—in Montana, where he hails from. We're sure he's quaking in his cowboy boots at the recent twist in fate, but everyone's favourite hot mess hayseed is decidedly better off back in his one-horse town.

RELATED STORIES
<u>Is Prince Billy the Most Hated Celeb in the World?</u>
<u>Billy's Fall from Grace: Splitting Heirs</u>
<u>Maple Leaf Undies Sell Out Online</u>
<u>Lady Sofia as Future Queen Consort?</u>
<u>Polls Reveal People Want Canadian Monarchy to Go?</u>
<u>Backlash Over Carbon Emission of Royal Private Jet</u>
<u>BREAKING: Fritz and Daffy to Debate with Prime Minister!</u>

Chapter Thirty

BILLY

I drive past the plank that says WELCOME TO LITTLE TIMBER, which now has a banner strung over it, with only the "Welcome" showing beneath.

WELCOME HOME, BILLY!

From the rope and neat handwriting style in paint, I know the Howard-Loyolas must have been behind creating the banner. I slow past the one-road town. It seems even smaller than I remember. Do I park and get out to have reunions with everyone?

On second thought, I doubt anyone's going to be hailing me as their hometown hero or jonesing to have me sign my autograph.

That's when I see something I must not have noticed earlier: rainbow flags and Canadian flags blowing from each storefront. Every single one.

They have my back. Maybe they've had it all along.

I smile to myself and keep on driving. I know I'll be back.

At the ranch, I pack for Canada, unable to believe I'm returning there so soon. I load up a backpack with the essentials: toothbrush, phone charger, wallet, passport. As I zip up my bag, I think about how reckless this is: going to the Citadelle to creep into Gord's central office, searching for dirt. But I'm ready to be reckless. There's nothing to lose. And I won't be alone. If our plan works, I'll leave Montana to dream big, but it will always be home. Always, always.

Even though the ranch hand's technically still on the clock, and has been, with no days off, I have time to help out for old times' sake. I ride Lucky Lady and herd the sheep. Do a perimeter check of the fence. And feed both horses carrots once they're back in their corral.

Mack sees me from the house and comes out to help, scraping grime out of their water bowls, scrubbing their buckets and their feed pans, without so much as a grimace. We sweep out the barn and hose it off together, not speaking but feeling comfortable in the shared silence. I know she hates this kind of labor, yet here she is. I can tell she doesn't want me to fly back. She's trying to be strong though, taking in the details of the moment, like capturing a memory to look at later when she's missing me.

As I wipe my brow, she points out a little shard of rainbow on the barn door. I nod. Maybe it's Dad. We each flash a little smile.

I cross the pasture and meet the hungry cows waiting by the gate. I cut the net wrap to lay out their food, and hand-feed a few clumps of hay into their slobbery, licking mouths.

At long last, I fire up the incinerator behind the house to burn up the used net wrap.

The flames lick the sky, dancing, free.

Finally, Mack and I head back in to clean ourselves up, our hair stuck with hay, our clothes damp and soiled, and our faces streaked with dirt. I try to savor each moment too, not knowing what the future holds, if I'll ever be back to living out of this tiny bedroom.

The sun sets over the Gallatin Range, sending long shadows

stretching through the den. After Mom gets home from getting supplies in town—mostly just sacks of corn, oats, and barley for the steers—I sit her down on the pullout couch and tell her everything. What Edward and I deduced. Gord's homophobic intentions to oust me. Our plan to find proof. And the fact that something that should take weeks to organize—the vote on the section 41 amendment at the House of Commons—was fast-tracked by the 338 elected members of Parliament. The prime minister won't likely get a unanimous vote because Quebec will surely vote against keeping the monarchy, nothing is certain.

Even if we can't find the proof to affect the votes, I hope whatever happens, we get justice. Someway. Somehow.

When I'm done talking, Mom nods solemnly. "Don't worry about leaving. We can manage things here." She pats my knee. "What's most important right now is that you're pursuing your dreams. You go, boy."

"Thanks, Mom."

"I can't wait to see *you* on the cover of *People* magazine."

"That hasn't happened yet?" I joke.

But Mom sniffles, fighting a cry.

I pull her into a hug. "Mom, it's not like you'll never see me back here. If this works, I'll have access to the royal private jet. I'll be able to fly you out to Canada or New York anytime."

"My heart is in Montana. You come visit me."

I laugh. "Okay. Every other weekend. It's a promise."

We hug.

Mack steps into the den, rolling a suitcase. "I'm going with Billy!"

We look at her. "Mack," I say, "how long have you been eavesdropping?"

She smiles sheepishly. "I'm all packed?"

"Mack, you're thirteen," Mom tells her. "Sorry, dear."

"Ugh, fine." Mack stomps back toward her room.

There's a knock on the door, and Mack runs to fling it open.
"Edward! Pax!" she says brightly. "You're holding hands! Yay!"
My best friend's eyes bug out at me, darting to their hand
gripping Edward's. I laugh and nod, glad to see Pax finally
got their happily-ever-after.

"Mack." Edward bows, blushing. "Connie. Lovely to see
you all again." He looks at me. "It's probably time to get going.
I didn't exactly tell my parents where I was, and they're going
to start wondering where I have gone if I'm not back soon.
Not to mention time is of the essence if we're going to influence the vote on Billy's title."

I drag my bag outside and hand it off to the driver, and hug
Mack, then Mom.

"I love you."

"I love you too."

I hop in the car and we're on our way. I give Dad one last
wave goodbye as the car passes his oak, which blows serenely
in a perfect spring breeze.

Within minutes, we're airborne, seated comfortably in the
private jet. I scroll through the many on-demand movies and
start watching *Poultrygeist*, a classic stop-motion kids' movie,
to take my mind off what we're about to do. Edward's fallen
asleep on Pax's shoulder. Pax gives me an elated thumbs-up.
It's nice to see them looking so happy again, their sparkle restored to its former glow.

I peek at my phone. There's #CrownBillyBoone trending at number one. I don't know what's more touching—the
fact that the public is being so supportive, or the fact that my
brother and sister thought to do this for me, that they and Pax
are fully in my corner.

An hour into the flight, I feel my eyelids grow heavy, and
I drift.

There's Dad again, standing in the pasture. Full head of hair. Full-on smile.

My joy at the sight of him starts to dwindle. I know it's the last time I'll see him in my dreams. I can just tell. It makes me sad.

"It's okay," he tells me. "*Go.*"

I don't want to. I can feel my body—my real body seated in the plane—wracked with silent sobs, my mouth drawn in a taut, clenched line, but I stay in the dream.

"*Son. Go.*"

Maybe, just maybe, I can move on—or at least take a tiny step into tomorrow. I inhale a deep, cleansing breath. I'm ready. It's time.

He fades before me, until he's gone. I don't scream for him. I don't even chase him. I let him go. And I feel, for the first time since his passing, a complete and utter sense of peace.

I wake as the plane descends onto the runway, and look over at my friends through tear-filled eyes.

"You okay?" Edward asks me.

I nod, blowing my nose into a napkin. "I'm good."

"Well, *I'm* not!" Pax exclaims. "Are we really doing this? Breaking into Gord's office to snoop?!"

Edward looks from Pax to me and gives a resolute nod. "Indeed we are."

Our dreams are just a hop and a skip away.

That is, if this all doesn't go south.

After staying overnight in Edward's heritage suite at a castle-like hotel, the Château Frontenac, the next morning, we meet Fi in the empty lot outside the Citadelle of Quebec, where we just spied Frederick and Daphnée leaving the premises. I remember what Gord taught me about the Citadelle, how the location, on the banks of the St. Lawrence River, is the second place the Royals now hold permanent full-time residence in Canada other than Rideau Hall.

It's also the location of Gord's central office.

Fi's wearing a fitted white suit jacket over a short white dress with black heels, and enormous sunglasses. "If it isn't the whole motley crew," she says with a smile as we approach.

"Fi," Edward says with a nod.

Although Pax and Edward are no longer holding hands, the way they stand so close to each other side by side *screams* couple—at least to me. It looks like Fi catches on too.

"Edward. Pax." She brushes a strand of hair out of her mouth and faces me. "Billy. I am so sorry. Mack's photos weren't mine to send, and I never imagined they'd end up as part of the whole tabloid scandal feature. By sending them, I hoped they'd at the most end up in a 'what not to wear' editorial. I was desperate to save the crown for the boy I loved—" she glances at Edward "—but I'm sorry I hurt you, and I'm sorry your family's reputation was damaged. That includes you too, Pax."

"I forgive you," I say. "The photos alone didn't do the damage."

"I forgive you too, honey. Even if you are pettier than a petticoat at times," Pax says. "Besides, we have a fashion empire to rule."

Fi nods in earnest.

"Were you able to dig up my mom's old emails and trace them back to Gord?" I ask Fi.

She shakes her head. "But I did hack into his calendar, and he's apparently out to lunch, meaning—"

"We can nose around through his office," Edward says quietly, glancing at the ceremonial guards watching us from narrow blue sentry boxes in their fuzzy black hats.

Pax gasps. "OMG. Scandalous, honey! Let's do it."

I knew this was coming, Still, my heart begins to race.

"We're just waiting on one more," Edward says, raising his hand to shield the sun as he looks down the drive.

"Did he ever call you back after you left the voice mail?" Pax asks.

Edward shakes his head, his arm lowering. "I guess it's just us, then."

Suddenly, a car approaches from down the drive. It pulls right up to us, the doors sliding up from the floor, and someone steps out in an army-green, short-sleeve button-down with matching shorts, each with bright orange pockets.

"Neel!" Edward hugs him. "I'm glad you decided to come. And I'm sorry. About everything. You were right. I went too far."

He grins. "Glad you finally came around, *bharā*." He regards Edward's less than formal attire, from windswept hair to casual sneakers. "And that you've *finally* loosened up a bit." A smile tugs the corner of his mouth. "Besides, you really thought I'd pass up your invite and miss out on the mischief?" He grins at the rest of us in a greeting. "Now that we're all here, let's get this party started!"

We form a sort of cluster and move toward the entrance, a tall arch in a wall of stone. The guards recognize Edward, welcoming him in salute as he leads us inside, as if he's been doing this his whole life...which he has.

We pass through the tunnel and onto the grounds, hurry up a grass-lined walkway bursting with tulips, and step into the private entrance of a long gray building. After emerging from a foyer, we hang a right at a carpeted grand staircase and stride stealthily down a long hallway on a runner, framed sketches on either side of us.

Edward takes a sharp right and we quicken our steps.

We pass through a dining room with crystal chandeliers and a hutch of china plates, before Edward pauses outside a door. After a moment, he opens it and beckons for us to follow him.

Inside, it's dimly lit, with puke-yellow walls, dusty drapes, and a large wooden desk in the center of the room on an intricate rug. A gold-framed portrait of Frederick in his youth hangs over the fireplace. There are bookcases, and leather sofas, and the royal flag of Canada. So, this is Gord's central office. It's honestly just how I'd expected it to look.

"We don't have long," Edward cautions us, yanking open a desk drawer and digging around inside while Pax does the same on the opposite end, moving aside inkpots and rubber stamps.

"What are we looking for again?" Neel hisses.

"Anything that might implicate him!" I whisper.

My hand reaches for a stack of magazines on a table at the same exact time as Neel. We touch for a split second, then apologize.

Fi begins rifling through a stack of paper in a shallow basket on the desk. Neel opens a glass door and starts combing through the ancient-looking books. I root around in a red-and-white despatch box resting on a table in the corner by an old clock.

My heart feels like it's going to pound right out of my chest, terrified we could get caught at any second.

I move to open drawers in a dresser under a framed oil painting of Rideau Hall. There are just files after files, blueprints, maps, nothing that screams suspicious or homophobic. I hear everyone else rustling around me. The metal clang of a desk drawer as it's closed. The rummaging whisper of more papers. Sighs, soft hums.

The sound of a double knock.

We all whip around to find Gord standing in the doorway.

"What's all this?" Gord asks Edward. His steel-gray eyes land on me. *"Billy?"*

"We were just taking a tour of your office, G!" Neel smiles.

Gord folds his arms. "I can see that. Now, if you don't leave, I'll have to call security."

"We're not going anywhere until you tell us what you did!" Pax shouts, standing protectively in front of me.

Gord smirks. "I don't have the foggiest clue what you're talking about." He looks at me again. "As for you, you're never to show your face here again. Understood?"

"You're the one who paid off my mom years ago to keep quiet. She might have been silenced, but I won't be."

"I'll give you till the count of five," Gord asserts coolly.

"And then you went and sold the story to the press," I continue, accusation dripping in my voice. "You're also the one who messed with my pants so that they'd rip when I bent over and got me booted out of the Royal Family! It was *you*." I jab my finger at him, heart racing, blood hot and in my ears.

Gord sighs. "So, you're not as dimwitted as you look." He glances at Edward. "No offense, Your Royal Highness."

My legs are shaking, and I feel like I could fall over, but I hold my ground. "So we're right!"

"Well, you're not wrong," Gord says. "I admit, I've worked too hard and too long to make sure the Royal Family of Canada had a long, successful, and stable tenure." A smug smile contorts his features.

"The last thing I needed was a scandal," he goes on. "Especially after your mother let it slip that you were *gay*—" he grimaces at the whispered word "—when she contacted me three years ago." He takes another step into the room and closes the door tight behind him. "I don't want a gay prince. My stunt at the Investiture Ceremony—sabotaging those pants so they'd unravel—ensured that the Canadian monarchy would be rid of you once and for all."

"You know what else worked, cupcake?" Fi asks with a satisfied smile. "The secret video I just took." She holds up her phone and Gord's voice comes through its speakers: *"I don't want a gay prince."*

I exchange a look with Edward, who's now standing by my side. Pax, Neel, and Fi hem in around us. Triumph surges through me.

At the same time, it feels like the twist of a knife. How can people act like they're fine with somebody being gay, while they're secretly doing everything they can to bring them down?

Gord blanches. He extends his hand out to Fi. "Give that to me."

Mack's face appears on Edward's phone screen via FaceTime, waving her own phone. "Thanks, Fi! And uploading the secret video of Gord's confession to my channel... And, done!"

"How dare you!" Gord snarls at her.

"Hey, no one talks to my sister like that!" I yell back, taking a step toward him.

Edward moves with me. "Sorry to say, but it looks like you'll be at the center of *this* media firestorm."

"Guards!" Gord calls over his shoulder.

In moments, infantrymen bust open the door.

"Seize them!" Gord shouts.

Edward points at him. "Gentlemen, as a prince of Canada, I command you detain this man, on the account of treason."

"And blatant homophobia, my God!" Pax adds.

Without hesitation, they seize Gord, who submits to being cuffed.

"What a jerk!" Neel murmurs.

"Seriously though," Fi adds with a shake of her head.

I exhale. "Well, we got what we came for."

Edward claps me on the back, chuckling. "Sure did."

"Not quite." Pax checks the time on their phone. "Umm... Your parents are about to weigh in on the official vote for the title transfer any minute now. We *might* want to hurry to Parliament."

Chapter Thirty-One

EDWARD

A short jet ride later, I burst emphatically through the heavy doors into the House of Commons at Parliament Hill, Billy and I in lockstep.

The 338 members of Parliament are pushing back their chairs and standing to applaud Mum and Dad who are seated on two olive-green thrones at the far end of the aisle running down the centre of the room, Mum in an elaborate gown with cape and crown, Dad in military regalia. The members of Parliament sit back down in the rows of desks and chairs on either side of the aisle. A hush falls over the packed room as all eyes land on us, including from various political parties and press in the upper level.

"His Royal Highness, Prince Edward," the Speaker says into an intercom.

Billy takes in the high-arched, stained-glass windows sending soft light streaming into the chamber, then at the TV cameras aimed at Mum and Dad, and goes white, but I grip his wrist and give a reassuring squeeze to say there's nothing to fear—not even with the members of the House of Commons staring at us in disbelief for barging in during a debate of upmost importance.

The fate of the monarchy.

"Edward." Dad's expression is one of sheer confusion.

"Dad!" I pull Billy across the green runner toward the thrones.

"What are you doing here?" Mum asks. "Is everything alright?"

"Our government is voting on the fate of the heir to the Crown," Dad says, eyeing the captive audience. "It appears most are in favour of the title transferring back to you, Edward." *Crisse.* We're too late.

"The Right Honourable Prime Minister," the Speaker says into his mic.

The prime minister steps up beside Mum and Dad, buttoning his jacket. "Your Royal Highnesses, the decision has been made." He looks at Billy. "The vote was unanimous. Billy, you are no longer Crown Prince. Edward is the official Crown Prince." He clears his throat then addresses the room again, repeating it all in French.

My heart sinks. "Mum, Dad," I say in appeal, "Gord orchestrated the whole thing!" I pull my phone out and show them the video cued up on Mack's YouTube channel, titled in true clickbait fashion: **Press Secretary's Shocking Confession!**

Dad gapes, and Mum touches her fingers to her lips, eyes widening—two expressions that would repulse dear, prim Granny.

"What's all this?" The prime minister sets his mouth in a hard line.

"Edward," Mum says softly, "this may not be a good time."

"It's the *only* time," I retort.

"Edward—" Dad starts.

I bow before the throng of people, and the room crackles into tense silence. I press play with trembling fingers as Billy bows beside me, holding my phone against a microphone. Gord's voice richochets around the vast space. I realize the video is also being projected, magnified on a large screen for all to see.

The video ends. The crowd takes a steeling breath, and looks from Billy to me.

We wait.

"I'm sorry," Dad says, so quietly I almost don't hear it.

Royals don't publicly apologize. What is going on?

He smiles. "Please know that Mr. Gord Lauzon's beliefs do not reflect those of the Royal Family. I cherish you both for exactly who you are." The way he says it, the way he stares, it's as if he knows.

As if he's known all along that I'm queer, too.

"You—you *do*?" I stammer, lowering the phone to my side.

"Thank you," Billy chimes in, sounding relieved.

Dad turns to the prime minister to discuss the sudden turn of events. I look at Billy, and then out at the attentive audience. The tension is palpable. What is going to happen? There's no going back now.

Finally, Dad addresses the room. "Our royal adviser is to blame for Billy's incident." He smiles, ignoring the hubbub. "Therefore, Billy's title will be reconferred."

I can hardly believe it. My chest swells with joy. I turn to Billy, who's holding his breath. He breaks into a laugh and joyfully tugs my sleeve.

As the room reacts with murmurs and outbursts, Dad repeats what he just said again, this time in French.

"We did it," I breathe to Billy, my grin spreading wider.

"We did it," he affirms, his laugh growing giddy.

"The title of Crown Prince remains with Prince Billy!" says the Speaker of the House.

The MPs applaud, and Pax, Fi, and Neel race into the room

and join us. Billy gives them a beaming thumbs-up, and they whoop and scream in a most undignified way, unfitting for such a formal setting. But who cares? I join in, cheering and laughing and bouncing up and down. I feel like I'm floating.

"Well done," Mum tells us, standing from her throne to applaud.

She and Dad embrace Billy, and I join in on the dog pile. Billy and Dad exchange a meaningful look, but my normal twinge of jealousy isn't there today. Not at all.

This is doing the right thing. This is choosing to be part of the right side of history.

And this is being a good brother, no ulterior motives in sight. There's nothing more princely than that.

After all, blood is thicker than maple syrup.

I wrap my brother in a hug and don't let go.

Some of the Maple Crown Rules are now a thing of the past. Certain traditions, like fruit cake as the traditional royal wedding cake, are meant to be tossed out.

After the debate, the Firm apologized publicly and privately and admitted our grievances are real. No more Only share what is necessary (Maple Crown Rule 77) nor Tradition trumps personal preference rhetoric (Maple Crown Rule 99). It's a new age for the monarchy.

I'm back at Rideau Hall, seated in the Small Drawing Room across from Mum and Dad. My teacup is shaking in my hand, I'm so nervous. More nervous than I was barging into the House of Commons meeting yesterday unannounced.

"You must have something of importance you want to talk to us about for you to want to join us for our afternoon tea," Mum says gently over the top of her own teacup.

I freeze up. But then I remember I want my life to begin.

That desire supercedes my fear, allowing me to push through the final layer of ice. "In the spirit of authenticity, which Mum, I know you're always preaching about, I have something I've been wanting to share with you both."

Dad leans forward on his armchair. "Alright, son. We're listening."

I take a deep breath, and just say what I've been too afraid my entire life to utter:

"I'm queer."

Mum and Dad show no reaction. They each blink, spurring me to continue.

"I realized I need to break away from the Crown, be my own person, leave this all behind. And I love to bake! Who knew?" I laugh, then grow completely flushed and go very quiet. My heart flutters a klick a minute.

Not quite the buttoned-up prince I used to be, at least not now.

Dad takes Mum's hand. "We understand if that's what you want to do, but you don't have to leave the family to be yourself or be happy." I can see love in his brown eyes.

"What about the queer thing?" I ask. "Neither of you seem surprised."

"We're a little surprised," Mum admits, smoothing her skirt over her knee, "but we've always loved you and always will love you, no matter what."

"We accept you as you are," Dad adds.

It feels like a gigantic millstone around my neck is lifting.

Before I know it, we're all hugging.

"We're sorry for putting so much pressure on you," Mum says.

"We are so proud of you for standing up for what you want and for being your true self—something we were brave enough to do when we were in your shoes and chose to break away from England," Dad says. "We've only ever wanted you to be yourself. To listen to your heart."

"Thank you. I love you."

"We love you too," Dad says, wiping his eyes.

"Are you comfortable with Billy being heir again?" Mum asks, recrossing her legs.

"Yes. I'm ready to step down and let Billy uphold his rightful mantle." I grin. "Besides, I was thinking maybe I could attend Chef Pierre's culinary school, even if it has to be via Zoom. You know, while also staying on as Billy's official royal adviser. After all, he's in the market for a new one."

"We can arrange that," Dad says. "It'll be nice to have a royal adviser who isn't trying to oust the Crown Prince through latent homophobia. I like this!"

"Even better—a royal adviser in full support of equal rights." All this time, I was being guided by someone with inherent bias and homophobia. I smile, relief flooding back through me knowing I can finally move on and be myself.

Now would probably be a good time for me to usher in my brother. "Billy!" I call, and he enters the room and perches on the arm of my chair, the maple leaf brooch pinned above his heart where it belongs.

"It'd be great if Edward could be my adviser," Billy says, flashing an easy smile.

Mum nods.

"Oh, and I know Billy's too nice to tell you himself, so I'll ask on his behalf," I say, shooting him a grin. "He really wants to be sure he still has time to continue with his music."

My brother turns to our parents. "I reached back out to Juilliard about rescheduling my audition. If I get in, can I still attend the music program this fall while continuing to train for Crown Prince?"

"Of course," Mum says. "We know it's so important to you, and it really seems like the one thing in your life that you truly did just for you, because it made you happy." Mum smiles kindly. "We are prioritizing happiness these days."

"Perhaps we could even introduce him to the Master of the King's Music," I add, thinking of the musical equivalent to the poet laureate who directs the court orchestra.

"I'd love that," Billy chimes in.

"Excellent idea, Edward," Mum says. "I bet Sir Nicholas would be delighted."

"Splendid." Dad checks his timepiece. "Is that everything?"

"There's one more thing." I spring out of my armchair, run to the door, and find Pax pacing in the corridor. When they see me, they freeze, their hand oscillating between a thumbs-up and a thumbs-down. I give them a big thumbs-up, and a smile washes over their face.

"Come with me."

Pax follows me into the drawing room.

Mum and Dad glance up at them, kicking up a swirl of nerves in my stomach. But Billy's presence calms me; I'm grateful my brother's here by my side, just like he promised he'd be.

Billy gives me a reassuring nod.

"Hello, Pax," Mum says.

"Hello, Royal Family!"

I slowly, carefully take Pax's hand in mine.

Dad blinks. "Oh." His eyes dart from me to Pax then back to me. "Are you together?"

"Yes," I say. "We're dating."

Mum claps her hands together. "Wonderful!"

"Indeed." Dad stands and pats me on the shoulder. "Glad to see it." He shakes Pax's hand.

Super. And no questions about Fi? I'm impressed—and grateful. The way Mum's looking at me, I know she understands now.

"So, who do we talk to about a royal wedding?" Pax asks. Before anyone can react, they add, "Kidding! Kidding!"

Everyone laughs.

The strange thing is, the idea doesn't absolutely terrify me like it once did. They would look nice in Jolee's ring.

I glance at Pax, and they smile back at me.

I'm thrilled at the notion of finally being able to be openly queer and in a real relationship. My first. With my Maple Heart. And who knows? Maybe one day Billy will find his true love and there will be a first-ever King & King, or a less gendered title combination altogether. It's truly time for a monarchy that supports all within its walls. A time of progress. A time of inclusion.

And now, the Canadian monarchy will flourish as was first intended, with no one left to set us off course. We're here to stay. If there's any more homophobia, or hate of any kind, we're on it.

This is going to be one hell of a story to tell my kids one day.

Progress has already begun. After the truth got out about Gord, Pax's fashion design business is back in full swing, with a focus on degenderizing fashion. They even asked Fi to be their official brand ambassador and champion of haute couture. Which means Pax gets to move back to New York with Billy and me and graduate from St. Aubyn's come mid-June. I've already booked a baking date with Pax to whip up Chef Pierre's take on pear and gruyere tart taught by the good chef himself, wearing my **KING OF BAKERS** apron with pride. Plus, I can't wait to partner with Chef Pierre on his cookbook. First, the sweet Mapleccino, then possibly my Queen Daphnée Cake, and then an even newer idea: what I call the Little Timber Yule Log.

Billy's doing just great, along with Mack and Connie. He taught me that to bear a crown of power doesn't mean you have to be alone. For that, I'm forever grateful.

My parents have continued to illustrate their support, although if they apologize one more time about always having said "We look forward to the day you find the perfect girl," I'm going to scream. Though it is nice to hear.

And as for Neel? My best friend is just excited that I can gallivant around the world with him, like old times, without fear of ruining my royal reputation. That is, within reason (nothing illegal). As he likes to say, there were many royal Edwards before me, but I'm by far the best—a few had some very suspicious friendships with notorious dictators, a rather low bar.

Oh, and **PRINCE EDDIE AND LADY FI ANNOUNCE THEY HAVE BROKEN UP** went over well in the press. Apparently, HeirHeads prefer me without her. Who would have thought? It's much better being platonic friends with Fi anyway. I know it's only a matter of time before she finds a new way to be Canada's hot topic—and before Pax and I go public, perhaps as a fairy-tale love story the likes of Mum and Dad's. "Royal baby steps," as they like to remind me.

If Pax taught me anything, it's that there are many types of perfect.

And they're mine.

CANADIAN ROYAL
COMMUNICATIONS

8th May

STATEMENT FROM HIS MAJESTY THE KING

The entire family is disheartened to ascertain the true depth of how trying the past few months have been for Billy. The points presented, particularly that of homophobia, are troubling. While some accounts may vary, they will be attended to accordingly by the family with discretion. We shall see to it that press secretaries undergo proper sensitivity training, as we have no tolerance for discrimination and hatred. A full investigation is also underway, and a diversity officer will be hired. Edward and Billy will always be much loved family members as well as Royal Members.

To this effect, the status of Crown Prince of Canada has been reinstated to Billy.

He will also regain his royal patronages, funds, and security.

It took an important vote to change the Succession Law. We thank Billy for his patience as he awaited his confirmation to the line of succession. We have sincerely apologized to him for any upset.

ENDS

Seven Weeks Later...

Sept semaines plus tard...

Chapter Thirty-Two

BILLY

It's a perfect last Sunday in June as the rainbow carriage we stand in glides past Stonewall Inn.

The crowds cheer, and cops on motorcycles with pride flags flowing off the back drive in front of us. I even manage to spot the Howard-Loyolas shaking noisemakers at us as we pass. I couldn't help flying them out here to pay them back for all their kindness.

Pax convinced Edward and me to wear rainbow capes with fake gold crowns, and get this? Pax made me the ultimate "gay cowboy" classic look—which looks so similar to what I used to wear in Montana, but it's all high-end maple leaf tartan and perfectly fitted. When I put it on, they stepped back and said, "Honey, when you asked me to design a sexy flannel shirt for you, I know I said it couldn't be done, but I went there and I DID!"

On the way over, Mom kept on saying how much I looked just like a Harlequin Romance cover, and the fans must have agreed, because they screamed and were dying over how "incredibly handsome" I am in my "true colors."

A photographer from *People* even took my photo before I got in the carriage, and I said to Mom, "I think you're going to get that *People* cover sooner than you expected."

Meanwhile, Pax is in an electric-pink cowpoke suit—looking sickeningly good in the matching hat and boots, the studs lining their lapel winking in the sun, as well as a choker and harness over a fitted mesh shirt, completing the look.

Mack and Fi stand beside them in matching Pax-designed rainbow gowns made up entirely of miles and miles of tulle. Neel's in jean shorts and a designer rainbow short-sleeve dress shirt. He jumps up and down, crushing me in a hearty side hug. Even the two white horses pulling our carriage have rainbow feathers in their headpieces. And then there's Mom, doing her comical robotic dance beside me, in a breezy rainbow sundress and vibrant sun hat, living her best life. It's nice seeing her happy again.

I glance over at Neel dancing beside me. "Aren't you going to miss all this?"

He flashes me a cheeky smile. "Nope. Because I'm not going."

"What?"

"I canceled my trip!" he yells excitedly over the music. "I realized this is my home. There are plenty of people here worth staying for."

He grins again, his dark eyes sparkling, and shimmies against me, his moves amusingly all shoulders.

"That's great!" Before I can ask any more questions, Edward appears from the other side of the float and dances toward us. In moments, he and his bestie are hip-bumping and roaring with laughter.

After losing Dad, my family felt smaller. I can't believe how much it's grown since discovering I'm a prince. I'd been dreading Father's Day earlier this month, and it certainly wasn't easy having to confront how much I miss him, but it was nice to get to spend the day with Frederick, who found a way

ERIC GERON

to honor Dad by unveiling a portrait of him at Rideau Hall. Like his oak tree back on the ranch, it helps me feel close to him in my new home.

Speaking of oak trees, we just planted a fifth, in honor of the baby Mom lost eighteen years ago. That was all Edward's idea.

I keep moving, dancing to the tune of hope, surrounded by friends and family. By love. It's like everything's lighter, freer. The music bumps loud from floats ahead and behind us. Everyone's waving flags and banners, and people on foot blow whistles, bang drums, and throw beads and other keepsakes. Signs read **LOVE TWINS** and **#TWINCES**. Fans hail me as the new Crown Prince, and Edward as out-and-proud prince in his own right. My Investiture Ceremony "Take Two" went off without a hitch last week, and wrapped up just in time for us to celebrate my first-ever NYC Gay Pride Parade.

Even though Frederick and Daphnée weren't able to attend, they're here in spirit.

And so is Dad. I can feel him in the high-rises and bars on either side of the street, in the joyful faces of people young and old, queer people and allies, children and babies, standing behind the barriers and rooting us on, cheering and yelling and hollering. He's all around us.

A confetti cannon explodes, showering us in rainbows.

And through the trees, over the skyline, a real rainbow breaks through the clouds.

"It's Dad!" Mack grips my arm, pointing. "He's giving us a rainbow!"

I smile and wrap my arms around her. "He is. He really is."

The horses clomp onward, and the sun warms my face.

The future is bright.

BRITISH ROYAL COMMUNICATIONS

26th June

STATEMENT FROM HER MAJESTY THE QUEEN

My family, along with the monarchy and the world, embraces Prince Edward for coming out as queer. We also want to express the same love, acceptance, and support to his twin Prince Billy.

Our government supports all people no matter their sexual orientation. We admittedly have not been very vocal about our support for the LGBTQIA+ community in the past. The history of the LGBTQIA+ community is vast, rich, and above all else, important. We vow to continue to show our public support, not just for my grandsons, but also for the equality and social justice for all. We wish you all a very happy Pride, today and always.

–ELIZA R.

THE END
FIN

★ ★ ★ ★ ★

ACKNOWLEDGMENTS

This book exists solely because of the unwavering support from so many special people to whom my gratitude truly knows no bounds. Without them, I may have given up long ago on a story that I had always wished for as a lonely queer teen.

Thank you first and foremost to Rebecca Kuss, who acquired *A Tale of Two Princes* and found it the perfect home at Inkyard. You believed in this story from its very first note.

Thank you to Brent Taylor, my superstar agent for whom I am astronomically grateful. I never imagined meeting anyone else who valued the importance of telling stories with queer characters for kids and teens as much as I did until I met you. Since then, I have been so thankful for your steadfast championing of my work, and for providing me with your optimism and reminders that stories matter. Thank you also to Dr. Uwe Stender for all of your support.

Thank you to Bess Braswell, Stephanie Cohen, Kathleen Oudit, Olivia Valcarce, and the rest of the team at Inkyard for being so thoughtful and for making the book beautiful in the process.

Infinite thanks to Lorraine Nam, whose gorgeous papercut artwork on the cover made the book complete and brought Edward and Billy to life.

Thank you to Emiko Jean, Jason June, Julian Winters, and

Brian Zepka for reading *Princes* and providing such brilliant blurbs.

Thank you to Alyssa Moon, Daniel Ross Noble, and Kamilla Benko, whose friendships mean the world to me.

Thank you to Disney Publishing, where I learned so much during my years as a book editor there, and to my Blizzard Entertainment family.

Thank you to my mom, who has been my rock through it all, with a special thanks to my siblings.

Thank you to Evie, who was by my side from the first draft to the very last.

Thank you to my loving friends, who have been rooting for me over the years.

Thank you to bloggers, booksellers, librarians, members of the book community, online pals, reviewers, and teachers.

And finally, thank *you*, the reader. I am endlessly grateful to you for picking up my book and filling your time reading it. When I was young, it seemed impossible to write this story and share it. My hope is that you found something in here that resonated with you, and that you felt like a part of Edward and Billy's family.

I see you. You matter. This book is for you. Find your joy.